KW-220-446

This is Des Wilson's second novel. He is also well known in Britain as a journalist, campaigner on social issues, and politician.

He was born in New Zealand in 1941, left school at fifteen to become a journalist, travelled to London in 1960, and eventually became a columnist on the *Guardian* and the *Observer* and a contributor to *The Times*, the *Independent*, the *Spectator*, the *New Statesman*, and for two years deputy editor of the *Illustrated London News*. He has written a number of campaigning books as well as his first novel for Sphere. He has also appeared frequently on radio and television.

As a campaigner he has been director of Shelter, the national campaign for the homeless, chairman of Friends of the Earth, chairman of the CLEAR campaign for lead-free petrol, chairman of the Campaign for Freedom of Information, and director of Citizen Action. He was President of the Liberal Party in 1986-87 and director of the Liberal Democrats 1992 General Election Campaign.

He lives in England.

Also by Des Wilson

COSTA DEL SOL

DES
WILSON
CAMPAIGN

WARNER BOOKS

A Warner Book

First published in Great Britain in 1992 by
Little, Brown and Company (UK) Ltd

Copyright © Des Wilson 1992

The right of Des Wilson to be identified as author
of this work has been asserted by him in accordance
with the Copyright, Designs and Patents Act 1988.

*All characters in this publication – save those clearly
in the public domain – are fictitious and any resemblance to
real persons, living or dead, is purely coincidental.*

Extracts from 'Take Me Home, Country Roads' (Bill
Danoff/Taffy Nivert/John Denver) copyright © 1971,
Cherry Lane Music Pub Co, USA.
All rights reserved. Reproduced by kind permission of
Cherry Lane Music Ltd, London WC2H 0EA.

All rights reserved.
No part of this publication may be reproduced,
stored in a retrieval system, or transmitted, in any
form or by any means, without the prior
permission in writing of the publisher, nor be
otherwise circulated in any form of binding or
cover other than that in which it is published and
without a similar condition including this
condition being imposed on the subsequent purchaser.

A CIP catalogue record for this book is available
from the British Library

ISBN 0 7474 0769 X

Photoset in North Wales by
Derek Doyle & Associates, Mold, Clwyd.
Printed and bound in Great Britain by
BPCC Hazells Ltd
Member of BPCC Ltd

Warner Books
A Division of
Little, Brown and Company (UK) Limited
165 Great Dover Street
London SE1 4YA

To
the best campaigners I know . . .
Ralph Nader
Michael Pertschuk
Maurice Frankel
Henry Witcomb
Jane Dunmore

Author's Note

CAMPAIGN is a novel and, except where, to inject a note of authenticity, real airlines, oil companies and newspapers are mentioned in passing, the companies, campaigning organisations, and characters are all as fictitious as the event portrayed.

I owe thanks to Tony Venables, Sam Smith, Chris Harvey, Juri Morizawa, Les Butcher, Geoff Bishop, Andrew Currie, Perrott Phillips, Marcel Berlins, all of whom helped my research or commented on the manuscript. I am specially grateful to two people; Barbara Boote for her faith and encouragement, and Michael Pertschuk for his particularly generous advice and assistance.

Des Wilson
May 1992

'Lobbying can be petty, tedious, boring and demeaning. But sometimes it's played out on a great stage full of bold strategies, fatal missteps, shrewd tactical feints, and intricate manoeuvres. The fate of the world – or at least a share in its fate – may rest not on grand policy debates or the massive realignment of political forces, but upon the play of greed, ambition, quirky alliances and coalitions, deep loyalties and deeper emnities, corroding envy, and yes, affection, even love.'

Michael Pertschuk,
Giant Killers, 1986

Part One

THE ENVIRONMENTALISTS

WASHINGTON

NOVEMBER

'So there he was, the Veep . . . *the goddamn Vice President of the United States* . . . drivin' the lane, and I just reached in and stripped the ball . . . just like that.'

He was a junior senator – one of the latest intake of lean, anti-smoking, non-drinking joggers who were making Washington politics a pain in the butt – and when he suddenly lunged forward his outstretched right arm almost took Ralph Nader's head off.

Up to then Nader had been indulgent – but enough was enough.

He was bored with the other's account of the weekly congressional basketball game.

Also, he preferred the Vice President's version.

So he took a step back, hoping to spot an escape route. Or, even better, Sam MacAnally, for whom he'd been looking for half an hour. In doing so he nudged the elbow of the *Washington Post*'s Jackie Brown, spilling her drink.

'Hi, Jackie,' he said. 'Sorry about that . . .'

'You're going to be, Ralph.' She good-humouredly nodded at the crowd fighting its way to the bar. 'Getting me another drink is going to be sheer hell.'

The campaigner laughed. 'Better than listening to another basketball story. You wouldn't *believe* how seriously these people take it.'

'Oh, I believe it,' she said. 'Those games are machismo-time with a capital M.'

'Well, I guess it's best they get it out of their system in the gym. Have you seen MacAnally?'

'Not yet.'

They looked around them. But what chance was there of finding him? The place was packed.

The ornate lobby of the Mayflower Hotel ran for most of a city block. Down its full length there hung glittering chandeliers and on either side of it, between huge mirrors, were the bars and banqueting halls.

And tonight everybody who was anybody was there . . .

Cabinet members, senators, ambassadors.

Publishers, columnists, lawyers, lobbyists.

Financiers, industrialists.

Stars from the arts and science, show business and sport . . .

All there to see the recently re-elected President honour 'America's finest' – men and women who would be given awards for outstanding individual achievement. The event was expected to raise a small fortune for the First Lady's latest cause, the sick and starving of the Third World.

This, Sam MacAnally said, as he finally made it to the East Room and found a friendly face, was ironic, considering that the jewellery on display would alone balance the books of the World Bank.

Unusually for MacAnally, it was said without humour. He was feeling sticky and irritable. It had taken an age to work his way down the crowded lobby. His face was flushed, sweat was trickling down his back. His shirt felt like a wet rag. And he was ill at ease in his rented tux – the jacket sleeves were embarrassingly short and the bow-tie he had fixed with a safety-pin was threatening to come apart.

'Hi Sam.' Jackie Brown had found him at last. 'Where's Marie? Isn't she coming?'

MacAnally shook his head and frowned. 'Not feeling well,' he said.

It was a poor lie, and he wasn't proud of it, but he didn't want to explain her absence.

It had caused their only really painful row.

Even now, immersed in this gossiping, jostling, sweating sea of people, he flinched at the memory of it.

'*For Christ's sake,*' he'd shouted, exasperated. '*It's the Environmentalist of the Decade award . . . from the President himself. I want you there.*'

She had laughed at him.

The whole affair was just a public relations stunt for the sponsors, Exxon – '*Exxon for God's sake!*'

As for the President, what had he done for environmental protection? '*Not a Goddamn thing.*'

About then he'd stormed out.

Angry because she was right.

Angry because she was wrong.

Right about the event.

Wrong about him.

As she would discover if she watched it on television. And he hoped she would.

'Sam!'

MacAnally became aware that Brown was trying to introduce him to Christopher Wilkins. The young senator from Connecticut was on that week's cover of *Time*, having been unexpectedly elected by an impress-ive margin with the help of an environmental-consumer-civil liberties coalition. By all accounts it had been a brilliant campaign. Already he was being touted as a possible Democratic candidate for President . . . 'the first 21st-century occupant of the White House', the *Time* article had predicted.

Wilkins had blond hair, blue eyes, and one of those political faces that looked as if it had a regular Super Wax Special at the local car wash . . . but his handshake, even in these now-steamy conditions, was as dry as it was firm.

'I've been looking forward to meeting you, Sam,' he said. 'I'm hoping we can get together, share a few issues. Maybe shake things up a bit.'

'Terrific. We need all the help we can get.'

For a split second the senator's smile faded.

This was not exactly the idea.

But before he could reflect on who should be helping whom, the President and First Lady arrived.

The effect was extraordinary. Everyone began edging in their direction. Self-consciously at first. Then with all the subtlety of a stampede.

MacAnally was amazed, amused, but, above all, relieved. At last he could breathe relatively fresh air. And get to the almost deserted bar. He still hadn't had a drink.

'You don't seem over-eager to meet our Chief Executive, Sam? Do I sense a lack of respect?'

MacAnally laughed. And cheered up. He was fond of Jackie Brown. Tiny – little more than five foot – but a ball of energy, talented and vivacious, Brown was a rising star on the *Post*. Now in her early thirties, with short dark hair, a round, friendly face, and big mocking eyes that never missed a trick, she had been a friend of MacAnally's since their college days. Once, on a camping trip in the Adirondacks, they had shared a sleeping bag together.

'So who let you in, Jackie? Not gate-crashing I hope?'

'You'll laugh at this. I'm doing a profile of you.'

'Oh God,' he groaned, unconvincingly.

'It's because of the award. Anyway, that's why I've fixed to be at your table for dinner.'

'Good,' he said.

'With Ralph.'

'Even better.'

'And Lionel North.'

'Oh *God*.'

'Come on, Lionel's OK. Just don't let him get to you.'

But MacAnally did.

North was an ultra-conservative syndicated columnist and television pundit whose views on liberals and campaigners like Nader and MacAnally made William F. Buckley Jnr sound like Jesse Jackson. He carefully cultivated what he fondly believed was an intellectual appearance, allowing his hair to grow longer than befitted a man in his early sixties. For this occasion he had chosen a burgundy-coloured frilly dress shirt and a crimson bow-tie in order to distinguish himself from the crowd.

'I'm surprised *you're* accepting one of these awards, Sam,' he began, literally as well as metaphorically wielding a knife. 'What was it you called the President recently . . .?'

'An environmental barbarian.' It was Brown who answered.

'Quite. And even I would grant you that Exxon's environmental record is . . . shall we say . . . controversial. Still, I guess when it comes to it, you professional liberals are competing for the same rewards as everyone else.'

'And you're not?' MacAnally snapped, glowering at him.

Brown quickly came between them.

'Oh, *come on*, Lionel,' she said. 'You're not pontificating on TV tonight. Anyway, from what I hear, the judges sent your entry back – saying the award was for writers, not butchers.'

Nader chuckled and joined in. 'You know, Lionel,' he said, 'Jackie's right. You should have your columns federally inspected . . . to check whether they're fit for human consumption.'

They all laughed at that, but before North could answer, the presentations began. One winner followed another into the spotlight, until, finally, the President spoke of a special award.

'We have, albeit belatedly, become aware that we face an environmental crisis. It's right that we should honour the one who's done more than any other to draw it to our attention . . . *Sam MacAnally*.'

The applause was warm but came mainly from the gallery and the fringes. MacAnally had over the years upset too many of the powerful at the centre tables to expect much from them.

He walked quickly to the front, shook hands with the President and turned to face the audience and the cameras.

What they saw was a slim, serious-looking man in his early thirties, about six feet tall, with a mop of black hair, a pale, boyish face, brown, intelligent eyes . . . humorous eyes . . . and a crooked bow-tie.

'Mr President,' he began, 'I *cannot accept this award* . . .'

He paused.

There were one or two gasps, but otherwise stunned silence.

Brown and North both reached for their notebooks.

The President took a small, almost indiscernible step back, as if preparing to remove himself from the danger zone.

'. . . I cannot accept this award for myself,' MacAnally continued, 'however, I willingly do so for the whole environmental movement.

'Mr President, if this event had been staged just a few years back, there would have been no environmental award.

'Until recently I and my fellow environmentalists were dismissed as eccentrics at best and freaks at worst, simply because we warned what would happen if we continued to squander finite resources, and to pollute our air, soil and water.

'It's our tragedy that you listen to us now only because we've been proved right.

'How much better for everyone if we'd been proved wrong.

'There is much I could talk about tonight . . . I could talk about the destruction of tropical rain forests . . . its probable effect on climate . . . and the consequent loss of hundreds of thousands of species of animal, insect and plant life . . .

'. . . about the poisoning of our oceans . . .

'. . . about the pollution of the air in our cities . . . and the damage to our lakes and forests . . .

'. . . about the terrifying threats to our planet from ozone depletion and global warming . . .

'Alas, time does not allow.

'Mr President, one of your predecessors, Jimmy Carter, commissioned the report *Global 2000*. It predicted that, unless we acted decisively by the turn of the century, the world would be more crowded, more polluted, less stable ecologically and more vulnerable to disruption.

'Mr President, we've *not* acted decisively . . . we've barely acted at all. Now time is running out.

'Your own administration has so far failed to grasp the nature of the problem, the urgent need for care and control.

'Too often it's put the short-term demands of big business or politics – and often it seems they're the same – before the long-term interests of the people and their planet.

'If this award, Mr President, *genuinely* acknowledges the importance of our cause, if it reflects a *real* desire to respond to it, it's a prize beyond value.

'If not, then it mocks our concern and the hopes of millions who share it . . .'

Once more he paused. '. . . but I prefer to believe the former, and in that spirit of optimism – one I hope you will justify in your second term of office – I accept it with thanks.'

He stood still for just a moment, then moved away, swiftly back towards his table.

For a moment there wasn't a sound.

Every eye was on the President, but if he was offended, he wasn't going to show it – not to a television audience of millions. Instead, he looked around, smiled reassuringly, and began to politely applaud.

It was all the encouragement they needed. Again the applause began in the gallery, but this time it spread throughout the room, building up to a roar of approval as the whole gathering rose to its feet, clapping and cheering, acknowledging – as *Newsweek* was later to comment – that '*an evening of banality and backslapping had been rescued by a fleeting moment of dignity and truth.*'

Even those who would willingly have seen him drop dead grudgingly stood to join in, conceding – if little else – his skill in exploiting the moment.

As the veteran Texan senator Ed Eberhard said to his neighbour, 'You have to hand it to the son-of-a-bitch, he took his chance.'

Back at the table Jackie Brown leaned over and planted a congratulatory kiss on his cheek.

Ralph Nader grinned. 'Are you a troublemaker, or what?' he said.

MacAnally smiled back.

The approval of his friend and one-time hero meant more to him than the award itself.

NEW YORK

Marie Doutriaux, wearing a jumper and faded blue jeans, sat on the floor in front of the television set, her legs folded under her, her glass of red wine untouched, shaking her head in half-amused, half-angry disbelief.

'Clever,' she conceded, speaking aloud to the image of Sam MacAnally on the screen. 'That *was* clever.'

There would be no criticism from the movement after that performance.

Yet still she felt cross with him.

Why?

Was it that he had let her attack him without explaining what he planned to do – that he'd allowed her to talk herself into a position she would now have to abandon, even apologise for?

Or was she angry at herself, for not trusting him?

She began to drink the wine and as it warmed her she felt her anger slip away.

Only to be replaced by disquiet.

In a way she hadn't anticipated – but presumed he had – he'd raised the stakes.

Tonight he'd taken the issue onto higher ground, heavily political ground.

Dangerous ground.

She hoped he knew what he was doing.

Suddenly she wanted to be there, not to share the limelight, but to be where the action was.

The programme was over now but she guessed everybody would still be mingling in the bars of the Mayflower. She picked up the phone and called Washington. She had to work at persuading the hotel staff to look for him in the crowd, but after several minutes he came on the line.

'Hi, Mac-O.'

'Hi . . . what did you think?'

'Not bad. Not bad at all.' She paused, then, contritely: 'OK, I admit it – I wish I was there.'

'It was *that* good?'

'Don't rub it in. I know I should have trusted you.'

'No,' he replied. 'No, that's not so. I had a rough idea what I wanted to do but you stiffened my backbone. I couldn't have done it without you. I mean that.' His voice softened. 'And I'm pleased you rang. Really pleased.'

She felt better. 'How about coming up this weekend?'

He pretended to be confused. 'Sorry . . . who is this . . . can it be that French bitch who told me to get my hypocritical butt out of there and not to bother coming back?'

'That's the one.'

'You're on. I'll take the shuttle Friday night.'

WASHINGTON, D.C.

MacAnally, cheered by her call, elated by his success, unaffected by doubt, was wandering back down the Mayflower's hall of mirrors, smiling at the reflection of his ill-fitting tuxedo, when he found himself blocking the path of the President and his party as they were leaving.

He began to step aside but the President called out. 'Sam.' For the second time that night he took the Chief Executive's hand.

'Well, you really handed it out to us tonight, Sam, but I don't blame you for that. Perhaps we have been lax on these issues. How would you like to come to the White House and talk to me about it?'

'I would welcome that, Mr President.'

'Good, good. We'll be in touch.'

Now on a real high, he re-entered the ballroom to find the party had broken up into gossiping groups, some gathered around the tables, others congregating at the bar, politicians chatting to journalists, ambassadors to ambassadors, lobbyists to anyone who would listen.

He saw the young Senator Wilkins talking to an elderly man, his short, thin frame bent slightly forward, his face looking as if it had been chiselled out of granite. Ed Eberhard was an old adversary of MacAnally's. The ranking Republican member of the Senate Environment and Public Works Committee, he was the only one to have opposed every single clause in every MacAnally-supported measure. MacAnally tried to by-pass the pair but Wilkins spotted him and called out, 'Sam, come and defend yourself. Senator Eberhard is accusing you of taking advantage of Exxon's hospitality.'

Eberhard's eyes, as they surveyed the campaigner's face, were shrewd but not unfriendly. 'Not really criticising you for that, young man. I guess everyone involved in this affair was trying to get what they could out of it. Taking opportunities . . . that's what life's all about.'

'I wish you'd "taken the opportunity" to back our improvements to the Clean Air Act, Senator,' MacAnally replied.

Eberhard laughed humourlessly. It sounded more like a bark. 'Improvements? If you environmentalists had your way you would have us back travelling across the country in covered wagons and hunting with bows and arrows.'

But MacAnally was in far too good a humour to be provoked. He grinned, winked at Wilkins, and moved on.

He was just about to seek out Brown and Nader when he heard someone call his name. He turned. Rising from one of the tables and coming towards him was a short, thick-set man. He was entirely bald, with a round parchment-white face and small nose and ears. His head looked like an unripened pumpkin. He was, thought MacAnally, even uglier than he looked in newspaper photographs.

Justin Lord was known as the 'commodities king'. He had made a fortune by predicting with extraordinary accuracy the commodities that would rise or fall in price, and buying and selling with near-infallible timing. It was said he only needed to hint that one could be temporarily going out of fashion for it to become a self-fulfilling prophecy.

Not that he ever dropped a hint; Lord, it was said, talked to no one. He was a loner. The *Wall Street Journal* had called him 'a man of mystery'.

'Mr MacAnally, that was a most impressive speech, sir.' It was said in an exceptionally deep, slightly guttural voice, and with almost exaggerated courtesy.

'Thank you. It's Mr Lord, isn't it?'

'I'm flattered you recognise me, sir.' He looked intently at the environmentalist and hesitated, as if reconsidering what he wanted to say. Then, suddenly decisive, he asked, 'Mr MacAnally, do you ever come to New York?'

'Frequently.'

'I know you're a busy man but I'd be grateful for your opinion on a matter of some importance. Could you spare me half an hour?'

MacAnally found the financier's modesty beguiling. 'I'm not too hot on the commodities market,' he said good-naturedly.

'I can assure you it's not business. Quite the contrary.'

'Of course I'd be pleased to see you, Mr Lord.'

'Then I'll ask my secretary to fix a convenient time. Once more my thanks for your speech tonight. It enhanced what I fear was threatening to be a rather tedious occasion.'

MacAnally watched him return to his table.

He couldn't imagine how he could help the man.

On the other hand the environmental movement was always looking for funds.

And Justin Lord was not short of those.

MacAnally decided that if he didn't hear from the commodities king, he would make contact himself.

NEW YORK

He decided to travel by Metroliner to New York. It would take longer than the shuttle but he needed time to think. In any case, he liked to travel by rail. It was a chance to look into America's backyard and, at least on this journey, into the past. At disused railway stations. Graveyards of derelict and stripped cars, sometimes piled upside down, three or four high. Broken glass windows like sightless eyes staring out from the empty skulls of closed factories. An abandoned drive-in movie theatre, its auditorium overgrown with grass, as forgotten as the stars who once shone from the big white screen that was still there, as if waiting for a late-night appearance by their ghosts.

But it wasn't all rocking chairs on the back porch, old people searching into their past. There were signs of regeneration too. Children's swings behind brightly painted box-like houses. Rows of yellow school buses, lined up like a uniformed regiment, waiting for action on Monday morning. Small boys playing on makeshift baseball triangles.

Despite spending all of his time in cities and thriving on the challenge, MacAnally was deeply attached to rural America, especially small towns with names nobody had heard of. His father, Ed MacAnally, was himself a small town college teacher from West Virginia. Tall and thin, with prematurely white hair and a beard, he had in his mid-thirties courted and married one of his students, a fair-haired beauty fifteen years his junior. They were committed conservationists long before it became fashionable and spent nearly all of their spare time photographing canyons and lakes, wildlife and fauna. Over the years they accumulated a huge collection of slides. These they would project onto the white-washed wall of their former farmhouse home, and look at in front of the fire on cold winter evenings.

From when he was old enough to talk, the young Sam begged to be allowed to stay up late and look at them too. From these pictures and from the journeys he made with his parents he learned of, and came to love the physical splendour of America.

Throughout his childhood the family spent the college vacations driving from state to state in an ageing Buick, the small boy kneeling on the back seat of the car, getting to know his country as it disappeared from view. They went everywhere. And there were pictures of Sam to prove it. Sam standing in front of Old Faithful at Yellowstone. Sam sitting cross-legged in front of a camp fire at Yosemite. Sam at the foot of a giant rock in Monument Valley. Sam peering over the edge of the Grand Canyon. Sam dwarfed by a giant seguaro plant in the Mojave Desert. Sam as far north as the Badlands of South Dakota and as far south as the bayous of Louisiana.

But also they went to the unknown places, down winding country roads into the heart of rural America, to the small communities still huddling around a general store, a white wooden church and a one-pump gas station.

Even now, sitting in a train, looking out of the windows, or driving across the country as he still liked to do, he would find himself humming John Denver's song:

> Country roads, take me home
> To the place I belong
> West Virginia, mountain momma
> Take me home, country roads . . .

Given their preference for staying near the land it was a cruel irony that it was on one of their few journeys by air, to visit Sam at college, that his parents perished together, killed instantly when their plane crashed – due, it was found, to engineering negligence.

They bequeathed Sam many things. They left an affinity with nature that drove him to follow them into the environmental movement. They left him an invaluable collection of 30,000 slides, all carefully filed, and now taken care of by a grateful environmental science faculty at Sam's former college. And they left him money. Not a fortune, but a tidy sum passed by his mother's parents to her and then to him. It was sufficient for him to be able to work fulltime in the movement while maintaining his financial independence.

Above all they left him with a deep sense of grief. This he converted into that powerful human fuel called anger. This was not expressed volcanically but in a ruthless, relentless drive to defeat those he believed to be desecrating the country his parents had loved and helped to protect for him. It was the anger that made him such a formidable operator.

Like many of his generation, MacAnally was encouraged by Ralph Nader. The country's most famous famous citizen advocate, then in his late thirties, had come to his college and inspired the young student. He spent the following summer vacation working as a volunteer in Nader's Washington headquarters and, when he left college, returned there, eventually being taken on the paid team. From there he went to work for a while at the Environmental Defence Fund, then as a regional organiser for the Sierra Club. Eventually and to no one's surprise he struck out on his own, forming a campaigning pressure group.

MacAnally had observed how difficult it was for the

big, all-embracing environmental groups to fight campaigns on specific issues with single-minded determination.

Their cutting edge was blunted by having to tackle too much.

So he created ECO to take on single issue campaigns.

It was an environmental guerrilla force – but non-violent.

A series of well-publicised successes, built on hard work, opportunism, and a lot of luck, attracted more and more young environmentalists to its ranks. MacAnally became a popular campus speaker, and also travelled to international environmental conferences. This led to the building up of a worldwide network and gradually the growth of ECO International, now with some thirty member countries.

He was, of course, not without critics, even within the movement. An articulate and aggressive debater, keenly sought after by television producers, he had, like Ralph Nader, become a star. The upshot was that other environmentalists would often struggle hard to get publicity for an issue only to find that it was MacAnally who was chosen for the interview. When challenged, he blamed the producers; they always wanted the biggest name they could get. But, truth to tell, he put up only token resistance. He *needed* the publicity. It was the key to his success. If his pursuit of it was misunderstood as ego-tripping then that was just too bad – a price he was willing to pay.

When accused, as he occasionally was, of being an autocratic leader, he was equally unapologetic, arguing that he fought his campaigns like wars. On one side were the public, their interests represented by the environmentalists, and on the other side were the enemy, the polluters and poisoners, the desecrators and destroyers.

You couldn't fight wars by committee. You needed generals. MacAnally was a general. Take it or leave it. There were plenty of other groups you could join if you didn't like it.

There had been another price for all this: he had become a loner, and for much of the time he *had* been lonely.

Then he met Marie.

It was at an environmental conference in New York. She was about five eight, slim, with small, firm breasts, stunningly long legs, and brown skin that made her appear permanently suntanned. She had black hair that she usually wore in a pony tail. This made her appear a lot younger than her thirty-one years. What struck MacAnally at that first meeting was the way she moved – proudly, with a hint of sensuality, but, above all, with astonishing presence . . . to MacAnally it seemed as if the centre of the crowded room was wherever she stood. He could hardly take his eyes off her.

When the panellists gathered for coffee before the debate, he went straight to her. In answer to his questions she said she was born and educated in France and had come to America in her late teens. She described her parents, now retired and back in the South of France, as having been 'something in the fashion business'. Whatever it was, they had made a lot of money. She lived in New York on an allowance.

Marie was an ecological fundamentalist, a 'dark Green', a believer that it was pointless fighting single issue campaigns when the entire eco-system was threatened. Now, cheered on by her supporters in the audience, she set out to give the famous Sam MacAnally a hard time.

'You fiddle while Rome burns,' she told him. 'You devote all your resources – your energy, money, and people – fighting to clean up one factory or one river, while ignoring problems that threaten the whole world.'

'Maybe that's because you care more about *the theory* than you care about *the people* actually being damaged,' he replied.

'Oh hell,' she retorted, 'I don't know how you can say that. The people you're helping often add up to only a few hundreds; I'm concerned about the *thousands of millions* who every day face disease, hunger, death.'

'OK, but what can you do for them today?' he asked. 'And I mean *today*. Let's say we'd realised what was happening in that factory in Bhopal: we could have saved 2,500 lives, and protected 10,000 seriously injured, 20,000 partially disabled, and more than 150,000 others adversely affected . . . are you telling me that if I'd been campaigning to protect that one community that it wouldn't have mattered?'

'Look, of course what you do is *worthy*,' she said, making 'worthy' sound wimpish in the extreme. 'But it's a question of priorities.'

'Exactly,' he said. 'That's where we differ. You determine your priorities by the size of the problem. I determine mine by what we can actually achieve, by what's possible. I'm interested in results. Furthermore,' he raised his voice as she began to interrupt, 'every small victory we achieve enhances our credibility as a movement and gets us the attention that enables us to raise the bigger issues. You run around talking about global warming and people will tell you they're more worried about the quality of water coming from their taps; you talk to them about their taps, maybe get their water cleaned up, and maybe – *just maybe* – they'll listen to you about global warming.'

It had been an argument that held its audience in thrall, not least because of the electricity between them.

Two actors on top form and with a good script had found in each other a performer to inspire their best.

Afterwards MacAnally had taken Marie aside and begged her to have dinner. They talked in Boxers, his favourite Greenwich Village diner, till late into the night and, as he had missed the last shuttle to Washington, he ended up sleeping on the couch in her cosy upper West Side apartment. A few weeks later, when back in New York, he had graduated to her bed, and in turn she began finding excuses to come to Washington more often.

They still argued, but with increasing respect for each other's point of view, and eventually Marie, after resisting for weeks, responded to his pressure on her to fill a gap by acting as New York organiser for ECO for a year.

Now, at the end of a tumultuous week, he took a taxi up Broadway, then down West 70th and, bag in hand, pressed one of the bells in the doorway of a tall brownstone in the block between Columbus Avenue and Central Park West.

'It's me,' he said as he heard her soft voice over the intercom.

The door clicked open and he bounded up the three flights of stairs, until he found her standing on the landing, wearing a simple white shift, her dark hair flowing over her shoulders. She was holding a half-full glass.

He dropped the bag and reached for her.

'My God, you look good,' he whispered into her hair.

She leaned back in his arms, the glass balanced perilously in one hand, and smiled into his eyes. 'Hi Mac-O.'

'I guess I'll *never* get you to stop calling me Mac-O,' he pretended to complain as he finally released her and picked up the bag.

'That's right, Mac-O,' she said, leading him in by the hand and laughing in the deep-throated way he loved.

He could smell something good simmering on the stove, but she took him by the hand and drew him down to where she had been kneeling on a cushion by the electric fire, and poured a second glass from a bottle of champagne in an ice bucket.

'What's this?' he said.

'Champagne; French champagne. The real thing. Because I was such a grouch when you told me about the award. I thought we should celebrate now – if only the look on the President's face. Christ, it was funny. I thought he was going to have a heart attack.'

'Well, to be fair, he took it all rather well.' He shifted to a more comfortable position on the floor, leaning back on the couch, his legs stretched out in front of him. 'Guess who's going to have a cosy chat at the White House?'

'You're kidding?'

'I'm not.'

Despite her previously cynical remarks about the President, she looked impressed.

'Anyway, what's the reaction in the movement?' he asked.

'Good. Even those who were sceptical before were positive about it afterwards. Everybody's happy.'

'That's great.'

'Yes. Mac-O . . .' She hesitated, then, reaching out, took his hand. 'I keep feeling that something's happening we're not completely in control of.'

'In what way?'

'Well, up to now the environmental issue has been *our* issue. Of course we wanted everyone to share it but we were in charge, we set the agenda. It worries me that we could lose control, that the issue could be taken over and somehow diminished . . .'

'I don't see . . .'

'. . . because the politicians and the multi-nationals have a way of picking up a thing and smothering it with bullshit so that everybody thinks something's happening when it's not.'

She got up, went to the stove to check the food, then knelt beside him again.

'With them, it's all façade, public relations, political rhetoric, but, just the same, they assume ownership of it as if they're saying, "*Well, thanks, you were right to draw it to our attention, but we're the big boys – we'll take over now*." And they will "take it over" – but to what end? To deplete it of its energy. So that in the end nothing really happens – at least nothing of any significance.'

He sat still for a moment, digesting what she had said. Then: 'I know what you mean. But we haven't any choice but to encourage them to get involved. For Christ's sake, that's what we've been campaigning *for*. All we can do is maintain our separate strength and act as their conscience on the issue. Keep watching what they're doing. Keep applying pressure for results.'

'I know that. But . . . well, I just think we need to be careful.'

MacAnally leapt up, and began restlessly to pace up and down. 'I'll tell you what we need,' he said. 'We need a new issue.

'Black and white.

'One that enables us to take on the big battalions and win.

'One that shows the politicians why we've a right to be an ongoing player at the table.'

He sat down beside her once more. 'That's what we need,' he said. 'A new issue.

'*We need a new campaign*.'

The World Trade Center occupies two gigantic

skyscrapers at the lower end of Manhattan, grey-white towers so high that they dwarf even the Empire State Building. Between them they house 1,000 organisations, nearly all commercial, and into them each day come more than 50,000 office workers, enough to populate a medium-sized town. Most of them enter the huge marble ground-floor halls from escalators fed by the Center's own subway station. From there they continue their journey skywards by elevator, some for more than 100 floors, their numbers diminishing as in twos and threes they decant into anonymous-looking corridors to even more anonymous-looking offices.

On this bright but cold Monday in November, MacAnally arrived by taxi at the Vesty Street entrance. He made his way across the crowded foyer, past the queues at the juice bar, the news stands, the drug store, the coffee and cookie shops, to WTC number one, where he took the elevator to the sky lobby on the 78th floor, transferring there to go on to the 98th.

There were only two words on the glass door.

Lord Inc.

He grinned.

Had the elevator over-shot? *Lord Inc.* Was that what it said on the door to heaven?

He knocked and entered a huge, thickly carpeted room, divided into two by a glass partition stretching from floor to ceiling. Behind the partition was what appeared to be an operations room. It was manned by a team of six, all sitting in front of an array of computer monitors, calculators, and telephones. The other half, where MacAnally was, appeared to serve both as reception area and Lord's outer office. It was occupied by two young women. One was little more than a teenager, blonde, pale, caked in make-up, and frowning with concentration as she attempted, apparently with some difficulty, to transfer shorthand notes to a word processor. The other was, MacAnally guessed, in her late twenties, tall and black, impeccably groomed, cool. She appeared to combine the role of receptionist and telephone operator.

MacAnally got the impression that not many people came to Lord Inc. The blonde girl abandoned her notes and looked at him as if he had come from another planet and even the cold-eyed receptionist allowed herself a show of surprise. When he explained that he had arranged to meet Justin Lord at nine she looked dubious, but carefully wrote down his name and disappeared. She returned almost immediately, a transformed woman, alert, bordering on friendly.

How did he like his coffee? Could she hang up his coat? Could he walk this way?

He followed her to the door. She wore a tight black dress. Extremely tight. He recalled the old joke; if he 'walked that way' he'd be arrested.

Lord's own office proved to be another vast, rectangular room, oak-panelled and impressively decorated with paintings. His taste was contemporary American and to MacAnally's unpractised eye they appeared to be originals.

At one end there stood a big oak desk, at the other a boardroom table and chairs and, in the middle, on a slightly lower level so that you had to take a couple of steps down to it, was a comfortable sitting area.

One wall was almost entirely obscured by four rows of television monitors showing the latest commodity and share prices from all over the world.

The room was empty and MacAnally stepped down onto the lower level and looked out of the window. To his left, far below, he could see the Brooklyn Bridge, the commuter traffic still streaming across on its way to work. He looked past the old Williamsburg Bank building to the Fulton fish market, down into the dark, man-made canyons of the Wall Street financial district, and then beyond them to Battery Park. Then he turned his gaze to the harbour, to the copper-coated Statue of Liberty shining in the late autumnal sun, to neighbouring Ellis Island, and, in the distance, to Staten Island and New Jersey.

'It's some view, isn't it?'

He turned and smiled at the man who had come quietly to his side. 'Breathtaking.'

'It has a special attraction for me,' said Lord, waving him to one of the armchairs. 'My parents and I came up that harbour when I was a baby, refugees from poverty in Germany . . . just three of the twelve million immigrants who came to this country by way of Ellis Island.' He pointed to the small piece of land seemingly floating in the water between Manhattan and New Jersey. 'I often sit and look at it and think of my own parents, queueing up before the immigration authorities, so full of hope.'

'I imagine that must be uplifting.'

'Uplifting?' Lord considered the word. Then, speaking so quietly that MacAnally had to lean forward to hear him, he said, 'I suppose so.

'Sometimes.

'Actually, I look at it with mixed feelings.' He paused. 'He was dead within a year, you know.'

Then, before the younger man could react: 'But their dream that America would prove a place of opportunity for their son has been fulfilled. When I look out there I still think of those words . . . "*sea of shining hope*".'

MacAnally was moved. Sitting down, Lord looked even shorter, rounder, yet it wasn't fat – MacAnally sensed a power in the stocky body. He must have been in his early seventies, but there were no physical signs of ageing. Like MacAnally, he had brown eyes, but these were so dark that when his back was to the light they looked like black orbs implanted on his disconcertingly white ball of a head.

MacAnally wondered what kind of man Lord really was. He had asked Jackie Brown to let him see the *Washington Post* clips on the financier but they revealed little except a passion for privacy. He was, apparently, a bachelor, lived alone in an Upper East Side apartment surrounded, it was said, by the same unlikely combination of expensive paintings and rows of flickering computer monitors that were all around them now.

According to the clippings he worked round the clock, accumulating more and more money.

But for what? The clippings provided no answer. MacAnally wondered if even Lord knew what it was.

There was a pot of coffee on the table and Lord poured for them both.

'Do you do much flying, Mr MacAnally?'

'Some. I lecture all over the country, and I travel abroad. And I'm on the shuttle between Washington and New York a lot. Why do you ask?'

'Have you noticed that air fares are one of the few things that are becoming less expensive?'

'Can't say I have.'

'Who gets your tickets?'

'We're serviced by an agency.'

Lord smiled. 'So even environmental tycoons don't always look at the bill.'

'Hardly a tycoon,' MacAnally laughed.

'I know. But I suggest you take a look. After steadily rising throughout the eighties and early nineties, air fares have fallen by twenty per cent and are still falling. Yet airline profits have substantially increased. Can you guess why?'

'I've no idea. Market forces . . .?' Then he remembered. 'No . . . wait . . . it must be because of plantacon.'

'*Quite so*, Mr MacAnally. A key factor in the economics of air travel is the price of fuel. Until recently this varied from fifteen to forty per cent of operating costs depending on the going rate for crude oil. Naturally the manufacturers came under enormous pressure to make planes more fuel-efficient. They succeeded to some extent, but it's only over the last four or five years that the industry's made a real breakthrough.'

Lord paused and poured himself a second cup of coffee. 'So you know all about plantacon?'

'Only what I've read in the papers.'

Everyone had heard of plantacon. It was an artificially created chemical that when added to aviation fuel helped to produce twenty-five per cent more energy per gallon.

This had cut costs dramatically. It had also enabled planes to fly further without re-fuelling, thus increasing route flexibility.

The plantacon revolution, the airlines had called it. For them, plantacon was little short of a miracle.

But what did this have to do with Lord?

Sensing that he was puzzled, Lord said, 'You're wondering why I'm rambling on about aircraft fuel, Mr MacAnally?'

He walked across to the desk and came back with two folders, one with a black card cover, one grey. 'These will interest you.'

He put the grey one on the table. 'This contains a history and an analysis of plantacon. You will find details of a number of deaths at the New Jersey factory where it was manufactured and tested. Go to the factory now and you'll see the workers dressed as if they're on the moon. You'll find they're taking an unprecedented range of safety measures. Why? Because plantacon is dangerous, Mr MacAnally, extremely nasty stuff.'

He leaned back in his chair. 'I believe you were involved in the campaign to stop the addition of lead to gasoline?'

MacAnally nodded.

'Well, this chemical seems to have the same effect on people as lead does? It's a neurotoxin, a brain poison. In high quantities it can drive people insane or kill them. This is what happened at the factory, but it's been well covered up, huge payments to the widows, arm-twisting of local newspaper editors and so on.'

He leaned forward once more, picking up the black folder. 'But the big question, Mr MacAnally, *the really big question*, is what effect it has in smaller quantities, for instance the quantities that are blasted out of the exhausts of jet aircraft, particularly when they're taking off and landing.'

MacAnally felt his heart beating faster. '*It's emitted from the exhausts*?'

Lord dropped the second folder on the table, still just out of MacAnally's reach. 'This report contains the results of research I myself commissioned, not just from one scientist but from five, not just in this country but also in England, Japan and Australia.

'The studies show contamination of the ground around airports.

'And they show that plantacon is reaching people. Some are inhaling it. Some are eating it because it's landing on their fruit and vegetables or getting into the soil they use to grow them. And children are licking fingers which have picked it up in playground dust.

'The research shows little effect on adults, at least so

far, but children are absorbing it into their bodies and the effects are alarming. There are signs of reduced IQ and all sorts of learning difficulties.'

He paused. 'Mr MacAnally, let me put it to you like this. *A huge number of jet aircraft are travelling around this planet, landing and taking off at airfields in the vicinity of the homes of millions of children, all of whom are being exposed to a dangerous pollutant – all of whom are at risk of brain damage.*'

MacAnally's mind reeled.

'But why have you kept this secret?'

'I haven't. I received the studies only the day before I heard you speak in Washington.'

'But what got you interested in this? What made you suspect this? What made you commission the research?'

Lord paused to call for more coffee. 'Mr MacAnally, I've only one relative in this country, a cousin who came as a child about the same time I did. He's a scientist of sorts, alas not a distinguished one. In fact, to put it bluntly, a failure. Over the years I've frequently helped him out of financial or other troubles. Yet he was the one who stumbled upon it. He was doing some work for one of the oil companies to do with the way they add plantacon to the fuel. Noting the highly toxic nature of the chemical he began to do a little extra research on his own. He came to me for funds to explore it further. Frankly I gave him the money without thinking. I was busy and just wanted him out of my office. Anyway, he came back claiming to have uncovered a scandal and, because I was afraid he was going to make a fool of himself, I arranged some backup work. That appeared to confirm his findings and led me to commission this whole-scale study. It's taken nearly a year.'

'And now?'

'That's where you come in. As you probably know,

I'm a private man, Mr MacAnally. I work at my business and I keep out of public affairs and especially the newspapers as much as they'll let me. I want this raised publicly and dealt with, but I don't want to be involved publicly myself.'

He moved the folders around with his hands, like playing cards, then put one on top of the other, and leaned forward.

'In any case I wouldn't know where to start. I'm a commodity dealer, Mr MacAnally. But you're an environmentalist, a politician.

'I wouldn't know what to do. But you would.

'I want to hand these files over to you.'

MacAnally walked to the window but this time he didn't see the view.

What he did see was a scandal of immense proportions.

And the prospect of a tremendous campaign.

Still looking out of the window, thinking aloud, he said, 'I can't imagine more powerful opponents than the airline industry, the oil industry and the plantacon manufacturers. Washington won't be sympathetic either . . . because of the energy savings.'

'I didn't think it would be easy, Mr MacAnally, that's why I'm prepared to give you the resources to fight with.'

He appeared at MacAnally's side. 'I'm not one for wearing my heart on my sleeve, but the fact is I've not given as much back to my adopted country as I should have. I've never really known how to. Now fate has given me this knowledge and introduced me to you. I believe that stopping this environmental damage is what I'm destined to do. But I can only do it with your help.

'If you'll run the campaign, I'll donate whatever you need to pay for it.

'Even if it runs into millions of dollars.'

*

MacAnally had four hours to fill. He strolled down to Battery Park and then, on an impulse, took the ferry to Ellis Island.

He walked up the short path from the jetty to a big rambling building and climbed the steps to the registry hall, where he knew that around seventy years ago the Lords must have sat with other immigrants, patiently waiting to be called to one of the tall desks at the end of the room. There, standing in front of the desk, they would have been interviewed and their fate decided. For the majority of the immigrants, including the Lords, it would be a new life in America; for a few it would be devastating rejection and a desolate journey back whence they came . . . to poverty . . . maybe even to a violent death.

On the ground floor he found an exhibit called America's family album. For it, thousands had submitted family photos and data. MacAnally was about to walk past when a thought struck him. He stopped and went back to the data board and pressed a variety of buttons until he came up with the name Lord. There were a number of possibilities. He tried them all. None was right. Then he remembered that one of the *Post* clippings had mentioned that the Lords had adopted a new name when they came to America. What was the old one? It took him a couple of minutes to remember, Lauda. He started pressing more buttons.

Then he found it: a faded picture of a man and a woman, standing close together with a battered old trunk at their feet. The man was short, thick-set. He looked disorientated.

The woman was thin, her face pinched, worry etched around her eyes. In the man's arms, his face almost hidden under a flat cap, was a small boy, probably only eighteen months to two years old. Under it were the words *Hans and Eva Lauda, and Justin, February 1924*.

MacAnally looked at the brave, bewildered-looking little family. Memories flooded back of his own parents, of the picture of the three of them that he kept on his dresser in Washington . . . a picture taken when he was only about two. He felt for Lord, orphaned while young. And he felt for himself. Tears pricked his eyes.

He returned to the ferry and, defying a wind that chilled him to the bone, wiping the salty spray from his face, he stood alone on the open deck as it returned to Manhattan, looking back to Ellis Island and then up to the twin towers of the World Trade Center. He imagined Lord up there at that moment, perhaps looking down at the island himself.

Remembering.

Or was he being overly sentimental? More likely Lord was engrossed in the figures from his flickering monitors, waiting for the right moment to buy and sell and, by that act alone, to send the price of some commodity soaring or tumbling. MacAnally thought, too, of peasants in some far-flung place, maybe working in sugar-cane fields or on banana or coffee plantations, whose meagre income would be raised or reduced by the speculative press of a button by a man they had never heard of on the 98th floor of a building they had never heard of in a city they probably would never see.

Some day he must ask Lord whether he ever considered the fate of those at the other end of the computerised world he inhabited.

But, then, what would be the point?

No doubt Lord had rationalised it to himself way back.

Still, why should a man who spent every hour of the day cold-heartedly playing a computer game with people's lives, and who seemed to have no room for human warmth in his own bizarre life, suddenly start caring about children being poisoned by plantacon?

Lord had said he wanted to pay back his debt to America.

Maybe.

MacAnally couldn't think of any other reason.

But he'd better have Lord checked out.

By the time they docked it was mid-afternoon and even colder. He pulled his jacket more closely around him and picked his way over the uneven pavements and between the human and other flotsam and jetsam of the Lower East Side to East 13th, to the address Justin Lord had given him. The graffiti-covered block between Broadway and University Place was full of small business premises, a photo laboratory, a lumber shop selling doors, shutters, and shelving, two antique shops, and, opposite each other on the corner, a Chinese restaurant and the offices of the Amalgamated Lithographers of America. He went up the stairs of an anonymous-looking office building until he found a door marked 'Aviation Technology Services'. He rang the bell and a panel opened. He found himself confronted by a woman in her fifties with sharp features encircled by wiry grey-black hair who looked him up and down suspiciously and then unenthusiastically nodded him into the untidy but cosy office of Ted Baker.

Lord's consultant was an affable, thick-set man, near to sixty, with silver-white hair, bushy eyebrows, and a good-humoured face.

'How much do you know about the way the engines on jet aircraft work?' he asked MacAnally as he sank back into an old leather chair behind a desk groaning with folders and charts and warmed his hands on the cup of coffee provided by the receptionist who, released from her cage, appeared tiny and birdlike but, MacAnally noted with relief, a little less hostile.

'Not a thing,' he said, 'and I'm no engineer. I'll need a child's guide.'

'OK, that's what you'll get.' He rested back in the chair and put his feet up on the desk.

'Put as straightforwardly as possible, a jet engine inhales air at the front and draws it into a piece of machinery known as the compressor where it's tightly squeezed.

'Then it enters a combustion chamber where the fuel's injected and the heat from the burning fuel causes it to expand – like a continuous explosion. From there the expanding air escapes into the turbine, and from there it's blasted out of the engine tailpipe and this propels the aircraft forward.'

He looked at the concentrating MacAnally and grinned. 'One of my over-sexed colleagues describes the four stages of the jet engine cycle as suck-squeeze-bang-blow.'

MacAnally laughed. 'You make it all sound simple.'

'Well, yes and no. In a way it is. Try inflating a balloon till its full of air and then let it go. It'll fly across the room at great speed as a result of the pent-up air being released from the narrow nozzle. If you compress a lot of air in an aircraft engine and then release the pent-up force from a comparatively small exhaust it has the same effect.'

He pointed to the wall where there was a complex drawing of a jet engine. 'Of course, there's a bit more technology involved. Some 20,000 parts to be precise.'

'Tell me about the fuel.'

'OK. It's not like car fuel but it's produced by the same companies. It's more like kerosene. For US domestic use its called Jet-A but everywhere else it's Jet-A-1.'

'What's the difference between Jet-A and Jet-A-1?'

'Not much, just in the freezing point of the fuel.'

He picked up a pipe and, beginning to stuff it with tobacco, continued, 'It's distilled from crude oil in the refinery, cleaned up to remove smelly sulphur compounds, and then made suitable for use in jet aircraft with a number of additives, an anti-static mixture, an anti-wear agent and so on.'

'Is that when the plantacon's added?'

'No, that's injected at the airport to avoid it getting lost in the pipelines . . . by sticking to the pipes.'

'*Pipelines?*'

'Of course. They use a lot of the stuff. If it was all moved by tanker you wouldn't be able to get your car on the roads.'

'You mean *all* the oil companies have pipelines into airports?'

'No, all the fuel is fed into one system.' Baker laughed at MacAnally's surprise. 'The fuel is all the same. It's manufactured to the same specifications, those laid down by ASTM, IATA, and the US and British defence authorities. So all companies just feed into the same pipeline.'

'But how does the customer who is, say, paying for Shell Jet-A, know he's getting Shell Jet-A?'

'He doesn't. And he probably isn't. It doesn't really matter. Each supplier feeds in the number of gallons their airline customer orders.'

'Well, if there's no difference, what's the point? Where's the competition?'

'In the quality of the service, security of supply, and in the financial deals, credit terms and the like.'

'How much fuel are we talking about?'

'Well, a Boeing 747-400, for instance, flying across the Atlantic or non-stop from a European capital to the Far East, could be carrying nearly 60,000 US gallons of fuel.

At the beginning of the 1990s the world's airlines, outside of the Eastern block, were consuming nearly 50 billion US gallons of Jet-A and Jet-A-1 a year.'

'Fifty billion! Holy shit! No wonder they're concerned about fuel efficiency.' He paused to take it all in. Then said, 'So tell me about plantacon.'

'Well, I expect you know the gist of it. The industry had already become exceptionally fuel-efficient, but given the volatility of fuel costs, and the effect of events like the 1991 Gulf crisis, it was always searching for a way whereby it could achieve more energy per gallon, thus cutting costs and enabling it to improve its services by flying greater distances on the same tankloads. Plantacon is the answer. It's an additive that increases the energy produced by the fuel. Its effect has been sensational. That's why you hear people talk of the "miracle additive" or "the plantacon revolution".'

MacAnally frowned with concentration. 'OK, now you said the fuel is burned up in the combustion chamber. But what happens to the plantacon?'

Baker shrugged. 'Frankly, I don't exactly know. But my guess is that it survives the burning process and is blasted out of the exhaust with the compressed air, probably in an invisible spray of tiny particles.'

'Would I be right in thinking that more power is needed when the plane is taking off and climbing than at any other time? That extra fuel is being burned then? Therefore greater emissions of . . . plantacon . . . whatever . . . are occurring then?'

'That's right.'

'So if plantacon was causing any environmental damage it would be in the vicinity of airports?'

Baker lit the pipe, puffed, and, looking MacAnally carefully in the eye, replied slowly, 'That would be a logical assumption.'

'Do you have evidence of such damage?'

Baker fiddled with the pipe. 'That's not the business I'm in, Mr MacAnally. I can't help you, I'm afraid.'

For a moment the environmentalist sat still, digesting all he had heard. Baker looked at him speculatively, then asked, 'How well do you know Mr Lord?'

'Not well at all. I've only met him once before today. He told me about the research he commissioned and suggested I talk to you. And that's it.'

Baker rose and walked to the small window, standing momentarily with his back to the environmentalist. Then, turning, he said, 'Well, I was hanging around the coffee bar in the World Trade Center once, waiting to meet Lord, when I got chatting to this guy who works in that operations room of his. He says that when the Lords came to the States they went to Ohio and Lord's father got a job with a corporation in Dayton. The people he worked for were manufacturing tetraethyl lead, TEL, the lead additive for gasoline. Lord's father was accidentally exposed to a lethal dose of the stuff. Went into a coma and was dead within a week. His mother died four years later, they say of a broken heart.

'Anyway, this guy says that Lord ended up in an orphanage. As soon as he was old enough to understand what really happened, he vowed to the other kids that he was never going to work for people like that . . . he was going to make himself invulnerable. And I guess that's what he now is.'

MacAnally remembered what Lord had said. '*He was dead within a year.*' He slowly shook his head. 'Christ.'

'I know. It's a sad story. But it explains his obsession with plantacon, doesn't it?'

MacAnally blinked uncomprehendingly at Baker. 'How? What do you mean?'

'Well, it's the TEL story all over. To him these are the

same kind of people as the ones that killed his father. And, indirectly, his mother. I figure it's not compassion for children that's driving him, it's a desire for revenge. The way he looks at it, he may not be able to get at the last generation of poisoners, but he can get at this one.'

He sat down and began to re-light his pipe, gratified by the impact of his words on MacAnally who was momentarily speechless.

Finally the campaigner got to his feet. 'You've given me a lot to think about.' He picked up his jacket. 'Thanks.'

'No problem. Come back any time.'

As he reached the door, Baker called after him. 'By the way, Mr MacAnally, have you worked out how much money is involved in all this?'

MacAnally stopped. 'I have a file on it. I haven't read it yet.'

'Well, think about it.

'I reckon this year plantacon will save the world's airlines thirteen billion gallons of fuel.

'The price has been fluctuating but, taking the latest supply crisis into account, the financial saving could be at least twelve and a half billion dollars.'

He looked at MacAnally grimly. 'There's not a *country* in the world that's going to like anyone challenging a twenty-five per cent *energy* saving.

'And the *industry*'s not going to like anyone challenging a twenty-five per cent *cost* saving.

'I don't know what you plan to do but – if it affects the plantacon revolution – you'd better be ready to face some powerful enemies.'

'It's an outrage.' Marie tossed the second of the two folders onto the floor in front of the fire and turned to Sam with her eyes flashing. 'Incredible.'

Sam looked up from the *New York Times*. 'But do you believe it?'

'Well, obviously we'll need to check out the studies but they have a ring of credibility about them.'

'That's what I think. Anyway, I'm going to see the two American scientists myself, and I'm asking Olly, Machiko, and Liz to see the ones in the other countries.'

Marie picked up the grey folder and skimmed through it once more.

The growth of the industry was mindblowing.

The major US airlines alone were carrying more than 450 *million* passengers a year and coping with thousands of millions of 'ton miles' of cargo.

Nearly 75 *million* people a year arrived or departed from just the three airports serving New York alone – JFK, La Guardia and Newark, New Jersey.

According to the figures Lord had provided, in the first year of the decade *more than 100 billion dollars* worth of new aircraft were on order or option.

There had then been a setback. Even historic names such as Pan Am, TWA and Eastern lost their lustre, and the 1991 Gulf War and its aftermath had a devastating effect on every international airline, one that far outlasted the war itself.

But even so the problems had proved temporary. There was never any question that the industry would recover, and now, not least because of plantacon, it had.

Marie thought of all those aircraft releasing an invisible spray of microscopically small particles of plantacon, poisoning the dust and soil and plant-life around the airports, in the gardens and on the playing fields of residential areas. And of millions of children unsuspectingly and slowly being damaged, their life chances reduced.

She became aware of MacAnally looking at her,

expectantly. She noticed his eyes were bright. Then she realised. 'Christ, of course – this is it, isn't it Mac-O? This is *the* issue. The big one – the campaign you talked about last night?'

'It's got to be.' He could hardly keep still. 'It's got it all.'

He began to pace round the room.

'Big powerful multi-national companies poisoning vulnerable little children.

'And it's winnable. They'll be hard to beat – they'll spend millions of dollars defending it – but they'll never be allowed to continue using the stuff once the facts come out.'

She was now excited too. 'So what do we have to do?'

'First, we'll check out the scientists and their research.'

'And Justin Lord?'

'Of course . . . but I must say I instinctively trust the man.'

Did it matter that Lord was driven by a desire to avenge his parents?

To MacAnally, whose whole life had been partly motivated by the same impulse, it didn't matter at all.

In fact, Lord's motives didn't really matter, period. As long as he didn't have a financial interest in the result. And that they could easily check out.

And as long as he wouldn't be running the campaign. And he wouldn't. MacAnally would. He would make that clear to Lord.

Still he said, 'Sure, of course we'll check him out.'

'What else?' she asked.

'Well, the campaign will have to be international. We'll have to persuade the ECO conference to adopt it as a priority.'

Marie frowned. That wouldn't be easy. The groups in

other countries were already fighting their own battles
. . . and had already chosen global warming as their big
international campaign.

'They won't want to change course,' she said. 'Especially the Third World countries. They'll say pollution
around airports is largely a problem for the developed
world . . . why should they care?'

'Goddamn it, Marie, I know that. But this is big, and we
can win it. Probably fairly quickly. It'll enhance our
credibility, and improve our prospects of winning other
campaigns.'

Marie slipped away to the kitchen to make some coffee.

She had nearly said, '*Who's* being "enhanced", Sam –
you or the movement?'

But that would have been unfair.

She knew Sam cared about the issues, as deeply as she
did.

Did it matter that he was excited by the challenge of the
campaign as well as angry about the children being
harmed?

Probably not.

It was the fusion of ambition *and* anger that made
MacAnally so difficult to stop.

When she returned from the kitchen she found he had
been working on his own reply to her question.

'Marie,' he said earnestly, 'we have no choice but to do
it. Otherwise we'll be deliberately deciding to ignore the
poisoning of millions of children. We'll be no better than
the polluters.'

She stood in the doorway, a coffee mug in each hand,
looking at him affectionately, and then began to giggle.

Then she was laughing so much that she had to put the
coffee down.

'Oh, Mac-O,' she said. 'Your other reasons were good
enough for me.

'Keep that one for the cameras.'

WASHINGTON, D.C.

ECO International

Urgent fax to:
　　Olly Witcomb (London)
　　Monique de Vos (Brussels)
　　Machiko Yanagi (Tokyo)
　　Mike McKenzie/Liz Scullen (Melbourne/Perth)

Confidential

It's been suggested that the aviation fuel additive plantacon represents a significant environmental and public health hazard.

Can you:

1) In the case of Olly, Machiko, and Liz or Mike, contact the scientist in your country (whose details I enclose) and check him out.

2) In the case of Monique check whether anybody in Europe is expressing concern about plantacon.

This is urgent.

Sam MacAnally

LONDON

Olly Witcomb's eyes didn't want to open. He felt lethargic to the point of paralysis.

Grudgingly, he reached out for the alarm clock. It was

nine o'clock. He had been asleep for ten hours. 'Christ,' he thought, 'I must have been wiped out.'

He looked down the dishevelled bed, then down the full length of the one big room that, apart from a separate bathroom, represented his entire space. He took in the polished wood floor, the rug he had bargained for in India last summer, the pine table and chairs, the breakfast bar and kitchen with their stack of unwashed ECO coffee mugs, the untidy piles of books and records scattered around the window to the small balcony overlooking the Thames, the jersey and jeans he had carelessly dropped on the floor the previous night, and . . . under the door . . . a folded copy of the *Guardian* and a white envelope.

Sally must have picked them up when she was collecting her mail and delivered them on her way back to the top floor.

Olly wished she would deliver herself as well.

He had dreamed of little else from the day he moved into the building.

He lay back on the pillow and recalled their meeting.

His was one of twelve flats in a recently converted warehouse in Wapping, right in the heart of Docklands. He had been the last one to arrive, just eight weeks back. It was late by the time he unpacked and he'd left the door to the landing open so that he could pile onto it the bags he was going to take down to the basement. She had stopped by to introduce herself.

She was on her way back from a late-night jog and was wearing a track suit.

She was about five eight, athletically built. Her face and blonde hair were wet with sweat, her blue eyes shining. She looked stunning.

From that moment he had been in love. Hopelessly.

In fact, such was her impact that, despite being one of

the country's more articulate campaigners, he could at that first encounter hardly speak.

He just grinned idiotically – and sort of stammered.

He assumed that as a result she considered him mentally defective because he had since asked her for drinks a couple of times, proposed a spur-of-the-moment dinner at the bistro on the corner, suggested the cinema, and the theatre, even a jog together (Olly hated exercise in any form). Always it had been inconvenient. Always it was 'another time'. He was getting nowhere.

Often at night he would fall asleep thinking about her up there, soft in her bed, alone.

At least he hoped she was alone.

Now, on this Monday morning, realising that he was more than capable of whiling away another hour in bed contemplating the problem, he rose and put on his dressing-gown. He went to the door and picked up the newspaper and letter, plugged in the electric kettle and busied himself making coffee while he listened to the *Today* programme on Radio Four.

He was just about to open the envelope when the doorbell rang. He answered it, still in his dressing-gown, unshaven and hair rumpled, and immediately wished he hadn't because there, bright and shining in a UK Ambassador uniform, stood Sally.

'Hi, Olly, how are you?'

'Great – at least I will be when I have this coffee and get myself together.' He looked down ruefully at his shabby dressing-gown and then at her uniform. 'I didn't know you were in the airline business.'

'You never asked.'

'You've never given me the chance.'

'Well, now you're getting one. You in tonight?'

He thought quickly. There was a meeting he could miss.

'It's just that I've got some friends coming round for a pizza and some wine, and I wondered whether you'd like to come up. Then I won't feel guilty about the noise.'

'I'd love to,' said Olly.

'Great. About nine?'

'No problem.'

He watched her walk down the stairs, his spirits rising. It had happened at last.

This was going to be a good day.

Then he opened the letter.

It was a copy of a fax from Sam MacAnally in Washington. Sent by messenger from the office.

Plantacon pollution?

Sounded a bit unlikely.

Anyway, where did that fit into their priorities? They were committed to campaigning on global warming.

Olly was a willing worker but for once he was tempted to ring MacAnally and complain.

They had enough to do already.

Didn't MacAnally realise that he – and, for that matter, Machiko in Japan, Monique in Brussels, and Liz and Mike in Australia – were on their own? That they didn't have the resources of the Washington office? That they were already stretched beyond the limits of what they could do well?

He poured another cup of coffee.

Oh well, to hell with it, he had tonight to look forward to.

Sally.

At last.

In the meantime, MacAnally and the plantacon would just have to wait.

TOKYO

On the same Monday as Olly Witcomb was reading his fax in London, Machiko Yanagi was arriving home to her flat in the Nishi Ogikubo district of Tokyo in the early evening after a long weekend spent with her parents in Kyoto.

She picked up the pile of letters lying inside the door and tore off a number of messages from the fax machine near by.

It was there because her flat doubled as an office.

She knew she was fortunate in the space she had, and also in its location. The ECO grant towards her rent made possible a much bigger flat than she could otherwise afford, and Nishi Ogikubo was one of the older, more characterful parts of Tokyo.

She put the correspondence on the table while she had a shower and changed.

It had been a good idea to go back to Kyoto. She felt rested, at peace with herself.

She relived in her mind the weekend's highlights: Friday evening wandering down crowded Gojo Street with her sister, pausing to sit on some steps and gossip with friends while they looked east to the imposing Higashiyama Mountains; Saturday resting by the dark-green lily pond at the gold pavilion at Rokuonji Temple and, in the afternoon, at the Zen stone garden in the Ryoanji Temple. Then, in the early evening, going with her family to light a candle at one of the shrines in the centre of the city. Yesterday she had driven with her father, a professor of philosophy at Kyoto University, to Mount Takao and from the Jingoji Temple looked down

on the Kiyotaki River winding between cherry trees.
There they had listened to the sounds of the singing frogs
and reminisced about her childhood days spent in these
mountains, especially the weekends when they came to
rejoice in the blazing red and orange colours of autumn.

She dried herself in front of the mirror. She was only
five two but stocky – a cuddly figure. Her good-
humoured oval face was dominated by big brown eyes.
Her black hair was grown long, in a style more Western
than Japanese.

She put on a towelling dressing-gown, poured a glass
of German wine, and made herself a salad with the
vegetables and the freshly baked bread she had
purchased on her way home from the railway station.

As she ate she picked up the pile of letters and faxes.
A note from a member of the Diet, the Japanese
parliament, asking her for an environmental briefing. A
request to speak to a university students' meeting on
tropical rain forests. Courtesy copies of other groups'
press releases.

And a letter from Perth, Australia . . . from Mike
McKenzie.

She put that aside. She would read it later.

But already she felt the warmth of his contact. She had
met him at the international ECO conference in Hong
Kong. Over six feet tall, and thus towering over her, red
hair, freckled, schoolboyish face, extrovert, he had
literally picked her up the first time he met her. 'Hi . . .'
he had said, lifting her up and holding her a foot off the
ground so that her face was on a level with his.
'. . . wow, you look even better up here than you do
down there.' Normally that would have irritated
Machiko beyond measure but this time, with this man, it
didn't; it was an act just too full of impulsive goodwill.

She had liked him immediately, and uninhibitedly

took a place next to him at dinner that evening. Within twenty-four hours they were inseparable, taking every chance between conference sessions to talk about themselves, their families, their countries, and their causes.

Then on the last night they had slipped away and taken the ferry round the huge harbour and into the Aberdeen shelter with its dramatic mix of giant, brightly illuminated floating restaurants and tiny, lantern-lit junks and sampans.

Later, after a Cantonese dinner on the water, they took the same ferry back, standing together by the railing, looking at the silhouettes of the tall buildings on either side of the water and at the darker, protective hills above.

It was Mike who voiced what they were both thinking. 'I don't want to say goodbye.'

'No,' she said.

'I wish we were in Perth; that you lived in Australia.'

She glanced at him, then smiled. 'Or you in Japan.'

He grinned. 'Yes, or me in Japan.' Then, 'Anyway . . .' He turned her round and looked searchingly at her up-turned face. 'I guess you know how I feel . . .'

She nodded. Then putting her head on his chest and pulling his arms around her, she hugged him.

It still wasn't enough for him. He wanted her to say it . . . that she felt the same.

And in a way she did. 'Let's go back,' she said. 'To my room.'

Once at their hotel near the water's edge in Kowloon, she had taken him straight to her room and locked the door and hand in hand they had walked to the window looking out over the majestic harbour. They could see the Star ferry on one of its hundreds of thousands of journeys across the water between Kowloon and Hong

Kong Island, could see the glittering signs on the island's crowded streets, the lights in the windows of the imposing row of skyscrapers at the foot of Victoria Peak. Then they were in each other's arms. They stood there, close, for a long time. He could feel her trembling, and she could hear his heart thumping. He could feel her nipples, hard against his chest; she could feel him, hard too, down there where she knew they were destined to be joined . . . then his hands were under her tee-shirt and cradling her small, firm breasts, and she was turning her face up to him.

And on that memorable night they became lovers.

That had been nine months back. Since then he had come to Japan on holiday. It had been a success. Even her conservative parents had been beguiled by the big, good-natured Australian.

But both Machiko and Mike knew a decision had to be taken.

Actually the decision was far more pressing for him than for her. Machiko was a self-contained woman, able to have such moments, keep them with her, know he was there . . . somewhere . . . part of her, and yet still get on with her own life. She had too much going on to be lonely. Or to fret.

He, however, could not settle for that. He wanted her with him all the time.

It was a problem that would have to be addressed.

That was what his letter would say.

That's what the last letter had said. And the ones before that.

They were all there, bound together, on the small table beside her bed.

So tonight she would read the latest. And she would think about it. And write back.

And, maybe this time, maybe next, she would give him the answer he was waiting for.

But first, there was a fax from Sam MacAnally in Washington.

She read it and shook her head.

She admired Sam immensely but for once she felt just a little bit irritated.

Why was he bothering with this when their priorities were well established? There was so much to do already. She had put a lot of energy into preparing the global warming campaign. Also she had been working hard at building up contacts with other environmental organisations, earning their goodwill by helping with their campaigns.

There was just no more time.

And this plantacon business didn't sound like much.

She put the fax on one side.

She would look into it, of course, because she was conscientious.

But it would have to wait.

MELBOURNE

While Olly Witcomb was opening his fax over breakfast and Machiko Yanagi was doing the same in Tokyo in the early evening, Liz Scullen in Melbourne was just swaying home from a party. Most of the city's environmentalists had been there. The cheap Australian wine had flowed freely. Too much of it into Liz.

She hadn't been home since the morning and there was a pile of mail on the table in the hall of the four-floor building.

She shuffled the letters as she slowly climbed towards her bedsitter at the top.

One was from her mother in Brisbane. That was going to annoy her. It could wait till Liz had sobered up.

A bill. That could definitely wait.

A hand-delivered letter from the office. That was unusual. She stopped on the second landing to rest, and opened it.

It was a fax from MacAnally in Washington.

About aircraft pollution.

Strange. They had been working for a year on global warming. They were nearly ready to go. It was going to be a big campaign. Why was Sam bothering them with this?

Liz needed plantacon like a hole in the head.

And talking of heads, hers was beginning to throb.

Tired and more than slightly drunk, she continued her upward journey. Already the nights were hot and humid and it wasn't even December. The combined effects of the drink and the heat were drenching her in sweat. She paused on the third landing and pulled off her tee-shirt. Then, naked from the waist up, she began her push for the summit.

She didn't meet anyone on the way, but it wouldn't have mattered if she had. The other tenants were used to her lack of inhibition. 'That's just Liz,' they would say to their goggle-eyed guests as, wearing only a flimsy pair of knickers, she bounded past them on her way up and down the stairs.

Not that she was bounding now. By the time she reached the door at the top she was almost on her knees.

As she turned the key in the lock she decided she would phone Mike McKenzie about plantacon when he got back to his Perth office from wherever he was . . . then she remembered, the rain forests conference in Tasmania. That was due to end tomorrow. He'd be home in a day or so. They would discuss who would follow it up.

Until then it could wait.

As she opened the door she tossed the letters and the fax towards her desk. The fax missed and fell down the back.

Where it remained.
For the time being, forgotten.

BRUSSELS

Monique de Vos was fighting to keep back the tears that were welling up as she heated some spaghetti in the small kitchenette attached to her first-floor bedsitter in the Rue Stevin.

For the umpteenth time she was reviewing last night's latest row with Pierre.

She couldn't believe she could have been so stupid as to get involved with a married man.

She had always sworn she wouldn't, always been critical of women who did.

It was wrong in principle and it didn't work in practice.

Yet she had done it. Why?

She was even angrier with herself when she considered the answers. They were all so predictable.

Because she had been lonely.

Because she believed him when he said his marriage was over.

Because every other man seemed so boring after she met him.

Because he pursued her so relentlessly. It had been irresistibly flattering. And Monique was not accustomed to that.

Equally predictable had been his behaviour once he had won.

He had plenty of time for her when he was wooing her; now he was always busy and she had to fit in with his schedule.

He had taken risks being seen with her until he got her;

now it all had to be secretive.

He had spent time dining in restaurants, going for walks
. . . *before* they became lovers; now all he wanted was to
meet at her flat and go to bed.

Now, on top of all that, he had picked up Sam's fax off
her desk and wanted to use it for his own political
advantage.

'No,' she had cried. 'No, no, no. That is confidential.
You should never have read it.'

'OK,' he had shrugged, dropping it where he found it.
'OK. Forget it.'

But he was giving in too quickly.

'I don't believe you,' she said. 'You're still planning to
use it. Well, I won't let you. If you use it you'll never come
to this flat again. Do you understand? I will never trust
you again.'

'If you loved me, you would want to help me,' he had
complained.

'If you loved *me* a lot of things would happen,' she had
replied.

All that day she had worried about it. On her way to
work, in the office, and as she walked home.

Monique was twenty-eight. She was about five six and
tended to hide her broad but shapely figure behind loose-
fitting shifts. She wore her hair so that it often fell over her
face. Her alert, sensitive eyes were also well camouflaged,
by big, round, shaded glasses. All this, of course, reflected the fact that Monique was shy. Until you got to know
her. Then, her friends would discover, she was able and
determined, loyal and giving.

She was also highly intelligent. She had graduated
from university with an impressive degree and begun her
career in the European Commission, rising quickly from
trainee to respected staff member of DGII (the office of
the Environment Director General). In the process she

had come to know and be trusted by the environmental groups all over Europe and, preferring them to the bureaucrats and politicians she dealt with in the Commission, she had taken a big cut in salary to join ECO.

As its Euro-lobbyist she spent most of her time in Brussels where the Commission offices were located, but she also regularly visited Strasbourg where the Parliament sat.

She had loved the work from the start and, as her confidence grew, she became less shy, more outgoing. While her affair with Pierre was blossoming, she had been happier than at any time in her life.

Now it had all gone wrong.

The affair was dying, as she knew it should, yet still she couldn't bear to end it herself.

In a way she hoped Pierre would just go away.

And plantacon too.

The fax had been unwelcome.

With the whole of Europe to cover, with ECO groups in twelve Community countries demanding her help in Brussels and Strasbourg, with the global warming campaign to coordinate, she was already over-taxed.

She had more than enough to do without plantacon.

Especially if Pierre was going to abuse her trust and get involved. She didn't know where his interest lay, but she suspected the worst.

She drained the water from the pan and poured the spaghetti onto a plate.

She put it on the table in front of her and looked at it.

She wasn't hungry now.

At last she began to cry. Softly at first, then bitterly.

It had all become such a mess.

Pierre.

Plantacon.

They were both problems she could do without.

Part Two

THE INDUSTRIALISTS . . .
THE SCIENTISTS . . .
THE POLITICIANS . . .

To: The Chairman,
       Executive Airways
From: ECO International, November 28.

Sir,

We understand that the high   xic fuel additive plantacon is being emitted fro   aircraft exhausts, especially in the vicinity of airports.

We would like to know whether you have considered the environmental or public health implications of this.

Yours,

Sam MacAnally
Director

To: The Chairman,
       Jet-A Supplies
From: ECO International, November 28.

Sir,

We understand that the plantacon you supply to airlines is highly toxic. As it appears that particles are released into the atmosphere, subsequently falling to earth, they could represent an environmental and public health hazard.

Have you considered this possibility?

Yours,

Sam MacAnally
Director

To: The Chairman,
       Fuel Efficient Industries (FEI)
From: ECO International, November 28.

Sir,

We understand your company is the inventor and sole manufacturer of plantacon, the fuel additive used in jet aircraft.

We assume that before persuading the aviation and oil industries to adopt this product you established that there would be no harmful environmental or public health side-effects. We would be grateful if you could confirm this.

Yours,

Sam MacAnally
Director

NEW YORK

DECEMBER

If the size of the airline had been the determining factor, Eugene Remington Jnr would not have been chairing this emergency meeting of the airlines' public affairs liaison committee. Someone from one of the majors would – someone from American, Delta or United, the big three.

But Remington had become chairman when he was himself with American, and had performed so well that it never crossed anyone's mind to replace him.

This is why the meeting was now taking place at 350 A Park Avenue, headquarters of Executive Airways, the airline that Remington had helped to found.

In addition to the passenger carriers, who were mainly represented by their public affairs directors, there were also present two people from the air cargo business – the PR head of Federal Express, the biggest, with in excess of two and a half billion ton miles a year, and – representing smaller carriers – the tough-talking Todd Birk, head of Airlift International, a thrusting new outfit operating out of Baltimore, Maryland.

There was only one item on the agenda – MacAnally's letter. The airlines were treating even the faintest wisp of a cloud over the miracle additive as if it were an approaching typhoon.

Remington was anxious they should act together. 'We know that ECO is influential and, at least from our point of view, potentially dangerous. MacAnally could be as big a menace to us as Nader was to the automobile industry in the Sixties. We mustn't let him divide and rule.'

'*Is* there any environmental problem?' It was a German, one of a number present on behalf of overseas carriers.

For an answer Remington looked to one of two men – not members of the committee – who were sitting together at the far end of the table.

'Dr Bain?'

Al Bain, chief scientific advisor to FEI, Fuel Efficient Industries, the manufacturers of plantacon, was a small, worried-looking man in his late fifties, with a lined face, thinning hair, and dressed in an uncared-for tweed suit. He now nervously pulled a sheaf of papers out of a battered old, brown leather satchel, scattering them on the table and sorting them as he spoke.

'Gentlemen, there's no question that plantacon is highly toxic.

'No one denies that.

'So of course it's potentially dangerous, but only in the way that many useful products are dangerous unless proper precautions are taken.

'And in this case they have been.'

'I understood there had been some kind of accident . . .' someone said.

Bain looked defensive. 'That was because safety procedures were inadequate.

'I can assure you the lessons have been learned.

'An industrial accident is now all but impossible.'

He described the care with which the product was produced, handled, stored and distributed. 'There is now no possibility of a leak, no possibility of anyone being harmed. It's safe.'

'Damn right it is.'

The others looked round in surprise.

Birk, the air cargo operator, looked back at them angrily. 'Damn environmentalists. Greens. Communists. They're just goddamn troublemakers. They'll say and do any goddamn thing they can to undermine industry, no matter what it does to companies, workers, or the country's economy.'

'Possibly so, Todd,' Remington said soothingly. 'Still, there are a few questions we could usefully address while we're all together.'

He turned back to the scientist. 'Dr Bain, the crux of the MacAnally letter is not that there are dangers to those handling plantacon *at the plant*, but that there's a threat *to the public* from the dissemination of particles from aircraft exhausts. Do you have a view on that?'

'Sir, it's dangerous if concentrated, but if any is emitted from the exhausts it would be in tiny quantities.

'Furthermore, it would be emitted at high levels and evenly dispersed into the atmosphere, much of it into infinity, and the remainder spread so thinly over the planet that it couldn't possibly harm anyone.

'It just isn't a serious threat. It *is no threat*. Period.' Bain looked round the room defiantly now, his initial nerves offset by a determination to defend his beloved product.

Remington now turned to the second man. Dr Bryce Kendrick was known to many in the room. A freelance industrial scientist, he was in appearance and manner the opposite of Bain . . . tall, distinguished-looking with a hint of good living above the belt, silver-grey hair, shiny, smooth face.

Remington asked him, 'At what levels could the toxic effects of plantacon impact on people?'

'If it were lying around in substantial quantities it would of course have serious effects on those exposed to it,' Kendrick replied, 'possibly a similar effect to lead. The properties are not dissimilar. So someone absorbing around eighty micrograms per decilitre of blood could suffer behavioural disturbances, and a lot worse – convulsions, paralysis, coma – and, in extreme cases, they could die.'

Some around the table looked shocked, but Kendrick remained cheerful.

'Don't worry, thanks to the safety measures Dr Bain has already described, no one *is* going to absorb such dangerous quantities.

'The point as far as you're concerned is that *the lower the level of exposure, the less the effect.*

'My guess is that even a child would need to absorb at least thirty-five micrograms per decilitre of blood before it showed any effect whatsoever – and I'm convinced we can show that any particles of plantacon found on the ground will be so minuscule and so thinly spread that there's no possibility of a child absorbing those quantities.'

That went down well.

But still Remington persisted. 'Presumably those most exposed to any sort of aircraft emissions are those living around airports?'

It was Kendrick who answered. 'Probably, and of course we could properly research all this, but I don't think you'll find much.' He looked round the room. 'Gentlemen, it's my view that MacAnally simply won't be able to demonstrate a cause for concern. The tone of his letter suggests he's only making initial enquiries. My advice is that you have no problem and would be wise not to over-react.'

Still Remington pressed on. 'Drs Bain and Kendrick, if we all contributed to the cost, would you test for signs of plantacon intake in children near airports, say Kennedy, Newark, and La Guardia? Also, would it be possible to compare the intellectual performance of children near airports with children living further away?'

Without waiting for a reply, he explained his thinking to the others. 'The environmentalists may have some scientific work. We can't counter that with assertions alone. Clearly if we can demonstrate we've done our homework and that there's no serious pollution, and that children near airports are just as bright as those further away, we're much more likely to settle the matter convincingly once and for all. We'll also look as if we care.'

They all looked at the scientists.

Kendrick nodded with barely disguised satisfaction. There could be a lucrative contract in this.

Bain indicated assent too, but with less enthusiasm. This, he knew, wouldn't be well received at FEI.

For the first time Remington relaxed. 'Right,' he said, 'I suggest we quietly commission this research but otherwise take Dr Kendrick's advice and leave it to the environmentalists to prove, if they can, that there's more to their letter than just kiteflying.'

'*I say hit them.*'

It was Birk.

'Why should we be spending money doing research to deal with these damn people? We've heard all we need to hear. Why don't we just tell them to fuck off? I say we should threaten to sue if they publish a single word about this. Turn the spotlight on them. Have someone look at their accounts, establish who's behind them politically. Scare the shit out of them.'

Remington looked affronted by the crudity of the attack. 'With respect, Todd, I don't think you know this man Sam MacAnally. He's highly regarded. Only a few days back the President himself honoured him with an award. He's well connected. Dangerous. It's best we treat him with some courtesy.'

As Birk started to protest, he added impatiently, 'Todd, we won't be wasting time. While the research is taking place we can also be preparing a response to any campaign that MacAnally and his friends are planning. And it can be as tough as it needs to be. I'm already working on who we could get to run it.'

He looked around the room. The others nodded.

'Chicken shit,' muttered Birk, and glowered as the rest of the group voted unanimously to adopt the Remington plan.

After they left their host returned to his desk and sat looking out from his window across Park Avenue to St Bartholomew's, the beautiful Episcopalian church tucked in between the tall office buildings directly opposite his own. It was the end of the working day and getting dark. The traffic was building up. Its roar even penetrated Remington's supposedly sound-proofed 20th floor office. In front of the church a man was arguing with a policeman about a parking ticket. An absurdly-long black limo was pulling up outside the nearby Waldorf Astoria. It was immediately surrounded by doormen and porters. From it stepped a short, fat man, cigar clamped between his teeth. He was immediately followed by a tall, curvaceous blonde, wriggling her way across the pavement in a dress at least a size too small. Remington grimaced. 'Gross,' he muttered to himself.

A handsome man with silvering hair, in his late forties, six feet tall, slim, and immaculately dressed in one of a number of pin-striped suits he had custom-made for him in London's Savile Row, Eugene Remington Jnr, came from Boston – old family, old money. Not satisfied with being a graduate of Harvard Law School, he had then spent a year at the Business School. From there he had gone to American Airlines where he developed a reputation as a whizz kid, rising to the position of Public Affairs Director by the time he was thirty.

Throughout his time at American he had dreamed of his own airline. He believed that the international industry was likely by the end of the 1990s to be dominated by nine carriers – American, Delta and United from the US, Air France, British Airways, JAL, KLM, Lufthansa and SAS. These were the ones with the aircraft, route networks, hubs, cost structures, information technology and financial strength to survive intense worldwide competition. There would, however, be opportunities for other airlines filling particular niche markets or providing specialist services. In his view there was a niche for an airline that set out to win the American domestic business traveller with an exclusive package. The invention of plantacon, coinciding with an upturn in the economy, provided him with the chance.

He left American and, taking three rising stars from other airlines as partners, launched Executive Airways with a spectacular burst of well-directed publicity and a range of special offers.

Executive Airways catered solely to the business market. It offered only one category of seat, Executive Class, and with its specially tailored service, including superb in-air communications facilities, it was upsetting the airline world in the way that, first Laker, then People's Express and Virgin had done in the past by its imaginative catering for the popular end of the market. A top Delta executive had once contemptuously described it as 'plantacon's baby'. The babe of the industry it may have been, but it quickly grew. Currently there was a greater demand for seats on its aircraft than it could meet.

And it wasn't only the planes that were flying high. Remington, head of a glamorous airline and rich, had become one of America's most eligible bachelors. After being linked to a number of desirable women he married a highly sought-after Broadway actress, beautiful but demanding and tempestuous, and the couple were frequently pictured in the gossip columns attending the most exclusive charity openings and society events. They had purchased a big house on Long Island, a penthouse overlooking Central Park, and a ranch near Santa Fe, New Mexico.

All this had stretched both the Remington family money and their combined earnings to the limits.

Not that Eugene Jnr had worried about that. Why should he? The airline had all the potential of a gold mine.

Thanks to plantacon.

But now, despite what the scientists Bain and Kendrick had said, and contrary to his own show of confidence at the meeting, he felt uneasy.

True, the MacAnally letter was framed as an enquiry. Yet Remington sensed there was more to it than that. Did MacAnally know something Remington didn't? Something Bain and Kendrick had missed? Or, worse, that they were covering up?

He considered telephoning the environmentalist and asking him point-blank what had prompted the letter.

But even as the thought crossed his mind, he rejected it.

He would have to be patient.

Either there was nothing in it, in which case he would know soon enough, or there was a genuine problem, in which case he mustn't let MacAnally know he was worried.

With a sigh, he turned his attention to the three folders on the coffee table before him.

Two of them he now picked up and tossed onto the floor. One of the men, Alexander Green, was said to have the best contacts on Capitol Hill but to be weak when it came to dealing with the media. Remington was convinced that, if there was to be a battle, it would be won or lost in the public arena as much as the corridors of power. The second, Ted Scroeder, was probably the best media manipulator in the business, but Remington was looking for someone who could put media coverage into the context of a wider campaign. He needed an all-rounder.

That left him with one folder. It contained a profile of the woman on the list, Nicola Kowalska.

From her photograph she appeared too guileless to be the kind of shrewd operator on whom to rest the fortunes

New York 69

of the world's top airlines, let alone entrust with his own
destiny. The photograph was of a fresh-faced, innocent-
looking woman in her mid thirties. But the accompanying report painted a different picture – according to it,
she was tough, ambitious, resolute in fostering an
impressive range of contacts across the media, politics,
and business. She had brilliantly handled at least two
crises for major companies, had even outwitted Nader
on one. She was ready, said his talent scouts, for 'the big
one'.

Remington liked what he read. He had a gut feeling
about Nicola Kowalska, a feeling that this was the right
woman for the cause and the right cause for the woman.

He walked back to his desk, picked up a phone and
called the number on top of the file.

'I say let's keep right out of this.' The speaker was David
Johnston, public relations director of one of the world's
biggest suppliers of Jet-A.

Johnston was not a happy man. This meeting of the
public affairs committee of the Oil Industries Liaison
Organisation (OILO) had caused him to reluctantly
abandon a much-needed holiday in Jamaica, leaving his
wife and two teenage children in the most expensive
hotel in Montego Bay together with custody of their joint
credit card. He had an uneasy feeling he was becoming
poorer by the minute. And without so much as a suntan
to show for it.

'Let the airlines fight them on their own,' he now
argued. 'Plantacon may be good news for them but it's
not so good for us. My company's profits are well down.
We could do with selling some more fuel. So who cares
what happens to plantacon compared to the risk of
having our image damaged by these environmentalists.'

'Well, it's not as simple as that, David.' It was the

representative from Shell. 'I know plantacon's reduced the demand for fuel and that's affecting our profits temporarily, but we expect increased aviation activity to compensate for that, so we're not likely to lose much in the long run. In any case, we welcome energy conservation. The longer fuel supplies last, the longer our business lasts. You have to take the longterm view.'

Johnston moved impatiently in his chair. 'Look at it like this,' he said, 'if plantacon pollution becomes a big issue, the public will blame us as much as the airlines.

'Yet all we're doing is complying with the airlines' requirements.

'And what happens if we try to explain that to the public?

'I'll tell you what happens – we sound like we're as guilty as hell but that we're trying to shift the blame.'

'I'm with David.' It was Cliff Anderson, the head of Jet-A Supplies, one of the new companies supplying a number of the smaller airlines, including Remington's Executive Airways. 'If the airlines want to fight this thing, let them. But we shouldn't join them. On the contrary we should establish our neutrality from the start. Then we should keep our heads down.'

'That's it,' said Johnston. 'We should simply say that we're happy to comply with whatever the regulatory authorities say. We should explain that we supply fuel to the industry's specifications and that if the specifications change we'll be happy to change too.'

'Hang on a minute,' the man from Shell said. 'Don't forget these are our customers. If we don't support them they'll move their business to someone who does.'

'Not if we all act together,' said Johnson. 'There'll be no point.'

'I think we should take an even tougher line . . .' It was Joe Pacino, the hard-bitten PR man from an oil company renowned for its uncompromisingly competitive approach. In fact, it had taken a lot of pressure to get Pacino to attend the meeting. As far as he was concerned, the others were competitors and he couldn't see why he should bother to talk to them. Now he was typically blunt:

'I say neutrality isn't good enough. Let's get on the winning side from the start. Let's tell the world that we're concerned about the charge that plantacon is a health risk and we call on the airlines to abandon its use until the matter is cleared up, one way or the other. That way we not only avoid public criticism, we actually get some Brownie points for a change.'

'Joe, that's going too far,' said Anderson. 'No one has proved there's anything wrong with plantacon yet. We shouldn't give the environmentalists any encouragement at this stage. For the time being let's throw the whole thing at the aviation industry and at FEI, the plantacon manufacturer, by telling MacAnally that we've passed his enquiry on to them and are awaiting their reply. Then when we get their reply we forward it with a letter saying we hope he's now satisfied. That will show we've acted promptly without us actually having done a thing.'

'I'll buy that.' Johnson looked at him approvingly.

The others agreed, Pacino with a resigned raising of his hands. 'OK, for starters,' he conceded. 'But if we look like getting bad PR, we're going to leave the airlines out there in space on their own. You bet your ass we are.'

Johnson nodded again. He would buy that too.

He looked at his watch.

He could catch the 5.30 p.m. plane back to Montego Bay after all.

The rum punch would taste all the better for knowing he had the situation under control.

HOBOKEN, NEW JERSEY

Dieter Partrell, the Dutch-born head of public affairs with FEI, was, thanks to heavy drinking and greedy eating, overweight and red-faced at the best of times, but today he was more flushed than usual, literally livid as he stared at the scientist before him.

Bain's report of the airlines' meeting had come as a bombshell.

'Fucking MacAnally,' he roared at the timid scientist. 'I don't believe it. This is persecution.'

He all but spat at Bain. 'Goddamn it, Al, what the hell were you doing . . . going there without telling me. Are you fucking mad?'

'You were away, Dieter. They asked me at short notice. Anyway, I assumed you'd want this pollution nonsense knocked on the head. And I believe that's what I've done.'

'Balls! You don't know MacAnally. I do.'

Partrell had been with a lead additive manufacturer when the battle had taken place over the levels of lead in gasoline. He had taken a beating from MacAnally then and would never forget or forgive the humiliation.

But there was more to his reaction than hostility towards the campaigner; what he was experiencing was fear . . . even panic. A threat to plantacon was a threat to all that he had worked towards for thirty years or more. Partrell, who survived a childhood in some of the Bronx's roughest streets and left school at fifteen, had bludgeoned, clawed, fought his way up, company by company, position by position, until he had finally reached the board of the lead additive company. When that folded, thanks to MacAnally's campaign, he had been left floundering. Then a Godsend – he had been approached by the men who were about to form FEI on the back of a revolutionary advance, an airline fuel additive called plantacon. Its potential was breathtaking. They were brilliant scientists, but needed someone to get the show on the road.

For seven years he had helped to set up the company, develop and test the product, and finally launch it at the right price to its highly sophisticated market. His relentless drive and determination made him the backbone of the operation, as essential to his boardroom colleagues as he was increasingly disliked by them. He had also ploughed every cent of his savings into it. And borrowed heavily to invest more. All being well, this was going to make him rich and powerful.

No wonder to Partrell another act of 'environmental sabotage' by MacAnally would be a' disaster beyond measure.

There was an issue of principle involved too. Partrell believed as passionately in his cause as MacAnally, his cause being the right of industry to get on with its business and earn the wealth upon which the nation depended. And hang the odd unfortunate by-product.

There were downsides in any activity, he would argue. Vast numbers of people died in road accidents. So were cars banned? No, of course not. The human price was paid.

So industry caused some pollution. The air wasn't as clean as it used to be. So was industry to be banned? If it was then you were banning jobs, wealth . . . 'Christ, you'd be banning the whole fucking American way of life.'

He had few friends. His reaction to the nervous Dr Bain's report would have surprised no one who knew him. He was a bully . . . an ungenerous employer, a brutal negotiator, a ruthless competitor.

But he had plantacon, and every airline now depended on it.

And that's the way it had to stay. About *that* Partrell had no doubts: whatever – *whatever* – was necessary to achieve it – *plantacon had to survive*.

So, having received Bain's report and been less than reassured by what he heard of the airlines' response, he picked up the phone and rang Eugene Remington. The airline chief was sympathetic but calm.

'Dieter, we have as big an interest in protecting plantacon as you,' he said. 'But whatever you say about MacAnally, you must on your own experience acknowledge we can't afford to under-estimate him. That's why we must play it carefully and calmly. If, as I believe, there's no problem, the whole matter will fade away within a matter of weeks; if there's some minor pollution we'll have to work out a strategy. But it's crucial we all work together.'

'*Working together*' was the last thing Partrell intended to do.

He didn't doubt that Remington and the other airline chiefs would do their best.

He *did* doubt whether their best would be good enough.

As for the oil industry, he didn't trust it at all. It had always been short-sightedly ambivalent about plantacon.

It took no time for him to persuade the company chairman to call an emergency board meeting.

'This MacAnally letter is a disaster. Potentially catastrophic,' he told it.

'And we'd better be clear about one thing. At the end of the day we're on our own.

'The airlines can afford to keep calm, but we can't.

'There's a fundamental difference between their position and ours. While a ban on plantacon would cut their profits, it wouldn't stop them operating. But it would put us out of business overnight.'

'Surely you're exaggerating, Dieter,' said one board member. 'No one takes these environmentalists seriously.'

Partrell looked at him almost contemptuously. 'Don't underestimate these people. They maybe be irresponsible, left-wing, industry-hating bastards, but they're damn effective. Too many people do take them seriously. You just look at what they've done to other industries.'

The chairman, in Partrell's view an ineffectual idiot at the best of times, was also unconvinced. 'MacAnally's letter falls well short of an outright accusation. By over-reacting might we not encourage him to think there's a problem where there isn't one?'

Partrell struggled to control his temper. 'I know this man. This is typical. He's covering his back and at the same time testing the issue. By writing to us and the airlines and oil companies he'll be able to claim that he made proper enquiries before launching a public attack. We should treat this as a warning shot. He wouldn't have fired it if he didn't mean business.'

He looked round at the doubting faces. Christ, he thought, these people had developed a great product – you couldn't take that away from them. But when it came to business . . . the stuff that went on out there in the real world where Partrell spoke for them . . . they were utterly hopeless.

'I really don't think you people understand,' he said, wearily. 'We only have one product. Plantacon. If it's banned, we're out of business. Finished.'

'We know that, Dieter, but we also know that, at the

levels of exposure MacAnally is talking about, the product's harmless.'

'Of course it's harmless, but that doesn't mean we'll win,' said Partrell. 'That's the problem.'

'If this thing gets into the open, all MacAnally's crowd need to do is run an emotive scare campaign and the burden of proof will be on us – and it will be an unreasonable burden.

'We could be totally in the right and still lose. It's happened before.'

The finance director intervened. 'I don't know whether Dieter is or is not over-reacting, but it would seem prudent to take some action in our defence. What's being suggested?'

Partrell looked at him contemptuously. He despised the finance director at the best of times, but today the patronising tone was too much.

'*Prudent,*' he roared. '*Prudent!* For Christ's sake, can't I get through to you. Everything we've built up, everything we've invested is at risk. *This man is a fucking lunatic . . . but a fucking effective fucking lunatic.* I tell you if we don't act he'll ruin us all.'

There was a stunned silence.

Partrell, red-faced, aware he had gone too far, opened the folder in front of him with shaking hands and, making a monumental effort to speak more quietly, began to list his proposals.

'First, we ask Al Bain and a scientific team to produce overwhelming evidence that plantacon is not being emitted near airports in quantities of any volume worth worrying about, that it's not reaching kids and it's not affecting kids. We should not only use our own people but commission studies using every friendly scientist we know. We'll build up a bank of evidence.

'Second, I set up surveillance on MacAnally and the

other leading environmentalists, try to get ahead of their plans, and also find out whatever we can use to discredit them.'

He saw doubt in their faces. 'It may *sound* over the top but, believe me, they'll be calling us all sorts of names, accusing us of heinous crimes against people, and we have to get them off the moral high ground by raising questions about them too.

'Third, we need to do a major PR job on plantacon. Glossy brochures. Wining and dining of politicians, media people, industrial opinion-formers, people from the regulatory agencies, etc. We must get across its benefits to the nation – not just cheaper travel and a healthier aviation industry, but also energy savings.

'To sum up, we get our case ready, get to know our enemy, and make as many political friends as we can.'

He looked round the room. He could feel the apprehension in the air. But there was not one dissenting voice. He had the go-ahead.

Later that day the two non-executive members of the board telephoned their dealers and off-loaded some of their shares.

They could always buy them back later.

But it was best to play safe.

BALTIMORE, MARYLAND

Todd Birk, on his third scotch, glared unseeingly out of the window of the office, a pre-fabricated shed on the piece of land he rented alongside his hangar at Baltimore International Airport.

Ever since the New York meeting he had been conscious of impending disaster.

Birk was fifty-five, short – about five six – but powerfully built, with a bullish head and small, distrustful eyes, all topped by thinning fair hair. Born on a small farm in Kansas, he had watched his father work and worry himself into an early grave, and decided there was *no way* he was going to do the same. 'No fucking way' . . . one of his favourite expressions.

He had always had a passion for planes, ever since he was a small boy. So, as soon as he was old enough, he joined the Air Force and trained as a maintenance engineer. When he decided to go into the air freight business he was so determined not to be restricted to maintenance that he started at a comparatively paltry wage on the ground floor as a loader with Federal Express. An exceptionally hard worker, he quickly became a foreman, and then continued upwards until he reached a middle management plateau. It took him some years to realise it was as far as he was going. He blamed his failure to reach the top on the college old boy network and on his lack of the social graces – he tended to be suspicious of anyone with an education, indeed anyone with manners – but the truth was that his refusal to suffer fools gladly, his red-hot temper, and the monstrous chip on his shoulder made him, at least in the view of Federal Express, unfit for higher things.

So he borrowed heavily, bought a second-hand DC-8, and set up his own small business. Soon he was moving enough freight to buy another plane. It had been tough going and more than once he had nearly gone under. He had worked with ferocious intensity. In the bars around the airport where workers from all the companies gathered he became a legend . . . the company boss who could actually be seen in overalls *polishing his goddamn' planes*, who would help to load them, who, long after his men went home, would still be there. One employee returned late one night to collect some shopping he had left in his locker and found Birk sweeping a hangar. '*Sweeping the fucking hangar – at damn near midnight! You wouldn't believe it if you didn't see it with your own eyes.*'

Then came plantacon and Birk borrowed again, this time to buy two more second-hand planes, a 727 and, his pride and joy, a 747. With the 747 and the extra fuel efficiency that was now possible, he set out with some success to under-cut the bigger companies on the longer international routes.

Now it was all starting to come together. He was just beginning to repay the loans. For Airlift International, profitability, then expansion, were just around the corner.

Federal Express were about to find out what they had lost when they offended Todd Birk.

But if these environmentalists got their way, if plantacon was banned, all that he had worked for could be destroyed.

He had asked his accountant to do some calculations, but in the meantime, no matter how he looked at it, goodbye plantacon meant goodbye Birk.

Well, it wasn't going to happen.

These blue chip college-educated New York assholes like Eugene Remington fucking Jnr could afford to be complacent, but he couldn't.

He hadn't fought his way to this point to be destroyed by these fucking environmentalists – a bunch of smart-ass college kids and their friends in the liberal media.

MacAnally and his Commie friends would have to be dealt with.

And he, Todd Birk, would see that they were.

*

Executive Airways
350A Park Avenue
New York City
New York

To Sam MacAnally, ECO International

Dear Mr MacAnally,

Your letter re. plantacon was discussed at a routine meeting of the Airlines Public Affairs Liaison Committee this week.

Let me assure you that every airline wants to be environmentally responsible. That is why we're exploring ways of still further reducing aircraft noise, and why we're seeking to still further reduce emissions of carbon and nitrogen oxides.

I'm therefore pleased to tell you that we've taken scientific advice on any possible environmental side-effects arising from the use of plantacon and are assured that fallout from aircraft is negligible and that there is no danger to people whatsoever.

In the meantime we congratulate you on your recent well-deserved award and wish you and ECO well in its splendid work.

Yours

Eugene Remington
Chairman

OIL INDUSTRIES LIAISON ORGANISATION (OILO)
3 New York Plaza
New York City
New York

Dear Mr MacAnally,

Our member companies have asked me to reply to your letter.

Our members manufacture aircraft fuel according to the specifications provided by their customers and also those laid down by national and international regulatory agencies.

In this context they have, as you say, been asked to add small quantities of the recently developed chemical plantacon to Jet-A.

This increases fuel efficiency and thus makes a major contribution to energy conservation, a concern we know you share.

Of course if there were any environmental or safety argument for not adding plantacon, our industry would be just as able and willing to respond to counter-instructions.

However, at the time of writing we know of no such argument.

We are, of course, passing your letter on to the airlines and to FEI for their comments.

We hope this deals satisfactorily with your query.

Yours,

David Johnston
Chairman, Public Affairs Committee

Sam MacAnally received no reply from Fuel Efficient Industries.

He also received no reply from Todd Birk's Airlift International.

He did, however, receive an anonymous postcard dispatched from the Baltimore area;

Hands off plantacon, MacAnally, or you and your Commie friends will wish you had never been born.

NEW YORK

If Ithaca, the up-state New York university, had a high reputation it was partly because of the internationally renowned papers on toxicology published by Dr Raynald Warner. A brilliant researcher, he had turned down a departmental chair because he didn't care for the administrative duties, even turned down prestigious offers from better known universities because he liked Ithaca and because it was where he could best take care of his wife.

Everyone knew that Dr Warner lived only for his research and his crippled wife. Dr Warner, the local community would tell you, was a good man, a loving and devoted husband and a thoughtful neighbour as well as a brilliant scientist. The town and university were lucky to have him. Such was their affection for the couple that when Alice Warner contracted her debilitating illness, neighbours and colleagues willingly clubbed together to raise money to adapt the Warners' home to cope with a wheel-chair.

They would also tell you that Dr Warner had not been looking himself recently. He was pale and red-eyed. And thin. Some speculated that he had received more bad news about his wife's health; others wondered whether he was unwell himself. When asked, however, he brushed off queries with reassurances and retreated even

deeper into the private world of his laboratory and scientific papers . . . literally thousands of scientific papers, all neatly piled high on shelves, on desks, on the floor, on the window sill, on the tops of filing cabinets, until there was only just room in his study for himself and one other. Even then Sam MacAnally had to remove a stack from the second chair.

From the start Warner had been reluctant to see the environmentalist. But the introductory letter from Justin Lord had been insistent. MacAnally, sensing the scientist's impatience, decided to waste no time.

'Justin Lord tells me he commissioned your research into plantacon pollution.'

Warner looked uncomfortable. 'It was a private contract.'

'Quite. But Mr Lord has already given me a copy of your findings and asked me to discuss it with you.'

'Yes. Yes, of course. Well, what do you want to know?'

'Sir, I know of your high reputation, but I have to ask this question: how confident are you that your findings are correct? Is there any room for error?'

'Error? What kind of error?'

'I don't know, Doctor. I'm asking you?'

Warner leaned forward. 'Let's be clear what we're talking about. Even the manufacturers admit plantacon is highly toxic. Now, they may dispute the level of emissions, and they'll undoubtedly dispute that they're harmful, but the point is that, because it's non-degradable, the plantacon does not just descend to the ground and then disappear. Its environmental presence is increasing day by day. So it's bound to become a threat to health eventually, even if it's not harming people now.'

MacAnally nodded his understanding. 'You report that it's already evident in dust, soil and plant life in the vicinity of airports?'

'And in the air.'

'Over how big an area?'

'You've read the report. I found significant levels up to five miles from where the planes were landing and taking off.'

'Can you help me put it in context, Doctor? How serious is the pollution compared with other environmental problems, and . . .'

The scientist interrupted him. 'No, I can't. And it's not my responsibility. I was asked specific questions requiring a scientific answer.'

He held up his fingers, one by one:

'One, is plantacon toxic? Answer, yes.

'Two, is it non-degradable? Answer, yes.

'Three, is there evidence that it's already contaminating areas around airports? Answer, yes.'

MacAnally pressed. 'You talk about long-term contamination. But is it harming people now? These other studies Mr Lord commissioned . . .'

'You'll have to ask the other researchers that. I can only comment on my own work.'

'And there's no possibility you could be wrong?'

The scientist's impatience increased. 'Really, Mr MacAnally, this is too much. I've already told you that I cannot see how. I could have conducted further research but there were no grounds for doing so. In my view it would have only replicated what I'd already done.'

MacAnally nodded, placatingly. 'And of course it's been replicated by others. Do you know these other scientists? Professor Barnes in England? Professor Tezuka in Japan? Abernathy or Cossens?'

'Abernathy and Cossens are not in my field. I know Barnes. And Tezuka by reputation.'

'Have you consulted with them? Or exchanged findings?'

number of tests to evaluate intellectual performance and learning ability.

The children in group C, the ones furthest from the airport, had no plantacon in their blood and were intellectually normal. *No problem*.

Group B, the medium distance group, had some plantacon in their blood and there was some, but not much, evidence of behavioural irregularity. *Cause for some concern*.

But Group A, the children nearest the airport, had higher levels of plantacon in their blood and – no question about it – were suffering devastating effects. Brain damage. *The nightmare finding*.

The children in Group A averaged between five and seven fewer IQ points than the others.

The Children in Group A also scored worst in a range of other behavioural tests. Compared with the groups further from the airport, they were more easily distracted, they lacked persistence, were more disorganised, were in some cases hyperactive and unnaturally impulsive. They were also more easily frustrated and more likely to day-dream, and they were less able to follow simple directions or sequences.

The effects appeared to be caused at levels as low as fifteen micrograms per decilitre. This indicated a relatively low safety threshold.

MacAnally studied the scientist's eager face. 'How sure are you about the findings?'

'Sure?' The young scientist's smile faded. 'You're not suggesting my work is flawed?'

'No, no. It's just that the implications are so serious.'

'I accept that. But I stand by my work.' He, like Warner, was defiant now. Looking Sam straight in the eye. 'Furthermore I understand it's been replicated by scientists in other countries. There doesn't seem to be much doubt about it.'

'Are you going to publish?'

'Mr Lord owns the research for the moment. But, yes, probably, if he doesn't wish to publish I will.'

'When?'

'I haven't thought about it . . . but I have the rights after two years.'

'We may be launching a major campaign on this issue. Would you be willing to appear publicly to describe your studies? At press conferences? Possibly even a Senate hearing?'

The scientist seemed in two minds. 'Would it really be necessary?' he asked.

'Vital. Is there a problem?'

Abernathy thought for a moment. 'No, I guess not.'

He thought some more and seemed to warm to the idea. Then he became positively enthusiastic. 'No. No problem. You just call and I'll be there.'

'Good. We'll be in touch then.' Anxious to get back to Washington MacAnally rose to leave.

Abernathy looked disappointed. 'Do you have to go so soon?'

Sam smiled apologetically. 'I would love to talk . . . but I have to get the shuttle and I'm already late. Listen, thanks for your time.'

'Sure.'

MacAnally left a five-dollar bill to pay for their drinks and, promising to be in touch, hailed a cab in Washington Square.

At least Abernathy wasn't going to be a problem.

And his findings were most damning.

He concluded it had been a good two days' work.

faint. He went white, and his hands began to shake so that he had to put down his cup, creating a lake of coffee in the saucer.

'Plantacon,' he exclaimed. 'I didn't understand that was what you said on the phone. Who told you about that work?'

It was Olly who was now surprised, although, having met Barnes, he could see the potential for confusion.

'I'm sorry if you're surprised,' he said. 'We were told about your study by the man who commissioned it.'

'We?'

Olly told him about ECO, Barnes listened intently, then, at first reluctantly, but after a while with encouraging lucidity, described how he had been promised a considerable sum to undertake studies in the UK similar to ones carried out by Abernathy and Warner in America.

Although he was semi-retired, his scientific curiosity had been aroused.

And he wouldn't pretend the money wasn't useful.

So he took the commission.

He took dust, soil and plant samples from close to Heathrow Airport and then from two places further away – but at distances comparable to those chosen for the American studies.

Analysis had revealed that the samples nearest to the airport were contaminated with plantacon.

Subsequently he had tested the blood of children in the three places.

'They were small samples, I have to say, but the levels of plantacon in their blood replicated the findings of Dr Abernathy.

'Finally I arranged a number of IQ tests and other tests of learning ability. You know, ability to concentrate, that kind of thing.

'I found the children with the most plantacon in their blood performed the worst. Once more, I replicated the findings of Dr Abernathy.'

Olly felt jubilant.

This was just what Sam MacAnally needed.

Supporting studies from more than one country would be much more influential than studies from one country alone.

'Are you intending to publish this work, Professor?'

Barnes, who Olly noticed with alarm had sunk further into the chair and appeared now to be in pain, shook his head and spoke, as if to himself. 'I shouldn't have undertaken this work at all. I wasn't well enough . . . I'm not well enough.'

Olly, remembering MacAnally's entreaties, groaned inwardly.

'We were hoping you would be willing to share your findings with the public . . . perhaps at a press conference in London.'

Barnes seemed to retreat into the chair even further.

Olly half expected him to disappear altogether. Barnes did have a ghost-like quality.

'London! I'm afraid that's impossible. In any event the work belongs to its funder.'

'I believe he's anxious it should be made public.'

'Well, then . . .' To Olly's relief Barnes appeared to be making one of his periodic revivals. '. . . let *him* publish it.'

Olly recalled what MacAnally had told him. They were not short of money on this one.

'We would send a comfortable car and driver, and have you put up in a good hotel. The press conference would only last about an hour and apart from one or two brief interviews that's all it will involve.'

'No, no. It's out of the question. You see . . .' Barnes

Well, if she knew Sam MacAnally, once the plantacon campaign got going, there would be plenty of those.

MELBOURNE

In Australia that same day Liz Scullen was planning to reorganise her life. She was sick of the bedsitter. She had chosen it because of its view of St Kilda beach and the sea, but it was too small and now that it was summer it was unbearably hot. When she had mentioned air-conditioning to the Greek landlord he had looked at her as if she was mad. Tomorrow she would look for another place. But still in St Kilda. Preferably near where she was now. She liked the tram ride from the city, the wide, flat beach, and the variety of small shops in the row opposite the house where she lived.

Yes, she would find somewhere else, then she would go to Brisbane and see her mother.

These damn letters had to stop.

Liz's mother came from an upper middle class English family. On leaving an exclusive girls' school in Cheltenham she had, while still only eighteen, precipitated a family crisis by running away with a feckless Australian jockey who had been working at a local racing stable. By the time they were located they were in Brisbane and she was expecting Liz. The family had decided it was better they stay there.

But Liz's mother had never relaxed into the Australian way of life. Putting the circumstances of her flight from England firmly behind her, she devoted all her time to desperate social-climbing, making her life wretched in the process – although she would, of course, not acknowledge that, least of all to herself.

As soon as Liz was old enough to understand she impressed upon her the importance of growing up 'a young lady'.

Liz disappointed from the start.

She became a real tomboy.

She liked the games her mother frowned on, made friends her mother believed entirely unsuitable.

Her father, to her mother's surprise, had become one of Australia's top trainers and a big earner. They also eventually inherited a considerable sum from the family in England, so they were able to send Liz to one of Australia's most expensive private boarding schools. But Liz, cheerful, fun-loving, always ready to respond to a dare, was expelled after a number of what most Australians would consider relatively innocent pranks; unfortunately an uptight institution for 'young ladies' judged them more harshly.

The episode of the head's bloomer's was the last straw. A severe sixty-three-year-old spinster, a firm disciplinarian who treated even a fleeting glance at a boy as if it were a near-expulsion offence, Miss Williams (no one ever knew her Christian name) had become known to generation after generation of her girls as Old Iron Knickers. This nickname was founded, in part, on her bloomers. Huge, tent-like, and pink, they flapped on the washing line behind her cottage every Monday. They were there, flying in their full glory, the day the men came to concrete the tennis court. Inevitably it was Liz who had the idea of filling the bloomers with cement. When the head came to collect them that evening they were no longer on the line, but forming a neat circle on the ground, each a concrete monument to her sizeable lower quarters.

The inquiry was exhaustive. But when it became clear that the whole school would be harshly punished unless the culprit was found, Liz confessed.

lengthening his stride. He led her to a spot right on the beach. 'Might as well eat outside.' Without asking her what she wanted, he ordered flounders and chips and two tubes of Fosters. This irritated her, but, well, what the hell, she thought, flounders would do. Very nicely, actually.

'Great house, Dr Cossens.'

'Sure.' He grinned again.

'Is there a Mrs Cossens?'

'Nope.' Another grin.

She was beginning to dislike the grin.

She thought it could be easy to dislike Cossens.

'Well, if you don't mind me asking, how can you afford the place? It must be worth—'

'A couple of million,' he replied with the same maddening grin.

'And . . .?'

'And what?'

'Well, I was asking . . .'

'Ah, yes, how can a mere lecturer afford it? Family money, I'm afraid. I thought I might just as well spend it on a decent house as invest the stuff on the stock market.'

'Lucky man.'

'Too true.' That grin again. Then, 'But it's time I asked the questions. Tell me more about your interest in plantacon.'

'Not much to say. I was asked to contact you because whoever funded the research wants it made public. And presumably wants some controls put on plantacon.'

She looked at him curiously. 'The airlines aren't going to like this. If you go public you'll be under a lot of pressure.'

'No problem. The study's straightforward enough. It's not my fault the bloody stuff's dangerous.' He paused. 'You think there'll be a lot of publicity, TV and the like?'

'I think there'll be a helluva lot.'

'Fair enough.' That was all he said but she got the impression he liked the idea.

Dr Cossens was no shrinking violet.

Still a shrinking violet was the last thing they needed.

As he led her up the grassy slope to the Watson's Bay bus terminal he said, 'Do you come to Sydney often?'

'I'm afraid so.'

He laughed. The rivalry between Melbourne and Sydney was as sharp as ever.

'And I come to Melbourne to lecture once a week. Maybe we could have dinner some time?'

'Maybe,' she said discouragingly.

Just for a split second the confident grin faded.

And just for a split second – a fraction of a split second – she liked him better for it.

Then the grin returned.

'That's OK,' he said.

And walked off.

Whistling confidently.

Liz considered it was almost worth making a date in order to see if she could find a way to wipe that grin away. Permanently.

Then she remembered they needed Dr Cossens, confidence intact.

HOBOKEN, NEW JERSEY

DECEMBER 23

Sam MacAnally had one more thing to do before Christmas.

He locked his office door for the last time this year,

She watched him eyeing the loaded oven tray.

'You have that glint in your eye my Patricia does when she sees fresh cookies. Would you like one?'

'You're very kind.'

She placed a mug of steaming hot coffee and a cookie in front of him and sat down, wiping her hands on her apron.

'What was it you wanted to see me about?'

'Mrs Jakowski, we're concerned about a product you know all about.' He paused. 'I'm talking about plantacon.'

The colour left her cheeks. She rose and, turning her back on him, began busying herself at the stove. 'I see. Well, how do you think I can help?'

'I'm sorry to arouse unhappy memories, but I understand your husband worked at the factory, that he died from plantacon poisoning.'

She turned to face him, leaning back on the sink, her hands gripping its sides. 'I'm sorry, Mr MacAnally, I'd like to help you but I can't.'

'They asked you not to talk about it?'

'I promised.'

'And, of course, I respect that. But we believe plantacon could be harming a lot of children. Possibly millions of children.'

'I haven't read about children dying . . .'

'They're not dying, Mrs Jakowski, they're being brain-damaged.'

She sat down, facing him. 'Brain-damaged?'

'Plantacon is a neurotoxin, Mrs Jakowski. That's a brain poison. Serious exposure, such as your husband must have experienced, can be fatal. Low level exposure doesn't have such a drastic effect. On adults maybe no effect at all. But children are more vulnerable. It can reduce their IQ, affect their behaviour.'

She looked at him, bewildered then, suddenly decisive, rose to her feet. 'Well, I wish I could help you Mr MacAnally, but I can't.'

'I don't want to know much, Mrs Jakowski. Just what happened to your husband and what he may have said about the plant. I promise no one will know we've spoken.'

She reached for the coffee pot and absent-mindedly refilled his mug.

Then, speaking as if to herself, she told him how pleased they had been when her husband Art had got his job at FEI.

'It was well paid and secure. We really thought things were going to be good for us. Then it all began to go wrong. Art began getting bad headaches and became all bad-tempered. He never used to be like that, Mr MacAnally. Art was one of the sweetest-tempered men I knew. One night he woke me up screaming and complaining about a dreadful pain in his stomach. He started to have convulsions. By the time the ambulance got here he was in a coma. They took him to hospital . . .' a tear began to run down her cheek '. . . they took him to a hospital and I went too. I waited for a while, then . . . then . . . they came out and said he was dead. Dead, Mr MacAnally. I couldn't believe it.'

She took a piece of kitchen towel and wiped her eyes.

He waited but when she didn't speak further, he asked, 'Then what happened?'

'What do you mean, what happened?'

'What did FEI do?'

'Oh, they were very good. A man came to see me. He explained there had been a leak in a pipe or something. Near where Art was working. Without anyone knowing he had been absorbing this stuff for days. They said they

Truly the plantacon revolution was a blessing to one and all.

WASHINGTON

JANUARY

The Monocle is a Capitol Hill restaurant accustomed to well-known faces but the pairing of the newsworthy new senator from Connecticut and the much-publicised environmentalist of the decade still turned a few heads.

Both had been on a media merry-go-round since the awards, Wilkins as the most interesting of the new senators to emerge from the elections and MacAnally as the controversial star of the nationally televised awards ceremony. Both had appeared on *Today* and *Good Morning America*, on *Face the Press*, and on *Johnny Carson*, as well as being profiled in all the major newspapers and magazines. That very week MacAnally had emerged in heroic mould from Jackie Brown's piece in the *Washington Post* and Wilkins' face was on the front page of *The Washingtonian* under the headline: '*The man on everybody's party list*'.

Of course, not all the publicity had been favourable: headlining his column '*Beware the new liberals*' Lionel North characteristically warned that people like MacAnally and Wilkins represented a threat to all that Presidents Reagan and Bush had done to lead America away from the self-indulgent liberalism that had begun with Kennedy and endured – except for the Nixon years – until the defeat of Carter.

'*I don't like these people,*' he wrote, '*self-appointed crusaders for what they claim to be the public good. I don't like the way they claim to know what's best for us. I don't like the way they impose their views upon the rest of us. In fact, I don't like them . . . period.'*

Between television appearances Wilkins had been putting together a staff composed mainly of bright young researchers recommended by Nader, MacAnally, Michael Pertschuk of the Advocacy Institute and a number of the other top citizen organisers in Washington, and was now looking for issues with which to make the running in the Senate. He had also got himself onto the committee of his choice – the Environment and Public Works Committee. This was a considerable achievement for a junior senator.

At lunch he made little attempt to hide his ambition from MacAnally. He wanted to get himself positioned right from the start as the people's champion. 'We can help each other,' he told the campaigner. 'I need your ability to identify the issues, to get them researched, to put together a grassroots campaign behind them. And I can offer in return a senator and a staff ready to run with it all the way on the Hill. We could make a terrific team.'

MacAnally took his time in replying. He welcomed Wilkins' honesty. And he didn't object to his ambition or his offer. But ECO had a number of senators and congressmen on the Hill ready to take up its cause; it always made sense to find the right horse for the right course.

Just the same, Wilkins was in the fast lane and provided he kept on his feet he could carry an issue a long way in a short time. And that could be just what was needed now.

'I know what you're saying, Chris,' Sam said. 'And, you're right, you could make a real difference. There are one or two things rising on the agenda . . . one in particular . . . if it checks out it could be a real scandal.'

'No.'

'Isn't that unusual?'

'Not always. If the work is privately commissioned my accountability is to the funder.'

'I thought scientists liked to publish . . .'

'Mr MacAnally, I'm a busy man. I undertook the commission and fulfilled it but I haven't the time to go beyond that. I understand Mr Lord wants the work published but at a time suitable to him. That's his right. He's paid well for that privilege. In the meantime I've done what I was asked to do.'

'What if he chose not to publish it? Do you have the right to do so?'

'I have a two-year time constraint, then I can publish if I wish.'

'If you wish . . . but surely . . .?'

Warner looked at his watch. 'Mr MacAnally, I'm not a crusader like you. I'm a scientist. I research and sometimes I discover. Often I do publish and often I share with other scientists. But this was a private commission, unrelated to my ongoing research. I don't know whether I'll follow it up, but I do know it won't be now. The work is in Mr Lord's hands for the time being.'

'But it suggests children are being damaged . . .'

'Not my study. Mine indicates environmental contamination – some now, and probably much more later. It's the others that demonstrate health effects, and I've no doubt Mr Lord will raise those findings with the companies concerned.'

MacAnally shook his head in wonder. This man lived in a world of his own.

He began to see how some scientists could develop weapons of mass destruction. Somehow they seemed able to divorce the invention from its practical effects.

'We only make it – we don't deploy it.'

Or, in Warner's case, '*I only discovered the pollution; it's not my responsibility to stop it.*'

He did his best to hide his growing impatience. 'What if I told you that Mr Lord has encouraged ECO to campaign for controls on the use of plantacon?'

'I would say that he's entitled to do so.'

'Would you be ready to testify publicly to your findings?'

Warner rose, clearly agitated.

He took a step towards the window, accidentally knocking over a stack of papers. As if pleased to be diverted, he took a moment to pick them up.

Then, looking across the sloping lawn outside, he said, 'I had hoped that my involvement would not be necessary, Mr MacAnally.'

'You don't think you have a duty?'

He turned now, and MacAnally saw to his surprise a look of panic in the older man's eyes.

'Look,' he said. 'I can't *cope* with this. Why do you think I choose to stay and work at this quiet university? I value *peace*. Value it beyond measure. And I need time for . . . for my wife. She's ill, Mr MacAnally. I cannot, I will not spend even one night away from her. I won't. Do you hear?'

MacAnally rose, concerned at the colour that had rushed to the older man's face.

'We'll try to keep the demands on you to a minimum, Dr Warner,' he said. 'I'm sorry if I've distressed you. But believe me, I wouldn't have come all this way if I didn't believe – and if I didn't expect *you* to believe – that this is serious.'

He waited for a reply but Warner, back at the window, staring out, now seemed oblivious to his visitor's presence.

MacAnally was dismayed.

This wasn't going to be good enough.

However, there appeared to be little more he could achieve today.

He would have to ask Justin Lord to talk to the scientist; presumably as the sponsor of the research he would have some influence.

He said goodbye and, after waiting fruitlessly for a reply, walked out of the building and into the town where he called into a warm, welcoming bar for a hamburger and fries before preparing to drive back to New York City.

An hour later, walking to where he had parked his rental car, he saw a man and woman crossing a small park, the woman in a wheelchair, wrapped up in blankets for protection from the damp early-winter air, the man, a familiar figure, talking to her as he gently steered her around the flower beds.

As they came closer, oblivious to him or anyone else in the park, he heard the woman laugh as she looked up to the man's face.

It was a laugh full of good humour, a look full of love.

Then he realised why the man was familiar. It was Dr Raynard Warner.

MacAnally's heart warmed to the careworn-looking scientist.

He hoped the plantacon campaign wouldn't trouble him too much.

On the other hand, it was essential that Warner testified – at their launch press conference, and at any Capitol Hill hearings that followed.

A compromise would have to be found.

NEW YORK

Dr David Abernathy was in his early thirties, short – no more than five foot five – and thin, with black hair and a small moustache.

He was also eager to please.

'Sam MacAnally, *the* Sam MacAnally . . . it's an honour, sir. I saw you on television receiving your award. Terrific. And I've followed your campaigns – for years.'

MacAnally found the young New York University scientist's effusive manner a little hard to take.

Still, he told himself, he shouldn't complain – after the dampening effect of his meeting with Warner, the enthusiasm was welcome.

Abernathy had suggested meeting at the Violet Café on the corner of West 4th Street and Washington Square, right at the heart of the University itself. It was bright, noisy, full of students. MacAnally noticed that when Abernathy's eyes wandered from time to time, it was only to passing men. He guessed Abernathy was gay.

'I had a letter from Mr Lord. He said you wanted to discuss my work.'

'Yes, I've read the report.'

'Read' was not the word. Sam had been stunned by it.

Abernathy had taken three sets of children aged eleven to thirteen. One group lived within a radius of five miles of John F. Kennedy Airport, one group between five and ten miles away, and one group between ten and and twenty miles away.

He had then measured the levels of plantacon in their blood and, having established those, he had arranged a

LONDON

Olly Witcomb had been on cloud nine all week. After going up to Sally's flat the other evening he had made what he believed to be the big breakthrough: he had asked her to dinner on Saturday night and she had accepted.

It was not the dinner that was significant.

It was *Saturday night*.

Saturday night, he figured, was not shared lightly with anyone.

The other thing about Saturday was that it opened up the possibilities of Sunday . . .

These, of course, were the thoughts of a man looking for encouragement from the woman's every word and deed.

A man close to being obsessed.

They slowed him down when he should have been concentrating on completing all his outstanding work.

In these circumstances a follow-up fax from Sam MacAnally was bad news. The plantacon thing was clearly gathering momentum. He had little choice but to respond. He decided to do so before the weekend.

He cancelled his monthly three-way liaison meeting with Friends of the Earth (FoE) and Greenpeace and took the crowded underground to Euston and from there embarked on a ninety-five-minute train journey north to Birmingham where he was met by a round-faced, ginger-haired, jolly-looking girl of about nineteen. She was a member of the local FoE Group. He had met her at an anti-nuclear power rally and she had offered help when he needed it in the Midlands. Chattering all the way, she piloted an old Volkswagen with more enthusiasm than skill up the busy Hagley Road and west into the Warwickshire countryside. Within twenty-five minutes they crossed the border into Worcestershire. It was raining and a gusty wind was blowing sheets of water into the windscreen. The worn wipers weren't really up to the challenge, but Olly doubted whether it made much difference to her driving whether she could see the road or not.

Still, to be fair, she got them there. By-passing the town centre of Kidderminster she continued a further three miles up a hill, then back down into the Wyre Valley. Bewdley, their destination, proved to be a picturesque town divided by the River Severn. They drove up an ancient main street, divided at the top by a clock tower, and turned right, past a newsagent's shop and a betting office, and then immediately left, climbing a steep hill until near the top they reached a big old thatched cottage.

There she left him, arranging to meet at the pub at the foot of the hill in an hour. Olly climbed up a bank, walked round the side of the house, unlatched the gate and found himself standing in a waist-high jungle of uncut grass and weeds. The path was hardly visible. He pushed his way to the door and knocked. There was no immediate answer. For a moment he thought that the journey may have been in vain. But, just as he was about to knock for the third time, he heard a shuffling sound and the door opened a fraction. He found himself looking into the deeply lined face of a man in his early sixties, white hair growing in tufts as if it had been attacked by a lunatic with shears. He was leaning on a walking stick and staring at the campaigner blankly, trying to recognise who or what he was.

'I'm Oliver Witcomb of ECO, Professor Barnes. I hope you remembered I was coming. I called last night.'

For what seemed an eternity the man looked at him,

puzzled, and then his face cleared and came alive. He straightened and to Olly's relief spoke lucidly. 'Yes. Yes, of course. How silly of me. I haven't been sleeping well . . . I'm afraid I drifted off.'

Barnes led Olly into a big room with a large stone fireplace. He appeared to have rekindled last night's fire for the grate was full of ash and the fireplace hadn't been cleaned. But the logs he had put on were blazing brightly. To the right of the fireplace was a comfortable-looking leather armchair, and in front of it a worn sofa. Otherwise the room was a shambles. It looked like the collection centre for a jumble sale. There were thousands of books, most of them in untidy heaps on the floor. There were filing cabinets, their drawers hanging out, discarded files lying around them. Olly noted at least three typewriters, all antique. There were newspapers everywhere, and letters, the torn envelopes left lying on the floor. An expensive-looking globe lay in one corner like a child's football. In another, by the door, there lay a tangle of walking sticks. Olly reckoned there must have been at least thirty of them.

He looked at Barnes apprehensively. Could this man really help them?

Barnes, on the other hand, was now looking positively bright-eyed. 'Let's have a coffee.' It wasn't a question. He just said it and then disappeared. Olly could hear a tap running and cups rattling and within a few minutes a call. 'Perhaps you would be good enough to carry it in.'

Olly leapt to his feet. 'Of course.'

He ducked under a low door and found himself in a dining room. The contrast with the sitting room was remarkable.

This was beautifully furnished with what appeared to be an antique table and chairs and with a superb display of hunting pictures on the wall.

The kitchen was absurdly tiny for such a large house but well equipped. But what struck Olly was that these rooms were immaculate, spick and span, polished till they shone.

Barnes looked at him and smiled. 'Now I know what you're thinking, young man. How can these rooms look so neat while the other one is such a mess.'

Olly began politely to disclaim the thought, but Barnes was not to be stopped.

'It's easily explained. I have a housekeeper who keeps the rest of the house clean. But I won't let her in there. No. Not in there. I would never be able to find a thing.'

He indicated a tray with two cups full of coffee and as they re-entered the cluttered sitting room he said, 'This may look like chaos to you, young man, but there is nothing I can't find here within a minute.'

He cleared a space for the tray on a small table by the fire and then said to Olly, 'Name something.'

'I beg your pardon, sir?'

'Name something. Anything. I promise you I'll find it within sixty seconds.'

Olly thought. 'Your electricity bill,' he said.

For a moment Barnes stood still. Then with a cry of triumph he grabbed his stick and shuffled to the far corner, tossed a pile of letters into the air and, seizing an envelope, held it aloft.

Olly laughed, but the effort seemed to exhaust the older man.

He shuffled slowly back to the leather chair and slumped into it. For a few minutes Olly left him in peace.

Eventually the scientist revived. 'I'm sorry,' he said. 'Truth is, I'm not well.' He noisily sipped his coffee. 'Now what was it you wanted to see me about?'

'The plantacon research. I wanted to ask about that.'

For a moment Olly thought the old man was going to

paused, then, shrugging his shoulders, said, 'Look, I don't want to appear difficult. You may as well know . . . I don't have long.'

'Long?'

'Long. I don't have *long*.' Then seeing Olly still wasn't grasping it, he virtually shouted, 'For God's sake man, I'm trying to tell you I'm *dying* . . . of cancer.'

He testily waved away Olly's gesture of concern. 'No, never mind. I'm not looking for sympathy. I'm simply stating the fact.'

Olly's mind worked feverishly, considering the options. 'Sir, could we send a small team, no more than three people, up here to make a video of you describing your report just as you've described it to me. It would only take about twenty minutes of your time. We could then show that at our press conference and make it available to the television people.'

Olly thought he saw a twinkle in the old scientist's eye. Grabbing his stick, Barnes pulled himself up. 'You're a resourceful young man,' he said. 'I'll think about it.'

He looked closely at Olly. There was a hint of a smile. 'Sorry, what was your name?'

'Witcomb, sir. Olly Witcomb.'

'You remind me of myself as a lad.' He opened the door. 'I'm not ruling your proposition out. I'll see what I can do. Ring me.'

In fact, later that night, Olly rang MacAnally. 'He's a bit eccentric, Sam, and old and sick. Dying of cancer. I'm afraid he won't make it to a press conference.'

'Damn.'

'Well, things could be worse. I asked whether we could send a camera team up to video an interview with him and he didn't say no.'

'That was a good idea. In fact, Olly, it was brilliant.'

'Thanks . . . except . . . he didn't say yes either.

Actually, although he's sick, I also got the feeling he was frightened. It's almost as if he'd been warned off publishing the results. You don't think the other side's got on to this?'

'I don't see how. The only people who know about it are the funder – and he *wants* a campaign – and the other scientists, and they wouldn't have any reason to do it. If he's sick, he probably just doesn't want to make the effort. I've already had this problem with one of the American scientists. In his case it's his wife who's ill.'

There was a lengthy silence. Then, just when Olly was going to ask whether Sam was still on the line, he said, 'Look, I have a feeling his contract requires him to cooperate with publication. I'll check this out with the funder.

'Obviously we don't want to come on heavy with him or worsen his condition, but I still think your idea of the video is terrific.'

Olly hung up, satisfied.

And turned his mind to other things.

Like Sally.

And Saturday night.

Maybe he'd better get some fresh coffee and orange juice in. Just in case she wanted to come down for breakfast the following morning.

Then he decided to take the sheets on his bed to the launderette.

He wasn't taking her for granted. But better to be safe than sorry.

TOKYO

Things were going well for Machiko Yanagi, too. Mike McKenzie had confirmed he would be at the ECO conference in Spain and they planned to holiday on the Costa del Sol afterwards. There they would resolve the unanswered questions.

Work, too, had been proceeding satisfactorily. It was a pity she had to spend time on this plantacon enquiry but Sam had been insistent. So, to see Professor Seiichi Tezuka, she made a three-hour bullet train journey to Tohoku University. Actually it proved enjoyable . . . a peaceful ride through green valleys and mountain tunnels. She arrived rested and took a taxi from the station to the university.

Tezuka's office was incredibly neat, even the pencils lined up in a row. He appeared to be a computer addict. There were two computers in the office, one on his desk, one on a side table, and scores of neatly catalogued disks.

She looked at him as he carefully saved the one he had been working on.

He was short, a bit overweight, with crew-cut black hair and a harassed-looking face.

Then, realising she was still standing, he apologised and waved her to a chair. 'I understand you want to know about plantacon? You've been told about my study by your American organisation, yes?'

'That's right.'

'Who, I understand, have been given copies of all the studies?'

'I believe so.'

'Well, I can confirm the information you already have.

'I was able by comparing samples close to and far away from the new Tokyo International Airport to establish that there is plantacon on the ground near the airport, less so elsewhere. It's clearly coming from the planes as they take off and land.

'There's a lot more detail in the report but that sums it up. There's not a lot more I can say.'

She nodded. 'You will know, Professor, that other studies suggest that children living near airports are already being harmed.

'We may decide to campaign for action to protect them. If we do, we'd welcome your support.'

'Well, it's a bit irregular.'

He picked up a pencil, then, another, then put them back, side by side with the others. He tidied the row so that they were in an immaculately straight line.

'In any case, I'm a scientist, not a politician, Miss Yanagi. I've done my work. Surely it's for others to take it from there.'

'Our campaign won't stand up without scientific evidence. If you weren't able to stand by your work publicly we would appear unconvincing.'

'Yes, yes, I see that.' He thought for a moment. 'It's not a question of not being able to . . .' He thought some more. 'All right, I'll give you one day. I'll come to Tokyo and announce the results of my work and give interviews. But that will be that.'

Machiko was about to protest that it wasn't enough, but then she thought better of it.

This would do for now.

The media and others would create their own demand and Tezuka would have little choice but to respond.

Yes, he was hooked.

So she thanked him and began to gather her things.

But he wasn't finished. He wanted to say that if there were an international conference, and if the other scientists were willing to appear, he would be happy to do so also.

'Naturally I would want to support my colleagues.'

'That could be helpful. Thank you.'

So Tezuka was one of those scientists who liked travelling to international conferences.

Still, she was bright as well as high spirited – and, incidentally, immensely popular – and got good results at a state school and a scholarship to university. So there were hopes that all would come right.

Then to her mother's horror, Liz started getting her name in the papers. She was arrested for allegedly kicking a policeman on the ankle while on a peace march. And fined. She was arrested on the top rung of a step-ladder while altering a poster advertising Good Luck cigarettes. By changing the ad from 'Have a Good Luck' to 'Have a Good Fuck' she was judged to have breached the peace. And fined. She was arrested on demonstrations over apartheid in South Africa (fined) and the destruction of rain forests in Tasmania (fined). And she was arrested at the Australian Rules final for running the full length of the field naked. The court was told that by taking up this 'dare' she had raised 300 dollars for charity. The court was unimpressed. Fined.

By this last act the media, on the other hand, was greatly impressed. Liz was a big girl, six feet tall, well built . . . and bountifully endowed with those features most appreciated by picture editors . . . hence her prominence on the front page of the next morning's tabloids.

Her mother nearly had a heart attack.

But what caused the biggest row between them was that instead of using her education to get a job suitable for a 'young lady', Liz joined the environmental movement fulltime and this year, at twenty-five, had become a campaigner for ECO. At this her mother wrote to say that she was stopping her allowance and would only reconsider when Liz got a 'respectable job'.

'This irresponsibility has to be checked. Until you reform, you'll never hear another word from me,' her mother wrote.

In fact what she got were *thousands of other words*.

By letter.

Regularly.

All of them in the form of lengthy lectures, some ending in stern denunciation, others in desperate pleas.

Liz hated the letters. There were three in her room now, unopened, waiting to be read.

It had to stop.

That was why she was planning to go to Brisbane.

She had rehearsed what she was going to say scores of times.

That while her mother claimed she was irresponsible, Liz could not have felt *more* responsible. She and her friends felt responsible for the whole damn world.

Too bloody responsible. Why otherwise was she working at least sixteen hours a day?

Liz wished she had the time to do all the things her mother imagined she did.

And if that didn't work, Liz decided, she would threaten to have the front pages of the Melbourne tabloids – the ones displaying her spectacular bust – posted to all her mother's high society friends with a request that their husbands get in touch.

That would shut her up.

Liz was nothing if not resourceful.

In the meantime there was work to do. There was the global warming campaign to prepare. There had to be a follow-up to Mike's tropical rain forest conference. They were due to publish a report about traffic pollution in Melbourne's streets.

And there was this MacAnally plantacon project.

She'd forgotten all about it until she got a follow-up call.

It was a damn nuisance.

She had listed her existing projects hoping that he

would tell her that if she was so busy she needn't bother, but, judging by what he said over the phone, it couldn't be ignored.

And she had to admit that if it was the scandal he claimed it to be, it could be just the issue she and Mike McKenzie needed to put ECO on the map in Australia.

She rang Dr Bruce Cossens and arranged to see him. The following day she took a plane to Sydney. Following his directions she boarded a bus from Circular Quay to Watson's Bay and made her way to a beautiful wooden house right on Sydney Harbour. She couldn't imagine what it cost but clearly Dr Cossens was making a lot of money, more than she imagined a Sydney University lecturer could possibly earn.

Nor did the man match her image of a reclusive academic surrounded by books and test tubes. He was young, probably in his early thirties, about six foot, well built, muscular, sun-bronzed. He was wearing only shorts and a tee-shirt. He greeted her with a lazy smile and led her onto the porch with a touch on the arm that felt irritatingly speculative.

She fell into a comfortable sun chair and gasped at the view. To her left she could see the Sydney Opera House and the Bridge, to the right a multi-coloured string of yachts making their way towards the ocean. 'My God, you do all right for yourself,' she said as he handed her a cold lager.

'A man's gotta live,' he grinned, throwing himself into another chair and resting his feet on the railings, stretching his long, brown legs out in front of him. His shorts were very short. And tight around the crotch. The bulge was impressive. Despite herself she had to force her eyes away from it. She looked back to his face. The grin had become wider. It took a lot to make Liz blush but this did it.

'So, you want to know about plantacon,' he said. 'How did you hear about it?'

'From America. The funder has involved our people there.'

'Right.' The answer seemed to satisfy him. 'Well, it's bad news all right. To put it in a nutshell, I got some kids near to the airport and some kids further away, and tested them for plantacon in blood and then for IQ and other behavioural problems. The kids near the airport are in trouble. They're picking up the plantacon, I don't know whether it's from the air or from the ground. And it's affecting their minds. They're definitely coming off worse in all the tests.'

'Will this stand up?'

'Well, not on its own. Science expects more than just one study. But I gather there are others that replicate the finding. Together they should make the case.'

'And you're ready to talk about this?'

'Sure.'

He swallowed the last of his lager and got up. 'Well, given you've come this far, how about lunch at Doyles?'

Despite a growing desire to put down the over-confident Dr Cossens, Liz saw no reason why he shouldn't buy her lunch before she went back. No reason at all. She liked fish and chips and Doyles was, after all, Doyles – famous throughout Australia.

'OK. You're on.'

He put on a pair of trainers and they walked out the front of the house, past a spotless white Porsche – bloody hell, what had that cost? – back round to the bay and down across a tree-covered lawn to the water's edge. A motor boat was just arriving at the small wharf with what appeared to be a party of Sydney business executives out for a boozy lunch.

'Better beat them to a table,' Cossens said,

took a cab to National Airport, and from there the shuttle to New York.

After leaving his bags with Marie and making a couple of calls in Manhattan he hailed a cab and asked the fare to Hoboken. He blanched at the reply but told himself that Justin Lord could just about cover the trip.

In fact Hoboken was close enough to be seen from the piers on the west side of Manhattan. A town fronting the Hudson River it was famous for three things: it was the site of America's first brewery; it claimed to be the home of baseball (the first modern-rules game was played there in 1846); and it was where Frank Sinatra was born. Now, thought MacAnally grimly, it could become famous for a fourth . . . as the place where they invented plantacon.

To get there the cab travelled under the Hudson via the Lincoln Tunnel, left the freeway immediately and cut down past Shanghai Red's wooden shed restaurant, across the newly developed Lincoln Harbour area where anchored yachts and glossy condominiums were being paid for with yuppie mortgages, then down into Hoboken's 14th Street with its row of ethnic restaurants.

They headed directly towards the river. MacAnally could see the Empire State Building dominating the skyline at the end of the street. When there was only a piece of vacant land between them and the river, they turned right, past Lady Jane's art deco restaurant and bar and into Hudson Street. Once a busy industrial centre it was now mainly wasteland. There were a number of derelict factory buildings, all broken glass and rusting iron. The sign on one of these abandoned structures proclaimed it to be the 'Industrial Relations Office'. MacAnally shrugged. Abandoned factory buildings meant lost jobs, lost pay. There had to be a lot of sad stories to tell about this place.

Only two factories seemed to be operational. There was the Maxwell House coffee-making plant at the end of the row. And there was another, set back from the front so that he hadn't seen it from the other end of the street. It was the one modern building on the block, a huge red-brick factory on the banks of the river, surrounded by a high fence capped with barbed wire. There were guards on the entrance and warning signs: DANGER – KEEP CLEAR. There was no other sign, apart from a small brass plaque by the gate: FEI. He walked by and from about fifty yards up the road could see round the back of the windowless building. There was a newly built wharf stretching out into the river and he could see a small tanker being fed by a thick pipeline. Another was anchored in the river nearby, no doubt awaiting its turn. Also at the back of the factory were a row of tanker trucks, painted black, with just the letters FEI painted on the side.

He wandered back past the factory to 14th Street and up a couple of blocks to Washington Street, clearly the main street of Hoboken. He walked past Kelly's Pub, the Washington Madison Square Sports Bistro and the Malibu Diner, then turned back towards the river. Between Washington and Hudson streets, parallel with them, was Bloomfield Street.

It was tree-lined and running up alongside the steps to the front door of each three-storeyed stone house were brightly painted, attractive wrought-iron railings, dividing the houses and yet somehow uniting the neighbourhood at the same time. There had been some snow the day before and children, on holiday from school, were building snowmen on the pavements.

He located the number he wanted and, after carefully climbing the icy steps, rang the bell. He had just about given up on a reply when he heard footsteps and the door opened. He found himself facing a small woman, probably in her forties but with hair prematurely greying. Piercing eyes stared at him warily out of a pinched face.

'Mrs Holmes?'

'Yes.'

'I'm sorry to bother you, Ma'am,' he began, 'my name is Sam MacAnally from an organisation called ECO. I wonder if I could talk to you for a moment.'

She looked even more wary. 'If you're one of those religious organisations . . .'

MacAnally laughed. 'No, Ma'am, we're involved in environmental protection.'

She looked at him uncomprehendingly. 'What has that got to do with me?'

He told her he wanted to talk about plantacon.

Her faced closed. 'Why? What do you want?'

'Mrs Holmes, I know this must seen an imposition, but I understand your husband died while he was working at the factory making it. I am hoping you could help me with some information . . .'

'I'm sorry, mister. I have nothing to say.'

She began to close the door.

MacAnally pressed her. 'Nothing you *want* to say or nothing you're *allowed* to say?'

She partly opened the door and looked at him defiantly. 'They've been very good to me. And if they don't want me to talk about it then I'm not going to talk about it. Goodbye.'

And this time the door was firmly closed.

Sam walked back into the street and, taking a piece of paper from his pocket, checked a second name. He was about halfway up Bloomfield Street when he felt a blow, then a chill between his shoulders. He swung round and saw a small girl, probably about five, standing open-mouthed with horror. She had hit him with a snow ball.

'I'm sorry, mister. I didn't mean to hit you.'

MacAnally grinned, picked up a handful of snow and tossed it gently back. 'That's OK. Maybe you can help me. Do you know where Mrs Jakowski lives?'

'Sure I do.' The girl pointed across the street. 'That house there. Look, I'll show you.'

And she scampered in front of him to the foot of another set of steps framed by another set of wrought-ironing railings. The house was red-brick, three storeys, framed by two trees. There was a holly wreath on the door and lights in the windows.

'Are you sure?' asked MacAnally.

'Of course I'm sure, silly. I live here.'

'Oh. Oh, I see. Well, is your Mum in?'

'Sure.' The little girl rang the bell.

Almost immediately the door was flung open and MacAnally found himself staring at a rosy-cheeked woman, blonde hair cut short, bright blue eyes, in her mid-thirties, wearing an apron and with her hands covered in flour. She took one look at MacAnally and the girl and said sternly, 'Patricia, have you been throwing snow at this man? I said you'd be in trouble . . .'

MacAnally quickly interjected. 'No, Ma'am, honestly, she's been extremely helpful. Actually, it was you I wanted to see. My name is MacAnally. From ECO.'

'Oh.' She looked at him closely, then, as if satisfied with what she saw, said, 'Yes, I see. Oh, well you'd better come in.' She ushered them into the kitchen where he was overwhelmed by the heavenly aroma of freshly made cookies.

'Coffee?'

'I'd love some.'

didn't want me to spend years tangled up with lawyers. They made a generous settlement, an extremely generous settlement. Even my lawyer said that. It will take care of Patricia and me for life.' She paused. There were more tears. 'Not that I wouldn't give you all of it to have Art back. Happy and kind . . . like he used to be . . . before . . .'

'I'm sorry.' MacAnally daren't look at her. He busied himself stirring his now cold coffee.

'Was it a condition of the settlement that you wouldn't talk about it?'

She looked at him, suddenly concerned. 'Yes. Yes, it was. Oh dear, I shouldn't have told you even this much.'

He hastened to reassure her. 'It's all right, Mrs Jakowski. I won't say a word. You have my promise. I just wanted to know a bit more for myself.'

He rose. 'Did your husband ever indicate that the work he was doing was dangerous?'

'He said it wasn't. As long as they were careful. Although . . .' she stopped.

'Yes?'

'I guess you know three others died too?'

'Yes, I do. Just one other thing, Mrs Jakowski. Do you remember the name of the man who came to see you from FEI?'

'Yes, yes, of course I do. It was Mr Partrell.'

'Partrell?'

'Dieter Partrell. He's one of the big men there. He was kind. I must say that. And very distressed.'

'I'm sure he was.' For a moment MacAnally looked grim. Then he took her hand. 'You've been very kind. And helpful. You'll hear no more from me, you have my word.'

'That's all right.'

As they got to the door she said, 'I only talked to you

because I saw you on television, Mr MacAnally. Getting that award.'

He smiled. 'Thank you. And I promise not to sue you for the snowball in the back.'

She laughed.

Her face lit up.

She suddenly looked younger.

MacAnally's heart went out to her. He swallowed, then, before she could see the pity in his eyes, he turned and began to walk back up the street.

He walked back down to Hudson Street and stood opposite the FEI factory.

It was getting dark and, as he stared at the anonymous-looking building, he thought of Art Jakowski working there, full of optimism for his family and their future.

He thought, too, of another family, back in the Twenties, of the knock on the door of their home in Dayton, Ohio . . . of the woman being told that her husband had died as a result of industrial negligence . . . and of the small boy who had grown up, so alienated from his fellow human beings. He thought of Justin Lord.

A big black block, framed by the lights of Manhattan across the water, the building without windows now seemed to him to take on a sinister appearance. Remote and hostile. It was almost as if it had been dropped there from outer space.

Then he told himself not to be melodramatic. And went looking for a cab. To take him back to Manhattan. And to Christmas with Marie.

Christmas and the New Year came and went.

Sam and Marie spent the holiday at Lake Placid, holed up in a warm inn where they drank hot punch in front of a roaring fire and otherwise surprised the staff by the inordinate amount of time they spent in bed. Eugene Remington was also at a ski resort. He had just purchased another house, a ranch-like place in Aspen, Colorado, and neighbours attended a big Christmas Eve housewarming.

His chosen campaigner Nicola Kowalska was with her family in Chicago and on Christmas Day did what she had done every year as a child – went ice-skating. The *Washington Post*'s Jackie Brown was with her folks in Omaha, Nebraska, devouring her mother's home cooking with all the gusto of someone who had spent too much of the past year eating TV dinners. The columnist Lionel North spent the holiday working on his latest book, to be titled *The failure of liberal America, from Roosevelt to Carter*. Dieter Partrell spent Christmas with his family in their brand-new New Jersey penthouse with views east towards Manhattan and south towards Hoboken and the FEI plant. But there was little the Partrell family could do to relieve his gloom. It was not a happy Christmas. Nor was Todd Birk's; he spent it in Witchita, Kansas, glowering at his ageing mother and complaining about Communist infiltration of American business. As far as is known Justin Lord never left his New York apartment, although his butler was heard to tell the doorman that he turned the computer monitors off for several hours on Christmas Day. Dr Raynald Warner and his wife spent it quietly, cosy in front of their fire, reading and listening to classical music and talking softly to each other. Dr David Abernathy flew to London, England, to stay with friends and spend his evenings at the theatre. Senator Christopher Wilkins and his family spent a lot of time attending Christmas and New Year functions in every corner of the state that was accessible in the snow. But then he was newly elected and not yet feeling secure. Senator Ed Eberhard never left his ranch outside Fort Worth, Texas. He was an old-timer and totally secure. Olly Witcomb, who had at least been kissed by Sally that Saturday night, and who now couldn't wait for the New Year and better things, was with his parents in Evesham, Worcestershire, only an hour's drive from where Professor Trevor Barnes was being cared for by his unmarried sister who had come from Norwich to share what would be his last Christmas. ECO's Euro-lobbyist Monique de Vos was with her family too, in Bruges. She hadn't received a card or present from her lover Pierre Courtois and didn't care. Courtois himself was skiing in Switzerland. With his wife. Machiko Yanagi was with her parents in Kyoto where she received a long and expensive and happy phone call from Mike McKenzie who spent Christmas Day on the beach in Perth. Liz Scullen got from Dr Bruce Cossens (spending Christmas on the Gold Coast) a suggestive Christmas card. She assumed he thought it was funny. She tossed it in the bin. And went to stay with her mother in Brisbane where, as always, they argued.

Anne Jakowski and Patricia went to church on Christmas Day, in the morning and in the evening. They prayed that Art was in heaven and being cared for as lovingly as he had cared for them.

For at least ten days no one did a thing about plantacon.

Except the airlines.

They added it to Jet-A.

And they flew a record number of holiday passengers a record number of miles, making in the process a record profit for the holiday fortnight.

But to be fair they offered good value. Fares were at a record low.

That was because fuel costs were at a record low.

Wilkins' face lit up. 'Good. What is it?'

MacAnally grinned. 'Hold it, Chris. I said *if it checks out*. Give me just a couple of weeks. I should know more. Then if it looks like holding up, it's yours. If not, we'll come up with another one.'

He called for the bill and added: 'There's just one thing.'

'Yes?'

'Some citizen groups take the view that once a senator or congressman takes up an issue, it becomes the politician's issue, and they become the politician's servant. We don't. As far as we're concerned it's a partnership. Equal input. Equal gains. You need to win votes; we understand that. But we have to raise money, and build support; and you need to understand that. We don't care whether your constituents think you did it all, but it's necessary that our supporters think we did. That way we both stay in business. And stay together.'

Wilkins looked at him with respect. 'I do understand that, Sam. That's no problem for me.'

'But do you understand what it means, Chris? It means an equal say in what happens to any measure we're promoting. It means not excluding us when the key meetings occur. And, above all, it means equal shares with the publicity. It's our life blood as much as it's yours.'

'OK, OK.' The senator laughed. 'I can see you've had some problems in the past. Look,' and he leaned forward earnestly, 'I *want* this to work, Sam. I need you too much to let you down.' He sat back. 'So, relax. We'll be in it together, all the way. I promise.'

'That's good enough for me.' MacAnally picked up the check and stood up.

'Do yourself a favour. Before we next meet, read up on the plantacon revolution.'

*

The 116 Club was usually frequented by Republicans and business lobbyists and it was there on that same day that Eugene Remington, on a visit from New York, was lunching with Ed Eberhard, Republican senator for Texas, ranking member of the Environment and Public Works Committee and one of the aviation industry's most valuable allies on the Hill.

Eberhard's support for the airlines was not surprising. American had its headquarters in Dallas-Fort Worth. And Remington's Executive Airlines had its operational base near Houston and was one of a number of airlines that contributed generously to Eberhard's election expenses.

For over an hour they reviewed matters rising on the political agenda and likely to affect the aviation industry. It was only when they were on to the coffee and cigars that Remington said, 'There's just one other thing . . .' he paused. 'I would be grateful if this could remain strictly between ourselves for the time being . . .'

The Texan nodded. Curtly. It was a request that didn't need to be made.

Remington, seeing his annoyance, apologised. 'Please don't misunderstand. I'm not questioning your discretion, Ed. It's just that this is not an issue I want you to *act* on for the time being.' He looked around the restaurant, then leaned forward. 'You know of course of the enormous savings of money and energy the industry has made by adding plantacon to Jet-A?'

'Yes.'

'Well, it appears we may be about to have some difficulty with the environmental lobby.'

The senator snorted with annoyance.

'The thing is,' Remington ploughed on, 'this man

MacAnally seems to have convinced himself that plantacon could be some sort of environmental hazard.'

'How can that be?'

'Well, he seems to be concerned that the emissions from aeroplane exhausts cause pollution harmful to people.'

'And do they?'

'No. My advice is that only small amounts are emitted from the planes and most of that disappears into infinity. Furthermore at the quantities that it's likely to be found on the ground it couldn't harm a fly.'

'Well, then, what's the problem?'

'There probably won't be one. But you know what it's like. When these environmentalists decide they're going to kick up a fuss they can cause a lot of trouble – it doesn't seem to matter whether they're right or wrong.'

The senator nodded. 'Well, keep me in touch. If I don't hear anything I'll assume there's no problem. But if there looks like being one, you let me know. And you better get yourself a good lobbyist down here because these environmentalists have got a lot more influence than they should have. In particular, this man MacAnally is a monumental pain in the butt.'

Remington, reaching for the check, said, 'Don't worry. If it comes to a fight we'll use anyone and anything we need. And we'll appreciate your help, Ed. You're a good friend of the industry. We know that.'

The senator rose. 'Why, thank you, Eugene. And fortunately for you I'm anything but a good friend of the environmental lobby.

'If what you say is right, they may have picked the wrong issue this time.

'And, if they have, you can be sure I'm going to kick ass. Yes sir, I'm going to kick ass.'

LONDON

Olly Witcomb and the Labour MP for Islington South, Nick Bell, had lunch on the first Thursday of every month at Joe Allen's restaurant just off the Strand. There, over chopped steak and salad and with a bottle of the house red wine, they regularly celebrated their by-election triumph, Bell as candidate and Witcomb as campaign manager.

The two went back a long way. They had come from the same two-up, two-down, red-bricked terraced housing in the same back streets of Nottingham. Together they had spent summer holidays at the county cricket ground, recording in a dog-eared scorebook the achievements of their Trent Bridge heroes, Hadlee and Randall. They played on damp Saturday afternoons on the same park in the same local football team. And, after attending the same local comprehensive school, they chose the same university – Bristol – and shared digs while there. They even lost their virginity on the same night, in the same room, although as all four involved were drunk, it was not clearly remembered. Finally, they had both come to London at the same time and rented a flat in Islington.

Olly Witcomb, his aim to become a sports journalist, began as a reporter on the local weekly newspaper. Nick Bell had got involved in politics at university, initially because he was in love with a beautiful West Indian girl who was secretary of the Labour club. He would have joined the Tories if she had been one of them. The girl preferred someone else but it didn't matter; by then Bell had found his real love. Politics. Above all he loved the manoeuvring and scheming. His heart set on a political career, he landed a job as a researcher at Labour Party headquarters in Walworth Road.

Together he and Olly had set about rejuvenating a lack-lustre local party, Olly as membership secretary and Bell as local elections organiser. Short of dedicated workers, the general management committee welcomed their enthusiasm and gave them their heads. The result was a landslide victory in the borough council elections.

There had never been any question that Bell would be the one they would promote for parliamentary candidate. It had been his objective since university.

Olly, less personally ambitious, more easy-going, more sceptical about what an MP could actually achieve, a born organiser, was happy to run his friend's campaign.

Their opportunity came unexpectedly early when the sitting MP died. Despite their achievements, many members of the Labour Party looked askance at fielding a twenty-four year old as the candidate in what would be a notable by-election, but Witcomb and Bell and their friends had got a stranglehold on the local party. Not even a determined drive by the older hands, backed by trade union votes, could stop them.

Olly ran a brilliant by-election campaign; the result for Bell was a 10,000 majority, an increase of more than 4,000 over his predecessor.

Now, with the council under Labour control and Bell in the House, Olly found himself without further political ambitions, so, spurred on by friends in the environmental movement, he went to work for Friends of the Earth and subsequently as UK representative of ECO. He and Bell no longer shared a flat but remained close friends.

In the meantime Bell, advised by the shrewder, more

patient Witcomb, bided his time. He knew that for the youngest MP to press too quickly for prominence would alienate the older hands and once that happened life could become decidedly unpleasant. So he concentrated on getting the feel of the House, being respectful to the more experienced backbenchers . . . and waiting.

There was, however, a definite limit to his patience. And he had reached it.

'If there was just one juicy scandal, Olly,' he said, 'that I could break with a well-timed series of questions in the House . . .'

Olly looked amused. 'There may be an issue coming up,' he said.

Bell leaned so far across the red and white chequered tablecloth that he nearly fell off his chair. 'What? For Christ's sake, *what*, Olly? Come on, man . . .'

Olly shook his head in wonder at the other's impatience. 'Nick,' he said. 'Will you just listen for a minute. I said there *may* be something coming up. If it does it will be big. Big enough not to take risks with. We're still checking it out.'

'Olly, Jesus wept, what's with the secrecy. It's *me*. Nick Bell, for Christ's sake.'

'Exactly.' Olly grinned. 'And I *know* you. Without me to hold you down you'll be up and off before we've got it right. Remember the Blackburn estate business.'

There had been a rumour that a Tory councillor had been taking cash bribes to support applications for council-owned homes. Before Olly could check it out, Bell had attacked the councillor in public, later having to apologise. He only narrowly avoided an expensive action for slander. It had been the one major setback in his constituency. He now grimaced at the memory.

'OK, OK, Olly, but I learned from that.'

'Well, do learn from it . . . have a bit of patience.'

'But you'll give this issue to me?'

Olly forked a French fry from his friend's abandoned plate. He was enjoying Bell's agony.

'Maybe. If you do it my way.'

'We'll do it together, Olly, you know that.'

Witcomb grinned sceptically. 'Do I?' Then before the indignant Bell could answer he said, 'OK. Maybe I'll know more next week.'

Bell looked at him crossly. But he recognised that stubborn ring in Witcomb's voice. He wasn't going to get more information today.

He also knew that gleam in the other's eye.

This was something big.

No doubt about it.

And he wanted it. All for himself.

So he gritted his teeth, feigned patience, and told Olly to ring him as soon as he was ready to talk.

BRUSSELS

Pierre Courtois, a Belgian MEP, was having lunch at Le Gigotin with Hans Fischer, a German who was chairman of the European Parliament Committee on Transport and Tourism.

The two men were not friends, but, as members of the same party, they had found it useful to help one another from time to time.

Now Courtois was trying to persuade Fischer to help him fill an unexpected vacancy for committee vice-chairman.

The German was not, however, responding, partly because he privately detested the Belgian, who, it was rumoured, had slept with his, Fischer's, secretary, upon whom Fischer himself had designs, but also because this rare chance to influence his successor (usually vice chairmen were appointed in pre-session deals) was one of the few bits of power he had. It was not to be dispensed lightly.

In any case he was in no hurry to make way as chairman. Putting an ambitious, well-connected, and thoroughly untrustworthy MEP like Courtois into the number two spot too early didn't make a lot of sense.

One final reservation: he knew Courtois was only using the committee, that he saw his ultimate destiny in Belgium's domestic politics. And Fischer cared about his committee. He wasn't going to have it used to such little purpose.

Courtois had ruthlessly but patiently pursued his ambition since university. First he had set out to make money, going into business and then, by way of a short cut, marrying the boss's daughter. Not that this had been too much of a sacrifice; she was beautiful as well as rich. The photographs of the pair with their young family regularly graced the pages of women's magazines.

With the help of his father-in-law, who was also influential in Belgian politics, he had been selected as candidate for a winnable seat in the European Parliament. Having got to Strasbourg at the age of thirty-six, his plan was to become conspicuous as a fighter for Belgian interests in Europe until he could get a safe place on the party's list for the Belgian parliament. There he hoped his reputation as an international advocate of the Belgian cause would help him to an early place in the Cabinet.

Courtois had, however, become bogged down. He had underestimated how powerless the European Parliament really was. While he hit the occasional headline with a 'Belgium won't stand for this' speech, he found that much of the time his activities were ignored. Nor was there a free place high on the party list for the Belgian Parliament. In this respect, his father-in-law had recently been surprisingly unhelpful. Courtois wondered, uncomfortably, whether the older man had heard whispers about his involvement with other women.

For if there was a flaw in the Courtois plan it was that he had no self-discipline when it came to women.

No matter who it was, once he met a woman he had to have her.

And inevitably that had become known. In Strasbourg. And increasingly in Brussels.

He pursued parliamentary assistants and Commission secretaries, journalists, female MEPs (he claimed to have slept with one from every country, one from every party), party workers and lobbyists, air hostesses and restaurant waitresses. He pursued them expensively, time-consumingly, shamelessly, sometimes humiliatingly, but more often successfully, because he was persistent, charming, good-looking – dark, thick hair, grey eyes, athletic build – wealthy, and simply wouldn't take no for an answer.

And once he got them he lost interest. Sometimes he slept with them several times. Sometimes he had three or four affairs going at the same time. But usually once per woman was enough.

Monique de Vos had lasted longer than most. That was because she had resisted his advances longer than most. Such women represented a challenge to Courtois. They got more of his time. That was because it wasn't enough just to get them into bed; they had to have their high and mighty attitudes fucked out of them. In the most humiliating way possible.

No wonder the Strasbourg secretaries had three times in a row voted Courtois 'shit of the year'.

But, in the case of Monique de Vos, there was another factor. He sensed Monique could be useful to him.

And now he had been proved right.

That brief fax message from ECO in the US aroused his interest. He knew a bit about the aviation industry, including the impact of what the Americans called the plantacon revolution.

If plantacon was an environmental hazard, and that's what the fax suggested, all hell was about to break loose.

It would be a pan-European issue.

One that belonged in either of the two committees to which he belonged.

And one on which he could fight the Belgian cause in the full glare of media attention.

He reckoned he couldn't lose whichever side he took.

Because if it wasn't in his interests to *defend* plantacon in the Transport and Tourism Committee, he could *attack* it in his other committee, Environment.

Which was the reason for this lunch with Fischer. Sensing now that the German was becoming bored with his pleadings for the vice-chairmanship, Courtois decided to play his ace in the hole.

'Look Hans,' he said, lowering his voice and leaning forward. 'I've got information on something coming up. A controversial issue, one that could be big, really big. But it has a lot of ramifications.

'There'll be others trying to put it into another committee.

'Environment.'

Fischer sat up. If there was an issue with transport ramifications, he wanted it in his committee. Definitely not in Environment.

'What is it?'

Courtois looked crafty. 'I'm still checking it out. I can't say yet. But I'll be blunt with you. I'm a substitute member of Environment and could steer it there just as easily as to the Transport. I'm minded to push it in the direction of the committee where I feel I've got some future.'

Fischer didn't know whether to admire the other's honesty or be appalled by the cynicism.

But it mattered little.

He, too, needed a new issue and he needed it soon. Above all, he couldn't afford to let a *transport* issue fall into the hands of the *environment* lobby. That would make him appear ineffective to politicians and industrialists alike. No, he had to be seen to be in control. If that meant accommodating this appalling creep Courtois, so be it.

'Well, as you know, Pierre, it isn't totally in my hands,' he said with a sleek smile, 'but I think I'll have considerable influence because of the way the vacancy has arisen.' He paused. 'Obviously I would look sympathetically on someone who could assist the committee to be more effective.'

Courtois looked directly back, not returning the smile. 'Quite.'

There was a silence.

Fischer spoke first. 'Well?'

'Well what?'

'Well, what's the issue?'

The other laughed. 'Oh, come on, Hans, you know better than that.'

This time Fischer didn't smile. 'Right. Quite. Well, let's put it like this. When you're ready to talk about it come to me. If I want to take the issue up I promise to fully involve you. And I'll back you for the vice-chairmanship.'

Courtois waved to the waiter for a couple of cognacs.

'Your word's good enough for me, Hans,' he said. 'We'll talk again in a week or two.'

The matter settled, he looked around the restaurant.

There was a woman at the bar, drinking cognac and dipping into a bowl of nuts. Maybe late thirties, red hair. She looked sexy. And alone.

Courtois caught her eye. She smiled. He smiled back.

An understanding reached, he switched the smile to Fischer, endured a recitation of the German's views on road haulage regulation, and waited patiently for him to leave.

He only had his constituents' interests to look after that afternoon.

And they would just have to wait.

TOKYO

Machiko Yanagi ran into Ichiro Hashimoto, one of the younger Diet members from the ruling Liberal Democratic Party, at a reception to welcome delegates to an international whaling conference. He had come over to her while she was carefully filling up a plate from the buffet.

'You need a bigger plate, Machiko,' he said, amused by her haul of sushi, tuna, salmon eggs and marinated raw fish.

She giggled. 'We environmentalists don't get to eat often . . . when we do we stock up.'

She looked at him. His pale, sharp face was topped by a mop of black hair. He wore glasses. He was unusually tall, over six foot, and exceptionally thin. 'You look as if you could do with some food yourself,' she said.

He laughed. 'Probably. I'll wait to see whether there's any left after your needs are met. So, how's our crusader?'

'I'm well, Ichiro. And you?'

'Frankly, Machiko, a little bored. Why can't you people come up with something I can have fun with? It would make a change from coping with constituents' suspicions about which Minister is on the take from whom.'

Then, taking her arm and guiding her out of the hearing of others, he said, 'Seriously, I do need some action.'

She put her plate down on a window ledge and delicately touched her face with a napkin, using the time to think. Then, cautiously, she said, 'Maybe I *can* help.'

His interest quickened.

'Really? What've you got?'

She giggled. 'You *are* eager,' she teased. 'Hasn't your name been in the *Asahi Shinbun* recently?'

'Hey,' he replied. 'Stop it. Sarcasm doesn't become you.'

She took a mouthful of food, enjoying keeping him waiting.

'Well,' she eventually said, 'I'm going to our international conference soon. Why don't I call you when I get back? There may be something . . .'

'Do that,' he said quickly. 'I mean it. I *need* an issue – a real *winner* of an issue.'

She giggled again. 'Don't we all.'

But that evening she jotted his name down in her diary. She would follow the contact up.

Hashimoto had sounded hungry for notoriety.

That meant he could be ready to go out on a limb.

And that mattered.

Because a campaign involving a member of the *governing* party would get more attention than one led by one of its traditional opponents.

If this plantacon campaign took off, he could be just the man they needed.

CANBERRA

Liz Scullen hated going to Canberra. It was too much of a man's town. And the men she lobbied there still treated women – and, for that matter, the environmental movement – as people to be indulged rather than to be taken seriously.

At least Keith Mullalay, the opposition environment spokesman, was better than most. An ambitious senator from Melbourne, at thirty-eight one of the youngest in the shadow cabinet, he had actually bothered to educate himself on the issues and keep in touch with campaigning environmentalists. His problem, as he told them over lunch – steak for him and Mike McKenzie, salad for Liz – was getting the shadow cabinet to take environmental issues seriously.

'They think you're all a load of wankers,' he confided. 'And I think they're crazy. We should make this *our* cause . . . it's a damn good one. You're in touch with the issue, Liz. You know what's coming up. And I need an issue. A new one. One that will get the environment high on the agenda.'

She considered telling him about plantacon but restrained herself. 'We'll come back to you, Keith. Maybe we have one . . . and if we do it'll be big, that we can promise you.'

He looked at her closely, made as if to press her further, then changed his mind. 'That would be good, Liz.'

They walked out into the bright sunlight. 'Can I get my driver to take you to the airport?'

McKenzie was about to accept but Liz bridled. 'We can take a bus.'

'But . . .'

'No buts, Mike, I don't think the taxpayers' money should be used to take senators' friends to airports.'

Mullalay laughed, amused both by Liz's obstinacy and Mike's obvious frustration. He got into the car and wound down the window. 'Mike, Liz, thanks for coming up. I'll look forward to hearing from you.'

McKenzie looked at her resignedly. 'Crikey, Liz, did it bloody matter that it was an official car? Now we've got to find a bloody bus.'

'I thought you were a man of principle.'

'My principles would have been unaffected by his car.'

'Your soul will be improved by the bus.'

'Well, all I can say is thank God I'm in Perth and you're in bloody Melbourne. I couldn't stand too much of this.' Then, as they walked to the bus station, he asked, 'What was the issue you hinted at?'

'Plantacon. You know. The stuff they add to aeroplane fuel. The stuff Sam keeps sending fax messages about.'

'Oh, yeah, have you been following that up then?'

'Well, someone had to. You were doing bugger all.'

'Anything in it?'

'Yes,' she said. 'I think there's a lot in it.'

At the airport, as they waited for their flights, she told him all about Cossens and his research.

And, as she waved goodbye and walked to her plane, he called after her. 'There's just one thing I don't understand, Liz.'

'What's that?'

'Well, given this plantacon business, what's a woman of principle doing flying in a bloody aeroplane?'

NEW YORK

The crowd packed into the ballroom of the Waldorf-Astoria rose, applauding, as to the sounds of 'Hail to the Chief' the President of the United States rose from his table and made his way to the podium.

This annual dinner of the aviation industry invariably attracted all the top airline executives to New York but it was especially crowded tonight for it was the first time this President had attended, although others had done so before him.

The President smiled, that election-winning smile that seemed to engulf the whole room. 'I flew here on one of your planes . . .' he began to loud laughter.

'OK,' he responded to the laughter, 'I know you're all in competition, but tonight you're one family, the industry that has done so much for this country, and it's good to see you all together.'

There was warm applause. He turned now to the notes prepared for him.

'This has been a good year for your industry. And for the consumer. More people have been carried to more destinations than ever before. You've helped make this great country into a place we can all get around, you've helped us to know each other and our country better . . .

'You've done a bit for this Administration, too. By getting your costs down, and lowering fares, you've cut down that inflation figure a bit. Why, maybe that even helped me get re-elected.'

There was more applause and laughter.

'Seriously though, the advance in fuel efficiency is not just a boon for you and the consumer but it's a boon for

energy conservation. And that's good news for the whole
country. A twenty-five per cent cut is a real triumph. I
congratulate all in the industry, the airline companies,
the oil companies and in particular the innovators, those
who invented plantacon, for what you're all doing for
America.'

From his table near the President, Eugene Remington
looked across to Senator Ed Eberhard and nodded
appreciatively. He knew Eberhard had been consulted
on the President's speech. Had he suggested that passage
about plantacon?

Whether he had or not, it had nailed the President's
colours to the mast. It would be harder for the
Administration to support any environmental campaign
now.

His guest David Johnston from OILO privately noted
Remington's reaction and thanked God he and the
others had not abandoned the airlines from the start.

What chance did MacAnally and his environmentalists
stand against these people?

He looked round the room at the applauding crowd.
Christ, they even had the President on their side. These
people were winners.

Dieter Partrell, on his third brandy, cigar in hand,
beamed at the guests at his table . . . airline purchasing
executives and their wives, and his new friend Todd Birk
(good man Birk – sound) . . . and flushed even redder
than usual.

He could already see the President's remarks printed
in gold letters on the FEI brochure.

Maybe MacAnally had beaten him before. And
beaten others.

But this was different.

Even MacAnally hadn't taken on and beaten a
President.

Part Three

PLANNING AND PLOTTING

NEW YORK

JANUARY

To determine its campaigning priorities, ECO International held a global meeting once a year. This year it was to be in the Spanish city of Seville.

Knowing that he would have to see Justin Lord before he left, Sam MacAnally asked Dominic Young to report on his enquiries into the commodity dealer's background.

Young was the only team member he could have asked to do it. A graduate of Browns University, he had initially worked for a Democratic senator, rising rapidly to become his top aide. Unfortunately for Young the senator was photographed by the *National Inquirer* with his hand up the mini-skirt of a transvestite go-go dancer in a sleazy club on Bourbon Street, New Orleans. This happened late at night in the middle of the Democratic convention. The senator claimed he was drunk and didn't know the girl was a boy. His Republican opponent wickedly campaigned on the slogan: '*He knows the difference . . . he'll make the difference.*' He won on a landslide, and the senator and Dom Young became unemployed together.

Young now combined the roles of ECO's economics advisor and chief administrator. A small, serious-looking, prematurely balding thirty-three year old, he was discreet, loyal, reliable. And he always told MacAnally the truth, no matter how unpalatable it may be. As a result he had become the campaigner's closest colleague, the one most capable of dissuading him from a rash act in one of his more headstrong moments.

He now came into MacAnally's office, a mug of coffee in one hand, a couple of folders in the other. He was wearing grey suit pants, a blue shirt, a red tie and red braces. MacAnally suppressed a grin. Young still dressed as if working on Capitol Hill. It was a standard joke within the office. As the campaigners, themselves dressed in cords or jeans and jumpers or faded shirts, passed him on the stairs they would always make a point of complimenting him on his appearance. 'Like the tie, Dom,' they would say. Or they would nod at his braces. 'Nice one, Dom.' Amazingly, Young never caught on. 'You like it?' he would beam, then continue merrily on his way, bustling from office to office, computer printouts in hand. They loved him for it.

'As far as I can see, the man's clean,' he now reported as he sunk into a battered armchair and tossed one of the folders onto the desk. 'We couldn't find a trace of a vested interest. No competing transportation interests . . . not a thing.'

'Any environmental downside in what he's doing?'

'Not really. The really dark Greens may question the business he's in . . . you know, its effect on the economies of Third World countries and such like . . . but there's not much they could make of it.'

He pointed to the folder. 'The details of his business are all in there.'

But MacAnally's eyes were on the second file. 'And you checked out his personal life?' He looked at Young and grinned. 'No go-go dancers, male or female?'

'That's not funny.'

'OK, OK.' MacAnally couldn't resist laughing at the other's reddening face. The fate of Young's former senator-employer was another popular subject of office humour – none of it appreciated by Young himself. 'Sorry. Go on.'

'Well, it wasn't so simple. As you know, he's avoided publicity like the plague. But we went to Dayton, Ohio, and looked at back files of the newspapers. Baker's account of the death of Lord's father stands up. It was on the front page of the local rag at the time.'

He handed over the second folder.

The main item was a newspaper story about the accident. It was headlined: *'Tragic end to immigrant's search for better life.'*

MacAnally flicked over the pages. 'I see you went to the orphanage.'

'Yep. Not only do they have him on their records but, once we got the administrator talking, he disclosed that Lord makes donations to it every year – big ones. They think the world of him there.

'Our researcher also had the idea of contacting charities helping families of German immigrants. He figured that if there was any other sign of Lord caring about his fellow man, that's where he'd find it. He was dead right. He's on the donors' list of three of them. Right there at the top.'

He finished his coffee, peered into the mug as if hoping to find another drop, gave up on it, and rose to head back to his own office. 'I reckon he's OK.'

MacAnally was impressed. 'That's terrific. Thanks Dom.' Then he called after him, 'Who did the detailed research?'

Young put his head back round the door. 'Adrian Carlisle. You should use him on the campaign. He's good news. One of the best we've got.'

Carlisle was a newcomer to ECO. After college he'd worked briefly with a Washington law firm and hated it. Not knowing what to do with his career he'd requested a sabbatical and had come to work with Young just before Christmas, initially as a volunteer helper, now on a small retainer and expenses. Only last week he had left a note on MacAnally's desk asking to be assigned to one of the campaigns. Young's recommendation was good enough for MacAnally. He decided to brief Carlisle on plantacon after the Seville Conference.

In the meantime there was Lord to see. MacAnally took the shuttle to La Guardia and a taxi into Manhattan. It was dusk, commuter time, and, although it was slow going, he drew comfort from the taxi's relatively steady pace compared with the immobility of the dense traffic bearing down on Queens. Once on the island it took another twenty minutes to get to the World Trade Center. There he struggled against the effervescent tide of office workers bursting out of overcrowded elevators on route to the subway, released from the duties of the day, free to do their own thing. As he rode alone to the 98th floor he wondered about that. For MacAnally the days tended to merge into the evenings and the evenings into the weekends. Apart from the time he spent with Marie, and even then they often talked about work; campaigning was his life. He wondered what all these people, descending the mountainous WTC Number One even as he climbed its slopes, would be doing in a couple of hours, and he envied them the range of options. It didn't, of course, occur to him that he had those options too.

He reached the 98th floor just as the blonde secretary from Lord's office was wriggling her way to the elevator in a too-tight skirt. To confront whatever adventures she had scheduled for the evening she had doubled the make-up quota. You could have scraped it off with a trowel. MacAnally pushed at the door to Lord Inc. He was much more respectfully received by the cool young black woman this time. She ushered him directly into Lord's office. The dealer was engrossed in a telephone conversation. He seemed to be talking entirely in figures . . . as if words hadn't been invented. Not wanting to appear inquisitive, the campaigner waited by the window on the lower tier of the big room. The largely deserted skyscrapers of Wall Street had become dark now, a mountain range against the grey of the sky. Beyond them, the harbour was silky black. He could see the probing light of a police launch. And, sparkling in the distance, he could see the illuminated outline of Staten Island. MacAnally could have happily stood there for hours. The view was hypnotic. But Lord soon ended his conversation and came to the window, shaking MacAnally's outstretched hand and collapsing into an armchair in one movement. 'How's it going?'

'Well, the scientists all seem confident their work will stand up. They're not all enthusiastic about getting mixed up in a public controversy, but that's not unusual. A lot of scientists actually prefer to have a paper published in some obscure journal read by only a tiny handful of their peers . . . for some reason they feel that wider publicity lowers the tone of whatever they're doing.'

'And, of course, they're right.' Lord was amused by MacAnally's evident indignation. 'Tell me about them.'

'Well, Warner's the most impressive, but he also worries me the most.'

'Why's that?'

'He's reclusive, suspicious. Lives in his own little world up there in Ithaca and won't leave his laboratory or his wife. That's understandable, of course . . . she's crippled. He also dislikes publicity as much as you do. I think he regrets getting involved.

'Abernathy is the opposite, enthusiastic, ready to help in any way we wish. In view of Warner's reticence, we'll need to use him a lot.

'Barnes is ill, I believe terminally ill with cancer. Sometimes he appears to lose touch with what's going on around him. So we plan to get him on video and to use that if we can't field him live.'

He hesitated, then added, 'By the way, my man in the UK got the impression he was frightened of something or someone. You don't think the other side have got wind of this and tried to intimidate him?'

Lord raised his eyebrows. 'I guess paranoia is an occupational hazard in your business. But it's highly unlikely . . . isn't it?'

MacAnally's hackles rose. In his experience it was being *accused* of paranoia that was the campaigner's occupational hazard, not the disease itself. But he could see Lord wasn't trying to be offensive. 'Yes. I guess you're right,' he eventually replied. 'It is unlikely. Although there's a lot at stake . . .' He thought for a moment, then continued. 'Anyway, his unavailability to testify in the UK is not helpful. We need to field a British scientist there. Maybe we should commission some more work?'

Lord frowned. 'I'd hoped five studies were enough. We don't want to delay any longer than we have to.' He looked troubled, then suggested, 'We could move some of the scientists round the world. They don't have to be restricted to their own countries. And it would show the evidence is international. Perhaps they like travelling and meeting other colleagues.'

'Some do. The Japanese, Tezuka, seemed positively anxious to do that and I gather the Australian, Cossens, fancies himself a bit. I don't think he'll mind getting on the international circuit.' Then, seeing that Lord looked a bit deflated by his report, he added cheerfully, 'But, not to worry, what matters is that they're all reputable scientists and we have the studies and they support each other. I'm only a layman, of course, but in my view the case for a ban on plantacon is unanswerable. My scientific advisor Jake Katzir would like to see even more studies, but then he always does. However, on the basis of what he's seen, he thinks the same as I do – that you've uncovered a scandal of immense proportions. It'll make one hell of a campaign.'

He told Lord about the exchange of correspondence between ECO and the top companies.

The older man looked surprised. 'Was it wise to warn them of your interest?'

'We had no choice. It would've weakened our position if we hadn't. Their first line of attack would be that we hadn't even bothered to raise the matter with them. To the media, and especially the politicians with whom we'll later have to deal, that would look bad.'

Lord looked impressed. 'I can see that. And, from what you say, their response has been bland, to put it mildly.'

'That doesn't matter. Our "responsible" approach is now on the record. So is their complacent answer. We're already one up.

'In any case,' he added, 'it makes sense to get a feel for the enemy's likely response before battle commences.'

Lord smiled. He clearly liked what he was hearing. 'Battle,' he repeated, as if trying on the word for size. 'Yes, quite. And what "feel" did you get?'

'They're playing it cool.' He began to think aloud. 'It could, of course, just be complacency. Companies as big as this aren't accustomed to challenge by mere citizens. They don't feel accountable to us. Shareholders, yes . . . to some extent. Customers, yes. Banks, yes. But ordinary people, no. Or maybe they're under-estimating us . . . thinking that if they reassure us we'll just go away. You'd be amazed how many polluters have treated us contemptuously in the past – until it was too late and they found their names plastered all over the papers. Or maybe they really don't think plantacon's a problem. It's incredible how people believe what they want to believe, even when evidence to the contrary is there for everyone to see.

'There's one thing, though. . . .'

He paused while the receptionist entered with a tray containing a pot of coffee and two cups and Lord for the first time showed impatience. He leaned forward eagerly. 'What's that?'

'Apart from a brief acknowledgement, in effect a brush-off, the airlines and the oil companies didn't reply as individual companies. Their main reply came via their industry liaison organisations.'

'And?'

'That suggests they're sufficiently worried to get together and develop an industry line.'

Lord was fascinated. 'Yes. Yes, I can see that. And you think that suggests guilt?'

'That's putting it a bit strong. As I said, it suggests they're worried.'

Lord poured coffee. 'So can I assume you're going ahead?'

'We're about to have our annual ECO conference – in Spain. I shall have to consult my colleagues from other countries. It'll have to be their decision too.'

Lord looked taken aback. 'You mean you haven't *decided*? Surely there can be no doubt . . .'

MacAnally interrupted. 'There isn't. Not in my mind. And I can persuade the others. But they must feel it's their decision. They must really want to do this.'

He stood up and, turning his back on the view, looked down at Lord. 'Don't forget, we'll be up against powerful forces who'll do whatever they have to to win. They'll spend a lot of money – and exert all the influence and muscle they've got. This is going to be all-out war. My people need to be totally committed if they're going to withstand what'll be thrown at them.'

He paused. 'And it's going to be expensive.'

Lord, relieved, spoke quickly. 'That's no problem, you know that. By the way, there's just one thing about the money. I want to be an anonymous supporter.'

MacAnally frowned. 'That won't be easy. People are bound to want to know where the money's coming from. They'll be suspicious if we can't answer. May I ask why the secrecy?'

'Mr MacAnally, if you're the man I think you are, you'll have had me checked out.' MacAnally looked apologetic and Lord smiled. It had the strange effect of making his face look like a rubbery theatrical mask. 'I see that you have,' he said. 'So you know I'm a private person. I don't like publicity. I would hate the kind of notoriety this would bring me.'

MacAnally nodded. 'Well, we'll do our best, but people will ask about the funding. And our opponents will investigate.

'You must have had anonymous contributions before?'

'Not of this size.'

'Couldn't you organise some extra fundraising so that you have other money as well. My money will have less curiosity value if it's not the only income the campaign has.'

MacAnally grinned appreciatively. 'You'll make a citizen group organiser yet, Mr Lord. We'll try. But it won't be easy. While we're talking about money, we're going to need some upfront. Once the decision is taken in Seville we'll want to act quickly.'

'Give me your bank account number. You'll have a million dollars in it by the end of the month.'

MacAnally gasped.

'I can't guarantee we'll win.'

Lord rose and took his hand. 'I know you'll do your best.'

That night Sam and Marie went to Boxers for dinner. They were lazing over their carrot cake dessert, Sam keeping half an eye on a football match on the television set above the bar, when Marie asked, 'How bloody is this battle going to be, Sam?'

'The higher the stakes, the rougher it's bound to get,' he said. 'And the stakes couldn't be higher. Shall we have an Irish coffee?'

'Sure.'

He caught the eye of a waitress and ordered.

'Fortunately we've enough experience of past battles to know what they'll do,' he said.

'What *will* they do?'

'Shoot the messenger.'

'Shoot the *what*?' She looked startled.

'The messenger. Haven't you heard that expression? It's what the more tyrannical dictators used to do . . . maybe still do. If they didn't like the message, they shot the poor guy who conveyed it. Well, it's going to be the same with these people. They'll start by doing all they can to attack and discredit us.'

'How will they do that?'

'Oh, they'll try to make people believe we're crazy. They'll accuse us of being emotive, hysterical, unreasonable. Or politically motivated. Or corrupt. Whatever it takes to undermine our credibility.'

'And if that fails?'

'You mean *when* it fails. It won't work, Marie. In fact it'll probably be counter-productive. I promise you. People are beginning to trust the environmental movement now. More than they trust business.'

'So what will they do then?'

'They'll attack the science. Produce their own studies . . . and claim inconsistencies or flaws in our studies. Try to confuse the issue so that people don't know what or who to believe.'

'And if *that* fails?'

'Delay. They'll buy time. Demand more research. Block legislative action.'

'And then?'

'If they're still losing, they'll go for a fix. A compromise. One that appears to cater to public concern but still enables them to use plantacon. This is their best chance. They can use the energy conservation argument. They'll offer some voluntary reduction in plantacon levels that sounds good and that gives the politicians a chance to have it both ways and save face. Then, if we reject it, we'll be made to look unreasonable.'

Marie shook her head angrily. 'These people are evil.'

'Maybe a few of them. But not the majority.'

'Well, what would you call them?'

'Depends. But most of them are plain desperate. Plantacon has led to the recovery of a huge industry.

Vast profits for a few. And work for many who otherwise would be unemployed. They simply won't want to believe what we're saying.'

'But surely they can't ignore the facts.'

MacAnally shrugged. 'There are 50,000 studies worldwide showing that smoking causes death and disease, yet there are still people in the tobacco industry who won't accept it's harmful. How *can* they reject so much evidence? Because they're so desperate that their minds have become permanently closed. For whole countries, even for areas in the south of this country, tobacco doesn't mean cancer . . . it means work, a living, a roof over their heads, food to eat. Anyone who threatens that by talking about public health sounds to them like a troublemaker. The worst kind. The kind that threatens their survival.

'Think about a ban on plantacon. Over the river in Hoboken, at the FEI factory, hundreds of men and women will be going home to their families to say they're out of work, that there's going to be no money coming in. All over the country airport and airline employees will be made redundant as profits fall. What do you think they're going to think of you and me and our campaign?

'What happens is that they grasp at every straw. At every bit of scientific evidence that offers hope. At every allegation or suggestion that the attacks on their beloved product are malevolently motivated.

'So, to put it in a nutshell, when we launch our campaign, there may be a few, like Dieter Partrell of FEI – I know him of old – who won't give a damn whether we have a case or not, but the majority in the industry won't just be cynically resisting it. They won't be covering up. They simply *won't believe it*.

'*Because they dare not believe it.*'

*

About three in the morning, when she woke to find him lying awake looking at her, he whispered, 'You know I always thought marriage was a ridiculous institution.'

Drowsily she raised herself on an elbow and said, 'So it is. But why are you saying so now?'

'Because I've found out why it's a good idea.'

'Oh. Why's that?'

'Because it's the only way . . .'

'The only way of what . . .?'

'. . . the only way to show . . . you know . . . how much you're committed.'

'What? A service and a piece of paper?'

'No. I'm not talking institutional. And I'm not talking religion. I'm talking psychology.'

'Psychological bullshit.' Then, 'Wait a minute,' she said, leaning over him so that he could feel her nipples brushing his naked chest. 'What the hell is this all about anyway?'

'Oh, didn't I make it clear?' he said. 'I was thinking of getting married myself.'

'What . . . *to* yourself?'

'Idiot.' He picked up a pillow and pretended to suffocate her. 'I'm probably insane – in fact I'm definitely insane – but I had thought of proposing it to you.'

She went still and for a moment he thought he had gone too far with the pillow, but when he moved it off her face he saw a silent tear running down one of her cheeks.

Then she reached up and pulled him down to her and, as he hardened, took him inside her.

He was still inside her when he fell asleep, for a few hours the cares of the world and its children forgotten.

SEVILLE

'I don't deny it's a scandal. If you can stand it up. But I think it would be crazy for ECO to make this its priority. We're already too advanced in planning the global warming campaign. And that will benefit everyone, not just people around airports.'

Mike McKenzie, the big, popular Australian, was leading a surprisingly well-supported protest.

'Why doesn't ECO America go it alone?' McKenzie asked. 'There's far more aviation activity in North America than anywhere else.'

MacAnally tried to look unruffled. He had assumed too much, had been taking them for granted. Now he mustn't appear to be pushing too hard. 'I understand your point, Mike, and I sympathise. But there's no reason why we shouldn't keep preparing our global warming campaign while we deal with this.'

He turned to the others. 'Look, I wouldn't be suggesting this if I didn't think it's a manageable campaign that we can win fairly quickly. Probably within a year. And, God knows, we need a success.'

He then tried the argument he had used with Marie. 'In any case, a decision to ignore the problem is a decision to ignore the fate of millions of children. Can we really do that?'

McKenzie was still unimpressed. 'Come on, Sam, that's bullshit and you know it. We don't have to ignore plantacon. We can draw attention to it. We can encourage other environmental organisations to take it up. And, as I've said, *you* can go it alone in America. No one's stopping you. I just don't think we should drop what we're already planning to do, especially when it's so crucial. Anyway, there'll be other environmental scandals. Will we always drop the big issues for the quick fix?'

There were more murmurs of support from around the room.

MacAnally took a deep breath. For once he was afraid he wouldn't carry them with him. 'A movement like ours,' he said, 'needs to consider three things when choosing a campaign:

'*Is the problem serious?* Well, I happen to think millions of kids having their minds blown by a poison being blasted out of aeroplanes is pretty damn serious.

'*Will it help the wider environmental cause if we raise it or win it?* Of course it will. People will be impressed and grateful that we identified the problem and fought and won. And it illustrates the cynicism of multi-national companies – it helps undermine their credibility, and that will strengthen our other campaigns.

'*Will it make ECO stronger, leave it better-equipped for the challenges that lie ahead?* The answer has to be yes. It will be good for its reputation, good for fundraising and membership, good for morale.'

He looked round the room. There were about fifty people there, two representatives from the thirty organisations around the world and an additional twenty members of the Spanish ECO who had organised the conference and who, as a reward, were allowed to attend as observers. Most were in their twenties or thirties, dressed in tee-shirts and jeans.

He could see his words had hit home.

Even McKenzie was now silent.

Then Olly Witcomb spoke. 'I must admit I wasn't too keen when Sam asked me to talk to Professor Barnes, but once I heard what he discovered I changed my mind. What the airlines are doing is just not on.'

Machiko Yanagi spoke similarly, and Liz Scullen was in no doubt. She had been arguing with McKenzie all the way from Australia on the plane.

'Christ, I don't know what the debate is about. I've already told Mike, I'm not giving an issue like this to Greenpeace or Friends of the Earth or anyone else. I want it . . . at least in Australia.

'In any case, global warming never was our issue alone. The others are all going on about it as well. Whereas this would be *our* issue, one we could actually make an impact with.' She turned to her fellow Australian. 'For Christ's sake, Mike, what choice do we have? Do you want to go back to Perth and see some other group making all the running on it? When we identified it first? You must be crazy.'

Mike McKenzie, who had listened more attentively to Machiko than to Liz, looked across at her, then at MacAnally and Witcomb. 'Well, you people have met the scientists, I haven't. Anyway . . .' and he grinned good-naturedly in defeat '. . . I can see I'm on a loser on this one . . . and the thought of another flight home being endlessly harangued by Liz is more than I can live with. I guess you can count Australia in.'

They all laughed, and MacAnally, sensing the moment was right, put it to a vote.

It was unanimous.

They would campaign for a ban on plantacon.

During lunch MacAnally sought Mike McKenzie out and dragged him off to a tapas bar. 'Sorry to have to fight you, Mike. Hope there're no hard feelings.'

'Hell no. I just wish we had more time to maybe carry out more research, maybe commission our own. Are you sure you're right, Sam? It's all so damn neat.'

'They're all reputable scientists, Mike. You call it neat. I call it solid – a solid case.'

'I guess so. And the rest of your arguments made good sense. Don't worry. I won't let you down.'

Sam squeezed his arm. 'Terrific. How are things with Machiko?'

McKenzie frowned. 'Good and bad. The good is that we're getting on just great. The bad is that I haven't persuaded her to come to Australia.'

'And Tokyo isn't on for you?'

'Sam, I know it sounds pathetic, but I could never learn the language. Honestly. Not because I'm lazy or wouldn't want to, but I have no gift for languages, no ear. I was a disaster at school in that area. I know I just couldn't make it work in Tokyo. I've tried to pick up some Japanese words but it's hopeless.'

'Have you explained that to her.'

'In a way.' He looked evasive.

'Come on, Mike, what do you mean "in a way"? Have you or haven't you.'

He looked stubborn. 'Well, not exactly.'

'Well, for Christ's sake, why not?'

'Because I want her to decide to come to Australia for its own sake, for me, not because I'm too inadequate to go to Japan.'

MacAnally laughed. 'Holy cow, Mike, you can be an idiot sometimes. Of course she would like you to say you would go to Tokyo, because it would show how much you care. Unless you talk to her about it she'll just think you're a typically selfish man, wanting things your own way. Explain to her, for Christ's sake. It's not that big a deal.'

McKenzie stubbornly chewed on a piece of serrano ham for a moment, then said, 'I guess you're right. As always.'

MacAnally laughed louder. 'Come on, have another San Miguel.'

After lunch Dominic Young told them how much energy plantacon saved, and how much money. The others gasped at the figures.

'Yes,' he said, 'we should be in no doubt that the economic and . energy conservation arguments for plantacon are damn near unanswerable. It's not just the airlines and the plantacon manufacturers who'll oppose us. They'll have the support of the workers' organisations and trade unions. More than half a million people work for the airlines in the US alone and that doesn't include people working for airplane manufacturers and at airports. Then there's the travel and holiday industries. And airline travellers – the consumers. And energy conservationists, even possibly some of our friends within the environmental movement. And above all governments. They see plantacon as a miracle worker because it helps keep down inflation and saves energy.'

'So how do we counter these arguments?' asked a campaigner from ECO Germany.

'We can't counter them directly,' Young replied. 'This is their strong ground and we can't touch them on it. It's so strong that our public health case is going to have to be much stronger than it should need to be.'

MacAnally agreed. 'It's Dom's *entrenched technology theory*.'

Young, noting a number of blank faces, explained. 'Once a particular form of technology becomes entrenched within an industry it's much harder to get it removed on public health grounds than if the hazard had been foreseen and the technology banned in the first place. That's because the money has been invested, the technology integrated into manufacture, and the economic and other benefits have become established. And because both the industry and the public have become accustomed to it and want, even need to defend it.'

'So,' repeated the German, 'how *do* we deal with the economic and energy arguments?'

'We don't,' said MacAnally. 'As Dom says, that's their ground. We can't win on it so we keep off it.

'In fact we go further.

'We acknowledge the strength of their case. We admit that plantacon would be good news if it weren't for the environmental pollution.

'We say that we greatly welcome the energy savings.

'Then we argue that, unfortunately, the pollution is so damaging and far-reaching in its effects that despite the product's advantages it still has to go.'

He leaned forward and spoke intently. 'I cannot overstress this. *We must fight on our ground, the environmental and public health ground, not on theirs*.

'Let them make their case. The more they talk about money, the more they'll appear uncaring about the children they're poisoning. We must make them seem only interested in the bottom line, show them to be cynical, greedy. Sacrificing children for profit.'

Next came Jake Katzir, ECO's scientific chief – a short, wiry man, thirty-five years old, black hair, small beard, with sharp features and intense dark-brown eyes. Katzir was responsible for ensuring the accuracy of ECO's environmental message. He was, he said, satisfied that the studies had been carried out by able men and that the findings were consistent.

'I'm surprised the industry's been so free from criticism on environmental issues,' he said.

'For a start there's the noise pollution, but that hardly needs explaining. As for air pollution, nitrogen oxides are unavoidably produced by the combustion of kerosene in modern aircraft engines.'

'Can't planes have catalytic converters?' someone asked.

'No. No one's invented one that will work in a plane. To be fair, the industry has been working hard at reducing emissions. With some success. But ultimately the only answer is to cut back on air travel. And . . .' he shrugged helplessly '. . . I don't see much chance of that.'

Then he moved on to plantacon.

He described the scientific studies, then talked about neurotoxins. 'To be toxic is to act as a poison. Neurotoxins affect the brain.'

'What I don't understand,' said one of the Spanish representatives, 'is why children are the ones being damaged at these low levels of exposure. Why not adults?'

'Well,' replied Katzir. 'it's likely that young children absorb more plantacon from the gut, almost five times that of an adult, and even more if they suffer from calcium or iron deficiency. Children have higher metabolic rates than do adults and their rapidly growing tissue is more easily affected by toxic substances. The poison affects both the central and peripheral nervous systems. Once more the young are especially susceptible because, compared with adults, they appear to have no barrier to entry to the nervous system and their nervous systems are still in the developmental stage.'

He paused, then summed up: 'So the bottom line is that children are absorbing more plantacon than adults and are also more vulnerable to its neurotoxic effects.'

That night they had a noisy dinner together in a restaurant near the Plaza San Francisco and afterwards split up, MacAnally, Young, Katzir, Olly Witcomb, Monique de

Vos and Liz Scullen and a number of others taking the old bridge, the Puente de Isabella II, over the river for a tour of tapas bars in the Triana district, while Mike McKenzie and Machiko Yanagi split off and wandered around the great Cathedral and then into the narrow, winding alleys and hidden squares of the Bario de Santa Cruz, lingering for a drink at first one bar, then another.

At the last of these Mike looked on with admiration as Machiko's request for *dos vaso e vino blanco seco* produced from the waiter the dry white wine he had suggested.

'You're good with languages, aren't you?' he said.

'Not exceptionally.'

'*Not exceptionally*' he mimicked her and laughed. 'Your English is better than mine. And look how you're picking up Spanish.'

'You could too.'

'No, actually, that's the thing . . . I couldn't.'

'But you're an intelligent man.'

'It's not intelligence we're talking about. It's a facility. Oh, I can pick up the odd words, even some phrases, but I have no ear for languages. It's the same reason I can't sing. I'm tone deaf.'

'Well, it doesn't really matter. You don't need a lot of Spanish in Australia.'

'But it's not just Spanish it applies to. I couldn't learn Japanese either.'

'You won't need that much in Australia either.'

'No . . . but I would in Japan.'

'But you don't live in Japan.' She looked at him big-eyed.

'I would have to if I wanted to be close to you.'

'Not if I came to live in Australia.'

'But you . . .' He stopped and looked at her, only half believing what he had heard. 'Say that again,' he said.

'In what language?' she replied, then laughed delightedly as he picked her up, in the same way as he had when they first met, and to the disbelief of everybody in the bar, carried her out into the square where he hugged her and where they sat under an orange tree late into the night, ignoring the cold, making plans.

'*Objective*: A phase out of plantacon within three years.'

'Why *three years*, for Christ's sake? Is this serious or isn't it?' The questioner was Liz Scullen.

MacAnally leaned back on the table. 'The decision to act on plantacon will be taken by balancing the risk to health or safety with the economic and other practical disadvantages of whatever remedial action we propose.

'We know from yesterday's briefings that the industries will try to minimise the environmental and health damage and maximise the economic cost and the energy loss. They'll hope at the same time to demonstrate we're unrealistic, that we're irresponsible industry wreckers.

'An immediate ban will be rejected as utopian and our calls for it will be shown to be unreasonable. But a *phase out* of plantacon will sound realistic and reasonable. It'll make it harder for them to claim we're irresponsible zealots. That's why we have to advocate a phase-out rather than an overnight ban.'

But Liz wasn't persuaded. 'I don't deny that what you're proposing is pragmatic but our role is to explain to people what's happening – that their kids are being damaged. How can we arouse their concern if we're at the same time talking about a phase-out? It just won't sound urgent enough.'

MacAnally sighed. First McKenzie, now Liz Scullen. Why were these Australians so damn argumentative? 'Liz, I take your point. But the reason so many campaigns fail is because their objectives are either unrealistic or can be convincingly portrayed by polluters as unrealistic.'

Olly Witcomb intervened. 'Liz, Sam's right. What you have to avoid at all costs is the industry convincing the public or the politicians that what you're calling for is impossible. Now, *we* know that it's *possible* to stop adding plantacon to airline fuel immediately, but *they're* going to claim it's *impossible*. If we're not careful *that* will then become the argument. We'll end up fighting on their best ground, arguing about costs and timetables.'

'There is another point.' It was MacAnally. 'Plantacon only affects children in areas around airports. That's a helluva lot of children, but still not *every* child. At least at the current level of contamination. So we won't have immediate wholehearted support from *every* parent. That limits the sacrifices we can demand from the public as a whole.'

He looked around the room. 'Anyone else?'

Silence.

'OK, objective settled.'

MacAnally then outlined the strategy: to concentrate on the health argument alone because it was their best ground and the industry's worst ground; to build on the innate suspicion of industry's defence when under attack on environmental issues; and to campaign worldwide.

Because the aviation and petroleum industries were international, with highly sophisticated communication systems, what ECO did in one country would need to be coordinated with similar activities in every country so that the campaign always had an element of surprise.

That meant all campaigning initiatives needed to occur simultaneously in thirty capital cities.

To enable all this to happen they would use a global computer network.

It was Witcomb who raised the question of funding. 'This is going to be incredibly expensive. They've got millions. How are we going to compete?'

'OK,' said MacAnally, 'this is how I propose we proceed:

'Five per cent of all your incomes will go into a central pool.'

There were groans but MacAnally was unapologetic.

'It's how we've done it before. Look, we've got to pay for it somehow. And it also commits you. If you put the money in you're more likely to do the work.

'Then we'll launch public appeals. I reckon we can produce half a million dollars to start with.'

'Start with?' exclaimed Mike McKenzie.

Reluctantly he told them about Lord, but wouldn't reveal his name. As he expected there was a gasp of surprise. Then an uneasy silence. Once more the abrasive Liz Scullen expressed their unease. 'Has this donor been checked out?'

MacAnally turned to Dominic Young.

'He has,' said Young. 'We can find no evidence whatsoever of a financial interest. Nor does he appear to have any other interest – other than the obvious altruistic one. The man seems to genuinely care about this.'

'Has he given money to any cause before?' asked Machiko.

'Yes, he has. I assure you . . . we've looked into his background carefully, both business and personal. He checks out.'

As the conference began to break up Monique de Vos raised the question of timing. For her a year wasn't enough. 'You may be able to get a decision in the US within twelve months but the European mechanism works more slowly,' she said.

'OK,' said MacAnally, 'I guess you're right. I propose

we launch worldwide in mid-February.

'In the US our aim will be early hearings, probably before the summer recess. Then we'll promote a bill over the autumn and winter.' He turned to Witcomb. 'What's the UK timing?'

'I don't think it'll require legislation in Britain,' Witcomb said. 'Just regulatory action.'

'So how long will it take?'

'A year's campaigning, minimum.'

'Liz? Mike?' MacAnally looked at the Australians.

It was Liz Scullen who answered. 'Provided things are happening in other countries, and especially the US, I think we can get a fairly quick decision. A year – maybe eighteen months.'

'Machiko?'

'I don't know,' she said honestly. 'I think what happens in the rest of the world will determine it. I don't think the Japanese will be motivated to act quickly on their own.'

'OK.' MacAnally looked round the room. 'How about aiming for a worldwide decision within eighteen months to phase out plantacon and then we give them another eighteen months to do it?'

'Christ.' It was Liz, still impatient for results. 'Three years. What about the kids in the meantime?'

MacAnally looked at her wearily. 'What about the kids if we fail?' he said.

NEW YORK

David Johnston had an office above the New York Health and Racquet Club in 3 New York Plaza, a glossy skyscraper at the harbour end of the Wall Street district, opposite the more staid-looking Chase Manhattan Bank and directly overlooking the green-roofed terminal for the Staten Island ferry.

Johnston was forty-seven. Dark-haired with a tinge of grey, he had retained the good looks that, together with a talent for duplicity and considerable charm, had helped him rise effortlessly in the public relations world to his extremely well-paid position with one of the biggest oil companies.

In addition he had become chairman of OILO's public affairs committee and saw no reason why he should not climb even higher.

If he was to do so, however, he needed to survive this plantacon business. Hence the troubled look in his eyes as he sat at his desk looking at *ENDS*, a British environmental newsletter. One of Johnston's colleagues in the UK had sent it to him with a circle round a paragraph on the back page:

The international campaigning organisation ECO held its annual conference in Seville last week. While its organisers are being uncharacteristically secretive, we're reliably informed they've decided on a high profile campaign likely to affect the aviation industry.

He took off his glasses and, sitting back in his chair, looked thoughtfully at the ceiling.

It looked as if the problem was about to surface.

This had to be handled carefully.

Johnston had to balance conflicting considerations:

On one hand, his *own* company must not harm its good relations with its airline customers by appearing to abandon them to their fate. On the other hand, the oil industry must not get trapped on the losing side.

This game had to be played both ways.

To put it another way, Johnston had to be two-faced.

This was where OILO came in. This was why his role in OILO was so crucial and why he had to keep everyone on it united.

As he had said to the liaison meeting, the airlines would continue to need fuel even if plantacon was banned.

All the fuel suppliers needed to do was *act together* so that, if it served them best to support a ban, there could be no possibility of the airlines retaliating by victimising any one supplier.

He asked his secretary to send a copy of the ENDS report to Eugene Remington of Executive Airways and another to Dieter Partrell of FEI. On his own company's compliments slip he wrote: *Thought you should see this. You know you have our support*.

That should keep them content. Reassure them that he was doing all he could.

Johnston looked at his watch. It was time for lunch. He would have sea scallops and Californian chablis at Gilmore's Deep Blue.

And well deserved too.

He was satisfied he had made a good start.

Unusually for someone who worked predominantly in New York and Washington, Nicola Kowalska had set up her first office in Philadelphia, approximately half-way between the two cities by rail.

It was not her home city. Nicola's grandparents on her father's side had come to America from Poland in the 1920s and settled in Chicago, where they had built a profitable business importing antiques from all over Europe. Nicola's father had joined it straight from school and got married when he was only twenty-one, to a bright, homely girl from Minneapolis whom he met on a Greyhound bus. Nicola was their only child.

From when she was ten her all-consuming ambition was to be a journalist. She contributed to the student magazine at college and, to learn her trade, went to work on a weekly newspaper serving a farming community in Oklahoma. For two years she covered the big stories in those parts, farm prices, local fairs, births, deaths, marriages, and the occasional fire. Then her mother died and her father all but fell apart. She returned to Chicago to live with him for a while and, journalistic jobs being hard to get, she temporarily went into a public relations consultancy as a drafter of press releases.

She took to the work like a duck to water and within a year was offered a huge raise to stay on as chief writer. Still she kept looking for work in what she called 'real journalism' but each time she almost got a break she was promoted by the consultancy and paid more. There is a moment in the career of a journalist-turned-PR person when it's too late to turn back. Nicola reached it. In Chicago at least.

By then her father had not only recovered but re-married, to the woman who had been keeping the antique business accounts. Nicola decided to go to New York and make one more attempt to break into straight journalism. But it was highly competitive and she didn't now have the right experience. Short of money, she once more joined a PR consultancy, this time one whose activities went well beyond big city PR, engaging in national campaigns, some of them exciting to work on. For the first time since she entered the business she began to enjoy it.

She sought a year in the company's Washington office to broaden her lobbying experience and soon demonstrated a gift for making things happen on the Hill.

It was a friend in the Senate who over lunch at La Colline one day said she should set up her own account.

'You're the best, Nicola,' he said. 'You wouldn't believe what a bore many of the people in your business are. OK, we work with them but we don't respect them. But people on the Hill really like you – you're efficient, know your stuff, stick to business, and know how to make things work so that both you and we come out of it well. Don't get your reputation damaged by associating with others who aren't in your class.'

The advice came at the right time. Nicola had been having an unsatisfactory affair with one of her colleagues. Six foot two, broad-shouldered, good-looking, a smooth operator, he was a high flier in the company. He was also a workaholic and this meant he was relatively undemanding and for Nicola, accustomed to her independence and busy herself, this for a while had worked rather well. She knew whatever they had wasn't love. But it was comfortable.

As her star had risen, however, he had become jealous, resentful of her success, and had actually on one occasion tried to block her, arguing that a particular assignment was too tough for a woman. At this she had seen red. When he got home to his flat that night the few possessions she had kept there were gone, his key was on the table.

So, encouraged by her friendly senator, she decided to take the gamble. Friends thought she was crazy to set up in Philadelphia. But she knew what she was doing. For one thing she preferred train to aeroplane (a point she would keep from Eugene Remington Jnr), and both New York and Washington were a relatively short journey from Philadelphia, in each case about an hour and a half. These days, with fax machines and telephones and computer networks and the like, you could be on the moon and still practise business. She could get much better office space there at half the price,

use the train journeys for reading and preparing for
meetings, stay over in either of the other cities if she
wanted to, and – this was the clincher – her first big client
was in Philadelphia. She had done some work with him
before and he had liked her style. He had offered her the
job of head of public affairs but she had suggested
instead she should become his agency, handling his PR,
corporate affairs, and lobbying. Her offer to set up in
Philadelphia had settled it. By opening an office there
she gave him confidence in her, also a hint of obligation.
He signed a three-year contract. And she was well on her
way.

As her reputation grew she rented a corner of an office
on K Street in Washington so she had a base there, with
access to conference rooms and a message service, and
also kept a tiny apartment on East 88th St in Manhattan.
This was used both as an office and stay-over. Both were
tax deductible and enabled her to claim that she had
facilities in all three cities; it looked good on her
notepaper.

Her big break came when she was called in to organise
a campaign in defence of the motorcycle industry. It was
faced with tough new exhaust emission and noise
controls which it claimed would cripple it. She lobbied
relentlessly and in the end the proposed regulations were
so melted down that the industry was able to emerge
looking environmentally conscious because of its
superficial compromises while hardly losing a cent in
profit.

The public affairs world gossips, and Eugene
Remington heard the talk. Also, Ed Eberhard
recommended her. So he had her discreetly investigated
by his head hunters. The report was good. That is why
this chilly February day she took the train from
Philadelphia to meet him in New York.

Remington found himself faced with a young woman with a warm smile but more character in her face than the glossy photograph in her file had suggested. There was the faintest hint of a line or two under her bright blue eyes. She had the same frizzy fair hair as in the photograph, and was medium height with a good figure well presented in a cream blouse and dark brown jacket and skirt.

He had his file on the desk but pushed it away and came round the desk to sit close to her.

'I'm not going to discuss your qualifications,' he said. 'You've been checked out. I'm not interviewing you for this task, Ms Kowalska, I want your services.'

She did her best to look as if this was an everyday offer, but could hardly believe her ears.

Getting new business without pitching for it was almost unheard of. She listened intently as Remington described the plantacon revolution . . . the increase in airline profits, the cuts in fares, the energy savings. A real American success story, now under threat from the environmental lobby.

'Is there any justification for their concern, Mr Remington?'

'As far as we can tell, no. We assume they're going to suggest there's contamination of areas around airports. But we find it incredible. We're currently conducting our own research and expect it to show the environmentalists have either got the wrong end of the stick or loaded their case in some way.'

She pressed him. 'If there *is* any strength in their case I need to know.'

'Of course. I can only say that, in so much as I can confirm it, because I'm not a scientist, plantacon is clean. It's an emotive and unjustified campaign.'

'And what is it you want me to do?'

'We don't know the size of campaign they're going to mount or the strength of their case. What we do know is that we can't afford to take chances. We must prepare to fight. I want you to coordinate our defence . . . lobbying, media work, the lot.'

Nicola did some quick calculations. She reckoned Executive Airways could afford a fair-sized fee, particularly with so much at stake. But, before she could raise the question, Remington added, 'I presume that you'll be doing it full time?'

Nicola was taken aback. 'I have *other* clients . . . but don't worry, your company will get as much of my time as necessary.'

Remington looked surprised. 'My company? I'm sorry, I don't think I've made myself clear.

'You would not be employed by my company.

'You would be working for the *whole industry*, building a coalition involving nearly all the commercial airlines, passenger and cargo, plus the oil companies and the plantacon manufacturer, and a whole lot more.

'The funds for the campaign are damn-near unlimited. But we want your undivided attention. We want results, whatever it costs.

'Ms Kowalska, *you will never have a bigger or more powerful client or a more generous budget if you work for another fifty years*.'

Nicola could hardly comprehend what she was hearing.

This was enormous.

It had to be the prize account of all time.

Doing her best to look unflustered, she said, 'You make yourself clear, Mr Remington. I can't neglect the others completely but I'll hire in help. I don't think you'll have cause to complain.'

When she hit Park Avenue she was trembling. She

took a taxi straight back to Pennsylvania station just in time to catch the five o'clock Metroliner and sank into her seat, her mind reeling.

If the environmentalists made a big thing of it, there would be a terrific battle . . . tremendous publicity. Coast to coast.

If she won she would be able to name her own price.

Everyone would want her.

Nicola was on the brink of becoming an American success story herself.

Then she opened the folder. Remington had put together a comprehensive brief. She flicked over pages of statistics about fare reductions, energy savings, increased employment. It was all good stuff.

At the back there was a section entitled 'The Environmentalists'.

She found herself staring at a picture of a dark-haired, pale-faced man with intense eyes and a confident, friendly smile.

Sam MacAnally.

It was late afternoon. Across the Hudson River, Dieter Partrell of FEI was just leaving the Hoboken factory for Manhattan. Boosted by the President's endorsement of the plantacon revolution, he had been busy preparing to take on ECO. 'This time,' he muttered to himself as he climbed into the back of his chauffeur-driven Cadillac, 'we're going to blow you out of the water, MacAnally.'

He had asked Al Bain to come up with a list of research projects and sympathetic scientists who could carry them out quickly.

He had put the word out that he was looking for a public relations company and a Washington lobbyist and that there were substantial fees involved. He had been deluged with calls.

The PR consultancy he had chosen was one of the biggest New York could offer. Its top media man Ted Scroeder had been on Remington's short list.

The lobbyist he had picked was Alexander Green, another on Remington's list.

It had been a busy week but there was one task left – a meeting with Charlie Orbell, not a man you asked to the office.

Their meeting place was a bar on the Lower East side. It had no name. Above the door a flashing neon sign said just '—AR'. It looked so run-down that, if it were not for the flickering sign with its missing letter, passers-by would never have given it a second thought, would have assumed it was one more casualty in the collapse of the neighbourhood. The interior was dimly lit. Some of the bottles on the shelf behind the bar were covered in dust. The juke box in the corner looked as if it were the first ever made. It didn't work. The barman was engaged in studying racing form. Requests for a drink were treated as a thoughtless intrusion on his privacy. At one end of the bar a woman, her hair dank, toyed with a near-empty glass. The ash tray in front of her was overflowing with the debris of countless cigarettes, yet she was in the act of lighting another. She gave Partrell a speculative smile. A tooth was missing. He looked at her with distaste and she shrugged and turned back to her drink. A small man in a shiny suit was sitting staring at himself in the mirror behind the bar. A salesman's case rested beside his stool. He looked defeated – but then, Partrell reflected, he had to be if he were in this place. A workman sat staring, cynically disbelieving, at the TV set behind the bar. It was a news programme, but the sound had been turned down. He didn't seem to care. It didn't seem to matter.

Then there was Orbell. A former New York City cop, drummed out of the force for corruption beyond the pale even by *its* standards, now an unlicensed private detective, he looked even seedier than when Partrell had used him last. Partrell looked with distaste at the pasty face and the sunken chest, and noted with irritation the shaking hand that quickly downed the double Bourbon on the rocks and gestured for another.

Charlie Orbell, Partrell concluded, was the kind of creature you found under rocks.

But Charlie Orbell had the qualifications he was looking for.

For money Charlie Orbell did whatever he was asked. And, in Partrell's experience, he delivered the goods.

Partrell briefed him quickly. He wanted to know all there was to know about Sam MacAnally. 'I want to know when he goes to bed and who with and when he wakes up, I want to know what toothpaste he uses.

'I want to know it all, Charlie,' he said brutally, 'from the size of his mother's tits to the length of his cock.

'And I want to know about this ECO outfit. Especially their finances. Where their money's coming from and how much. Down to the last fucking dollar, Charlie?'

His eyes narrowed. As always the detective appeared far away. He viciously squeezed the other's arm. 'Are you hearing me, Charlie? Am I getting to that booze-fuddled thing you call a brain?'

Orbell nodded, impervious to the insults, and moved his empty glass pointedly in front of Partrell.

The businessman reluctantly ordered another.

'Usual money. And I want it done quickly. Do I need to say more, Charlie?'

'No, Mr Partrell, and thanks for the drink.'

Partrell stood up, looked at Orbell, and shook his head in disgust. 'For Christ's sake, Charlie, have a bath. Put on some clean underwear. Have one decent meal. And try to go one day without a drink.'

He buttoned up his coat. 'You'd be fucking amazed how sweetly you could smell.'

Orbell looked after him morosely.

He couldn't give a damn what Partrell thought about him.

For one thing he detested Partrell as much as Partrell obviously despised him.

For another, Partrell could be as contemptuous as he liked, but the truth was the mother-fucker needed Orbell more than Orbell needed him.

And, he thought, the shit that Partrell gave him to do was the kind of shit Partrell wouldn't want anyone else to know about. One day that could be worth even more to Orbell than the money Partrell paid him now – and to be fair, the money was already good.

He looked down the bar. The woman gave him a half-hearted smile, more automatic reflex than touting for his business. She didn't really think he had the money. Anyway, even she had her standards.

Orbell read her mind, shrugged, and spat on the floor. Deliberately in her direction. Silly goddamn bitch. She didn't even remember that he had already fucked her.

By the garbage cans round the back.

She was that kind of whore.

But then Charlie Orbell was that kind of man.

BALTIMORE

Todd Birk sat behind his desk late into the night, wearing a thick, brown leather jacket, heavy blue jeans, and Texan-style boots, drinking one beer after another from the fridge in the corner of his untidy office, reading and re-reading first one piece of paper, then another.

One was a note from his accountant. It was the analysis Birk had requested, and the answer was as unpalatable as it was predictable: a ban on plantacon would put up costs by twenty-five per cent. That would set back the company's break-even date by three years. And it would rule out the longer flights that were the key to his expansion.

Birk scowled and turned his attention to the other – his copy of Remington's letter to MacAnally. '*We congratulate you on your recent well-deserved award . . .*' Christ, Remington and company were chicken shits. If they thought this was the way to deal with publicity-seeking Reds like MacAnally these New York dick-heads were even stupider than Birk had thought.

He walked to the door and looked at the corner of the airfield that was his. At his beloved planes. The hangar. The warehouse. The transport vans. All painted with his logo – a spinning globe and the words Airlift International. Then, taking a deep breath, he called an unlisted New York number and asked for Theodore Jordan.

Until the environmentalists had attacked plantacon, Jordan had been the only shadow over Birk's life.

When he had borrowed all he could from respectable sources and still needed more, he had been advised to turn to Jordan and his company, the International Investors' Trust . . . IIT.

It had been a desperate act. The terms had been horrendous – inevitably when you had no choice – but that wasn't all. He knew that if he failed to repay Jordan and IIT he would face more than bankruptcy.

Birk didn't dare even think the word 'mafia', but if Jordan wasn't involved with the mafia, he definitely was into organised crime. In a big way. Jordan was a launderer of illicit cash. Drugs money. He cleaned it up by investing it imaginatively and untraceably.

And by loaning it to desperate people like Todd Birk.

Birk had met Theodore Jordan only once. Tough as he was, he had been intimidated by the man. Somehow he got the feeling – probably deliberately engendered by the money-lender – that in dealing with Jordan and IIT he had entered an alien world, one untouched by all civilised rules. Jordan, a tall, bald man, who walked with a limp, had a sinister way of speaking quietly and courteously, always calling you Mister . . . 'Mr Birk' . . . in a gravelly voice while at the same time conveying a sense of spine-chilling menace. Birk had been told that when his men dared to whisper to each other in bars they called him The Skull. There was no need for him to spell out what would happen if Birk failed on the payments. He only had to say at their one meeting, 'You *will* meet your payments, Mr Birk . . .?' to raise in Birk's mind that indelible image of a concrete coffin.

It was that unpleasant thought that preoccupied Birk now.

Yet he wasn't without hope.

For, cunningly, he had concluded that his potential enemy could just as easily be a friend.

What was the point in Jordan terrorising Birk and probably going without his money, when by terrorising MacAnally and his friends he could save plantacon and thus get his money?

'Mr Jordan?' He was surprised to have been transferred to the money-lender so quickly.

'Mr Birk. I trust this is not bad news.'

'I'm not dropping behind in payments, Mr Jordan, if that's what you're suggesting. But I do have a problem.'

He briefly described it.

He half expected Jordan to say that it was *his* problem – that he should fuck off and solve it – but the response was . . . well, if it were not beyond the realm of possibility, Birk would have said it was almost friendly.

'I see. Not good news, Mr Birk. For you . . . but I'm afraid also for me.' He paused and then, as if thinking aloud, added, 'We've invested fairly heavily in the aviation industry since the plantacon revolution.'

There was a pause. Birk didn't know what to say. Then to his gratification he heard: 'Yes, well thank you, Mr Birk. This information is helpful. Keep me in touch with all that develops and we'll consider what action to take.'

Birk put the phone down and wiped the sweat off his face.

'*What action to take!*'

He hadn't considered the possibility that Jordan and his friends had been investing in the industry generally.

He began to feel exhilarated.

That meant *Jordan had his own vested interest in plantacon* . . . a much bigger interest than just Birk's survival.

All he needed to do was fire Jordan up and that would be that.

If Jordan could frighten someone as tough as he, Todd Birk, God knows what he would do to MacAnally and his faggot friends?

He got himself another beer and went to stand in the doorway and look out across the airfield. In the distance he could see the lights of a jumbo jet as it landed and began to taxi towards the terminal. The temperature was falling well below freezing. But as he surveyed the world he loved, Birk didn't feel the cold. He felt great – just great.

Jesus wept . . . he, Todd Birk, was going to save plantacon.

Not those New York college boys who ran the fancy airlines. What the fuck did they know?

He was going to do it.

Because he had the ace in the hole.
Jordan.
The Skull.
Who even now was considering '*what action to take*'.

HOBOKEN, NEW JERSEY

Looking even more harassed and burdened with problems than usual, Al Bain proposed to Dieter Partrell that their scientific surveys be conducted on a number of issues:

To what extent were plantacon particles emitted from aircraft – on takeoff, on landing, and at cruise speed?

What happened to them? How widely were they dispersed?

'*Were they reaching people? If so, at what levels of exposure could they be harmful, if at all?*

Partrell scowled. 'Christ, Al, you know all this is bullshit don't you?'

The scientist looked at him mildly. 'If you mean we'll discover nothing that's harmful to us, Dieter, I share your view. But I did once suggest we should carry out some tests for environmental effects before going full steam ahead.'

Partrell sat up, reddening. 'What? When?'

Bain took out a sheaf of memos and detached one. 'Five years ago. But no one replied and I assumed no one thought the expenditure worthwhile. You will recall developmental costs were high then and there was no revenue coming in.'

Partrell stared at the memo. He recalled getting it – and throwing it into the wastepaper basket.

'Al, I think we should forget you ever wrote this.'

Bain blinked. 'Forget?'

Partrell glared at him. 'Fucking *forget*, Al. Am I making myself clear? Just think what mischief MacAnally and company could make if they could show that we were advised to check on environmental hazards and didn't do it. *Forget it*.'

Bain shrugged. 'And the research I'm proposing?'

Partrell looked at the questions. 'Yes, well, I suppose these are the ones we'll have to answer. What about this list of scientists you sent me? Which are the ones we can count on?'

Bain looked annoyed. 'I hope you're not suggesting they can be bought, Dieter?'

Partrell looked at him grimly. 'That's exactly what I'm suggesting, Al. For Christ's sake man, you've been in this business for years. What for? Hardly the scientific distinction. It's because we pay you a helluva lot more than you would get anywhere else.'

Bain rose, white-faced. 'How dare you, Dieter. I won't stand for this.'

Partrell knew he had gone too far. He despised the spineless little scientist but he needed him now. So he waved him back to his seat. 'OK, Al, I'm sorry, I'm not suggesting you've been bought in the sense that you would do anything wrong. Just that like me you work here for the fucking money. That's a simple fact. And I want scientists who earn their money from our industry, who are at least not biased against us, who will at least be sympathetic to our concerns. Is that unreasonable?'

Bain was still fuming but at least calmed down enough to say weakly, 'Well, I don't know, Dieter. I can only guarantee they're good scientists.'

Partrell let it drop. After all he could check out the scientists later, find out who they worked for, who funded their research. He didn't need Bain's involvement. One thing was for sure; he wasn't having some fruitcake from the environmental movement doing the work. 'OK, Al,' he said, 'let me pick five from this lot. I'll read the files and let you know.'

Once he was alone, he cross-checked Bain's list with one he had compiled himself. Some names were on both lists, in fact six in all. Partrell didn't imagine these six could actually be bought – well, maybe one of them could – but he knew they had been unconvinced by environmentalists in the past; hopefully they would be equally unsympathetic to them on plantacon.

And they came from the range of countries he needed to cover.

Of the six, he eventually dropped two.

One had been so over-zealous in publicly attacking environmentalists that he now lacked any credibility at all.

The other's reputation for integrity was a byword in the business. The guy could stuff his integrity; Partrell didn't need it. He believed without question that the science would support plantacon and discredit MacAnally but, as MacAnally was likely to field a bunch of fanatical anti-pollution scientists on his side, he didn't see why he shouldn't put together as strong a hand as possible.

Partrell's favoured four scientists were drawn from the US, Europe, Japan and Australia – the areas where, his advisors had told him, ECO was strongest. He added to them another American. Bryce Kendrick. A good man Kendrick. Sound. He wouldn't let them down.

'Tell them we want a good clean job and we want it within a month, Al,' he told Bain when he went to the other's basement laboratory to give him the list.

'When MacAnally strikes we must be ready to strike back.'

WASHINGTON, D.C.

It was bitterly cold this morning. There was more snow in the air. MacAnally felt in the wind the worst blasts of the winter so far. He shivered and, pulling his jacket closely round him, walked briskly around Dupont Circle and up 19th Street to the ECO office.

MacAnally guessed every environmental pressure group's office looked the same . . . posters on the wall advertising long-past international conferences on pollution of the oceans or rallies on nuclear power, posters demanding their readers save tropical rain forests, save the whale, save the national parks. Most were out of date. There were even faded posters calling on voters to Dump Watt (a long-forgotten Secretary for the Interior). Every room was overcrowded with people and computers, filing cabinets, and paper. The atmosphere was slightly frantic . . . as if everybody, everything was late. Which in a way it was.

On the ground floor, in a big reception area, a busy and harassed receptionist and two volunteers dealt with orders for leaflets, posters, car stickers.

On the first floor, the library, packed high with books, reports, newspaper files, leaflets, was run by a dumpy, good-natured girl with long ginger hair who was perpetually munching a horrendous-looking dark brown loaf.

The first floor, managed by Dominic Young, also harboured the administrators, fundraisers and membership recruiters, their rooms all small and relatively tidy compared with the second floor.

It was on the second floor that the campaigners

worked in an open plan office, each with their little kingdom – a desk surrounded by partitions. Every available piece of wall and partition was covered in notes, cuttings, posters, memos, reminders. Each campaigner had a computer. Some even had volunteer helpers sitting on the floor round their desks, like slaves, sorting files, opening letters, leaping up at their master's or mistress's command. Here were the rain forest campaigners, the acid rain campaigners, the pollution campaigners. The stars of the ECO show.

The top floor held a conference room, a kitchen, and, alone in a roomy office, Sam MacAnally. On one side of his desk was an in/out tray, on the other two phones, one internal, one external, and his computer. Beside the desk was a TV set. Outside, in a small cubby-hole of her own, sat the reason why his office was tidier than the others – MacAnally was the only one with a secretary.

It was to this office he climbed now with a cheery 'hi' to anyone he met on the way. Half-way up he bumped into Adrian Carlisle, wearing a suit and looking out of place and confused amid the jean-clad, casually dressed campaigners.

Carlisle was about twenty-seven but had a younger face. He was medium height, dark-haired. And eager, but at the same time he had an aura of professionalism. Maybe it was the suit. MacAnally could see why Dom Young had liked him. Christ, someone else who wore a suit. *Every day.* (MacAnally wore one when it was politic; most of the other campaigners never did.)

'Dom says you want me to work on the plantacon campaign,' Carlisle said.

'You want to?'

'Sure.'

'OK. Come on up. Sit in on my morning.' He waved Carlisle into the office and to one of the chairs and tossed him the campaign file. 'You'd better read up on this.'

Explaining that he needed to pull the scientific evidence together for the launch, he picked up the phone to ring Raynald Warner. Instead he got his secretary. MacAnally remembered her, a motherly woman in her fifties, clearly devoted to her boss.

'I'm sorry, Mr MacAnally, I don't think he can speak to you now. He's talking to his lawyer and in any case he is, as you can imagine, still deeply shocked. Sometimes I wonder whether he'll ever recover.'

MacAnally was confused. 'I'm sorry, I don't understand. . . .'

'Oh, no,' she stopped him. '*I'm* sorry. It's me who should apologise, Mr MacAnally, there's no reason why you should have known . . . Dr Warner's wife died last week. He's been inconsolable ever since.'

MacAnally remembered the scene in the park, the scientist lovingly pushing his wife's wheelchair through the autumn leaves. 'I'm sorry.'

He thought for a moment. 'Look, of course I won't disturb him now, but there *is* a problem. We're having a press conference soon to raise the scientific questions over plantacon and naturally we're hoping Dr Warner can attend. When will I be able to discuss this with him?'

'My guess is you're wasting your time, Mr MacAnally,' she said. 'I can't see him wanting to go anywhere. Not for a while. And he's busy off-loading things. I know he mentioned this project as one of them.'

MacAnally was stunned. 'But he can't . . .'

At his impatience, a chill came into her voice. 'I can assure you he *can*, Mr MacAnally.'

'I'm sorry.' How many times had one or the other apologised during this conversation? 'What I meant is that it would be a tragedy if he did. So much hangs on his work.'

'Well, I'll mention it to him, Mr MacAnally, and try to get you an answer.'

Sam hung up just as Marie was coming by. 'Christ, Marie,' he said, 'this is bad news. Warner's wife has died.'

'I'm sorry,' she said. 'How sad.'

But MacAnally's compassion had temporarily deserted him. 'Sad? *Sad*? It's *disastrous*. You don't understand; he's talking about *dropping out*.'

He stood up. 'I'll have to go up there.'

Marie stood firmly in front of him. 'Oh no, you don't, Mac-O. I can just see it . . . if you lose your patience with him, and start demanding he come to Washington, you'll really blow it. Ithaca is in New York State. That's my territory. Let me go. I think this calls for a softer touch.'

MacAnally flopped back in his chair. 'You're right, I suppose,' he said. 'But for Christ's sake don't fail. We *must* have him at the press conference. It's essential.'

'I was going back to New York at the weekend,' she said. 'I'll go up on Friday.'

'You'll have to get someone to drive you,' said MacAnally. He looked across to Carlisle who was listening in the corner. 'Do you drive, Adrian?'

'Sure.'

'Would you mind . . .'

'No problem,' he said. 'It'll be fun. And Marie can brief me on her end of things while we drive up.'

'Terrific,' said MacAnally, then turned back to Marie: 'For Christ's sake, turn on the charm. We need Warner's work. I wouldn't want to launch this campaign without it.'

The following Friday, while Marie and Adrian Carlisle went to Ithaca to see the scientist Raynald Warner, Sam MacAnally lunched at Adirondacks in Union Station with Chris Wilkins and Jay Sandbach, the amiable, bustling, prematurely balding ECO congressional lobbyist.

'Chris,' Sam said once they had ordered, fortunately at the senator's expense, for Adirondacks was expensive. 'You remember our last conversation – my reference to an emerging environmental scandal?'

The young senator was eager. 'Yes. Tell me more.'

So MacAnally did. Wilkins listened engrossed, occasionally shaking his head in surprise.

'My God, Sam, this is serious. Outrageous. Of course you must campaign on it – and if you want this taken up on the Hill, count me in. I think I'm better placed to do it than most.'

MacAnally was amused by the senator's anxiety to make the issue his own. But he didn't doubt that Wilkins was their man.

He would be single-minded, and on this campaign that was crucial.

Adrian Carlisle had spent the previous day researching Wilkins' career. He was ambitious all right, opportunistic, even ruthless. But he hadn't always chosen the easy issues, had stood up to powerful interests, and on a number of occasions had, when tested in Connecticut politics, done what was right rather than what was expedient.

'We plan to launch fairly soon, Chris. If you're willing to lead in the Senate I'll want you at the press conference to endorse the campaign and publicly promise support.

'In the meantime Jay here will assist you to discreetly brief our other friends, those on the Hill we can trust, so that we can guarantee you have help.'

'What are we aiming for?'

'We'll want to go with a bill to phase out plantacon within three years.

'We don't know how long we can keep the issue in the headlines so we must get an early hearing while the temperature is high. You'll need to persuade the committee chairman. Fortunately it's Hal Frankle. He's good on these issues.'

Wilkins could hardly wait. 'I'll see him as soon as possible. I'll cancel whatever I've got.' He looked at Sandbach. 'Come up to my office tomorrow morning. Let's get cracking then.'

MacAnally looked at him thoughtfully. 'Chris, just one thing. I think you should take a day or so to think through the implications for you personally.

'Of course you're right to believe this could be the environmental *cause célèbre* of the decade but it will make you a lot of enemies. The Administration won't like it. Half of Congress won't like it. Some of the biggest industries in the country won't like it. The trade unions won't like it.

'And if we win it will cost the airlines billions of dollars of profit, the country billions of dollars of export earnings, and both the industry and the country a lot of extra energy.

'This is going to be one hell of a fight. There's bound to be some blood spilt.'

But Wilkins was not to be discouraged. 'What the hell, Sam. We're on the side of the angels. That's what matters.

Eugene Remington Jnr and Nicola Kowalska arrived late at the 116 Club for their lunch date with Senator Ed Eberhard. But he was even later.

'Ed's all right,' Remington told her as they waited. 'Bit crusty. But a real fighter. And devoted to the aviation industry. We couldn't have a better man to argue our case in the Senate.'

'How will he fare in a fight with Wilkins?'

'My guess is he'll walk all over him. He's got the experience. He won't want to be beaten by a newcomer.

And when you've been there as long as he has you have a lot of friends – or at least a lot of markers to call in.'

He rose to greet the Texan. 'The President's speech was most encouraging, most encouraging, Ed,' he said. 'I could detect your hand there. Many thanks.'

'Well, one does what one can, Eugene,' the senator replied, suitably flattered. 'The President has been known to value my opinion.'

Pompous ass, thought Nicola, but her smile was winning. 'I'm only glad you're on our side, Senator. Your influence will be enormously helpful.'

Remington produced the paragraph David Johnston had sent him from the London newsletter *ENDS*. 'I know this is not much to go on, Ed, but it does look as if this environmental lot are planning a campaign.'

Eberhard grunted. 'Campaign! *Goddamn campaigns*. I tell you, Eugene, these so-called campaigners haven't helped the democratic system one little bit. Governing this great country of ours is difficult enough without these self-appointed crusaders.'

'Quite.' Remington picked up the menu. 'I'm afraid we'll have to take them seriously though. I guess they'll have friends ready and willing to back them on the Hill?'

'Not as many as we'll have. But there are one or two of the new lot – this man Wilkins for a start – whom we won't be able to count on. Still,' and he smiled in anticipation, 'we've seen off their kind before. Dare say we can do it again.'

Nicola spoke up. 'What do you suggest we do first, Senator?'

'Well, we can't reply to an attack until one's made. But we can prepare.

'So get the homework done, young lady. Get the answers ready. And in the meantime I'll have a little chat with the committee chairman, Hal Frankle. We don't want him over-reacting before he gets both sides of the story.

'And I'll have a talk with Wilkins too. He may be misguided but he's not a fool. He may respond to the political facts of life.'

NEW YORK

The journey was unexpectedly difficult. It had snowed heavily and although many of the roads had been ploughed and sprinkled with grit, they were still treacherous. It took all Carlisle's concentration to maintain the car's grip on the surface. But, during the easier parts of the drive, he kept Marie busy answering questions about ECO.

'How did it start?'

'Sam was bored with committees. He wanted a single issue pressure group that could move quickly. I guess it was initially a one-man band. Then he started to recruit help. People like Dom Young, Jay Sandbach and Jake Katzir – good people. And people just started setting up local ECO groups and he decided to let them grow – to give him grassroots support.'

'How does he control them?'

'In a way, he doesn't. It's like a business franchise. They contract to have the name in return for obeying a few rules.'

'A franchise – you mean like Kentucky Fried Chicken?'

She laughed. 'Don't say that to Sam. He loves fried chicken. You could give him ideas.'

Carlisle wrestled with the wheel as the car momentarily lost its grip. Then, as it straightened, he slowed a little and asked, 'What are the rules?'

'Oh, to campaign non-violently, to base their campaigns on the truth, not to libel or slander people . . . that kind of thing. And to take financial and legal responsibility for their own activities.'

They had been travelling west but when they reached the town of Owego they turned off the main road, heading north now, up route 96.

Marie asked Carlisle about himself.

'Not much to say really. It was always kind of assumed I would follow my father into law. After college he arranged for me to start with a friend's firm in Washington. You know how it is?'

'Sure, I know how it is,' Marie said dryly.

Carlisle laughed. 'Yes, well, OK, but I didn't like it either. Anyway the truth is I don't need to earn money, I'm going to inherit more than I know what to do with, so I decided either my life was going to be a write-off or I was going to make myself useful. That's why I'm here.'

'How did you come to work for ECO?'

'I approached Dom Young at a party.'

'At a party?'

'Sure. I'd been thinking about working for ECO for months and someone pointed him out to me at this party. So I just walked up and said that I was a lawyer and wanted to work for ECO and didn't want a lot of money, and he gave me the number of his direct line and told me to ring him. So I did, and went down to 19th Street, and he took me on.'

'Just like that.'

'Well, I wasn't costing him much money, only expenses really, and I was keen. Half the people in the Washington office are the same. They're either volunteers or graduates working for damn-all before they start earning a proper living.'

'I guess so.' Marie looked out of the car window at the Ithaca town sign. 'Well done, Carlisle, we made it.' She said it with some relief because the snow had been even heavier in these parts and the roads for the past few miles noticeably more treacherous.

It was just 12.30 p.m. They asked directions and half drove, half skidded to the university, missing the main entrance and finding themselves by good fortune outside the science faculty.

'This looks like it,' said Marie.

'Right. Presumably that's Warner's car.' He pointed to a battered-looking old Chev sitting in a bay marked 'Reserved for Dr Warner'.

'Look, I don't want to sound like a male chauvinist but the whole idea was that you turn on your womanly charms. I'll be in the way. Shall I stay in the car?'

'You'll freeze. But you're right. And you need a break. Look, you drive back to that inn we passed about a quarter of a mile back, down the hill. Get some lunch. I'll walk down when I'm done.'

Carlisle, cold and hungry, took no persuading.

Marie got out of the car. It was getting even colder and she shivered as she walked quickly to the entrance. She found herself in a lobby. It was being painted and there were ladders on either side of the door, paint pots lying about, but no sign of the painters. Presumably they were at lunch. There was a sign above a bell saying 'Please ring for reception'. Remembering what MacAnally had said about the over-protective secretary, she decided to ignore the bell and, pushing past the double doors in front of her, she walked down a corridor looking at the names on the doors. She was about half-way along when a motherly-looking woman called out, 'Wait a minute. Who are you? Who are you looking for?'

'I'm sorry,' Marie said. 'I was trying to find Dr Warner.'

'Well, you can't just burst in. You have . . .'

Just then the door ahead opened and out came a small, untidy-looking man, deep lines etched on his face.

'What's the fuss, Betty?' he said.

'This young lady has come to see you. We have no arrangement . . . I explained . . .'

Marie interrupted. 'I've come all the way from New York to see you, sir. I'm Marie Doutriaux from ECO. I'm a colleague of Sam MacAnally. I would be grateful for just a few minutes of your time . . . it really wouldn't take long.'

The secretary looked furious. 'This won't. . . .' she began, but Warner interrupted her.

'No, Betty, best get this matter dealt with.' He stopped and looked at Marie and his face softened. 'You've come all the way from New York in this weather? You must have had a rough journey. Have you had lunch?'

'No, sir.'

'Then you'll be my guest. There's an inn at the foot of the hill.'

Marie gasped her thanks and Warner, ignoring an annoyed look from his outmanoeuvred secretary, grabbed her arm and half pushed her into his office where she waited, standing, for about five minutes until, having shuffled some papers from one pile to another, he appeared to remember her and, pulling on a thick overcoat that engulfed him almost completely, he guided her out into the cold air and towards his ageing car.

'I've been meaning to give Mr MacAnally a ring,' he said as they got in and he turned the key in the ignition.

It took several turns and some impatient pressing of the accelerator with his foot before the engine fired. He reversed the car out of its parking space and steered it towards the gates.

'The fact is, my wife's death has altered a lot of things.'

'I'm terribly sorry, Doctor . . .' Marie began.

'Yes, yes,' he said curtly, as if unwilling to allow a stranger to enter his private world of grief. 'It's not that.'

He paused to concentrate on his driving. They were now heading down the steep hill, the car slipping and sliding on the icy road.

Then he suddenly said, '*Her* name was Marie, you know.'

She couldn't think of a reply, so she looked around them. 'I've not been to Ithaca before. Is it a good place to live?'

'We like it . . .' He stopped and bit his lip as he realised what he had said.

Marie's heart filled with compassion, but Warner didn't have time to dwell on his mistake. The icy surface was making their short journey increasingly difficult. While experienced in the conditions, he was wishing he hadn't chanced the hill. He drove as slowly as possible in low gear, knowing that if he needed to brake it had to be done gently but, when he touched the pedal, it gave way and his foot went straight to the floor.

'Oh God,' he said, 'hold tight!'

'What's the matter?' cried Marie, alarmed by the panic in his voice.

'I don't know . . . the brakes aren't working.'

He began to twist the steering wheel frantically, first to the left, then to the right, hoping to slow the car down, but it didn't help.

Instead it began to speed up towards the crossroads and traffic lights at the foot of the hill.

Marie caught a fleeting glimpse of brightly painted houses, a snow-covered park, a school with children playing outside in red, white and blue anoraks, a baker's delivery van . . .

Her heart pounding, she grabbed the door handle, desperately weighing the pros and cons of making a jump for it.

She should have done, because even as she dismissed the idea it became clear that the car was completely out of control, skidding as if on skis towards the lights which were changing to red.

They were now going too fast for her to jump. She looked desperately to Warner, who was breathing heavily, tugging on the wheel, pumping on the unresponding brake, his face contorted with fear.

'Try turning us right round,' she screamed.

But he had simultaneously had the same idea and was already pulling desperately on the wheel. In fact the car did respond, but the only effect was that it now slid backwards.

Just as fast.

Past white-faced onlookers.

Past the STOP sign.

Past the red lights.

Straight into the path of a big silver-grey truck.

They collided with a terrible bang, then, apart from a hissing sound from the truck's broken radiator, there was only silence.

By the time the diners in the nearby inn came running out – one of them a white-faced Adrian Carlisle – Raynald Warner and Marie were already dead.

LONDON

Olly Witcomb didn't wait for his regular lunch with Nick Bell at Joe Allens. Instead he called for him in the Central Lobby after a vote at seven and the two left by the St Stephen's entrance of the Commons and walked across the street, down the alleyway between Westminster Abbey and St Margaret's Church and up Victoria Street, past Scotland Yard, to a wine bar just off the main street. There they ordered a bottle of the house red, and grabbed a table in the corner. The place was crowded so their conversation was conducted in little more than a whisper.

'Remember that issue I told you was coming up?' Olly asked.

The other's eyes positively gleamed.

'Yes, yes,' he said.

'Well, it looks like a runner and it could be a big one.'

For five minutes he spelled out the details. As he talked Bell could hardly contain himself.

'*Fuck me!*' he eventually said.

'Hardly a parliamentary expression.'

The other grinned. 'OK, bloody hell then. This is terrific.'

Olly shook his head in wonder. 'Whatever happened to the man I helped get elected?'

'What do you mean?'

'He would have said this is terrible.'

'Well, of course it's bloody terrible. But it's a terrific issue for me and you bloody well know it.'

Olly reached out and took the other's wrist and squeezed it.

'OK, Nick, calm down. It's not just for *you*. You can make the running in the House but it's got to be teamwork. This has got to be done my way.'

'Sure. For *fuck's sake*, Olly, what *other* way is there? You've got me this far.'

'As long as we understand each other.' His grip tightened. '*I mean it*, Nick. You're right, this is big, and you can make your name on it and I'm all for that. But

ECO's got to get its share and it's got to be done right.'

'OK, OK. For God's sake, let go of my wrist.'

Olly leaned back. 'And don't think it's going to be easy. No one's going to want to hear this news. I'm not just talking about the industry but Whitehall too. Since the Gulf war, and with North Sea oil on a downturn, they've become increasingly energy conscious. Then there's their obsession with inflation. This'll put costs up. They're going to resist it like mad.'

'So? That'll make victory even sweeter.'

Olly sighed. 'Christ, Nick, you're not listening. I agree it's winnable in theory but I know these people. They'll begin by delaying, setting up committees of inquiry, spending money on lengthy research, etc. . . . you'll find it hard to keep the parliamentary momentum going. There's another thing.' He paused.

'What? What other thing?'

'Well . . . how do you know you can count on your own party? I don't think the unions are going to like this much at all. And if your party wins the election, you'll be facing the same economic and energy problems the Tories are facing now.'

Bell thought. 'Good point.' He thought some more. 'Well, I'll tell you what. No one can argue that we're not right. So I'll launch into this without consulting anyone . . . an instinctive response, an act of conscience. I'll probably get a tongue-lashing from the Whips, but once I've done it the party will have little choice but to support me. Especially if I can make the Tories look bad.'

Olly nodded. Act of conscience! There was no limit to Bell's gall. 'OK, that'll work.' He recalled what he had heard about the Labour Chief Whip. 'Rather you than me,' he thought.

'Presumably you'll be stirring it up in the country?'

'That's right. But it has to be coordinated with what you're doing. That's why I'm telling you we *must work together*.'

'OK. *For Christ's sake*, we *will* work together . . . why are you making a meal of it, Olly? Don't you trust me?'

'I trust your ambition, Nick. I just want to be sure it's harnessed properly to this cause. I don't want you to run away with it and screw it up.'

'Look, what do I have to say . . .?'

Olly grinned, taking pity. 'Nothing more I guess . . .'

'So, what do I do?'

Olly told him.

When the campaigner got back to Wapping he ignored his own door and wandered up to Sally's. From inside he could hear music. He knocked and to his dismay heard voices. One was a man's. Before he could retreat she opened the door and smiled.

'Hi, Olly, want to come in?'

Behind her he could see a young man relaxing full length on the settee. He wore what looked like a fawn cashmere sweater and brown corduroy trousers. He had taken his dark-brown shoes off and dropped them carelessly on the floor.

'No, I won't disturb you. I was just going to suggest a drink tomorrow night,' he lied.

Her smile faded. 'Oh, I'm sorry, I can't do that.'

'Never mind,' he said, already on his way down the stairs, half running, his face scarlet, 'another time.'

He fumbled with his key, pushed open his door, slammed it shut behind him, threw his briefcase at the wall, and collapsed on the couch.

'Damn,' he said aloud. So there *was* someone else. And by the look of him a yuppie, the kind who were buying up all the best flats in the Docklands, roaring up and down the narrow streets in their flashy sports cars, pushing up the prices in the wine bars, and generally making Olly want to take to the streets with a machine-gun.

Now one of them was lying up there in Sally's flat, as if he owned the place.

He got up and, seeing a cushion on the floor, kicked it across the room.

It was his own fault.

He was letting the plantacon campaign take up too much of his time.

If he wasn't careful he would lose her.

Two days passed before he next saw her . . . on her way upstairs.

'Hi, Olly,' she said, 'I wish you'd popped in the other night. You could have met my brother.'

BRUSSELS

Also on that momentous February day Monique de Vos called at her old office. Her former boss, Claude Chevallier, the Head of Division 3 (Clean Technologies and Soil Protection) of Directorate A (Nuclear Safety, Waste Management, and Prevention and Control of Pollution) of DG (Directorate General) XI (Environment, Consumer Protection and Nuclear Safety) was not to be found in the huge European Commission building in the heart of Brussels. Instead he worked in an anonymous-looking building in the Rue Breydel, this day made to look even more depressing than usual by the driving rain. It had formed a river in the gutter and lakes on the pavement, and, having soaked everyone's shoes, made a squelchy mess of the lobby.

Monique, who didn't have the money to spare for a taxi, shook the rain from her hair and, after exchanging hugs and news with former colleagues, knocked on Chevallier's door.

'Monique!' He had always described her as his right hand and he greeted her warmly. 'What does this mean? Are you coming back to me?'

She laughed. 'Never.'

They chatted while they waited for a coffee, then he said, 'Well, I guess this isn't just a social call.'

'No,' she said. 'Tell me, have you been looking at aircraft emissions at all?'

His smile faded. 'That's strange . . . why do you ask?'

'No, you answer *my* question first . . . why is it strange?'

'Well, because it seems to be coming on to our agenda.'

He took out some documents from the filing cabinet beside his desk. 'We just got some papers from the European Parliament. There's an issue coming up on the agenda of the Transport committee that I felt would have been better in Environment.' He flicked over the pages. 'Here it is.' And he passed it to her.

Monique looked at the page:

Draft resolution:

This Parliament calls upon the Committee on Transport and Tourism to consider any economic, energy, safety, or other side-effects associated with the fuel additive plantacon, and to report.

Chevallier looked over her shoulder. 'It doesn't mention public health or environmental effects, and that's what worries me. Why not? If you're raising a range of questions about a technological process, why leave those ones out?

'It's almost,' he said, 'as if someone was anticipating trouble and decided to get plantacon well established on the agenda of another committee first, a committee more favourably inclined towards the industry.

'Do you know this man who is being proposed as rapporteur?'

Monique looked to the foot of the page.

The leading signatory and proposed rapporteur was Pierre Courtois.

She froze, anger and sorrow at the betrayal competing for her emotions.

But this one act settled it.

Even as she sat there her feelings about Courtois crystallised. Suddenly she no longer felt hurt, sad, confused.

Now she felt only anger. More . . . worse . . . she began to hate.

That man . . . that man who had shared her bed . . . consumed her body . . . for that's what he had done . . . consumed it . . . ravaged it . . . and she had let him, wanted him to . . . because she believed he loved her.

The bastard.

Right. Whatever he was up to, she was going to be on the other side.

She pulled a chair up to Chevallier's desk and began to speak intently.

She told him about the five scientific studies, about the planned ECO campaign.

'Claude, Courtois has got hold of this and is obviously determined to keep it away from this department. There can only be one reason for that. You've already said it. He wants to keep it in what he believes to be safe hands. If *Transport* is in control of the debate, then the aviation industry will have far too much influence. You've got to fight to get it into DG XI. You've got to.'

Chevallier grinned. 'Same old Monique. Still bullying me, and you're not even working here any more.'

'I mean it, Claude. This is really important.'

'OK, OK. But it's going to be harder now that Courtois has got it moving.' He looked at her curiously. 'What do you know about him?'

She turned away so that he couldn't see her face. 'Only that he's a ruthless shit.'

He looked at her back.

'Personal?'

She turned to him. 'It was. But this isn't. This is an *environmental* issue. It *belongs* in DG XI. If we don't get it under the control of DG XI it could lead to a disaster. If it gets into the Transport directorate or even the Energy directorate they'll block action for years.'

'Not necessarily. They're not completely in the hands of the industry.'

'When have you ever known Alain Jurgensen oppose the airlines on any issue of importance?'

'Didn't you hear? He's leaving soon. There'll be a new head of the Air Transport Division.'

'Probably not soon enough. This has to be sorted out now.'

'Hmm. Well, even if it starts in the Transport committee it can still be handled by this directorate. It'll take a bit of manoeuvring but it's not impossible. Let's see what we can do?'

She hugged him. 'Good. And we'll help.'

'How can you do that?'

'We'll build up a major Europe-wide environmental coalition to campaign on the issue.

'We'll mobilise the Parliament's Environment committee.

'We'll create the political heat you need.'

Monique left the building. Her mind was so full she hardly noticed the rain.

She walked down the Rue Belliard, past the semicircular European Parliament building, past the railway station with the new conference centre looming behind it, to her tiny office in the Rue du Luxembourg.

As she did she considered the first moves.

These would have to be in Strasbourg.

She would have to get the Committee on Environment, Public Health and Consumer Protection to table amendments to the Transport and Tourism Committee's resolution – injecting an environmental pollution factor and proposing that *it* should be responsible for the report, rather than Transport.

She would then have to get sufficient political support to guarantee, if a battle developed between the two committees, that Environment won.

It was a challenge, but she relished it.

This – not global warming – would now be her first big European campaign.

With an added ingredient.

By winning it she would also be defeating Pierre Courtois.

TOKYO

Machiko Yanagi hardly ever drank more than a glass or two of wine but the previous evening had been exceptional. It had begun with a meeting of half a dozen environmentalists around a circular table in a noisy, informal sushi bar in the Akasaka district, and then unexpectedly turned into a party that went on late into the night. They drank mainly chilled Japanese saki and Michiko now uncharacteristically was suffering from a hangover.

She would have liked to have stayed at home and tackled the problem with an aspirin but Ichiro Hashimoto had only been free to see her at 9 a.m. and this was why she now faced him across the desk in his busy little office in the Diet, gratefully accepting a coffee while he studied with a frown the file she put in front of him.

Eventually he put it down and looked at her thoughtfully. 'This is trouble,' he said, '*big* trouble. The battle with the more extreme of your movement over the siting of the international airport was bad enough, but this is likely to be even worse.'

He looked out of the window.

'I don't know,' he said. 'I don't know . . .'

'What don't you know?' she asked.

'Whether I want this trouble.'

'But what about the children? Don't you care about them?'

He sighed. 'I care about a lot of things. But I can't possibly get involved in them all.'

'So you choose the easy ones.'

He looked at her coldly. 'I choose the realistic ones. Politics is the art of the possible.'

'Well,' she rose and reached for the file, 'if you don't care or . . .'

'Wait a minute.' He too put his hand on the file, pinning it to the desk. 'I didn't say I *wouldn't* take it up. I said I didn't know whether I could.'

He paused. 'Look, let me think about it for a day or two. Will you leave me the file?'

'I can't do that. But I won't show it to anyone else for a couple of days.'

'Good.' Then he smiled. 'I'm sorry if I seem unhelpful. But I'm not paid by my constituents to act recklessly. I must consider the matter carefully – all of its aspects.'

'Try starting with the children,' she smiled back.

He stood at the window until he saw her emerge from the building and walk across the street. Then he reached for the phone. 'Get me Ryuji Hirose, at Yamamura Kikatu,' he said.

In less than half a minute he was talking to the head of the Global Communications public relations company to whom he was a parliamentary consultant.

'Ryuji? How are you? Good . . . Do you still work for Japanese Airlines? . . . In that case it's worth having lunch . . . no, not next week, Ryuji. Today. Shall we say at one today?'

MELBOURNE

Liz Scullen was unable to make the date with Keith Mullalay on the one day that week he was due in Melbourne (although she hoped to be there by the end of the meeting) so Mike McKenzie was the one who, with Dr Bruce Cossens, delivered the plantacon file.

They met at Mullalay's constituency headquarters, the two sitting quietly while the senator quickly read the notes. Eventually he dropped them on the desk in front of him and whistled an exclamation. 'Christ, this is not good news,' he said.

He looked interestedly at Cossens. 'You don't have any doubt about the results?'

'They've been replicated in other countries.'

'But you don't have any doubts? About yours.'

'Why should I?'

Mullalay looked at him sharply.

'I'll tell you why,' he said. 'Because if this blows up politically all hell will break loose and you're going to be on the firing line. And the fucking ammunition's going to be nuclear.'

'That's OK.'

Mullalay looked at him sharply a second time. He didn't like Cossens. Too confident. Slick. He turned to McKenzie.

'What do you people intend to do about this?'

'Well, the big fight will be in the United States. And in Europe. But we need other countries to support whatever starts there. After all, this is harming our kids, too.'

'Hmm. Can I see the other studies?'

'Of course. And you'll be backed up by our whole operation. And put in touch with politicians overseas. You won't be on your own.'

'OK. Feed me the material and make the contacts and, if it still looks OK, I'm your man.'

As the two were leaving, a taxi pulled up and Liz Scullen leapt out.

'Damn, I missed it,' she said. 'How did it go?'

McKenzie, waving to the cab to wait, quickly filled her in.

'Well, that's OK then,' she said, relieved. 'Well done.'

'Careful, Liz,' he teased, 'you'll be discovering we can do without you.'

'Not while you're the best we've got,' she said.

He got into her taxi, wound down the window and, with a broad grin, raised two fingers.

'See you,' he called.

'Not if I see you coming first.'

That left her with the grinning Cossens.

'Do you two always communicate by abuse?' he asked.

'*Abuse*?' she said. 'Bloody hell. That's friendly banter. If you want to hear abuse, just get on the wrong side of me . . .'

'No thanks,' he said, 'I can imagine . . .' Then: 'I'm staying in Melbourne overnight. How about dinner?'

She wanted to say, 'How about a kick in the groin?' but, still mindful of his importance, she reluctantly accepted.

They went to a Greek taverna near St Kilda where she lived. Over lamb kebabs and a salad of goat's cheese, tomatoes, onion rings and lettuce, and a bottle of retsina, he prompted her to talk to him about ECO. She was surprised to find he was a good listener.

At some point, while they were on the second bottle, they got on to music. He shared her liking for jazz, in fact turned out to really know his stuff.

By the time they finished the third bottle they were into her life history.

As she unsteadily climbed the stairs to her oven of a room, stripping as she went, she decided that after three bottles of retsina, Cossens became almost tolerable.

Unfortunately the way she felt now . . . sick, dizzy . . . that was two and a half bottles too many.

The price of liking Cossens was far too high.

WASHINGTON, D.C.

It was cold but bright, a crisp day, and MacAnally, feeling in need of exercise and fresh air, walked back to his office from the Wilkins meeting, briefing Jay Sandbach as he went.

'Keep a grip on Wilkins and those guys working for him. He'll be put under colossal pressure. If he doesn't have a lot of support he could crack.

'And there's another problem: if he does stick with it there'll be publicity . . . it's like a drug to politicians. Once they start getting a regular fix they develop an uncontrollable desire for more. That makes them harder to control. We need to be in daily contact with his office, with his aides Tom Gamell and Carl Hanson.'

'What else do you want me to do?'

'Start lining up some other senators. And their aides. And do some research on those who have links with the airlines and all their associated industries. Let's know who we'll be dealing with.'

'Well, there'll be Ed Eberhard for a start. He'll be a real pain in the butt.'

'Why do you say that?'

'Because he not only gets campaign money from the airlines but he's genuinely committed to them. They've always been one of his causes.

'Also he has a lot of influence, not least with the President himself. I reckon he'll be their leader on this.'

'OK, you'd better get a brief on him for Wilkins. Especially the bit about getting money from the airlines.'

As soon as they reached the ECO office door MacAnally knew something was wrong. The phones weren't in action. People were standing around in groups. The receptionist took one look at him and burst into tears.

'What in God's name's happened?' he asked, standing, astonished, in the doorway.

One of his senior colleagues, Molly Macintosh, their grassroots coordinator, took his arm and half led, half dragged him into the storeroom at the back and slammed the door behind them.

'Sam, sit down.'

'What the . . .?'

She pushed him down onto a packing case. '*Sam*. Just *listen* . . . it's Marie . . .'

He went cold, knowing already, knowing by the look on her face, knowing he didn't want to hear . . . wanting to stop her talking, but knowing he couldn't. Knowing everything, knowing nothing.

He heard a voice, he presumed it was his, say, 'Marie? *What about Marie?*'

'Sam, I'm so sorry.' She stood close to him, put her hands on his shoulders, looked down into his face with sad eyes. 'There was an accident. She's . . . dead.'

He just looked up at her. Blankly. He wanted to fight the news, wanted to shout and scream and cry and . . . throw things . . . but he was paralysed . . . couldn't move, couldn't react.

He heard the voice ask, 'How did it happen?'

And he half heard the reply, '. . . don't know much . . . going down a steep hill . . . ice . . . brakes failed . . . hit a truck . . . both killed . . . instantaneously . . . doctors said . . . no pain.'

He still felt numb. 'Adrian . . .?'

'He's OK. He wasn't in the car.'

'Well, who was? You said . . . both . . . and Marie doesn't drive.'

'Dr Warner. They were in his car.'

Warner's car? Why were they in Warner's car?

But then . . . who cared? He didn't care what car. He didn't care now . . . when . . . who else was there.

He was starting to feel now. To care now. To hurt now.

He stopped asking questions.

He no longer wanted to hear the answers.

What did they matter?

All that mattered was that . . .

. . . *Marie was dead*.

Christ, Christ, oh, *Jesus Christ* . . .

Marie was dead.

Part Four

WAR IS DECLARED

NEW YORK

The blizzards – severe enough in Washington to cause the President's January inauguration to be moved indoors – had continued into February. It was another month of frozen pipes and snow ploughs, cancellations and cold . . . cold . . . cold.

But the temperature was rising on the plantacon front.

ECO was now committed to its campaign.

The industry was preparing to defend itself.

The scientists were steeling themselves to go public.

And the politicians in the know were manoeuvring themselves to realise the full potential of the controversy – whatever that potential may be.

Given the growing concern within the industry, Eugene Remington had moved this key meeting from his own offices to neutral territory across Park Avenue in the Waldorf Astoria.

It was just as well.

Their numbers had doubled, in fact almost trebled.

He noticed also there had been an upgrading of the status of those attending. In addition to public affairs directors there were a number of chief executives. His former boss at American Airlines was there, hardly surprising when you considered what he had at stake. When Remington had left it in 1989, American Airlines had 500 aircraft, 75,000 employees and, with over 800,000 flights a year carrying more than 70 million passengers plus cargo, were reputed to have made an operating profit of over 700 million dollars and a net profit of more than 400 million dollars. It had experienced ups and downs during the 1990s but was now thriving on the plantacon revolution, as were its main rivals, Delta and United, who were represented by their general counsel – their top legal officers.

There were also top men from the major air freight companies, including the deputy chief executive of Federal Express and the number ones from his nearest rivals, Northwest, Flying Tiger and United. Sitting there, truculent as ever, was Todd Birk of Airlift International.

Remington was not surprised by the turnout. He himself was under growing pressure. Executive Airways, uniquely operating at full capacity, should have been expanding to reap the full benefits of its popularity. It couldn't do that without additional aircraft and Boeing and McDonnell Douglas were competing to get its order. The company had been on the brink of going ahead; the MacAnally letter had changed all that. Now it didn't know what to do.

As if that wasn't bad enough, Remington also had personal problems. The ski lodge in Aspen had been one purchase too many. He either had to make drastic economies, with a corresponding loss of face, or earn even more money. That would, of course, have been no problem were it not for the crisis over plantacon.

Remington's morale was not helped by having to admit that they were still ill-prepared to meet the threat.

They didn't even know the nature of the charges the environmentalists would make, or the scientific evidence that would back them up.

'You mean we still don't know what we're facing?' the Delta chief executive asked angrily. 'What's been going on?'

Remington bridled at the criticism, but contrived to sound reassuring.

'Until they unveil whatever evidence they've got we can't confront it,' he said. 'It's a pity our own research isn't ready yet, but that's no one's fault. Scientific studies need to be conducted in a scientific way. You can't hurry them. . . .'

He stopped, aware that someone else was trying to speak. It was the representative of JAL, a polite, generally cheerful man. 'I think I can help,' he said. 'My associates in Tokyo have been given a summary of the ECO research.'

He could not have achieved a greater impact if he had lobbed a hand grenade into the meeting.

Remington was stunned. 'The *environmentalists'* research?' he asked.

'Yes, sir. There are five studies from four countries, America, the UK, Japan and Australia, and they purport to have found plantacon in children's blood. They say that it's affecting their intelligence and behaviour.'

As he spoke, he circulated the information the Diet member Hashimoto had given the airline's PR consultancy.

It was sketchy, but . . . there it was.

At last the charges against plantacon were known.

Remington saw consternation and disbelief on every face. But, the first to recover, he moved quickly to regain control of the meeting. 'If we're not careful,' he warned, 'we'll be on a hiding to nothing. Once the charge is made, there'll be a lot of concern, especially in the areas allegedly affected. We need to put together a well-coordinated, united defence based on sensitivity to growing environmental concerns.'

'Jesus Christ!'

Remington inwardly groaned at the interruption.

It was Todd Birk, red-faced and impatient. 'What is this? *Sensitivity to environmental concerns*? What about my company's survival? What about the jobs of my workers? What about sensitivity to them? I say we nuke the bastards.'

One or two looked shocked, others embarrassed. Someone laughed. Remington, furious, wondering why they'd ever invited Birk to a meeting of this calibre, nevertheless managed a cool smile. 'I understand exactly how you feel, Todd. I sympathise. But we're dealing with other people's perceptions, not our own.'

He reported the results of an opinion poll. Two thirds of those questioned had said they believed environmental threats were as serious as environmentalists claimed. Only twenty-five per cent believed they were exaggerated.

'Maybe that's because we're not tough enough in answering the troublemakers,' said Birk.

'Well, we may have problems there. The poll shows the public are much more inclined to trust the views of the environmentalists' scientists than ours.

'More than two thirds say they would rely on the opinion of an environmental group scientist, while only fifteen per cent would trust a government scientist and only six per cent would rely on the findings of a corporate scientist.'

There was a shaking of heads, but he went coolly on.

'I'm sorry to say seventy per cent of the public

disapprove of the way industry and business meet their environmental responsibilities, and the same number want prison terms for officials of companies found guilty of deliberately violating pollution laws.'

He now spoke directly to Birk. 'Todd, we have a huge credibility gap to close. If people are going to listen to us we have to persuade them to trust us, and to do that we'll have to do more than wishing we could "nuke the bastards".'

The air cargo man subsided muttering, encouraged only by a nod of approval from Dieter Partrell of FEI who was pleased someone in the room saw it his way.

Remington continued. 'This is what I propose: we combine resources of finance and contacts – political, media and other contacts – behind one coordinated campaign.

'A coalition.

'That is vital, both so that we can combat the attack as efficiently as possible and so that the environmentalists can't divide us or embarrass us with inconsistencies.

'The coalition should form a coordinating committee, let's call it the war council, and it alone should conduct our campaign.

'Its work should be carried out by a campaign coordinator – let's call her the quarterback on our team.'

'Her?' Partrell looked surprised.

'Yes,' said Remington. 'Her. I have her standing by.'

And, picking up the phone, he asked his secretary to usher in Nicola Kowalska.

WASHINGTON, D.C.

For forty-eight hours MacAnally was lost to ECO, lost to the plantacon campaign, lost to the world. He had stumbled away from the pitying faces, the hesitantly offered hands reaching out to touch him, and forgetting even his jacket had crashed through the downstairs door and into the street, walking in a huddle of pain and disbelief, oblivious of the cold, into Dupont Circle. Then down P Street towards Georgetown, past the Italian restaurant Donna Adele where he and Marie had often had lunch when she was in Washington, past the Georgetown Hotel where she had once stayed after they had a blazing row, past the church where they had once sheltered from the rain. Unthinking, he crossed the bridge over Rock Creek Parkway, occasionally almost bumping into joggers, and walked on to the Georgetown residential area. Eventually he found himself at the Potomac. There he sat on a seat looking across the river to the state of Virginia.

Only then did he realise that he had followed the path they had taken so often when Marie came to Washington, their steps full of new life in the spring, their progress slow as they enjoyed the warmth of a summer evening, their journey so full of pleasure at the colours of autumn, their walk brisk, sometimes almost a jog during the icy winter.

Now she was gone. How could she be gone? He'd known the pain of death . . . his parents . . . but they had been old . . . he had always known they would die one day . . . but Marie . . . she was not old . . . he thought of her warm apartment in New York . . . of his cosy bed in Washington . . . their arguments, her eyes flashing, her way of taking his hand and holding it so tight the knuckles went white.

'No, oh no,' he cried to himself, bending double with pain. He wanted something to hit. Then something to do, and suddenly he was running, running along the banks of the Potomac, running in the snow, running past the Kennedy Center and Watergate, up to the Lincoln Memorial where he paused . . . she had loved this place . . . then up to the Washington Memorial and up the mall. Even in the cold he was sweating now, he was slowing, he was panting, he looked wild-eyed. People moved away, but he wasn't aware . . . wasn't aware of anyone or anything except an all-consuming grief. Then he saw a taxi and he was exhausted. He called it and went back to his room. There he stood under the shower and then went to bed and finally wept.

The next day he woke up unable to feel a thing. When the office rang he answered in a voice that was dead. He willed himself to cry, to feel angry, to feel something, but he couldn't . . . he couldn't feel.

All day he lay around doing nothing. Later, when the phone began to ring again, he ignored it.

At about seven the doorbell rang. He didn't answer. But it wouldn't stop. It rang and rang and rang. Finally he went to it and found his old friend Jackie Brown.

'Sam.' The *Post* reporter came to him, gently pushed him back through the door, kicked it closed behind her, and wrapped her arms round him and held him. At last the tears began to flow. For about five minutes they stood there, he weeping into her hair, then she led him into the sitting room. And shivered. The room was like a refrigerator. She quickly turned on the electric fire and getting a bottle of Scotch poured them each a large one, then another, then another. They didn't say much but she saw him physically warming and then getting slightly drunk. After a while she led him by the hand to the bed, undressed them both, and taking his hand, drew him down beside her. Almost immediately he fell asleep in her arms.

For more than two hours she lay still, listening to him breathing, then, slipping gently from his grasp, she turned over and went to sleep herself.

When she woke he was gone.

She dressed quickly, gulped down a mug of coffee, and then went to Dupont Circle and found him in the ECO office, telephoning, dictating letters, issuing instructions, making plans.

Most people noticed little difference from the MacAnally they were used to.

He's coming through it well, they said.

But she saw it in his eyes.

The anger.

She had last seen it at college when Sam's parents were killed.

He was avenging Marie's death with his work.

As she left the building she shivered, and it wasn't from the cold.

She didn't know whom he was planning to campaign against next.

But, whoever it was, they didn't stand a chance.

NEW YORK

Nicola Kowalska sat quietly for ten minutes or so as they speculated about the nature of MacAnally's opening press conference.

Then Dieter Partrell proposed that the industry hold a press conference on the same day. They should throw whatever they had at the environmentalists, right from the start . . . refute the charges, and explain the cost to the nation of banning plantacon.

Now Nicola spoke for the first time. 'With respect to Mr Partrell I think that would be a mistake . . .'

He went red, but she pretended not to notice:

' . . . At that point we won't be able to refute their scientific evidence because ours won't be ready. We'll sound unconvincing . . . like people who don't *want* to believe what they're hearing, rather than people who can authoritatively answer it.

'And, as Mr Partrell has just demonstrated, all we could talk about is money, the cost of banning plantacon. That is exactly what MacAnally wants, because he'll sound caring and compassionate while we sound mercenary.'

Partrell glowered at her. 'What do you suggest . . . we lie back and do nothing?'

'Not at all.'

She was praying they couldn't see her hands shaking under the table.

This was her opening move with these people. Now that she had made it she had to win. Otherwise she would have lost her authority right from the start.

'I suggest we issue a holding press release, not too combative; we should appear quietly confident that plantacon will be proved to be safe, but declare ourselves willing to consider what they have to say – and ready to openly debate the matter.

'Then we sit tight for at least seven days. By then MacAnally will have had to maintain momentum for a week without confrontation.

'We must never forget that MacAnally *needs* confrontation and it's not in our interests to give it to him.

'If he blows all his evidence on Day One and he hasn't elicited an aggressive response, how can he keep plantacon in the news . . . how can he keep the story going?

'Then, just when he's running out of steam, we hold our press conference and produce our own research.

'We'll have turned things around – *we'll* then be the story. It will be *our* research that calls for an answer.

'With luck the headlines will be saying "*plantacon cleared*". There will be a general sigh of relief.'

She saw doubt on one or two faces. 'Of course that won't be the end of it. But we'll have the environmentalists on the defensive and the resulting confusion over the conflicting research will make it difficult for them to get the kind of quick response from the politicians that they'll be hoping for.'

'I still don't like the idea of lying quiet for a week.' It was Partrell.

Nor did he like being contradicted in front of half the industry, least of all by this slip of a girl. What could she know about the jungle they were operating in?

It was, thought Partrell, typical of an Ivy Leaguer like Remington to hire her instead of a tough operator who would take on MacAnally with no holds barred.

But Partrell and Birk were the only dissenters; the remainder were solidly behind Nicola Kowalska. It had been a good start.

'Mr Chairman, how do we know that our research will clearly disprove what these environmentalists are saying?' It was the general counsel of Delta.

Partrell answered. 'First, because there never was any possibility that plantacon is damaging. It's safe. Our research will show that. Second, because ours are not a bunch of publicity-seeking, anti-business scientists; these are people we can trust.'

'People we can trust?' The British Airways man was frowning. 'I hope . . .'

Partrell interrupted. 'I don't mean people *we own*, I mean people we can trust to approach the task responsibly.'

The BA man looked unhappy but said nothing.

Someone asked, 'Who's likely to be against us in Congress?'

'Actually my lobbyist has already made some enquiries.' It was Partrell.

Remington and Nicola Kowalska glanced at each other apprehensively. What did Partrell mean by '*my lobbyist*'?

They really didn't want Partrell and his people trampling all over this in hob-nailed boots.

They couldn't blame Partrell for wanting to do all he could to protect his wonder additive, but Partrell was a crude operator, a street fighter, totally unsuited for the sophisticated campaign they had to run.

Partrell was still talking. 'There's this new man from Connecticut . . . Wilkins. He was elected on an environmental ticket. He's looking for a cause. And he's known to be talking to MacAnally.'

Nicola looked at Remington again. He was frowning.

In fact he was wondering how Partrell knew who MacAnally was talking to.

He didn't like the sound of this. Not one little bit.

'Maybe that's so,' he said quickly, 'but we must play it cool. Not do anything that will rebound on us.' He looked hard at Partrell.

'Still, we'll be talking to Wilkins ourselves. He's new and inexperienced. It may help to remind him of a few facts of life. He may not have thought through the consequences . . . the effect on the economy and energy conservation and exports. Our friend in the senate, Ed Eberhard, plans to talk to him before he introduces a bill and becomes trapped by his own rhetoric.'

He looked at his watch and suggested they move on to Nicola Kowalska's campaign plan.

'Right,' she said. 'Let's begin with the coalition. I believe we should draw it from nine groups:

'There are *the airlines* of course, both passenger and cargo.

'Then there are *consumer groups* representing air travellers who would have to pay higher fares.

'And there's *business generally*. We should involve the Chamber of Commerce and other business organisations. Higher fares would affect their costs considerably.

'Of course – as we've heard – we can count on *the aircraft manufacturers*.

'There's *the travel and holiday and hotel industries*, all of whom stand to lose heavily if fewer people are travelling.

'I would hope for support from *the unions*. With 500,000 jobs at stake in the airlines alone, and maybe as many more associated with the industry generally, we should have their support.

'There are all of *the trade associations* and related institutions from the Air Transport Association and the American Freight Association to IATA.

'Then we can look to *everyone concerned with energy conservation*, up to the White House. I also think we have a chance of dividing the environmental movement on this one. Some environmental organisations rate energy conservation above all else.

'There's *the defence industry* – the Air Force and the Pentagon, whose costs will also be dramatically affected and who have a lot of friends on the Hill.

'We mustn't forget *international organisations*, from airlines to governments.

'And, of course, there's *FEI, the manufacturer*.'

Then, almost as if it were an afterthought, she said, 'Then there's *the oil industry*. We'll be looking for a major contribution from the fuel suppliers.'

There was an embarrassed cough. It was David

Johnston. 'I'm afraid I haven't had a chance to consult my industry on the detail of this,' he said.

Remington looked at him sharply. 'Surely there'll be no problem there?'

Johnston looked back impassively. 'Of course, Eugene, you have our sympathy and support,' he said. 'It's just that we haven't discussed the matter in any detail. That's all I'm saying.'

The others looked at him suspiciously.

'Christ . . . what the hell is going on here?' It was Birk again. 'Are you people trying to play this both ways?'

'No, Mr Birk. But, with respect, it *is* primarily your problem. You specify you want plantacon added to the fuel and we add it.

'But if you specify you don't want it added, we won't add it.

'It's to meet your needs that it's added, not ours.

'So, while, as I say, you have our support, it's for you to satisfy the public on this one, not the oil industry.'

'So what does your so-called "sympathy and support" add up to?' Birk sneered.

'Well, it's a bit difficult to know what we can do.' Johnston looked round the room with an oily smile. He was beginning to feel uneasy. He hadn't handled this well. He could see one or two of his own company's customers looking at him intently. 'Naturally, if you have any suggestions . . .'

Nicola Kowalska stepped in quickly. 'I've no doubt we can make some, Mr Johnston. But, gentlemen, I would be grateful if we could stick to the structure at present. We can follow through on the detail later.'

Damn Johnston, she thought. He had undermined the effect of her opening. They had been impressed by her proposal to that point. She could see it on their faces. Now they were looking disconcerted, some of them positively alarmed. If the fuel suppliers abandoned them they could be in real trouble.

She worked hard to regain the initiative.

'The coalition I've described could be enormously powerful . . . probably the most formidable opponent the environmental movement has ever encountered.

'As for the oil companies,' she said, looking at Johnston, 'we can understand their position. But I have no doubt we can work it out to everyone's satisfaction.'

Johnston, aware of glares from both Partrell and Birk, and hostility in other parts of the room, nodded encouragingly, grateful to the young woman for helping to get him off the hook.

His nod helped her too. She moved confidently on.

'Our overall policy must be to establish a holding position for the moment and go on the offensive when we have our scientific defence assembled.

'In the meantime I suggest each company prepares a letter to go to all shareholders and employees the day before the ECO press conference so that they receive the first news of the anti-plantacon campaign from us. Assure them of your environmental record and that there's no cause for concern, and advise them that your own counter research will be published soon. Remember, these are *your* people. All they need to know is that you've not been taken by surprise, that you have the matter in hand, and that in your own time you'll deal with it.

'I'll call a meeting of your Washington lobbyists and brief them personally so that everyone is working on a common line and so that we all know who's talking to whom.

'It's vital we're all saying the same thing. *Vital*. The smallest of inconsistencies and the environmentalists will leap on it and make it seem sinister.

'We'll ask lawyers to look at what ECO says and see if there's any legal action we can take that will have an inhibiting effect. I'm doubtful about this but it's worth a try.

'We must also be ready to fight internationally. I have a list of ECO organisations around the world. I will establish a key contact in each country and have them operating a similar defensive campaign to ours.

'I'll have a plan for further work ready by our next meeting, say in ten days' time, but the most urgent thing is to get the coalition established, the war council appointed, and our communications working.'

They were impressed. Even Partrell was silent. Only Birk still glowered, unconvinced. 'Chicken shit,' his neighbour heard him mutter.

Nicola went straight from the meeting to Pennsylvania Station and sank into a seat on the Metroliner. She was exhausted, but exultant. She felt she had won their confidence and was in control. The worst was over.

However, the Japanese information had come as a blow.

Up to then she had expected the environmentalists' charges to be flimsy; now it seemed there was a real case to answer.

Nor was she as sanguine as she had pretended about MacAnally's inability to sustain his campaign.

Nor did she like the look of Partrell. Would he be containable? She remembered his reference to his own lobbyists. Remington had been right to frown at that. She would have to get in touch with Partrell's people quickly and try to persuade them to play a team game.

The last thing she wanted was MacAnally playing divide and rule.

She opened the file and looked again at the picture of MacAnally and the thought came:

'Know thine enemy.'

Why not?

She decided to give him a ring.

Dieter Partrell, being driven back to Hoboken, was also thinking about MacAnally. Damn the man.

He must get on to Charlie Orbell. Find out what the little shit had come up with.

His mind turned to Nicola Kowalska. There was no doubt she was impressive. Made a lot of sense.

Yes, let her do her best.

But he, Partrell, was not leaving the fate of plantacon in anyone's hands except his own. Not Remington's. Not those of his war council. And not Nicola Kowalska's.

That night he would call a meeting of his own team . . . the ad agency, and Green and Scroeder.

And then – an afterthought this – he would get together with Todd Birk.

He liked the look of Birk.

He was sound.

More than you could say for that motherfucker of an oilman, Johnston.

Something would have to be done about him.

He would add Johnston to Charlie Orbell's brief.

Birk, on the train to Baltimore, was feeling confused and desperate. He was an airline man, not a political animal. He hadn't found the meeting easy, and couldn't judge whether their tactics made sense or not.

This woman Kowalska talked well, but the problem, it seemed to him, was that they were all playing MacAnally's game. By treating him seriously they were playing into his hands. Building him up.

No one was talking about going for the jugular. Discrediting MacAnally and the rest of his anti-American, anti-business, knee-jerk liberals and Reds. Or frightening them off. What were these environmentalists if they weren't a bunch of jumped-up students? All they had to do was hit them where it hurts. They would fold quickly enough.

But hit them how?

Should he telephone Jordan? He hadn't heard from him since that first call. Maybe he should update him on what the Jap had said?

Yes, that was the answer.

The Skull would know what to do.

He got up from his seat and went to the bar.

On his way he passed Nicola Kowalska, also on the train *en route* for Philadelphia, her head resting back, her eyes closed.

Asleep, she looked about eighteen.

Fucking hell, he thought, if Remington and the rest believed that he, Todd Birk, was going to gamble his company, his life, on this girl, they must be stark, raving mad.

WASHINGTON, D.C.

For two weeks the whole office had been turned over to organising the launch of the plantacon campaign.

Given that the key to winning worldwide was to win in the US itself, because most of the planes were made there and most of the regulations set there, MacAnally chose to spend most of his time on the American campaign, delegating almost totally to Olly in London, Monique in Brussels, Machiko in Japan, and Liz and Mike in Australia.

The phone was constantly ringing from all over the world, the fax machine overloaded as the forthcoming press conferences were coordinated.

A press kit was ready. The plastic folder was headed 'Victims of the plantacon revolution'. Inside was an eight-page tabloid newspaper. It featured the scientific studies and laid out the objectives for the worldwide campaign. It also contained news of campaign initiatives, personalities supporting the campaign, and a message from Senator Chris Wilkins. And there was an article by Sam MacAnally,

In it he wrote:

'Sometimes society has to make hard choices.

Today is one of those days.

We have to choose between cheap air travel and the health of millions of children.'

He didn't deny that it was asking a lot to throw away the fruits of the plantacon revolution.

'Yet we do have to ask it. We have to ask it because the price for using it is a human one of terrifying proportions.

'We publish evidence today that millions of children are at risk of brain damage, their learning ability undermined because of pollution from plantacon.

'In those circumstances who would hesitate?

'After all, we always got by before without plantacon. Planes don't need it to fly. Airlines don't need it to make a profit. And our wealthy country doesn't need it.

'On the other hand, children do need their intelligence, their ability to learn.

'You would think in these circumstances a campaign would not be necessary. You would think the industry would say "Much as we wish it were not so, the human cost of plantacon is too high. We'll let it go."

'Not a bit of it. They won't even discuss the issue.

'They are already preparing their public relations

response. We can predict what it will be.

'They'll say environmentalists are hysterical. That you shouldn't listen to us.

'They'll fault the scientific evidence and produce their own well-paid scientists.

'They'll use all their powerful contacts. And they own plenty of those.

'In short, they'll do whatever they have to to protect their profits.

'That's why we have to turn to the people of this country and say "Join us. Fight for your children."

'If you do, we'll win.

'We'll win because the most irrepressible form of power is parent power.'

In addition to distributing the material at the Washington press conference ECO would mail it to the media throughout the US.

ECO supporters would be sent copies with a special 'what you can do' briefing, and ECO groups in the vicinity of airports would be given a leaflet for door to door distribution. It would contain a contact number of a local group or organiser, and would advertise an ECO-sponsored meeting within the next few weeks.

Not only would every senator and representative receive a mailing, but so would their key legislative assistants and researchers, as would all key Administration officials. And, of course, the White House would be sent copies.

There was to be one other mailing. ECO would send the studies and the newspaper to every airline company, every oil company and to FEI.

'Surely we're giving them more help than we should,' Adrian Carlisle said, amazed at the generosity of the gesture.

'Don't you believe it,' replied MacAnally. 'I'm not

helping them at all. If they're going to reply to the launch, as they will, it's better they reply to the facts and to what we're actually saying, rather than to unreliable media reports. If there's going to be a war let's all know what we're fighting about. It also helps if we can show that we have at each point, before planning the campaign, then before launching it, given them the chance to act responsibly.

'They'll get the stuff anyway, from some friendly journalist or politician. We gain a lot and lose nothing by sending it ourselves.'

LONDON

Following the pattern established by MacAnally for ECO America, and tried and tested by the more seasoned of British pressure group campaigners, Olly Witcomb had begun by building up substantial pre-launch support.

He was especially anxious to anticipate the charges that the campaign was emotive and hysterical by recruiting as many influential names as he could. He spent several days either writing confidential letters, making telephone calls, or calling on members of the House of Lords and Commons who had proved trustworthy supporters of the environmental movement. He also contacted well-known names in health prevention, including a number of TV and radio doctors or medical columnists, leading trade unionists not likely to be affected by the ban, people whose names were associated with care for children, educationalists, and people in the arts or show business who were involved in such campaigns as *Parents for Safe Food* and *Parents against Tobacco*.

Helped by a budget much greater than he was accustomed to, he commissioned a writer and designer to adapt the Washington print material and press releases so that they would make sense in a British context.

He also hired an experienced grassroots campaigner to put together a list of citizen organisations, district and county councils, and media near to all of the country's airports, beginning with the four London ones, Heathrow, Gatwick, Luton and Stansted, plus Manchester, Birmingham, Cardiff and Glasgow.

'We've got to stimulate parent concern to take advantage of the politicians' vulnerability in the run-up to a General Election,' Witcomb urged his small organising committee when they met over pizzas and wine at his flat.

'You don't think there'll be a media leak?' one of the team asked.

'Yes. I know for a fact there will be.'

'How? Who?'

'Because I'll be doing the leaking.' Witcomb laughed at their surprise. 'For some reason – I don't know why – journalists believe what they read in newspapers. The best way to get the media to sit up and take notice is for it to be told by one of its own that a big story's coming up.

'My plan is to negotiate a limited story with the *Observer* for publication on the Sunday before the launch.

'It works for both of us. The paper gets the benefit of not being left behind by the daily newspaper coverage and we get a reminder of the event hand-delivered to every news editor via their Sunday paper.'

The day after the press conference the grassroots campaign would begin. Local groups would be asked to

write letters to newspapers, call their MPs and council-
lors, organise petitions, and set up public meetings in areas
near airports.

Someone suggested a 'boycott planes' campaign,
encouraging people to declare that they would make
domestic journeys by train and would holiday in the UK
rather than fly abroad.

'Terrific,' said Witcomb. 'I don't think many people
will do it but it'll scare the shit out of the industry.'

When they had all left he climbed a few stairs to see
whether there was a light under Sally's door or to listen for
the sound of music. It was dark and silent.

Damn plantacon, he thought, it's really screwing up my
life. I haven't seen Sally for days.

He was climbing into bed when a disconcerting thought
struck him.

If the campaign succeeded, Sally could be affected.

If there were cutbacks, she could even be out of work.

Then one thought led to another.

She mustn't know what he was doing.

She worked for the enemy.

He fell back on the pillow. Christ, he couldn't believe
the way he was thinking.

Sally, the enemy? *The enemy!*

This was insane.

But he couldn't get to sleep for hours. And when he did
he dreamt of Sally. She had drilled a hole in her sitting-
room floor and was watching him as he slept. She was in
her British Ambassador uniform and surrounded by other
British Ambassador officers, also in uniform. They were
armed and waiting for her to give the order to attack.

He woke, bathed in sweat.

Damn plantacon.

Why the hell couldn't they have stuck with global
warming?

Memo To: Public Affairs Director
          UK Ambassador
          London

From: Nicola Kowalska, February 12.
          For urgent attention

We are reliably informed that the ECO campaign for a ban on plantacon is to be launched on February 19.

Our scientific response is likely to be ready within a week of that date.

We propose therefore that you call a meeting of all appropriate companies/organisations in the UK to fully brief them on our strategy and form a coalition to handle the industry's response in the UK.

You should also issue on the day of their launch a holding press release on the lines of our own one (to follow later), and prepare to deal with public concern in the vicinity of airports.

Good luck
Nicola Kowalska

Trevor Richardson, UK Ambassador public affairs director, dropped the fax on his desk with a sigh. This he didn't need.

UK Ambassador was the latest British aviation success story. It had followed the lead of Executive Airways in the US and set out to attract the business traveller. Like Remington's company it offered only one class. It called this Ambassador. Also like its American counterpart, its success owed much to plantacon.

He had, of course, been expecting trouble having been briefed by his New York representatives. Personally he couldn't believe it was going to be the problem everyone was making out. Who would listen to these environmentalists? Always preaching doom and gloom. The Government knew the importance of plantacon. It was saving the airlines and the consumer a fortune. It was saving energy. Such an improbable scare story about kids being affected by plantacon would be laughed out of court.

Richardson was damned if he was going to over-react. UK coalition? Fullscale press conference? Christ, these Americans always went over the top.

He pressed a button and called for Peter Kingman, the new eager-beaver public relations officer he had employed.

Kingman would be just the person to take this on.

On Fridays most MPs are back in their constituencies. The main political writers take the day off. It's a quiet day at Westminster. So few people noticed the written question and answer in that day's edition of *Hansard*.

Nicholas Bell (Islington): Will the Secretary of State for Transport state whether consideration was given to possible pollution by plantacon before it was cleared for use by the aviation industry?

Secretary of State for Transport: Plantacon was cleared for use after the usual procedures were observed.

Hardly world-shattering stuff. Just one of thousands of written exchanges buried in *Hansard* every session.

But Bell had put his marker down.

He was now on record having raised the question.

This would give him the advantage when the storm broke.

The Observer, *Sunday, February 16*

ENVIRONMENTAL ROW COULD REVERSE 'PLANTACON REVOLUTION'

By George MacDonald, environment reporter

A major storm is set to break this week over claims that a fuel additive used for jet aircraft is causing widespread pollution and damaging the health of millions of children.

The charge will be levelled by the international environmental group ECO.

They will publish evidence suggesting that plantacon, the revolutionary additive which has increased fuel efficiency and cut airline fares, is polluting areas in the vicinity of airports and that children have been found with high levels of it in their blood and with corresponding learning and behavioural problems.

The industry is bound to contest the claims strongly for there are billions of pounds at stake, while for Environment Secretary Tom Muldoon this will come as a particularly unwelcome headache, possibly forcing him into confrontation with both Energy and Transport colleagues in the Cabinet.

ECO UK director Oliver Witcomb told the Observer *last week that 'what we have to say will shock the nation. This is a classic case of the financial interests of multi-nationals with huge resources being put before the health and well-being of vulnerable children, and I don't believe the British public will stand for it.'*

'Bloody hell!' Trevor Richardson sat up in bed, spilling coffee all over his Sunday newspapers.

'What's the matter?' mumbled his half-awake wife.

He looked at her dispiritedly. 'Not a lot. We're only facing a bloody disaster, that's all.'

He got out of bed, pulled on a dressing-gown and, going into his study, fumbled in his briefcase for his address book and Peter Kingman's number.

He had to wait a long time for an answer and it was clear from the befuddled voice at the other end of the phone that he had woken up the young executive.

'Christ, it's Richardson,' he heard Kingman whisper in answer to a female voice; Richardson thought of his own sexually apathetic wife in curlers next door and imagined some nubile young blonde in Kingman's bed. This did little to improve his temper.

'I was expecting your report on the plantacon business on my desk on Friday,' he said coldly.

There was a silence. 'Well, yes, sir, and it's all but ready. Sorry, I didn't realise it was vital for Friday. You didn't seem to be taking it that seriously. I can have it with you by lunchtime tomorrow.'

'No, you won't,' said Richardson sadistically, thinking that with luck the nubile young blonde wouldn't be getting any more of Kingman this Sunday.

'What you'll do is leave that poor bloody girl alone, get yourself an *Observer* and read it, and be in my office with your report by nine in the morning. Have a nice day.'

'Bloody hell.' Tom Muldoon put down his knife and fork and stared at the *Observer* over his bacon and eggs. His wife, who had been absorbed in the review section, looked up enquiringly.

'Another Cabinet reshuffle, dear?' she said.

He gave her a dismissive glare.

He couldn't understand why she insisted on always making that joke . . .

. . . if she considered it a joke.

He didn't find it funny at all.

'I wish it was,' he said.

'Why?'

'I've just emerged from about six bloody months of bloody infighting with Ted Ingham over the environmental effects of his so-called transport policy and now, according to the *Observer*, we're heading for another bloody row.'

'What over, dear?'

'Plantacon.'

She looked at him blankly.

He pushed away the plate, his breakfast ruined. 'The stuff they put in aviation fuel . . . the so-called "miracle additive". Apart from that I don't know much about it and up to now I didn't bloody care.'

'Darling, I wish you wouldn't say bloody every second word. What would the voters think if they heard the way you talk at home?'

He stood up, the *Observer* in his hand. 'I don't bloody well care about that either,' he said.

Trevor Richardson dropped the report onto the desk and looked at the young man standing apprehensively in front of him. 'Not bad,' he said grudgingly.

Richardson had already asked his secretary to call a meeting of the other major British airlines, including British Airways and Virgin. It was fixed for the following day. The leading oil companies, BP, Shell, Texaco, and Mobil were also invited. Everyone had read the *Observer*. Everyone was coming.

Now he discovered that since being phoned on Sunday morning Peter Kingman had been remarkably active. He had already prepared an adapted version of Nicola Kowalska's press release and had provisionally booked a room at the International Press Centre for the industry's own press conference. He had also put together a list of politicians, officials and organisations to be lobbied in the meantime.

It wasn't a bad effort, thought Richardson. No, it wasn't bad at all. He took the unusual step of calling his secretary and asking her to bring Kingman a coffee – a rare sign that he was pleased with an underling.

'I think I'd better chair this first meeting myself, Peter,' he said. 'But you should be there, and we'll establish you as coordinator of the industry team. I'll reassign all your other duties so you can concentrate on it.'

Kingman looked pleased. 'So you really do think this is serious?'

'Well, I know the Yanks do. Up until now I've been assuming that the environmentalists didn't have the weight to make any impact on it in the UK. Probably they haven't, but I tell you this – I don't want to be in the position of explaining why we under-estimated them.'

He stood up and walked to the window, looking out across the Thames. UK Ambassador was what its chairman liked to call a tightly run ship; its headquarters staff was small. So it fitted neatly into three floors of a high-rise office block on the patch of embankment between Parliament Square and the Tate Gallery. From there Richardson absent-mindedly watched a barge chug by. Otherwise the river was deserted; it was too cold for tourist boats. Down below the traffic had slowed to a halt; there appeared to be a problem between the drivers of a taxi and a red London Transport bus. However, one car had got past. He watched the Rolls-Royce cruise to the front door thirteen floors below. The round figure who emerged was unmistakable. It was his chairman Sir Humphrey (Pinky) Brooks . . . he of the over-fed belly and face that flushed pink at the slightest provocation.

'I'll tell you what worries me even more than the

Yanks and more than the *Observer*,' he told Kingman.
'The chairman is going to call me upstairs in about . . . '
he looked at his watch '. . . two minutes. That's because
he's got telephone messages on his desk to ring the
offices of three Cabinet Ministers – Environment,
Energy and Transport – plus the Civil Aviation
Authority and the British Airports Authority. It's bound
to be about this plantacon business. I can't think what
else they're worrying about. And if they're worried, you
and I had better get worried. Because I have a feeling
that someone is going to be made a scapegoat if this all
goes wrong . . .'

The Secretary of State for the Environment hurried into
the ugly Marsham Street building which housed his
ministry. It was ironic, he thought, that those charged
with the environment should occupy such an eyesore. It
looked more like a multi-storey public lavatory. He
hated the building. And, for that matter, he hated the
job. The sooner the PM reshuffled the Cabinet the
better.

Muldoon had a meeting at 11 a.m. every Monday with
his Minister of State and two Parliamentary Under
Secretaries of State, his Parliamentary Private Secretary
(a backbench MP), and his senior officials. The purpose
was to look at the week's business, assign responsibilities
and confirm policy.

Lying on his desk this Monday was the *Observer*, open
at the page three article on plantacon.

'Before we get to the agenda, what do we know about
this?'

His junior Ministers looked blank. It was left to the
Permanent Secretary, his senior civil servant, to reply.

'I've already spoken to colleagues at Transport and

Energy, Minister, and to some others,' he said soothingly.

Muldoon restrained a grin. I bet you have, he thought. He could imagine how the telephone lines had buzzed as the Whitehall response was negotiated and coordinated.

'The Department of Transport says that banning plantacon would be a devastating blow to the British aviation industry just when it's become a notable success.

'The Department of Energy say it's one of the biggest breakthroughs ever in energy conservation and must be defended at all costs.

'Trade and Industry says the resulting lower air fares have been enormously helpful to business and should be protected.

'The Treasury says it doesn't dare think about the effect on inflation if plantacon were to go.

'The Foreign Office says we must stand together with our European partners, all of whom are bound to defend plantacon resolutely.

'To sum up, Minister, the case for banning plantacon would have to be incredibly convincing before we got these departments to even look at it.'

This time Muldoon could not suppress a grin. His Permanent Secretary had surpassed himself. 'I'm glad you're on my side,' he murmured sarcastically. Then: 'Well, what *is* the case?'

'We don't know, Minister. Obviously even the *Observer* didn't know or they would have spelt it out.' He smiled deprecatingly. 'My guess is that it's just another environmentalist scare, Minister . . . it won't last the week.'

Muldoon frowned. 'Maybe so. Just the same I don't like reading about possible environmental problems in the papers. If these pressure groups are genuinely concerned and if they're responsible people they should come to us.'

He considered for a moment, then turned to his Parliamentary Private Secretary. 'I've met this Witcomb a number of times at environmental events. He seems reasonable enough. I think we should get him in for a briefing before he goes public.'

His PPS hesitated. 'We don't want to inflate his sense of importance too much.'

'Well, why don't we get one of his friends on the back benches . . . Hal Robbins is well in with the environmentalists . . . to give him a ring and suggest that it would be wise if he were to brief the Secretary of State. He could suggest there's a chance of getting half an hour with me in the House after the vote tomorrow evening. That way the meeting will be at his request, not mine.'

'Will he fall for it?'

'I can't see how he can refuse if Robbins proposes it, especially as Robbins is a good supporter of the environmental movement and would clearly be trying to be helpful. It would also weaken his public position if we made it known that he'd refused to share his concern with us. It would suggest he's more interested in publicity than results.

'Oh, he'll come all right.'

FRANKFURT

The day after Pierre Courtois was elected vice-chairman of the European Parliament's Transport and Tourism Committee and rapporteur of its inquiry into plantacon he flew to Frankfurt to talk to a meeting of European airline executives.

He was met at the airport by an imposing black limousine and instead of going into the city was driven to an exclusive country house hotel on the outskirts where he was greeted by Erhard Piermont, the German who was Brussels lobbyist for a number of airlines and who was to chair the meeting. Piermont was a thick-set, ruddy-faced man with protruding eyes and veins standing out on his temple. There was a whiff of alcohol on his breath. Courtois was not surprised; Piermont was a notoriously heavy drinker.

'Pierre,' Piermont said, putting his arm round the other. 'Good to see you.' He lowered his voice. 'Can I have a quick word before you meet my colleagues?'

He led the Euro MP down the corridor to a smaller, quieter bar. 'Look, I want you to know that we're grateful to you for letting us know about this plantacon business and getting it before the transport committee. Really grateful.'

'No problem.'

'Can I ask you a direct question?'

'Sure.'

'What's in it for you – taking this initiative?'

Courtois smiled smoothly. 'Just doing my duty, Erhard. I heard rumours the environmentalists were likely to be raising the issue and took the view that we in Transport and Tourism were best able to consider it . . . shall we say, objectively.'

'Objectively? Quite.' Piermont looked at him hard. 'And that's it?'

'As of now.'

'Ah.' Piermont now looked thoughtful. 'Well, if we can be of help you only have to ask. We don't like to be considered unappreciative.'

'Thank you. I'll keep it in mind, Erhard.'

Back at the bar they met the remainder of those who

had come for the meeting and adjourned to a conference room on the first floor.

It didn't take Piermont long to spell out the nature of the threat.

'We take the view that there's going to be no stopping this coming on to the Community's agenda. That being the case the first essential is to keep it away from DG X1 – the environmental people – who are likely to look at it in . . . shall we say . . . an unbalanced way.'

Courtois confirmed this. 'It's vital to get it raised via the *Transport* committee. Our brief is wider. Daniela Bonetti and her *Environment* committee will go straight for the environmental impact of plantacon, whereas we'll consider the energy, tourism, transport and other advantages. But even if we succeed, you mustn't forget we have few powers. All we can do is voice opinions.

'The Commission alone can initiate legislation. It may wait for our report or it may begin immediately to respond to the ECO campaign, especially if pressed to do so by any of the member countries. That's why it's crucial to get the right directorate in the Commission to handle it.'

'How can you do that?' a Spaniard asked.

Erhard Piermont stepped in. 'That's where I come in. I shall be lobbying within the Commission.'

Courtois continued. 'If there's a real fight within the Commission, the Presidency decides. That changes from country to country every six months. The UK will hold it at the crucial time. So we'll need help from our British friends.'

Peter Kingman from UK Ambassador nodded. 'We'll do what we can.'

'So what happens then?' It was the Frenchman.

'Well, if the Commission is persuaded that there needs to be regulatory action, it produces its proposal for action, probably in the form of a draft directive. This goes both to the Parliament, for comment, and to the Council of Ministers.

'Usually the Council of Ministers at its first meeting argues unproductively. The Commission has then to go back to the drawing board and return six months later with a revised compromise proposal more acceptable to the disputing countries.

'So to prevail we need, first, to have the Commission on our side.

'Then, ideally, but not crucially, we need to have Parliament on our side.

'And, if all else fails, we need to have sufficient member countries backing our line to ensure any move to ban plantacon is blocked by the Council of Ministers.'

'So what are we going to do?' asked a representative of KLM.

Piermont responded. 'We set up a coordinating committee in Brussels, serviced by my office if you're all agreeable. And we resist every proposal, comma by comma, fullstop by fullstop. At the same time we need a tough response in every member country.'

'How long will all this take?'

'Could be as long as eighteen months unless there are special circumstances.'

'What special circumstances?'

Courtois answered. 'Well, if, for instance, the North Americans banned plantacon, making it impossible for our airlines to fly in there.

'Or if plantacon was, in fact, proved to be highly dangerous.'

Piermont shook his head vehemently.

'That's not possible,' he said, 'plantacon is safe.'

He looked at them defiantly.

No one contradicted him.

But few met his eye.

The fact was they didn't know.

When Pierre Courtois got back to his room he found a small white envelope under the door. It contained a note from Erhard Piermont. 'I'm sending you a little present,' it said.

Five minutes later there was a discreet knock on the door.

The 'present' was five foot ten, brunette.

She was wearing only a pair of knickers under her leather coat.

Courtois took them off.

The knickers, that is.

To a man with a jaded appetite the leather coat provided welcome novelty.

STRASBOURG

While Courtois was in Frankfurt, Monique de Vos was in Strasbourg preparing for the monthly plenary session of the European Parliament due to begin the following day.

Her first port of call was Daniela Bonetti, the popular, radical, and vivacious chairwoman of the Parliament's Environment committee. She and Monique were old friends and had helped each other on numerous occasions. It took less than ten minutes to wind up Bonetti, and for the following forty-eight hours she and Monique lobbied extensively.

Their aim was to get the plenary session to pass an amendment to the Courtois resolution, making the *Environment* committee – *not* the *Transport* committee – responsible for debating plantacon.

Bonetti, who had quite a few favours to trade, pulled out all the stops to get the support of both the major groupings in the parliament, the Socialists and the Christian Democrats.

By the time Courtois arrived in Strasbourg to find an urgent message to contact Fischer, the two women were well on the way to a deal.

Courtois found Fischer in the members' bar. The German hastily ushered him to a quiet corner. 'We've got problems. Bonetti is on the war path and she's running an amendment that will give the issue to her. I gather the Socialist leadership has already agreed to back her. That means, at least in theory, she's got one hundred and eighty votes of the two hundred and sixty she needs before we even start. She'll get the Greens. It'll be desperately difficult for us to win a majority.'

Courtois thought quickly. 'I don't think it can be that bad. We've a good chance of splitting the Socialist vote. They've only heard the environmental case. Just wait till we talk to them about the economics and the energy considerations and the impact on their national airlines. If we can whittle down the Socialist vote to nearer one hundred we'll be safe.'

Fischer looked more cheerful. 'Sounds worth a try.'

For two days the lobbying was intense. Euro MPs of all parties from all countries were approached, first by Bonetti and Monique de Vos, then by Courtois and Fischer. Favours were called in. Promises and threats were made. Arms were twisted. The prospects of poisoned children and bankrupt airlines were graphically described. Fischer promised German support for an Italian intiative on another unrelated matter in return for guaranteed support. Bonetti conceded a vacant vice-chairmanship to Spain in return for its sympathy.

By the end of the second day of the plenary, with the

Transport and Tourism resolution nearing the top of the agenda, it was neck and neck.

Then came good news for Fischer and Courtois. The German SPD delegation were not going to support the leadership of the Socialist group despite sitting with them in the Parliament. Airline lobbyists had done their stuff. And that meant the loss of eighty votes to the environmentalists.

Bonetti located Monique in the lobby. 'We're losing,' she said. 'But I don't believe the Germans will hold their present line once the public campaign gets going in Germany. Not with the Greens so influential there. So we have to get the decision postponed until after the ECO campaign is launched.'

'Can you do that?'

'The President owes me a big favour. I'll ask for the debate to be postponed until the last session and then slow down the other business so that we don't get to it. It'll then be held over. That'll give us the time we need.'

It was the one move Fischer and Courtois hadn't anticipated, and it succeeded.

Just.

When the session ended the plantacon resolution was the very next item on the agenda.

On his way to the railway station Pierre Courtois found himself standing next to Monique de Vos on the crowded bus.

He smiled at her and she looked away.

'Monique,' he whispered, touching her arm.

She turned and looked at him with hate in her eyes. 'Would you mind not touching me,' she said coldly and loudly.

Everyone on the bus turned and looked at him. One woman hissed. She heard another tell her neighbour his name in a loud whisper.

He went a bright red and looked back at her in fury.

'You may have won a reprieve in Strasbourg,' he whispered viciously, 'but we'll win in Brussels.'

She replied, no longer loudly, but in a voice so chilling that he winced.

'You *won't win*, Pierre. Your winning days are over. From now on you're going to be a loser. A loser all the way. That I promise you.'

He leapt off the bus when it reached the railway station, and hurried away from her and the still-critical eyes of the other passengers.

As he sat at the front of the train her words stayed with him.

He hadn't liked the look in her eyes.

The woman could turn out to be bad news.

He felt tired.

He also felt a bit itchy around the crotch. Christ, he hoped that girl in Strasbourg hadn't given him more than Piermont had intended.

Sometimes he wondered whether it wasn't time to give up chasing women.

It was expensive. It was tiring. It was time-consuming. And it was increasingly dangerous.

And he was bored with it.

Yes, maybe he would buy a big bunch of flowers when he got to Brussels.

For his wife.

He should be more thoughtful about these things.

He left the train quickly, then, just after he passed the ticket barrier, he heard a woman's voice call his name.

He turned. It was a freelance reporter from Holland, a sort of Euro-political 'groupie', a rather attractive woman in her late twenties who was ever-present in Brussels and Strasbourg. Courtois had seen her around.

'Can I give you a lift, Pierre?' she asked.

He looked at her. She was wearing a red dress, with a black belt pulling it tight round her waist. One hand clutched a small holdall. The other some car keys. She looked free. And to the practised eye of Pierre Courtois she looked easy.

'That would be kind of you,' he said.

He took her arm as they walked to her car.

On their way they passed the flower stand.

Courtois didn't even notice it.

TOKYO

Something was wrong.

Ichiro Hashimoto was not returning Machiko's calls.

But she had received an unprecedented invitation to a Japan Airlines reception.

Why would an MP who had been so friendly, so anxious for her help, now be avoiding her?

And why would a company that previously had never heard of her be asking her for drinks?

No matter what way she looked at it, she kept coming back to only one conclusion. Hashimoto had tipped the airline off. They would know all about the five studies and were bound to have passed the information on to others.

She sat in her flat, almost weeping with rage and humiliation. How could she explain to Sam that she had let them down so badly? And what would Mike think of her when he discovered that she had carelessly caused them to be betrayed?

Then an even worse thought crossed her mind.

Hashimoto would have noted the name of the scientist, Seiichi Tezuka. What if they tried to get at him?

It was too late to get him at the university so she rang the operator and asked for his home number. Fortunately she found him in.

'Mr Tezuka, have you by any chance been offered hospitality by Japan Airlines?'

'How strange you should ask. I received an invitation today. To have lunch and discuss some possible research for them.'

Machiko talked long and hard but even when she had put the phone down she wasn't positive she had convinced the scientist he shouldn't go. So she rang Sam MacAnally in America and apologetically explained what had happened.

'Machiko, Machiko, for God's sake stop apologising,' he eventually interrupted her now-tearful saga. 'It was bound to happen somewhere. It's not your fault. Look, don't worry about Tezuka. I'll talk to his sponsor here. He'll sort it out. What plans have you got for the launch?'

She explained what she had arranged . . . a press conference, interviews with Tezuka on a number of television programmes and a major feature in the widely read *Asahi Journal*. Also there was to be a token demonstration at the airport by representatives of every Japanese environmental group and the presentation of a petition to the Diet by leaders of twenty child-care organisations.

'It's not a lot, Sam, but it's the best we can do in the time.'

'It sounds great. Listen, Machiko, you're doing well. Don't worry about this other business. Carry on the good work.'

She hung up feeling much better.

But there was still Mike.

She felt she must tell him what had happened.

She tracked him down in Australia and, over the phone, poured out her story.

He was furious, but not at her. 'Get the bastard, Machiko,' he bellowed down the line. 'Give the issue to one of his opponents and if Hashimoto opposes you in Parliament get someone to ask him about his links with the industry. Condemn him as a defender of child poisoners. Make him pay.'

She giggled.

'You would have made a great Samurai warrior,' she said.

And then she telephoned Mit'sura Hasegawa of the opposition Socialist Party.

Hasegawa was fiery, unpredictable, not particularly influential, but, if he took the issue up, there was no way it wouldn't be noticed.

Another thing. Hasegawa and Hashimoto were bitter enemies.

Once Hasegawa heard of Hashimoto's betrayal of confidence there would be no stopping him.

SYDNEY

Liz Scullen had got the bit between her teeth. Besides the usual things, press conference, media coverage, parliamentary lobbying, she planned a 'boycott Qantas' campaign that she knew would cause an uproar.

Her other big idea was a 'hands around Sydney airport' demonstration. She hoped parents and children would link hands and form a giant circle right around its perimeter. It would make great TV.

The opposition senator Mullalay was being more than helpful. He planned a major debate in Canberra immediately after the launch and had apparently got the Shadow Cabinet enthusiastic. 'We look like having a lot of fun up here,' he promised. Mike McKenzie was given the task of liaising with him.

The only bad news for Liz was Dr Bruce Cossens. He had become obsessed with becoming a media star and telephoned her daily with fresh suggestions of radio and TV phone-in shows and magazine interviews. While she was as anxious as he was to get him on the airwaves she could have done without the calls, and without the impression he gave of being far more concerned about becoming famous than he was about protecting children.

He had also become obsessed with her. When he wasn't pestering her about publicity he was suggesting dates – drinks, dinner, a swim, various parties, the lot.

She thanked God he was in Sydney and she in Melbourne because, while he seemed to be in the Victorian city a lot more these days, there were usually a few hundred miles between them. And the advance work for the launch of the campaign provided a ready excuse for her non-availability when he was closer at hand.

Admittedly she had liked him a bit more that evening in Melbourne, but she was convinced that was because of the drink.

She still found the grin maddening.

On the other hand she was also aware that he was the only scientist she had, so she did her best to discourage him without being downright rude. That, together with being worn down by his persistence, was why, when in Sydney, she accepted an invitation to a barbecue at his place. The thought of a steak and cold beer overlooking the harbour on a summer's evening was not unappealing.

She did her best to ignore the grin that greeted her, took the proffered beer, and sank into a hammock-chair on the balcony. There was just the slightest breeze but this and the sunshine meant the harbour was alive with sailing boats.

'This can't be bad,' she thought as Cossens began grilling prawns on the barbecue.

Later, as the sun slipped away to the other side of the world, they sat side by side with their feet up on the railings, looking out at the dark expanse of water and back to the lights of the city. For all the jokes about the rivalry between Melbourne and Sydney, she had to admit she liked Sydney.

She glanced at the man beside her. He appeared lost in thought.

'What do you want to do with your life, Bruce? Is your heart really in science?'

He laughed. 'You don't think much of me, do you?'

'Why do you say that?'

'It's the truth, isn't it?'

'No,' she lied.

Actually, she considered, it wasn't really a lie. While she didn't rate Cossens's social conscience, she had decided that – as someone to have a beer and a steak with – he wasn't too bad.

'It's just that you seem so keen on the publicity,' she added.

'Sure. Why not? Tell you the truth, I wouldn't mind becoming one of those TV scientists. You know. Like on *Tomorrow's World.*'

'Why?'

He opened another can of beer. Liz had to duck to avoid the spray. 'Sorry,' he said. He took a sip of it and reflected. 'I guess it must be because I've always been a loner. Well, I suppose if I was honest I'd say lonely. Only child. Lost my parents young. Live alone. I guess a psychiatrist would say I crave attention.'

Liz looked at him, surprised.

There could be no questioning the honesty of the self-analysis.

Or that it had hurt him to say it. He was staring out towards the water now, almost defiantly avoiding her eyes.

'Fair enough,' she said, lightly. 'Good a reason as any.' Then, fearing she had responded too flippantly, she added, 'Actually, Cossens, you're not a bad sort really. When you're not grinning that inane grin.'

'Sorry,' he said. 'Nervous habit. I've been told about it before. I don't even know I'm doing it.'

She began to feel guilty now. Cossens was hardly the superficial narcissus she had imagined. The arrogance was for show.

She had been right that evening in Melbourne. When he wasn't operating under the cover of excessive self-confidence, Cossens was all right.

She suddenly realised that he was looking at her in the dark.

She turned and faced him.

She felt herself go still. For, shed of its arrogance, without the maddening grin, it was a vulnerable face, almost a shy face . . . it reminded her of the face of a small boy. The way he was looking at her now she would have sworn he was desperate for her approval.

She felt her heart fill with . . . what? Affection? Compassion? She didn't know.

What she did know was that she was too confused to commit herself further tonight.

So she reached over, took his head between her hands, and kissed him on the forehead.

'I think I'll go before I do something I regret,' she said.

'Would you regret it?' he asked.

'Well, I'm not going to find out. At least not tonight.'

And, grabbing her bag, she left him.

He followed her to the front door. At the gate she turned. He was watching her from the doorway.

He looked attractive in his tee-shirt and shorts. She felt her resolve weaken.

Then he grinned.

She turned and walked away.

She would have to do something about that grin.

If she was going to get involved with Cossens that grin would definitely have to go.

WASHINGTON, D.C.

Sam MacAnally called his top team together for a final meeting. Each member made a brief report.

Jake Katzir said that the New York scientist David Abernathy was already on his way to Washington, now eager to get started. The good news from the UK was that Professor Barnes had bowed to pressure from Justin Lcrd and, having been promised comfortable transport and the chance to see his specialist while in London, was after all going to attend the press conference there. After receiving a phone call from New York the Japanese scientist Seiichi Tezuka had decided not to meet Japan Airlines, and was on course for the Tokyo launch. And according to Liz Scullen, the Australian, Dr Bruce Cossens, was raring to go. Raynald Warner's work was ready to be published as a separate report.

MacAnally was pleased. 'Well, that's all looking good,' he said.

Jake Katzir, looking slightly sheepish, said he just had one fear.

'What's that?' asked MacAnally.

'Well, the Tezuka business worries me.'

'What Tezuka business?'

'The attempt to woo him with research contracts. As you know, I'm not a conspiracy theorist. But there's so much money involved in all this that I'm afraid someone may try to get at one or two of the others.'

'Who would do that?'

'Not the reputable companies. But who knows how many people stand to lose if plantacon is banned? Or how much they've got at stake. Or what they'll do to protect it. I tell you, this could turn nasty.'

MacAnally looked incredulous. 'For Christ's sake, Jake, next you'll be suggesting someone will try to bump them off?'

'No, no. Of course not. Maybe just bribe them. Or frighten them . . . I don't know. Don't forget what Olly said about Barnes . . . that he appeared frightened.' He looked at the doubt in their faces and became even more sheepish. 'Look, forget I said it.'

Molly Macintosh chipped in. 'Actually, Sam, if they're going to bump anyone off, it'll be you.'

MacAnally laughed.

She reddened. 'I'm not joking, Sam. I think we should have someone with you all the time. I'm not suggesting a blackjack in a dark alley, but if the other side organise worker demos, they could become violent.'

MacAnally hesitated for a moment. Then shook his head and chuckled. 'No. No, no, no. Come on. Let's keep our sense of proportion here.'

And shrugging off their concern, he asked the others to report.

Molly Macintosh said she had her grassroots operation 'all ready and waiting for lift off'.

Jay Sandbach said that the news from the Hill was

mixed. Wilkins was 'on a high' but not getting the encouragement from his administrative assistant Ted Gamell that they hoped for. Apparently Gamell, whose responsibility was to help the senator get re-elected, feared Wilkins would alienate significant groups in the state. On the other hand, the senator's legislative assistant Carl Hanson was all for it. Wilkins had sounded out the senators on the 'environmentally friendly list' and the response was good. But there were reports that Ed Eberhard was being unusually active. That could mean the other side were already lobbying too.

Dominic Young had been trying to find out what industry was up to. 'We know from Machiko that they have at least some idea what our research says. And we know that there have been a couple of high level meetings in New York. Also a number of lobbying and PR consultancies were asked to pitch for the FEI account. That would suggest they're getting in shape for a battle. But apart from that we don't know a lot.'

MacAnally turned to Carlisle. 'Are all the mailings set up?'

'In their envelopes, stamped, and ready to go.'

Carlisle also reported that there was considerable interest in the press conference. The main television networks were all sending crews. CNN was thinking of covering it live. C-Span definitely would. So would national public radio. And he was getting enquiries from the media all over the country, all wanting a local angle. At this rate the coverage would be enormous.

'Good.' MacAnally looked round the room. 'Well, that's it then. We're in business.'

Later he walked back to his apartment.

It was cold – he kept forgetting to get the central heating fixed – and there wasn't any food in the refrigerator, but he was too tired to go out and buy some.

So he went to bed.

As he lay there, he turned his mind to what lay ahead. The campaign was in good shape. His collegues – Dom, Jake, Jay and the rest – were a terrific bunch. And they had been wonderfully supportive since Marie's death – not saying much, but just shoring him up in any way they could.

He guessed the effects of his loss hadn't really worked through yet. All he knew was that he was finding it harder than usual to get motivated.

Still, that would change once the bullets began to fly.

He looked at the picture by his bed of himself and his parents. How he wished they could have seen one of his campaigns.

'This one's for you, Mum, Dad,' he whispered.

He looked, too, at the picture of Marie, the one he had taken at Christmas. She was standing in the snow, her legs apart, wrapped up in a black leather jacket and thick woollen leggings, about to hurl a snow ball at him. It had marvellously captured her vitality – and the laughter in her eyes.

As he did every night, he lay there for hours thinking of her.

He had stopped crying after that first night.

Sometimes he wished it wasn't so.

He wondered whether part of him had died with her.

Then he thought . . . maybe that was best.

He was fed up with people he loved dying.

Memo from Sam MacAnally
To all member countries, ECO

re campaign launch

All systems go for February 19.

Reports from all countries encouraging.

Good luck
Sam

PHILADELPHIA

Nicola Kowalska was also in bed, reviewing in her mind the events of the past few days.

The companies had responded well. They had appointed a war council that combined experience with influence.

She had been given an enormous budget and access to creative and other talents from a number of other industries.

Even FEI had reluctantly cooperated and she had already met the men Partrell had hired, Green and Scroeder, and was impressed with them. They would be an asset.

The coalition was taking offices in Washington and she was busy recruiting staff.

And Remington was proving a gem. Calm. Supportive. And available when needed, but without imposing.

Yes, things were on course.

But she would be glad when she had their own research.

She was apprehensive about what the environmentalists were actually going to produce.

What if they were right?

It didn't bear thinking about.

She switched off the light and lay in the dark.

She wasn't as happy as she had expected to be.

It wasn't the campaign that was the problem. That was exciting – hard work but rewarding.

It was just that she missed having someone to come home to – someone to talk to about it.

Her lover in Washington may have turned out to be an asshole, but while they were together and working for the same company they had been able to share experiences, gossip.

She now realised it was that, more than the sex, that she had looked forward to when they were together.

Not that the sex had been bad.

She switched the light back on, got up, and raided the refrigerator. Then with a glass of milk and a ham sandwich she returned to bed and switched on the TV.

There was an old film on one channel. She had seen it. Football highlights on another. She wasn't interested. A quiz show. Jesus Christ! A couple of news programmes; she watched but didn't really listen.

Then she switched it off.

It wasn't television she needed.

It was company.

The truth was, she told herself, she was lonely.

Work wasn't enough.

From Nicola Kowalska
To the Plantacon Coalition

ECO campaign launch confirmed for February 19.

Our own plans well advanced.
Please remember the importance of coordinating all of our activity.

Keep in touch.

Good luck
Nicola

WASHINGTON, D.C.

AIRLINE SHARES DROP AFTER CHARGES THAT
PLANTACON IS ENVIRONMENTAL THREAT

New York Times, *February 20*

Airline shares fell yesterday after environmentalists claimed that the fuel additive plantacon was becoming a major environmental pollutant.

Leading environmentalist Sam MacAnally told a press conference that 'millions of children living in the vicinity of airports all over the world were being brain-damaged by an invisible spray of toxic poison emitted from aircraft as they take off and land'.

MacAnally's organisation ECO has launched an international campaign for a worldwide ban on the use of plantacon until a way can be found to prevent the pollution.

The economics of the aviation industry have been dramatically improved by what has become known as the 'plantacon revolution'. Fuel costs have been cut by twenty-five per cent and aircraft have been able to travel longer distances without refuelling. The aviation industry is believed to be saving twelve and a half billion dollars a year.

Spokesmen for the industry said yesterday that a ban on plantacon on the basis of 'flimsy scientific work' was totally unjustified. It would 'spell disaster for the industry and its customers and for energy conservation. It would also adversely affect the country's export income.'

This concern was reflected in a panic selling of shares on Wall Street. By closing time they had plummeted by 170 cents.

ECO's allegations are that:

- plantacon is a neurotoxin, a brain poison, and the industry made no attempt to consider its environmental effects when deciding to add it to fuel

- scientific studies had shown considerable contamination of the areas surrounding airports, including New York's JF Kennedy

- other scientific studies showed that children in the vicinity of airfields were now plantacon carriers and that the higher their intake the more their intellectual performance was being under-mined.

Mr MacAnally, last year named as Environmentalist of the Decade, was harsh in his criticism of the industry. 'They have put increased profit before public health. In response to our enquiries they have chosen to ignore genuine concerns and reply with a public relations exercise.'

Also at the ECO press conference was Connecticut Senator, Christopher Wilkins. He said that he intended to press the Public Works and Environment Committee to hold hearings on the issue. 'I am, of course, more than willing that the industry should have the chance to put its case because plantacon is an energy saver and that is a conservation plus. But if the price of plantacon is damage to our children's health then the price is too high.'

Mr Dieter Partrell of the manufacturers Fuel Efficient Industries (FEI) was scathing in his response. He told us that 'MacAnally is a renowned anti-industry trouble-maker who would not be content until he has bankrupted half the corporations in the country.' The plantacon that was emitted from aircraft exhausts was, he claimed, *minimal and was largely blown into infinity. The quantities reaching the ground could harm no one.*

Mr Partrell said the industry would be publishing its own studies within a few days. They would contradict those of the environmental lobby and show there was no cause for concern.

He said his company was considering suing Mr MacAnally and ECO for heavy damages for their unwarranted charges.

- *Details of the scientific studies Section A page 3*
- *Story on the economics of the industry Section B page 16*
- *Profile of environmentalist MacAnally Section B page 17*

The press conference had been held at 11 a.m. in the Senate committee hearing room in the Russell building, just over twelve weeks after the first meeting between Lord and MacAnally.

After MacAnally and Wilkins had outlined the case the questions came thick and fast.

'Aren't you as conservationists concerned about the energy loss that would result from a ban?' asked the *New York Times*.

'Of course. But you have to balance the energy benefits against the threat to public health. Can there be any question that the health of millions of children must come first?'

'Given what's at stake,' asked a reporter from *Nature*, 'would you accept that your scientific evidence will have to withstand the closest examination? And are you satisfied it will?'

'We have five studies conducted in four countries, five scientists replicating each other's work and ready to stand by it.' He paused. 'Actually, alas, four . . . as you will know, Dr Warner was tragically killed before he could attend today. I think that represents a convincing case.'

Then from the *Washington Post*: 'If you win this it will be the end of the plantacon revolution. There's a lot at stake. You presumably anticipate the industry will fight?'

MacAnally: 'My experience is that these multi-national companies always put profit before the public interest. I've no doubt they'll do so in this case. But we've beaten big vested interests before.'

The publicity was considerable. It was not, as MacAnally had hoped, the front page lead story but it made most front pages with background stories inside.

Some papers also published their own editorial comment.

The *Washington Post* said:

The airline industry is entitled to take time to make a considered reply to the charges made by the environmental movement but the reply must be to the charge that children are being harmed. Citing economic and energy conservation statistics will not impress concerned parents.

The plantacon revolution has been accepted without question. The Environmental Campaigns Organisation (ECO) do a public service in raising questions about its safety. We hope that from everybody's point of view they can be answered satisfactorily.'

Lionel North's syndicated column was typically abrasive:

Mr Sam MacAnally is in the headlines again.

Not satisfied with undermining three or four worthwhile industries with his genius for publicity and scare stories he now wants to end the plantacon revolution.

He claims to be an energy conservationist but apparently he wants to destroy the one great energy-saver invented over the past quarter of a century.

He claims to be a citizen representative but will increase the fares of millions of his fellow citizens who fly each year, on holiday or on business.

He claims to be a patriot but will lose the country billions of dollars in exports.

And all for what? Some dubious studies by relatively unknown scientists about which more questions can be asked than are answered.

I expect the industry to answer these charges satisfactorily, plantacon to be cleared and Mr MacAnally to be run out of town.

And about time too.

The environmentalist of the decade is about to become the laughing stock of the decade.

MacAnally noted with interest that apart from Dieter Partrell, an old adversary, whose comments he noted with amusement, the industry's reply was low key, muted. He wondered what the industry were up to. Presumably holding back their response to let MacAnally fire all his shots first.

Well, he wasn't going to.

He had something in reserve. It was in a brown envelope in his locked desk drawer.

He would use it when the time was right.

LONDON

The evening before the British press conference Olly Witcomb walked from his office to the House of Commons. It was a cold, clear night and Parliament Square was deserted apart from a couple of policemen and a passing jogger. He had thirty minutes before the House voted at 10 p.m., after which he was to meet Hal Robbins in the Central Lobby of the House of Commons, so he walked up on to Westminster Bridge.

He looked up the silently flowing river to the lights of the City, then back at the Palace of Westminster, the light at the top of Big Ben indicating that MPs were still sitting.

It had been a long but good day. All the mailings had been posted at lunchtime. Replies to the press conference invitation suggested they would get massive media coverage. The number of MP supporters was now well over 200, albeit mainly Labour and Liberal Democrat. In addition to the original ten supporting organisations there were now another thirty signed up or at least expressing concern.

He had spoken that day to Professor Barnes who had, instead of making the video, been persuaded to come to London.

He had sounded nervous on the phone, saying he didn't like public appearances, but nevertheless he would do his bit. Olly warmed to the old man. He was a good sort. A real trooper.

MacAnally had sent Adrian Carlisle from Washington. He had brought with him copies of the final American mailings and had spent an hour briefing Olly on what was planned on the other side of the Atlantic. Olly was glad to have him there; he would be a useful additional speaker at the press conference.

Nick Bell had signed Olly on as a researcher. This got the campaigner a pass to the Houses of Parliament and this he now waved at the policeman at the St Stephen's entrance before making his way up to the Lobby where Hal Robbins was waiting. Chatting affably, he steered the campaigner to Muldoon's office where they found the Secretary of State in shirtsleeves signing letters.

'Hal, come in.' He warmly greeted his party colleague and then shook Witcomb's hand. 'Good to see you, Olly. I think last time was at the European consultative conference.'

'It was, Secretary of State.'

'Well now, Hal here said you wanted to have a word about this plantacon business.'

He listened to Olly without interrupting, then sat looking thoughtful. 'Olly, of course I'll look into the matter thoroughly. But it would be unlikely we would give up the benefits of plantacon just on the basis of some unofficial studies from the US. We'd have to do a lot more work on it ourselves.'

'With respect, Minister, it's not just from the US.'

'Yes, but commissioned in the US to a specific brief.'

'Does it matter to whose brief it was? What matters is that millions of children are being brain-damaged and you have the power to stop it.'

Muldoon smiled reassuringly. 'That's a bit over the top, isn't it? We haven't had a single complaint from a single child or parent that anyone's been damaged.'

'Of course not, Minister. Because no one realised that plantacon was falling to the ground or that it was being absorbed into children's bodies. Thus if they were not performing to their full potential, no one would necessarily know, or know why.'

'Quite so, quite so, but can you really expect us to forsake the colossal benefits of plantacon on the basis of a few initial studies that have no official status? At the very least we need to take a look at the position over, say, a five-year period of studies and follow-up.'

'Five years!' Olly was shocked. 'Sir, do you realise the damage that could be done over five years? And even then there would be further argument over the studies, then a phasing out period. We could be talking about ten years. This simply won't be acceptable.'

'Acceptable to whom, Olly?' The expression on Muldoon's face hardened slightly. 'You have only one interest in this, one point of view. We have to weigh in the balance a great deal more. The economy. The need to conserve energy. Above all the need to take responsible decisions on the basis of the best advice and research.'

Olly looked at Robbins, then back to the Secretary of State, then rose to his feet. 'Sir, one of the things you will need to weigh will be the opinions of the voters.'

Muldoon too rose. To Olly he was maddeningly cheerful. 'Oh dear, we're going to experience one of these so-called campaigns. Well, I don't deny your ability to raise public concern, young man. But the voters expect more of me than to just roll over in the face of it. I've promised you I will look into this matter and that promise will be kept.'

Olly shook his hand unenthusiastically and as Robbins thanked the Secretary of State for the meeting he preceded the back-bencher out into the corridor and back to the lobby.

'He's not a bad man, Olly,' Robbins told him. 'And he heard what you said. I think it was worthwhile.'

'I wish I felt the same,' Olly said bitterly. And walked out into the night.

Olly Witcomb was later to recall that February 19 began to fall apart within seconds of his waking up.

He looked at the clock and realised the wake-up call he had ordered had not been made. The BBC taxi was due within five minutes. As a result he cut himself shaving, spilled some coffee on his best shirt and left a folder of key facts behind in the flat.

The day was going to get worse.

There is no more influential programme on British radio or television than Radio Four's *Today* show. Broadcast every weekday between 6.30 a.m. and 8.45 a.m. it not only has a substantial public audience but is listened to by most people in politics, the media, and other professions of influence. The Prime Minister was known to be a regular listener between 6.30 and 7.30 a.m. while taking a bath and having breakfast, and it was at 7.10 a.m., immediately after the news, that Witcomb was booked to appear.

Today had a habit of staging confrontations and to Witcomb's annoyance they had also invited Trevor Richardson of UK Ambassador. He had hoped to have the interview to himself. He was even more angered by the decision of the programme's presenter Brian Redhead to give Richardson the first word.

'How vital is plantacon to the airline business, Mr Richardson?' he asked.

Richardson took a fair chunk of the time allocated for the item to spell out the economic and energy advantages of plantacon.

'Altogether it has been good news for everyone, Brian,' he finally purred.

Olly, still irritated by his meeting with the Secretary of State, further irritated by the programme's undermining of his launch, and uptight about the day that lay ahead, began badly, losing his cool and attacking Richardson's complacency without properly spelling out the scientific case. As as result Richardson was able to reply soothingly, 'Really, I can't see what Mr Witcomb's worried about. He's making accusations without a shred of acceptable evidence.'

Olly realised he had made a weak start and tried hard to pull it round. He began to quietly summarise the evidence but then saw Redhead getting a one minute signal from his producer. He hesitated just for a moment and Richardson seized the chance to jump in.

'As far as I can see, Mr Witcomb is asking us to abandon the huge benefits of plantacon on the basis of some rather dodgy American work.' He made the word

American seem like a bad smell. 'He hasn't any official support at all. And no British work of any substance. I suggest he go back to the drawing board and consider this matter in a calmer fashion. There is too much at stake for big decisions to be taken on the basis of emotion and, if I may say so, hysteria.'

Redhead looked at the environmentalist. 'Thirty seconds, Mr Witcomb.' Olly looked at him in fury. *Thirty seconds* to recover from what he knew to be a disaster.

He spoke in short, sharp sentences, trying to make each one tell. 'The facts are these. Plantacon is a dangerous neurotoxin. It's falling from planes and contaminating areas around airports. Children are absorbing it and being brain-damaged. There are five studies including one British one to show this. It has to be stopped.'

He stopped with five seconds to go and immediately knew he had blundered, for the experienced Richardson seized the precious few seconds for himself. 'Naturally we'll listen carefully,' he said. 'Because we have children too. But until there's real evidence that *British* children are being harmed I suggest that nobody gets alarmed.'

Witcomb began to protest that there was no difference between British children and American children but was silenced as time ran out. He left the studio furious with himself.

But worse was to come. He had hired a portable telephone for the week and was in a taxi on his way from Broadcasting House to the office when the call came.

It was the ginger-haired girl from Birmingham, the one who had driven him to see Barnes, the one who had been charged with the task of going with the hired limo to bring him to London.

And she was crying.

'Olly? Olly, you're not going to believe this.'

'What?'

The phone went dead. He cursed. He sometimes wondered whether these mobile phones were worth the aggro.

Eventually it rang again. 'Olly?'

'Yes.'

'Olly, is that you . . .?'

'Yes. For Christ's sake, yes . . . what's the matter . . .?'

'Olly, oh God . . . this phone . . . are you there? . . . Olly, I don't know how to tell you . . . it's Professor Barnes . . .'

It had still been dark when they arrived. The thatched cottage was shrouded in mist. The overgrown garden helped to make it look like those haunted houses she had seen in old black and white movies.

She had shivered as they went up the path.

They had knocked on the door repeatedly, she and the driver.

She remembered what Olly had said, about Barnes being ill, old, vague. Could he be asleep upstairs? Or lying ill somewhere else in the house?

She had shouted out, 'Professor Barnes.' So had the driver, in a louder voice than she could muster.

No answer.

Then he had reached past her and tried the door handle.

The door had swung open and there before them was the most cluttered room she had ever seen.

Once more they had called his name.

Still no answer.

Tentatively they had walked inside, picking their way around the filing cabinets and the piles of books.

There had been a door to the left of the fireplace.

They went into a beautiful old dining room. All antique furniture. And oak beams.

And from one of the beams Professor Barnes was hanging, a rope pulled tightly around his neck.

At his feet . . . below his feet, out of reach . . . a chair lay upturned on the ground.

Olly collapsed into a corner of the cab. His heart felt as if it had ceased to beat. His mind had stopped working, as if someone had pulled out the plug.

It took a tremendous struggle to pull himself back. '*Killed himself*? When? Where? Why?'

'I don't know all the answers. We found him hanging. In his dining room. There was a note. Oh, Olly, it was awful. That poor man . . .'

But Olly was not in a compassionate mood. Under the stress of the moment all he could think was that Barnes shouldn't have done this to them. It wasn't fair.

'A note. About this business?'

'I don't think so. The driver read it, I didn't. As far as I could gather it was about his cancer becoming worse. It said he couldn't face going on.'

'Oh God.'

Olly couldn't grasp it. Only yesterday the old man had talked to him about coming to London. Had he lost his nerve?

Then he had a sobering thought. Had the pressure he had applied caused Barnes to end his life?

At last he became conscious of the human tragedy.

For the first time he pictured Barnes hanging from one of those great wooden beams.

He felt weak, suddenly deprived of energy or enthusiasm.

He felt as if the world had become as untidy as Barnes's room.

He felt as if he were responsible.

And now he had to face the press conference without a scientist.

It took place in a conference hall near Parliament Square and was even better attended than Olly Witcomb expected.

He had in the taxi briefly considered calling it off because of the death of Barnes but decided there was no choice but to continue.

Speaking as calmly as possible, so as not to sound over the top, he spelled out the details of the charge, concluding with a call to the Secretary of State to introduce regulations to phase out plantacon over the shortest possible time scale.

Then, in the absence of Barnes, he called on Adrian Carlisle to review the international research and describe the worldwide campaign. The young American lawyer was impressive. Olly thanked God he was there.

The first question was inevitable. From *The Times*: 'Why is there no scientist for us to question directly? Where, for instance, is Professor Barnes?'

It was the moment Olly had been dreading. 'I'm sorry to have to say that Professor Barnes died last night. He has been suffering from cancer.'

There was a stunned silence, relieved in the end by a sympathetic journalist who asked about the likely response from the rest of Europe.

'We'll know better in a day or two after we've seen reaction to the Europe-wide campaign being launched in Brussels today by my colleague Monique de Vos.'

A reporter from an aviation industry magazine rose. 'Trevor Richardson of UK Ambassador has just said the industry will soon produce findings that contradict yours. He's described your campaign as hysterical and

emotional. What do you say to that?'

'I say that typically the polluters are attacking the messenger instead of addressing the message.

'As for emotion, the main emotion being expressed today is fear. It's the airlines who are emotional. They're afraid of lost profits.'

And on that note the press conference ended.

WASHINGTON, D.C.

The reports came in to MacAnally for twenty-four hours. All over the world the press conferences had gone well. The campaign was off to a flying start.

The only bad news was the suicide of Professor Barnes.

MacAnally recalled Jake Katzir's fears.

Two scientists dead out of five seemed incredibly bad luck.

Could someone have frightened Barnes?

Apparently his note had talked about not wanting to 'go on'.

Did he mean with the pain from cancer, or with involvement in the plantacon controversy?

But Sam couldn't believe the loss of two of their scientists was other than coincidence . . . just plain bad luck. Still, it wasn't good. They had only three scientists now. It was necessary, more than ever, that they had their wholehearted cooperation.

He decided to ask Justin Lord to speak to each of the three, to remind them of their contracts, maybe even to commission some more work.

Whatever happened the scientists must not become vulnerable to pressure from the other side.

LONDON

At the headquarters of UK Ambassador all hell had broken loose. Within hours of the ECO press conference Trevor Richardson had messages to ring the company chairman, BBC and ITN, and ten national newspapers as well as colleagues at other airlines and in other industries, a total of forty requests for return phone calls by lunchtime. He arranged for all the media calls to be dealt with by Peter Kingman using a standard comment: 'UK Ambassador has been in consultation with the US aviation industry and is informed that further scientific evidence, to be published in approximately a week's time, will invalidate the environmentalist claims.'

Kingman was also given the task of liaising with other industries in order that their comments were similar.

The following morning they looked together at the newspapers. *The Times* ran the story at the foot of the front page. The *Independent* and *Guardian* and *Financial Times* all led on it. And nearly every major newspaper ran leaders. *Today* splashed its centre-spread with '*The invisible cloud*' and the *Daily Mail* launched one of its campaigns with: '*We ask the questions: will the Government face up to the plantacon challenge?*'

In addition there were stories about the death of Professor Barnes and tributes to his distinguished career.

The *Mirror* was the only one to note that it was the second death of a scientist involved in the plantacon controversy. '*Boffin dies as plantacon jinx strikes again*', it said.

Richardson was called to see UK Ambassador chairman Sir Humphrey Brooks just before lunch. 'What do you make of it, Trevor?' the latter asked, dispensing a generous pre-lunch sherry.

Richardson, who despised sherry as much as he despised Brooks, and who was desperate for a hefty gin and tonic, responded cautiously.

'Obviously I'm concerned at the suggestions being made, Sir Humphrey,' he began. 'The environmental movement is gaining strength and influence and if they have a case then we have a problem.'

Brooks looked at him suspiciously. The normally bellicose Richardson was being uncharacteristically careful. He shrewdly guessed what was happening. Richardson was covering his back.

Brooks had a small round head on a round body, the latter cultivated by regular ingestions of rich food and late-night port. He was a former aviation minister in a Tory administration and the chairmanship of UK Ambassador had come to him late in a previously mediocre business career. Anxious to cash in on the plantacon revolution before he retired he had encouraged the company to invest heavily in expansion. He now felt personally exposed. And he was damned if he was going to let the ambitious and ruthless Richardson expose him further.

On the other hand he knew few operators better than Richardson at dealing with a crisis of this kind.

So he kept his feelings in check. At least, he thought he did – it was an astonishing fact about Brooks that he was unaware that everybody knew exactly how he was feeling by the colour of his face. As Richardson had once told Kingman, light pink meant either he'd had a few drinks or was irritated; medium pink meant either he'd had a good few drinks or was feeling under real pressure; bright pink meant either he was drunk or deeply upset.

However, there was a confusing factor – he also went

pink if things were going well.

When he had heard about his knighthood he had apparently gone through the pink barrier. He had gone red. And extraordinarily for someone who coloured in the way he did, Brooks never went red.

This morning, Richardson noted, he was a light pink. Brooks wasn't panicking yet.

Probably he was too bloody stupid to realise what was at stake.

But Brooks was being, for him, quite clever.

'Whatever happens, it won't be your fault, Trevor. You didn't introduce plantacon,' he said reassuringly. Then, observing his public affairs director visibly relax, he continued in exactly the same tone of voice. 'But of course your experience will be of immeasurable value in helping us to take the flak. How do you intend to handle it?'

The responsibility for dealing with the crisis had been moved so deftly that even Richardson didn't notice it. 'Well,' he said, 'I'm waiting to see what the Americans come up with. I gather they've set a scientific study of their own in motion and are convinced they can invalidate the charges. Also they've set up a high-powered international campaign in defence of plantacon and we'll want to link into that. But it would help if you could have lunch with one or two people . . . the Secretary of State for Transport, perhaps?'

They sat down and worked out a list of six key people the chairman should contact.

As he got up to leave, Richardson smiled to himself.

Brooks was at his most enthusiastic when arranging a lunch.

Now he had six to look forward to.

No wonder he was on his way to bright pink.

NEW YORK

The panic buttons had been pushed all over the planet, and the pressure on Nicola Kowalska's war council was enormous. Airlines in scores of other countries wanted reassurance. Shares had fallen. Their telephone lines were jammed with enquiries from parents living near airports. The media wanted a detailed response. As a result it assembled in sombre mood.

Except for Dieter Partrell.

He arrived with Al Bain in tow looking extremely pleased with himself.

Impatient to share his good news he proposed a change in the agenda so that the results of their research could be presented immediately.

Bain, harassed by Partrell into wearing his best suit but still managing to look untidy and worried, did the reporting.

'With the financial resources you put at our disposal we also commissioned five studies to address the three key charges the environmentalists are making. We now have the American results in full.

'The first study involved taking samples of dust, plant life and soil from around three major airports, JFK in New York, Washington International, and Chicago's O'Hare. We analysed the samples and found virtually no trace of plantacon whatsoever.'

He showed the results on the screen.

'The second study involved blood samples from 250 children in the vicinity of each airport, 750 in all. We found no traces of plantacon in blood. We also tested for plantacon in hair and found no sign.'

Once more he showed the results on the screen.

'In the circumstances the third study was difficult to undertake. We could hardly test for the effects of plantacon on children if they hadn't absorbed any plantacon.

'Nevertheless we compared one hundred children living close to the three airports with one hundred children living well away from airports and found no significant difference in intelligence, learning ability, behavioural tendencies, etc.'

Partrell interrupted. 'What this means,' he said triumphantly, 'is that plantacon has been completely cleared.

'It's *not* falling to the ground in significant amounts.

'It's *not* being picked up by kids and it's *not* affecting them.

'We can blast these environmentalists out of the water.'

He could not hide his glee. 'This is the end of MacAnally. The goddamn end.'

Bain, much to his superior's annoyance, interrupted. 'Indeed the science does appear to exonerate plantacon totally,' he said mildly, 'although I have to say that in the time available these studies were limited in size. Also the environmentalists may argue that plantacon has only begun to be used in large quantities over the past two or three years, so it could be accumulating in the environment. The position may have to be re-evaluated later.'

Partrell frowned. '*Thank you, Al*,' he said icily, furious that the scientist had gone beyond his brief.

Impatiently he turned to the others. 'The point is that there is no *evidence* of harm. And we haven't referred to the overseas work yet. We are due to get the reports from Australia, Japan and the UK in a couple of days but we've spoken to the three scientists by phone and their preliminary results support these findings.

'Now,' he said, the note of triumph returning to his voice, 'given the weakness of the scientific case against plantacon, we went on to commission studies to show the economic and conservation advantages of the product.'

He reported these results himself. The first study, by a team from the Harvard Business School, showed that over the next ten years the use of plantacon would lead to a saving of 150 *billion* gallons of fuel, representing a colossal energy gain.

Study number two by the same people predicted financial savings of up to 120 *billion* dollars over the same decade.

'And the export earnings for this country will be worth at least fifty *billion* dollars.'

He looked around the room. 'What it adds up to is this: at our press conference we can show that there is no cause for alarm, but what we can also show is that the benefits of plantacon economically and in terms of energy saving are massive.

'I repeat: we'll blow them out of the water.'

He sat back, his face shining with virtue.

There was relief and even glee on almost every face.

Then Nicola Kowalska spoke.

'Dr Bain,' she said, noticeably addressing him rather than the ecstatic Partrell, 'how do you explain the remarkable discrepancy between the two sets of studies? After all, MacAnally is fielding five scientists from four countries and they all have reputations too. How can they come up with one set of results and your people with another?'

Bain shrugged. 'I can't explain that. Of course there could be differences in methodology that could explain some difference in the results but the contrast is so sharp that . . .'

He paused and looked uncomfortable.

Nicola pressed. ' . . . that somebody either did incredibly bad work or produced deliberately false work. Is that what you're saying?'

Partrell interrupted, speaking forcibly. 'Either is possible with these environmentalists. They'll grab any work that sustains their paranoia, no matter what it is. They're capable of taking bad science and using it, or misinterpreting good science.'

'But publishing fraudulent science?' It was Remington. 'I find that hard to believe.'

Partrell flushed. 'I hope you're not suggesting—'

Remington interrupted. 'I'm not suggesting anything. I'm just reminding you that the opinion poll showed that only six per cent believe our scientists and sixty-eight per cent believe the scientists produced by people like ECO. We have a problem of credibility – that's not our fault but it is a reality.'

Then, seeing Partrell was struggling to control his temper, he responded more positively. 'Still, these scientists you've used are well established. Provided they're willing to stand by their work and speak for it I think we can, as you say, prevent any groundswell behind MacAnally and put him on the defensive.'

'For Christ's sake, we should hit them with everything we've got. This stuff is dynamite.' It was Todd Birk, who Remington had failed to keep off the war council, if only because Birk had flatly insisted on being there. 'It's just what I expected, of course. I think we owe Mr Partrell and Dr Bain our thanks.'

Partrell, welcoming Birk's support and anxious not to prolong the discussion about the differences in the results, now took the initiative from Remington.

'Let's move on to how we use these studies,' he urged.

Remington hesitated. He was still disconcerted by the

contrast in results, but was unable to see any reason not to comply with Partrell's request.

'Very well,' he eventually said, turning to Nicola.

She had thought carefully about their line. 'Well, clearly we adopt a firm stance, but in so much as we attack the environmentalists it should be more in sorrow than in anger.

'We should regret that a good cause is undermined by irresponsible and emotive over-reaction to perceived threats – threats not substantiated by fact.

'At the press conference we should present the studies, say that we're content that plantacon is one hundred per cent safe, but at the same time say that as part of our general sense of environmental responsibility we'll be carrying out regular six monthly tests. This will be seen as a generous response.'

She then produced what she believed was the master stroke.

'I then suggest we go even further than we could reasonably be expected to. We should say that this unwarranted plantacon scare shows that there needs to be ongoing work in this area. The industry would, therefore, set up a special Aviation Environmental Commission with a budget of ten million dollars to finance studies in major medical centres, universities and nonprofit research institutes throughout the country. It would investigate ways whereby the industry could contribute further to environmental protection.

'We could also underline our contribution to energy conservation by announcing a set of energy conservation awards.

'The effect of all this would be to make us look extremely generous in the face of unwarranted attacks and provocation.

'It would inspire confidence.

'And it would strengthen the hand of our political supporters.

'All at minimal cost – at least, compared with the cost of losing plantacon.'

Birk exploded. '*I don't believe this*. We've won. We've got the facts to finish these motherfuckers off.' He paused, nodded an apology to Nicola for the language, then belligerently continued, 'We don't need all this bullshit.'

But to his surprise Partrell supported their campaign coordinator. 'No, Todd, I think it's a good idea. I admit this environmental attack has scared the hell out of us. If we can do a few things like this to prevent any further attacks it's all right with me.'

They got down to planning the press conference. Remington, who had been furious at the remarks Partrell had been quoted as making on the day of the ECO launch, urged discipline.

FEI should play a minor part in the press conference because it had the biggest vested interest.

The whole thing must look dignified and responsive to public concerns.

He accepted Nicola's advice that the attacks on the environmentalists should be more in sorrow than in anger.

The press conference would be backed up by widespread paid-for advertising, by mailings to all interested groups, and by presentations on the Hill.

Finally, if people were still concerned, they would hold public meetings around the airports and show the studies and field the scientists.

They would do special presentations to local councils, school boards and other organisations.

An information pack would be sent to every local newspaper and taped radio interviews to every local radio station.

They would spend whatever money it took.

They had a defence now and by God it was going to be heard.

Washington Post, *March 3*

STORM AS FRESH STUDIES CLEAR PLANTACON ON POLLUTION CHARGES
by Jacqueline Brown, Environment reporter

Five new scientific studies, financed by the aviation industry, and published yesterday, have failed to replicate the findings of earlier research suggesting the fuel additive plantacon is an environmental pollutant harming the mental health of children.

The studies found little evidence of plantacon fallout near airports and no difference in the intelligence or learning skills of children near airports compared with children living further away.

The industry claimed that plantacon had been cleared.

The five scientists who appeared at a series of press conferences around the world yesterday, could not explain the contrast between their results and those of the scientists whose work was published by the environmental organisation ECO last week.

ECO leader Sam MacAnally said yesterday the difference could lie in who funded the research. 'It's no coincidence that all the scientists who found plantacon to be dangerous work in the public sector and presumably in the public interest, while all those who claim it's safe work in the private sector and presumably in their employers' interest.'

Last night Ms Nicola Kowalska, coordinator of the air industry's plantacon advisory committee, said Mr

MacAnally's remarks were an outrage and a slander on scientists of the highest standing. 'If the best he can do is make unfounded attacks on the scientists' integrity then it suggests he has no real confidence in his own scientific work.'

At the industry press conference Mr Eugene Remington of Executive Airways said that plantacon's benefits to the economy and to energy conservation were enormous. He predicted savings of 120,000 million dollars over ten years and a huge energy saving.

'Nevertheless if the industry believed for one minute that plantacon harmed human health we would forgo those benefits,' he said. 'The opposite is the case. We are one hundred per cent sure that it's safe and the environmentalists' charges are based on faulty scientific work and a desire to attack our industry irrespective of the consequences.'

The industry promised to:
- *set up an aviation environmental impact review board*
- *conduct regular review studies on plantacon and other environmental questions arising from air travel*
- *cooperate fully with any official inquiry*
- *hold public meetings in all areas alleged to be affected*
- *make their scientists and scientific work available for national and international conferences*
- *set aside a special fund to carry out environmental research to do with the industry generally, and to promote even greater energy conservation.*

Mr Remington said, 'We could not be doing more to address the questions and the public anxieties.'

Last night Senator Ed Eberhard, (Rep., Texas), said that he was satisfied the matter had been cleared up. 'I will oppose a bill and believe there is no need for hearings. They would be a waste of congressional time.'

He said the industry could not have been more respon-
sive to public concern. 'Its package of proposals is
generous in the extreme.'

However, Senator Christopher Wilkins, (Dem.,
Conn.), said that nothing the industry had said or done
altered the fact that five studies in four countries had
implicated plantacon in IQ deficiency and behavioural
problems of children. 'The questions must be properly
answered. Only a congressional hearing will achieve that. I
will proceed with preparing a bill to outlaw this pollutant.'

The industry's press conference had gone well. Eugene
Remington, in particular, performed with conviction.
Nicola found herself feeling grateful he was on their side.
He sounded reassuring. He looked honest. He exuded
charm. And it was clear that he had already made
personal friends of most of the aviation journalists
present.

But from the daily newspapers the questions had come
thick and fast:

'How do you explain the difference in the research?'
(The *Los Angeles Times*.)

'I don't wish to impugn the motives or the ability of the
environmental lobby and its scientists but it's just possible
that they formed a view about plantacon and simply read
all their findings that way. We were anxious to establish
the exact truth.'

'But it's not the interpretation of the findings but the
findings themselves that are different,' the reporter said.

'Well, a lot of questions have to be asked about
methodology and so on. I hope the scientists will get
together and maybe even do some combined work. But,
as I've said, in the meantime there is no scientific
justification for even considering a ban on such a valuable
product.'

'What if damage is proved? What will your industry do?' (The *Boston Globe*).

'It won't be.'

'But what if it is?'

Remington looked serious. 'If plantacon had the effects that the environmentalists claim, action would have to be taken, obviously, and we would support it, either in terms of devising a way of reducing the pollution or finding an alternative to plantacon, if that's possible. We will do what is right. But at present I have no reason to believe the damage will be proved. I think the environmental lobby have made a serious and damaging mistake and one they may ultimately have to pay for.'

'What do you mean by that?' (*Village Voice*.)

'I mean that while we support the work of men like Mr MacAnally there must come a point where they have to think twice before slandering a great industry and all who work in it. They cannot make these irresponsible charges with impunity.'

The television coverage that night was balanced, with the airline research getting the headline but with MacAnally appearing at the end of each report, thus ensuring that the argument remained alive.

The newspaper comment writers were unanimous:

Plantacon questions still require an answer, the *New York Times* headline summed them up.

The paper said:

The plantacon controversy rages on. We now have two sets of scientific studies contradicting each other. There are many reasons why the questions they raise must be answered: we must know the truth about plantacon (and this newspaper hopes it will be cleared, for the economic and energy benefits are obvious). We must know how two sets of studies can produce such contrasting results. And we may learn much about the attitudes and actions of both industry and the environmental lobby. In our view Senator Chris Wilkins is right to press for a hearing. Whether he needs to press for a bill at this point is another question, but if it gives added urgency to the hearings and the debate generally it is probably a useful initiative.

Lionel North's syndicated column took a different view.

With every day Mr Sam MacAnally looks a more likely candidate for fraud of the decade than for its outstanding environmentalist.

This column raised questions last week about his attacks on plantacon, one of the great cost and energy savers of the last fifty years.

Those questions are given fresh weight by the work of no less than five reputable scientists who have all looked into the questions Mr MacAnally raised and found them without foundation.

Plantacon particles are not falling onto the ground in significant quantities.

Children near airports are not being affected by plantacon.

Children near airports can be just as bright and alert as children elsewhere.

That's what these scientists say.

So what does Mr MacAnally do?

Does he apologise and withdraw? No.

Does he scientifically criticise the scientists? No, he can't, because he is not a scientist. He has no qualifications.

Does he raise any factual or methodological or any other serious question over their work? No, because presumably there are none.

What he does is attack their integrity. He suggests they have been bought.

This is the behaviour of a charlatan.

While I sympathise with Senator Ed Eberhard who says Congress should forget the whole thing, I don't agree.

Let them go ahead and hold a hearing. The issue will soon not be plantacon but Mr MacAnally and his Green friends.

And the humiliation of Mr MacAnally is a consummation devoutly to be wished.

MacAnally read the newspapers in his office. On the whole things were going according to plan.

The industry was bound to have its day but, apart from North's column, the newspaper editorials were still supporting a congressional hearing.

And a hearing was objective number one.

Still, a little bit of discrediting of the industry would do no harm at this point.

He took a key from his pocket and opened his desk drawer.

Inside it was the brown envelope with the New Jersey postmark, just as it had arrived a few days earlier.

He took out the slip of paper, re-read it, smiled, and rang Jackie Brown.

Washington Post, *March 4*

PLANTACON MANUFACTURERS WERE WARNED TO TEST FOR ENVIRONMENTAL THREAT

by Jacqueline Brown, Environment Reporter

Plantacon manufacturers FEI (Fuel Efficient Industries) were warned by their own Chief Scientist that they should investigate the product's possible environmental effects before persuading the aviation industry to adopt it as a fuel additive.

This is revealed by a confidential memo, leaked to the Post, *and written by FEI chief scientist Alfred Bain nearly five years ago.*

The memo says:

> It's probable that not all of the plantacon will be burned up with the fuel and that particles will be released from the aircraft exhausts. These will probably be minimal but given its toxic nature we should perhaps carry out experimental work to ensure that there will be no environmental effects.

Sources close to the company say that no such tests were undertaken, probably becuse they would have delayed the mass production of plantacon for some time.

Testing of plantacon by aircraft manufacturers such as Boeing, McDonnell Douglas and Airbus in the US and engine manufacturers such as General Electric and Pratt and Whitney in the US and Rolls-Royce in the UK had already taken seven years and cost many millions of dollars.

Further delays would have stretched FEI's borrowings to the limit.

In any case, sources say, the company would hardly have been anxious to discover any environmental downside to plantacon as it may have caused its miracle additive to be 'still-born'.

Dr Bain last night refused to comment, and the company's Director of Public Affairs, Mr Dieter Partrell, said that he had no knowledge of the memo. 'It's conceivable that my colleague Dr Bain reconsidered the need for this work and therefore did not send the memo; I will discuss the matter with him tomorrow,' he said.

Environmentalist Sam MacAnally, head of ECO, said last night, 'This blows sky-high the industry's position that

*it is environmentally sensitive and that it's acted
responsibly. It's clear its own scientists were worried
about plantacon but the company didn't want to know
because it would delay the flow of profit.'*

In their Dupont Circle office MacAnally and Adrian
Carlisle read the story and chuckled with glee.

In his car on his way through the Lincoln Tunnel from
Manhattan to Hoboken Dieter Partrell heard the story
recounted on the radio and raged at his bewildered
chauffeur. 'Fuck Al and his bloody memo. Fuck
MacAnally.'

In his laboratory in the basement of FEI's factory, Al
Bain read the story expressionlessly.

There would be a row with Partrell today.

Still, Bain didn't regret his decision to post the memo
to MacAnally.

No one could prove it was him, and if this all went
wrong he was damned if that bastard Partrell was going
to take him, Al Bain, and his scientific colleagues down
with him.

WASHINGTON, D.C.

Senator Chris Wilkins arrived at his office in the Taft
building pleased with the way things were going.

He had already received nationwide TV coverage and
his office had lined up more interviews with influential
newspapers and magazines.

And judging by his postbag, the campaign was being
well received in his own state. 'I voted for you because I
believed you would put people first. You have vindicated
that vote,' wrote one constituent.

Wilkins was Connecticut-born and bred. His family had been relatively poor but a series of scholarships had earned him the education and the contacts he needed to get going in politics. He worked conspicuously hard in the election campaign of the Governor and thereby won an influential friend who was to be decisive later when Wilkins and two others of his own age fought a highly competitive primary to be Democratic candidate for the US Senate. Any one of the three would have made a good representative for the state but it was Wilkins who sensed that there was a liberal swing taking place. So his environmental-consumer-civil liberties coalition was formed. 'Quality of life' was his slogan. That, and undenied hints that he was the popular Governor's choice, did the trick. He won the primary, and by polling day was heading for a landslide.

He was convinced the plantacon bill would give him a dream start in Washington. This made all the more irritating the tension in his office caused by a difference of opinion between his top aides.

Tom Gamell, who as administrative assistant was his most senior advisor, continued to argue strongly that they should play it cool. From the start he had been unconvinced by the environmental case and the studies published by the industry had strengthened his view that the whole campaign was too risky for Wilkins at this point in his career. In particular, Gamell opposed the introduction of a bill. Wilkins could achieve his political objectives by raising questions without becoming inextricably linked to the black and white plantacon-must-go argument.

On the other hand, his number two aide, Carl Hanson, his legislative assistant, argued that it was a remarkable opportunity for Wilkins to prove that he could get things done.

Hanson, who saw his man going all the way to the White House and already had himself measured for domestic policy advisor when they got there, argued that the trouble with arriving in Washington with a reputation as a rising star is that expectations were high and, if you didn't make an early impact, people quickly decided you were all glitz and no substance.

When he saw the publicity Wilkins was getting, and the pleasure the young senator was obtaining from it, Gamell realised he was probably fighting a losing battle. Just the same, when Ed Eberhard got in touch, he changed Wilkins' diary in order to guarantee an early meeting.

Eberhard was accompanied by Eugene Remington and Nicola Kowalska, but it was the presence of a fourth person that Wilkins noted with some apprehension. Mick Graham, a silver-haired sixty-five year old, was a lawyer from his own state, a senior member of the party, and extremely influential.

Seeing that Wilkins was puzzled as to why he was there, Gamell slipped him a note. *'Mick Graham's a non-executive director of a small outfit that hires out executive aeroplanes to companies. And he has legal clients in the aviation industry. He's got a vested interest in the other side. Careful!'*

Remington began, oozing reassurance. He talked of the savings and the energy and export benefits of plantacon, and then spelt out the industry's response . . . the promised environmental impact studies, the energy conservation awards, the regular reviews of plantacon and other aircraft emissions. 'We could not be doing more or spending more, Senator. If any problem emerges we will spot it and respond. But at this time there simply is no cause for concern.'

Eberhard chose this moment to join in. 'Chris, I

appreciate your concern for children, but the studies the environmentalists produced have been discredited. There really is no justification for pressing ahead unless they can come up with more convincing evidence than this.'

Mick Graham now engaged in the argument, bringing the pressure nearer to home. 'You know, Chris, in our state there are thousands of people who depend for their living on the aviation industry . . . not just companies like the one I'm associated with . . . it's engaged in air transport . . . but private air taxi firms, travel agents, and a number of technical support companies in the aviation industry. And of course I need hardly tell you we're the home state of United Parcel Service. I know they'll expect their senator to consider their problems.'

Wilkins nodded. 'I assure you, Mick, I'll take the needs of business into account. You've put its case well – and fairly. Tell me,' he said, looking to Remington, 'how do you account for the differences in the research results?'

'Senator, I'm not a scientist, but I understand that there're a variety of ways whereby different findings could emerge. It's partly to do with the way the work was done. And even if there were IQ differences between groups of children there could, I'm told, be a variety of reasons for it other than plantacon. But, as I've said, we're happy to support further research.'

Wilkins rose. 'Well, I'm relieved to hear that you believe this matter can be cleared up. As I've said, I'd be as pleased as you if we can.'

Then came the sting in the tail. 'One thing's for sure,' he said, 'given your confidence in plantacon, you've obviously got nothing to fear from hearings.'

Eberhard, already on his feet, confident that the senator was backing off from hearings, now looked at

Wilkins with a combination of respect for his nerve and dislike for his confidence. 'Quite so,' he said between clenched teeth.

As she reached the door Nicola Kowalska suddenly turned. 'Just one thing more, Senator. Given your desire to approach this with an open mind, you may wish to let us see a copy of the bill at the draft stage – before it's introduced. We would be happy to make constructive comments.'

'No problem,' smiled Wilkins. 'Get in touch with Carl here. He'll arrange it.'

Nicola smiled back. She had, she felt, achieved the one gain for her side from the meeting.

And it was a considerable gain.

They wouldn't just comment on the draft bill. They would seek to water it down, word by word, clause by clause.

It was amazing what you could achieve with behind-the-scenes negotiation.

A senator, confronted with the political facts of life, could compromise in private in a way he wouldn't feel able to do in public.

Once they were outside she turned to the others. 'Obviously we'll try to block a hearing if we can. But I'm afraid there's little chance. That being the case, it would make sense to be more positive about it. Let's aim to surprise everyone by publicly welcoming it.'

Eberhard began to raise doubts but the Maine lawyer Mick Graham took him by the arm. 'The young lady's right, Ed. If you can't beat 'em, join 'em.'

Later, when they were on their own, sitting in the back of his car, Remington smiled at his campaign director. 'You handled that well. It strikes me you really want this hearing.'

'The way I look at it, Mr Remington . . .'

'Eugene . . .'

'Oh . . . yes . . . thank you . . .'

She smiled at him.

He felt warmed by it. He had been so worried about plantacon that he hadn't really noticed before – but she was a good-looking woman.

'The way I look at it, Eugene, plantacon is either good news or bad news.

'If it's bad news, it'll be difficult to save it, hearing or no hearing.

'If it's good news, then the hearing will work for us.

'In any case, if the hearing's going to take place we have to try to dictate the plays.

'Wilkins wants to make it *his* court of inquiry. I believe we can make it into an inquiry of *our own* . . . into MacAnally and his irresponsible approach to the whole affair. He's applied a lot of pressure to get a hearing. He could find the whole thing blows up in his face.'

She turned to look at him and, not for the first time, he noticed the glint of steel in her eyes.

Thank God, he thought – I've picked the right one.

She was a fighter, this woman.

And, he reckoned, a winner.

He began to relax. For the first time for days he felt it was probably going to be all right.

Nicola Kowalska gave him confidence.

He gave her another sideways glance.

She really was good looking.

She was wearing a short skirt and his eyes strayed to her legs.

For a fleeting moment he wondered . . . then . . . no . . . he had enough problems . . .

The car pulled up at the sidewalk. She thanked him for the lift, and he watched her get out of the car and begin to walk towards her office.

She was damn good looking . . .

The President of the United States was angry. He glowered at his Special Advisor for Domestic Affairs, Jack Donaghue. 'Why the hell wasn't I warned of this plantacon business before I made that speech in New York?

'You realise that I've been put in a damn difficult position.

'If I express concern, it'll look as if I go around praising people and products without knowing what I'm talking about.

'If I defend it, I could look as if I don't care about the kids involved.'

Donaghue was apologetic. 'I'm sorry, Mr President, but it hit us without any warning.'

'Well, Ed bloody Eberhard knew about it. He must have known about it when he made his input into the speech. The son-of-a-bitch has nailed us to the mast.'

Donaghue looked at the papers on his lap and shuffled his feet, embarrassed.

'Well, what do we do?' The President looked at him.

'Well, sir, knowing MacAnally, there'll be a question planted for your Press Conference tomorrow. I've drafted a reply.'

'Let's see it.'

The President put on his glasses and leaned over the desk, frowning with concentration. The draft reply was brief:

'*Plantacon has, as I said recently, revolutionised the aviation industry, cutting costs and saving energy, and these benefits have to be welcomed. And I do welcome them. However if environmental or public health disadvantages can be proved, my Administration will naturally weigh them in the balance and act, as always, in the overriding public interest.'*

He grunted. 'OK. It's bullshit and they'll know it, but it will do.'

He called in his Appointments Secretary.

'I promised Sam MacAnally of ECO a meeting. Fix it, will you?'

Washington Post, *March 10*

PRESSURE GROWS FOR EARLY CONGRESSIONAL HEARING INTO PLANTACON

by Jacqueline Brown, Environment Reporter

The likelihood of an early Congressional hearing into allegations that the fuel additive plantacon is an environmental hazard increased last night when Nicola Kowalska, coordinator of the industry's response, stated that it would not oppose hearings.

'We don't think hearings are necessary but are so confident of our case that we will not oppose them,' she said.

The President was asked about plantacon at his weekly press conference yesterday. He praised plantacon's contribution to energy savings but said if environmental or public health problems were identified the Administration would 'act, as always, in the overriding public interest'.

LONDON

It was the day for parliamentary questions to the Secretary of State for the Environment and Nick Bell was ready.

'Is the Right Honourable Gentleman aware of the five scientific studies indicating that pollution caused by plantacon is a threat to children? Will he investigate these charges immediately and if necessary place a temporary ban on the additive?'

There were a number of cries of 'hear, hear,' from his own side.

Tom Muldoon looked at the note carefully prepared by his civil servants. 'Plantacon is of enormous benefit to the aviation industry and to the nation. We would naturally look carefully at any environmental downside, but I'm informed that there is no evidence as yet that justifies the claims the honourable member and the environmental lobby has been making.'

The Speaker took the unusual step of allowing Bell a second stab at the question.

'Does the Secretary of State really believe that he can brush aside five studies as *insufficient evidence*? How many does he need? How many children must be harmed before he becomes less sanguine?'

Muldoon leaned over the dispatch box. 'The honourable member neglects to mention the five studies that contradict his own selective list in every way.'

There was laughter from MPs behind him but Bell was back on his feet. 'On a point of order, Mr Speaker, in view of the unsatisfactory nature of this reply I demand an emergency debate.' There were catcalls from the minister's friends and demands that Bell 'Sit down'.

The Speaker looked cross. 'Really, the honourable member knows this is not the time . . .'

But Bell knew what he was doing. He was going to irritate the Speaker and annoy other MPs but the headlines the next day would justify any passing unpopularity in the House.

'Mr Speaker,' he shouted, 'there are millions of

children being affected by this poison. If this House does not care, who will? I demand a debate.'

The Speaker rose. 'This is *not the time* and the honourable member knows it.'

Still the MP remained standing . . . still shouting.

The Speaker, furious now, pointed a threatening finger at Bell. '*Sit down. If the honourable member does not sit down he will leave me no choice* . . .'

Defiantly Bill stood firm.

He had no intention of leaving the Speaker with a choice.

And as he was forced to leave the chamber he looked up to Olly Witcomb in the gallery with a satisfied smile.

In fact, Bell was more than satisfied . . . he was over the moon.

Unless World War Three broke out overnight, he would be all over tomorrow's front pages. '*Uproar in House over plantacon; MP suspended after allegations of children being poisoned.*'

By this demonstration he had made the issue his own.

WASHINGTON, D.C.

It was 3 a.m. but still MacAnally was at his desk.

It was the first opportunity for some days to look at the reports from overseas.

He hadn't realised what an international *cause célèbre* the plantacon affair had become.

There had already been one furious row in the British House of Commons and more confrontations were expected. Olly Witcomb was doing well, keeping the story in the papers. The BBC television programme *Panorama* was due to do a forty-minute special. There were rumours of a row between British Airways and UK Ambassador on how to handle the crisis. And the Cabinet ministers responsible for environmental and transport matters were said to be at loggerheads.

The European airlines were engaged in a war of words with the Greens in Germany and France, and a European Parliament debate was scheduled. In addition the issue was getting parliamentary attention in almost every one of the EC member countries.

In Japan there had been a spectacular row in the Diet between two MPs, one from the Socialist party accusing a Liberal Democrat, Ichiro Hashimoto, of being on the payroll of the industry. Both had been suspended for a day.

The Socialist, Mit'sura Hasegawa, was threatening to take it further.

His charge was that Hashimoto had been provided with information in his role as a member of the Diet and had then used that information for financial gain. Hashimoto was, therefore, acting corruptly.

Hasegawa now threatened to make the charges outside of the Diet chamber.

He was confining Hashimoto to two options: either he sued for libel, or he did not – the latter meaning, claimed Hasegawa, that he was guilty.

All this was keeping plantacon on the Japanese front pages.

Liz Scullen had brilliantly wound up the Australian media and Dr Bruce Cossens was having the time of his life appearing on radio and television daily. So enthusiastic was the coverage that the Australian television programme *Seven Days* was being sued by an airline for libel over charges it had made that the airline's management was environmentally irresponsible. (Even Liz Scullen thought the programme had gone over the top.)

From all over the world ECO groups had sent in press clippings and reports of growing concern.

MacAnally noted that a view gaining common currency throughout the world was that what happened in the US would determine the fate of plantacon everywhere.

It was typically expressed in an editorial in the London *Times*:

The world will watch with interest the upcoming plantacon hearings in the US Senate. Because half the world's aviation activity takes place in North America, and because of the overwhelming American influence on the whole industry, the American response to this challenge to their 'wonder additive' will undoubtedly determine what happens elsewhere.

His own overseas colleagues had been making the same point, including Machiko. 'I can get the publicity,' she told him on the phone, 'but Japan will only ban plantacon when everybody else does. All I can do is make people aware of what's at stake so that it's more easily accepted when the time comes.'

MacAnally tossed the file onto his desk.

They were right of course.

It was the battle on American soil that mattered.

And it was really only about to begin.

Part Five

BATTLEGROUND USA

WASHINGTON, D.C.

MARCH

Everyone knew it – the environmentalists, the industry, the politicians.

If it was to win world-wide, ECO had first to win in the United States.

Its best chance of doing that was to mobilise the people in greatest danger . . . those who lived near airports.

MacAnally made it clear to grassroots organiser Molly Macintosh that he wanted quick results.

'The industry's going to throw money at this like it's going out of style,' he said. 'Its aim will be to neutralise the issue at federal level. *Our best chance is to put pressure on Congress at state level . . . at the grassroots. We've got to make this whole thing about votes . . . and we've got to do it soon.*'

Macintosh, an irrepressible, ginger-haired, thirty-one year old from Wisconsin and with ten years' experience, now set out to find local organisers.

They had to be good.

They had to be self-starters, capable of taking full responsibility for the campaign in their own area.

They had to be able to use the nationally provided information intelligently, be presentable, and be efficient.

Kathy Smith was ideal. A thirty-seven-year-old school-teacher who lived and worked near Portland International Jetport in the state of Maine, she was a passionately committed environmentalist, already a member of other local groups. And, being a schoolteacher, she was accustomed to speaking to, and organising people.

Molly Macintosh met Smith in De Milo's waterfront restaurant in Portland. Over bowls of steaming clam chowder and plates of scallops and salad, they plotted a campaign to take place in communities around the airport.

Kathy Smith committed herself to put together a local organising committee from friends, neighbours, members of the PTA, and members of other local environmental groups.

They would leaflet the whole community, advertise in the local newspaper, and hold a press conference – all intended to attract a big crowd to a public meeting.

They hoped the meeting would help to launch a petition and letter-writing campaign to apply pressure on the state's representatives in Washington, and also to activate local councils, the state legislature, and the Governor.

Once all this was under way, there would be a major demonstration by parents and children in the vicinity of the airport.

The public meeting took place in a school hall in a leafy street half a mile from where the planes landed and took off.

Because this was the home state of Hal Frankle, the key Senate committee chairman, Macintosh decided to make a flying visit to support Smith. Also on the platform was Teddy Dalgleish, a local science lecturer who had been briefed by ECO to answer the more technical questions.

There was an encouraging turnout; more than 250, many of them members of the school's PTA.

They began by showing the campaign video. Professionally made, it told its viewers all about plantacon, described the five incriminating studies, and concluded by asking parents to launch their own local campaign. The aim: a ban on plantacon.

When the video ended there was silence in the crowded hall. Many of the parents were visibly shaken.

Then Kathy Smith spoke . . . providing still more facts . . . asking for support.

Molly Macintosh was impressed by the schoolteacher's style – informative, concerned, but not emotive.

But she also observed that the first speaker had taken a seat near the front, on the right-hand side of the hall. Thus, when he stood, he had only to turn slightly to his left to have the whole gathering within his sights. It was the mark of a professional.

'I've seen him before,' she whispered to Smith. 'His name's Turner. He's a freelance lobbyist for the airlines. He gets hired to go wherever there are meetings like this . . . you know, about night flying, or people objecting to the siting of an airport . . . that sort of thing.'

Turner was fair-haired, tubby, tanned, glossy-looking in a fawn mohair suit. Smith felt he had all the instant likeability of an encyclopedia salesman.

But she soon realised that he was good at what he did.

'Let me be straight with you,' he began. 'I work for the airline industry.'

There was a stir of interest, someone called out 'shame', and others began to hiss.

But Turner was unperturbed. 'It's easy to hiss,' he said calmly. 'It's easy to shout down those we don't want to hear – much harder to listen.

'But, if you *really* care, you should want *all* the facts.

'I just want you to hear a bit more.

'If you then still feel like hissing me, then that's OK with me. Hiss away.'

Someone called out, 'We don't need to hear more', but other voices began to demand that Turner be heard.

He waited patiently until there was quiet.

Then he waited some more.

It was beautifully done. By allowing himself to become the underdog – a man asking only that he should be heard – Turner had succeeded in obtaining the audience's undivided and even sympathetic attention.

'The video you've seen and the presentation by Ms Smith were based on five scientific studies. And, of course, they do exist.

'But you should have been told that there are five other scientific studies that completely refute them.

'She didn't mention those.

'Not even in passing.

'Ask yourself, why not?

'If ECO really wants to tell you all they know, why didn't they tell you that?

'Second, they haven't told you that the industry refutes all their claims: it denies that plantacon contaminates your land. It denies that your children are affected.

'Why haven't they told you that?

'And have they told you that the industry has offered more research, regular monitoring, cooperation with any governmental inquiries?

'No, they haven't told you that either. Why not?

'So the first point I make to you is that – while you're of course concerned by what you've been told . . . as I would be in your place – you've not been given the whole story.

'OK, they've got you worried about plantacon.

'But *don't panic*.

'Ask to know more.

'Ask to know *a lot more* before you're conned into premature action.'

Seeing the audience was impressed, Molly Macintosh decided enough was enough.

They had to regain control of the meeting – and quickly.

So she interrupted.

'Mr Turner says we haven't told you all we know. Let's look at what *he* hasn't told you,' she said.

'*He* hasn't told you he's a professional PR man paid to travel the country attending local meetings to cover up for the airlines whenever they're causing environmental damage. In the old days they would have called him a hired gun.

'*He* hasn't told you that the five scientists who've refuted the findings are all paid for by the industry – they were hired to refute the evidence – whereas ours are all public servants, professors and lecturers in universities.

'That's why we didn't mention their studies. Frankly, we took for granted – and we expect you to take for granted – that the industry would produce its own highly paid scientists.

'But who's going to believe them?'

'That's not fair . . . ' Turner tried to interrupt.

But Macintosh, raising her voice, talked him down. '*He* also hasn't told you that the reason the airlines are anxious to refute the evidence is that banning plantacon will cost them billions of dollars. That's why he's here.

'Who do you think he cares about?

'The community?

'Or the industry?

'Who would you trust to care for your children . . . Kathy Smith, a local schoolteacher, or Mr Turner, a professional PR man from out of town?

'Kathy Smith is paid to care for your children; Mr Turner is paid to care for the airlines.'

But the PR man had his supporters. A man in his fifties, with a weather-beaten face, greying hair, dressed in overalls as if he had come to the meeting on his way home from work, rose hesitantly to his feet.

'With respect to you, Miss, I work at the airport and so do many others in this community.

'It's our industry you're saying tells lies and is poisoning our children.

'If there are two sides to the story then we should hear them both. This should be properly investigated.

'I'm happy to support an inquiry. But I'm not happy to support a campaign to ban plantacon until that's happened.'

He sat down to considerable applause.

Kathy rose to reply. 'Of course there should be further investigation . . . we're not afraid of that. Despite what Mr Turner says, we're not afraid of the facts. But how do we get an urgent inquiry of the right quality? Only by demanding it – and making clear to the authorities and the airlines that if they don't cooperate we will insist on an outright ban. And by making it clear that we won't vote for a congressman unless he's committed to putting our children first.'

Macintosh judged that at this point the mood of the meeting was evenly balanced.

But such had been the tension in the hall that she and Smith had forgotten Dalgleish, the local scientist.

A thin, pale-faced young man with a small moustache, he took off his glasses and gestured with them while he spoke.

'Look, I haven't conducted this research but I've studied the findings.

'I have to tell you, as a scientist, but also as a local parent – I have two kids myself – that we have every reason to be concerned.

'The research was not just done in this country but other countries. It's solidly based.

'But the main point I want to make to you is this:

'If ECO is wrong, we lose nothing, because that will emerge from further research. In which case, plantacon can be re-introduced.

'But if they're right, and plantacon is the hazard we believe it is, any delay could make things worse for our children.

'So what makes sense? I think we should at least press for a ban until the questions are answered.

'Otherwise our children are being used as guinea pigs for ongoing research.'

That did it. There was loud applause. They were winning.

Molly Macintosh leaned over and whispered to Kathy Smith to break the meeting up while they were on top.

'Let me say I respect what the gentleman who works at the airport has said,' Smith said, looking to the man in the overalls. 'But I also think Ted Dalgleish is right. We should take the safer course until the industry can prove its case. I'm going to end the main meeting now, but those who would like to be involved should stay behind so we can get your names and plan our campaign.'

At the end of the meeting thirty stayed and were formed into a local group.

In the days that followed things moved quickly,

Kathy Smith proving a live-wire of whom MacAnally himself would have been proud.

A petition of 5,000 names was compiled and presented to Senator Frankle in front of local television cameras.

As local organisations came on board, they issued their own press releases, thus maintaining the flow of media stories.

A debate at another local PTA was covered live by local radio and well reported in local newspapers.

Confronted by questioners while attending a state fair, the Governor promised to take the issue seriously.

And the demonstration and rally in front of the airfield, climaxing in the action – pioneered by Liz Scullen in Australia – of thousands of men, women and children holding hands in an unbroken chain around its perimeter, was heavily featured on local television.

So the grassroots campaign got underway.

The Portland campaign was repeated all over the country . . .

In San Diego, California . . .

Columbus, Ohio . . .

Des Moines, Iowa . . .

San Antonio, Texas . . .

Nashville, Tennessee . . .

Tampa, Florida . . .

And the letters and petitions mounted in congressional offices.

Under pressure from local media, one congressman after another promised constituents they would 'look into it'.

One meeting that received little media attention but was more than usually explosive took place in the town of Glenburnie on the fringes of Baltimore–Washington International Airport. Held in a school hall in Meadow Brook it drew its audience from three neighbouring districts, Glenbrook, Meadow Brook and Willow Dale, all of them close to the airport and the industrial park where Todd Birk's Airlift International had its depot.

Free for an evening and wanting to test grassroots reaction for himself, MacAnally had personally driven over from Washington D.C. in company with Adrian Carlisle.

It was, however, to turn out to be an unrepresentative meeting, not only because of MacAnally's attendance but because sitting in the front row, glowering as usual, was Todd Birk.

The air freight man hardly waited for MacAnally to complete his speech before getting to his feet and launching an attack.

'I see at least ten people here who I know work at the airport. Their families depend on it for their living.

'I see two men here who work for me.

'Are you telling them your anti-industry campaigns and loaded scientific studies justify their industry being crippled and their families losing their wage packets?

'Because I'm telling you and I'm telling this meeting that if you and your fellow weirdos prevail my company will fold and those two men over there and several hundred others will be out of work. And that's only the start. It'll hit the whole industry.'

He pointed at MacAnally. 'This man has not mentioned jobs. Not mentioned the economy. Not mentioned your standard of living.

'Because he doesn't damn well care.

'He's a typical rich college kid on an ego trip, abusing a system you decent people finance with your work.'

MacAnally, contriving to look unsurprised by Birk's furious intervention, calmly sat it out, then quietly said: 'Of course we care about the economy, about the ability of people to work, and of course we appreciate what plantacon offers.'

He turned his eyes from Birk and addressed the rest of the audience. 'But we also care about the health of your children.

'Sometimes we have to make difficult choices.

'Surely if the scientific evidence shows that the children in this area – *your* children – are being brain damaged, or threatened with brain damage, you, their parents, would want their well-being to come first.'

'If? *If?*' roared Birk. 'That's the point, isn't it? You're not even able to be definite about it. There are as many studies to say plantacon is safe as there are studies to say it's dangerous. You want us to destroy our industry and economy *just in case* you're right. Why the hell should we?

'You talk about difficult choices.

'When did you ever have to make a difficult choice?

'You haven't done a proper day's work in your life.

'We're the ones making the choices and I, for one, choose not to have my life screwed up by you.'

There was a smattering of applause as Birk sat down. A man leaned over and enthusiastically patted him on the back.

'You let him have it, Todd,' called another.

MacAnally did his best to spell out the scientific evidence with Birk muttering to his neighbours at the front and swelling with indignation like a simmering volcano. But the air freight man had his employees and other supporters well organised. They began barracking.

When other members of the audience called out that they wanted to hear more, they too were shouted down.

The mood became ugly, neighbour turning against neighbour. Those uncommitted parents who MacAnally needed to reach began to slip away.

The campaigner judged there was little point in going on. They had achieved all they could. But, when the meeting ended, only a handful volunteered to help and they had to run a gauntlet of jeers from Birk's employees as they walked to their cars.

As MacAnally and Carlisle were themselves just about to drive off, there was a tap on the window.

MacAnally wound it down and found Birk's malevolent red face thrust almost into his own. He could smell the alcohol on the other's breath.

'Listen, you mother-fucker, you're not going to screw up my company.'

MacAnally drew back from the shouting head that was now right in the car.

'Look, Mr Birk, I understand your problem . . .'

'*Understand . . . understand*', roared the head. 'I don't give a fuck whether you understand or not. I don't need your understanding. I don't need you at all. So let me make it clear, asshole . . . if you and your crazy Commie friends don't lay off plantacon I'm going to make damn sure you aren't able to damage anyone else . . . ever again. Is that fucking clear?'

MacAnally, heart thumping, tried to look calm. 'Are you threatening me, Mr Birk?'

'Too fucking right I'm threatening you. Just like you and your Commie friends are threatening my company. So get the hell out of here while you still can.'

The head vanished.

MacAnally looked at Carlisle who had gone white but said nothing.

Then a frightening banging began, as Birk's supporters gathered around the car and began to hit it on the roof with their fists.

It was followed by a shattering of glass at the back of the car.

'Christ,' said Carlisle. 'They're smashing your lights. Let's get the hell out of this place.'

MacAnally turned on the ignition, hit the accelerator, and seconds later his vehicle literally burst out of the car park.

Without speaking to each other, they drove away from Baltimore.

Back to Washington.

Just as fast as they could.

Only later did MacAnally recall Birk's words . . . and in particular the threats about what would happen if he didn't 'lay off plantacon'.

It was exactly the same threat that had been on the postcard.

The one he received in reply to his initial letter to the airlines and air freight companies.

The one he received with a Baltimore postmark.

Within a few weeks Molly Macintosh was able to report to Sam MacAnally that there were highly visible and vocal anti-plantacon campaigns in 44 of the 51 states, and in nearly 300 communities within those states. Congress was feeling the pressure.

But lobbyist Jay Sandbach's report was mixed. 'The bad news is that most of the politicians are simply saying they'll listen to the evidence. They're not promising to act.

'But the good news is that it's on their agendas and they're getting sufficient pressure from their constituencies to want to be let off the hook.'

'What lets them off the hook?' asked Carlisle.

'Hearings,' said Sandbach. 'That's why I said it's good news. I think you've got the head of steam you need to get the hearings.'

Encouraged, MacAnally arranged a planning meeting with the man who would be his congressional spearhead, Senator Chris Wilkins.

*

'They're raising a storm within the communities close to airports,' Nicola Kowalska told the war council when it met in her hastily rented suite of offices in K Street. 'And this is beginning to filter back via their congressmen.

'My guess is that a hearing's inevitable.'

Eugene Remington frowned. 'What are we doing to counter their local campaigns?'

'We've had people at the meetings, skilled PR people, and we've also been encouraging local union members to go. While the mood of the meetings is favouring the environmentalists, we've raised some doubts.

'We're also conducting a major media operation using Ted Scroeder's consultancy.'

Scroeder was a short, thick-set man with massive thighs. When he stood he looked so securely anchored to the ground that Nicola doubted even a tank could knock him down. Scroeder was also the best in his business. Crisp and confident, he said, 'We've issued press briefings to every local newspaper, radio station and TV station within the vicinity of airports.

'We've sent media people in wherever the environmentalists have been most active.

'As you can see from the file of cuttings, almost every story has at least had a rebuttal from us. Also of the two hundred and ten local TV and radio stories to date, we've had a spokesman on seventy per cent.

'But the problem is that we can't initiate the stories. It's the environmentalists who make the charges and set the pace; we're inevitably on the defensive and this shows in the coverage.'

'Let's not mince words,' said Dieter Partrell, red-faced as always, and impatient. 'What we've just been told is that we're losing the local media battle. Getting less coverage.'

Nicola Kowalska spoke quickly. 'Mr Partrell is right, but what's happening now was to be expected.

'The environmentalists are fighting on their best ground. We were bound to be on the defensive at this stage.'

'So what do you propose to do about it?'

'Do what we did at national level. Let them use up their energy first, and then we respond with our own press conferences, local meetings, scientific presentations, etcetera. Also mobilise the trade unions and others to fight back.

'Above all, we have to use the *national* media to counter the *local* media . . . because we stand a better chance of getting more balanced debate going nationally. Less emotion, less hysteria.'

Seeing they were still concerned, she attempted to calm them by arguing that the pace of their campaign was about right. There were dangers in doing too much too early.

'The key to success is to manipulate the other side into peaking too soon. We're still months away from the moment of truth.'

She outlined the programme.

'For a start, we seek to avoid a hearing. But only privately, because *publicly* we have to maintain we're not afraid of a hearing.

'If there *is* a hearing, we try to turn it to our advantage. In particular we aim to stop a bill emerging from the Committee. If *that* fails and there *is* a bill, we seek to water it down at the mark-up stage.

'Then we try to influence the Senate vote. If we lose *that* vote, we apply pressure on the House of Representatives to water the bill down.

'If it still survives, we undermine it in the conference committee . . . that's the meeting of a small group drawn from each House and charged with producing the final compromise bill.

'If we're still unhappy, we try to affect the final Senate vote.

'Finally, *if all else fails*, we go for a Presidential veto.'

The lobbyist Alexander Green explained that even that was simplifying it.

There were hundreds of ways to delay and frustrate the measure.

'My own view is that we're going to win and that the environmentalists will be routed, but if it goes wrong we must make our number one priority avoiding an outright ban on plantacon.

'That's crucial because a ban gives you no room for manoeuvre.'

'How do you do that?' asked Partrell.

'By opening up another front. We'll try to get the bill to set plantacon emission standards. And a timetable for reductions in levels of emission. By the time we play around with that and make it as complex as possible the heat will be out of the issue. So, even if we've lost the argument we could well come out of the whole thing having lost very little else.

'In my view the worst that's possible is having to comply with fairly relaxed emission standards. The environmentalists will have been thrown a bone, but with hardly any meat on it.

'The politicians can claim they've taken action.

'And the public will get bored.'

Partrell looked unhappy. What the lobbyist was describing – 'opening up another front' – a compromise – sounded a lot like a sell-out to him.

But – his temper under control for once – he decided to let it ride.

The scenario Nicola Kowalska had outlined gave him

plenty of time to decide what to do.

One thing: *he* was paying Green, not the war council, and Green would be making no further proposals of that sort. Not after he, Partrell, had spoken to him.

He turned his attention back to the meeting. Nicola Kowalska was summing up their strategy: 'We slow the controversy down. Get the heat out of the issue. Keep it low on the political agenda. Then, once it's off the boil, we quietly but steadily build up our side of the story. We produce another series of scientific studies, a poll of workers demanding fair play for the industry, more figures on cost and energy savings, etcetera.'

Green intervened. 'Also, we've found a conservation group concerned with energy. It's prepared to say that the pollution evidence is not sufficiently strong to counterbalance the enormous benefits of energy savings. We're going to build this up as an "environmentalists divided" story. It will do ECO no good at all.'

Remington looked pleased. 'Good,' he said. 'With a bit of luck we'll find the environmentalists have shot their bolt.'

Then, almost as if reassuring himself, he began to tick off on his fingers what he saw as their advantages:

'They've no more news stories coming; all they can do is repeat the same message. We're the one with the new stories.

'Remember, they have to force change. We only have to protect the status quo.

'They have to keep building momentum, but we only have to ride it out.

'Once the initial skirmishes are over the pressure will be on them, not us.'

Afterwards Nicola adjourned to her office for a meeting with Scroeder and Green.

They decided on a three stage plan:

First, there would be an intensive local media operation on the 'plantacon cleared' theme. ECO must not have it all their own way at the grassroots.

Second, Scroeder would encourage national newspaper features calling for a balanced review of the facts. He would also seek articles challenging the credibility of the environmentalists from columnists such as Lionel North.

Third, there would be a programme of national advertising, all with positive messages about plantacon.

They reviewed an advertising campaign for TV, radio and newspapers.

The TV commercial began with warm pictures of people at airports and on planes.

'. . . *Americans fly every year . . .*

'*It's the aviation industry that keeps families together* . . . (picture of grandmother greeting parents and children at airport) . . .

'. . . *The airlines who make your holiday trips possible* . . . (picture of families on a beach) . . .

'. . . *The airlines who create unprecedented opportunities for travel throughout the world* . . . (pictures of Rome, Paris, London) . . .

'. . . *The airlines who enable business to operate efficiently* . . . (picture of man working on plane) . . .

'*In the past this important industry has had two problems* . . . *energy* . . . *cost* . . .

'*Plantacon solved these. It made it cheaper to fly. And it conserves energy . . .*

'*Now some extremist groups say plantacon should be banned* . . . (pictures of long-haired, violent-looking protestors with placards; not ECO people, but who was to know?) . . .

'*Why do they want it banned? Because, they say, the*

emissions from airplane exhausts can harm children. But it isn't true. (Picture of headlines saying 'plantacon cleared by fresh studies') . . . *Five top scientists have all produced reports clearing plantacon of being a pollutant.*

'*You know, we care about our environment . . . and our country . . . that's why we donated several million dollars last year to environmental causes.*

'*We care about safety . . . that's why we spend millions of dollars a year improving it . . .*

'*We care about being sure . . . that's why we'll review exhaust emissions every six months, that's why we've set up an independent research institute, why we're cooperating with governmental agencies on pollution monitoring and action.*

'*We are convinced we can have plantacon and a clean environment.*

(Picture of children looking up at an aeroplane in the sky.)

'*Don't let the doomsday merchants destroy progress. Progress with care. It's the American way. It's our way.*

'*Back your airlines.*

'*And, remember . . . we're parents too.*'

A second commercial, for local television, showed a working man standing by a fence with an airport in the background.

'*Hi. I'm Colin Dennison and I and my family live close to O'Hare, one of the world's busiest airports. So if anyone has to be convinced plantacon is safe it's me.*

'*And I am convinced.*

'*I've been to a briefing by independent scientists. They've proved there is no cause for alarm.*

'*And I know my own children. And frankly I resent the suggestion that they're backward. My son is top of his class. My daughter has won a scholarship to college. Who*

*are these outside environmentalists and what gives them
the right to scare our neighbourhoods? To undermine our
property values? To frighten our children? What are their
scientific qualifications? I can tell you our local ECO
campaigners have none.*

'*I say, let's not be talked out of the benefits of plantacon
by such people playing on our fears.*

'*Let's back our airlines and those who work in them.*

'*Let's tell our congressmen, we're not afraid.*

'*Let's tell them to back plantacon.*'

The campaign hit the air waves later that week.

At first MacAnally tried to counter the advertising
campaign by condemning the ads and the money being
spent on them.

On this point, NBC's *Today* programme staged a
furious debate between MacAnally and Lionel North.

'Why's Mr MacAnally running scared?' taunted the
columnist. 'Has he gone too far this time? Is he afraid he
and his nutty friends are going to be shown up as
scaremongers?'

'Our science stands up and our case stands up,'
MacAnally replied. 'But the industry is spending
millions ensuring only their case is heard. They're trying
to buy their way out of trouble.'

'That's not true. You get the free publicity, they
don't,' countered North. 'The publicity has been
completely unbalanced in your favour.'

'This should not be decided by money or TV
advertising,' MacAnally replied. 'It should be decided
soberly, scientifically. What we need is a Congressional
hearing. I believe we'll get one now, because senators
and members of the House of Representatives will be
appalled by this attempt to buy the argument.'

'Why should they be appalled?' asked North cynically. 'Don't they use the same techniques to get elected?'

Afterwards the two met in the TV studio's guest room. North, stirring his coffee, walked over to the environmentalist. 'Good knock-about stuff, Sam.'

MacAnally looked at him contemptuously. 'For Christ's sake, Lionel, why do you have to treat this like a game?'

'Because it *is* a game, Sam. Come on, admit it, if not to me, at least to yourself. It's a game. To you, it's goodies and baddies. You see yourself like the good gunfighter who rides into town, helps the decent, hardworking homesteaders see off the evil ranchers, then rides off into the sunset, heading for another right to wrong.'

'Bullshit!'

'Is it, Sam? You think about it. What matters to you most? The issue itself? The children you claim you care so much about? Or is it the fight?'

He looked at MacAnally shrewdly. 'You know, I hadn't seen your name in the papers for nearly a year before you got that award. Were you running out of campaigns, Sam? Were you looking for a cause? Did you need a new issue? Did you need plantacon as much as the airlines do? To survive?'

MacAnally hesitated.

He knew he had said exactly that. To Marie that night in New York. '*We need an issue*', he had said, '*black and white . . .*'

'I probably have said that at some time, Lionel,' he eventually conceded. 'But so what? It doesn't follow that we manufacture causes. Or even have to search for them. There are more environmental causes than people to fight them.'

He turned defence into attack. 'Why don't you ask *yourself* a question, Lionel.

'Ask yourself what happens if I'm right and I win. I'll tell you what happens – we save a lot of kids from damage.

'Then ask what happens if I'm right but *you* win. What are you going to feel like when the truth comes out? As it eventually will. Will you feel any guilt about the kids harmed because you didn't give a damn . . . not even enough of a damn to consider the matter objectively?'

'*Objectively*', snorted North. 'I'm surprised the word doesn't stick in your throat. Since when have you been objective?'

'Maybe I'm not required to be. But you set yourself up as a commentator, advisor to the reading public. Aren't they entitled to some objectivity from you?'

North laughed. 'Good God, no. They read me because they know I'm not objective. They *know* I'm prejudiced. They share my prejudices. That's why they're with me all the way.'

MacAnally shook his head in wonder. He couldn't remember when he had disliked a man so much. 'Your cynicism leaves me speechless,' he said.

'I wish it did,' said North.

MacAnally struggled to control his temper and, perhaps fortunately, was rescued by the announcement of the arrival of his taxi.

While in New York for the *Today* show, MacAnally called on Justin Lord. He found the commodities king looking pleased to see him.

'How's it going?' he asked, waving MacAnally to a seat.

'It looks like you already know that,' MacAnally said, amused by the huge pile of clippings on the coffee table.

Lord chuckled. 'I've not missed much,' he said. 'I must admit I'm having more fun than I can ever remember. I only wish I could be doing the campaigning myself.'

MacAnally thought that it was the first time he had heard Lord laugh.

He watched the older man shuffling the clippings. Rubbing his hands with glee. Stopping to point to one story, then another.

He was like a child with a scrapbook. Or a stamp album.

Christ, thought MacAnally, Lord really *was* having fun.

For the first time, he found himself actually liking the man.

'How did you get all this media publicity?' Lord asked.

MacAnally described how it worked.

Influential journalists were listed under a number of headings: environmental reporters, writers on health and safety and children's issues, political reporters and columnists, and so on.

A press officer was assigned to each.

Then newspapers were listed and broken down into sections, opinion writers and columnists, op-ed pages, letters columns, news pages.

Each was used in the most appropriate way.

Media enquiry desks were set up dealing with the scientific argument, the political struggle, and the general campaign, all of them either manned by specialists or ready to refer journalists to a panel of experts who could easily be reached by phone.

Radio and TV sound bites were prepared on every angle of the debate and circulated to local groups for use on local radio and TV stations.

Everybody involved was fed a small number of key slogans or lines to use repeatedly . . .

. . . Like, '*Is it right people should be able to fly more cheaply at the expense of our children's health?'* . . .

It was hoped that if these things were said often enough they would start to sink in.

The campaign was also encouraging parents in target communities to create photo opportunities with their children.

One involved children carrying placards saying, *'While they're flying you on your business trip they're driving me out of my mind'*.

This had caused considerable controversy within the campaign. Some felt it was going over the top. MacAnally, infuriated by the industry's advertising campaign, had brushed the complaints aside.

All this MacAnally now told Justin Lord. 'This is why we'll get the hearings. It's the only way the Congressmen can appease parents in their constituencies.

'But we've got a way to go to win the national debate.

'I'm getting worried that the scientific world is obviously unconvinced and divided.'

Lord looked surprised. 'I wasn't aware of that.'

'No, well, it hasn't shown up in the newspapers yet. But it will. We're bound to annoy a lot of scientists by questioning the integrity of the industry's studies. Scientists don't like scientific arguments reduced to personalities. They especially don't like the suggestion that scientists can be bought. Like any group, they tend to unite when attacked.

'But it's more than that: they're genuinely not convinced that plantacon can have any effect at that level of exposure. And the medical and scientific journals remain dubious too. The scientific world is inherently conservative.'

'How are we going to counter that?'

MacAnally noticed the 'we' and smiled to himself. Who ever said Lord was only excited by commodity prices?

'By reducing the importance of the scientific argument and building up the political one,' he replied.

'You mean stirring up public concern beyond the point where the scientific facts matter?'

'Well, if you put it like that . . .'

'You surprise me, Mr MacAnally. I knew you were good, but I didn't know you were so ruthless.'

'We have to do what we have to do, Mr Lord. I've been in this kind of game before. The point is, scientists can't *always* let politicians off the hook. Clearly they can't in the case of plantacon or there wouldn't be so much scientific controversy.

'It's where there's uncertainty that politicians have to earn their money – face up to their responsibilities and take the best decision possible in the circumstances.

'That's what's about to happen. The plantacon decision is becoming a *political* decision, not a scientific one. That means votes. So what we have to do now is make it look like they're choosing between the financial interests of big business on the one hand, and the entirely separate interests of the people on the other . . . and get the people watching and the politicians sensitive to the fact that the people are watching.'

Lord was enthralled. 'What are you going to do about all this television and radio advertising?' he asked.

'Well, we're doing our best to counter it. Actually I think their advertising may be counter-productive.'

'Why?'

'Because it's keeping the issue before the public just when we were beginning to have trouble keeping it there.

'They're contributing to the pressure on Washington, not reducing it – and at their expense. We would have had difficulty maintaining the publicity momentum; now they're spending millions of dollars doing it for us. It's what in football is called an own goal.'

'Are you planning any TV advertising of your own?'

'Can't afford it.'

'Is the money I've provided insufficient?'

MacAnally paused. The truth was he hadn't thought about it. He had never had such resources before, and therefore had not even considered TV advertising. But he knew its value. It was the one way you could guarantee you got your message across in exactly your own way, at the time you wanted it heard or seen, and to the audience you wanted to reach. Not only that but paid advertising tended to generate even more media interest. It had the effect of telling the public that, 'there is a real row going on here; you'd better be aware of it.'

'I guess we could do some,' he said.

'Well, if you want some more money, just ring me.' Lord rose and taking MacAnally's hand said to him, 'I know the pressure you're under. And I appreciate what you're doing. If my money can help, don't hesitate . . .'

Sam told Lord he would come back to him and, as soon as he was back in Washington, discussed it with his team who were all for it. Molly Macintosh suggested the best value would be TV and radio spots on local stations in target communities.

So was born what became famous as the 'invisible poison' commercial.

The opening scene was a field with corn blowing in the wind.

In the distance planes could be seen taking off and landing on an airfield.

Slowly the camera panned up until all you could see was blue sky.

Then the voice:

'You can't see it.

'It's invisible.

'*But it's there . . . just blowin' in the wind . . .*'

(Low background music, Bob Dylan singing 'Blowin' in the Wind').

'*Eventually it will land . . . on the fruit or vegetables in your garden, on the grass or in the dust where your children play . . . and slowly, inexorably, it will build up in their blood until it begins to damage their brains . . .*

'*For some it's already too late. Their IQ has been reduced. Their ability to learn has been diminished. Their chances of success in life have been undermined.*

'*And all because the airlines want to increase their profits.*'

(A tiny speck appears in the sky now, growing slowly larger as a plane begins to approach.)

'*They call it the plantacon revolution.*

'*We call it the invisible cloud . . .*

'*The cloud over your child's life.*

'*The plantacon cloud.*'

(The plane roars into view and straight out of the picture. The camera pans back down to the field where a child is now seen running.)

The voice concludes: '*Tell your senator, tell your congressman, that the price of plantacon is too high.*'

The commercial appeared all over the US on local television stations near to airports.

The following week Congress received more letters and phone calls on one subject on one day since the heights of the controversy over the Vietnam war more than thirty years before.

That evening Senator Chris Wilkins was telephoned by Senator Hal Frankle, chairman of the Environmental Pollution Sub-committee of the Senate Public Works and Environment Committee. 'We'd better talk,' he said.

*

Before the meeting MacAnally and Wilkins got together to review their political objectives. These were:

a) go for an early hearing;

b) get politicians and staff members on the Hill under pressure from their constituencies, so that a Wilkins Bill would get priority over the hundreds of others queueing up in both Houses.

Wilkins had with Sandbach's help now won the support of another Senate pollution sub-committee member. Leighton Taverner, a Republican senator from Oregon, had been defeated by the airlines in a row about night-flying over a key Republican ward in his state. As a result he had nearly lost his Senate seat. He had reason to want revenge.

But when it came to getting a hearing, the key man was the chairman of the Public Works and Environment Committee, Senator Hal Frankle from Maine.

There could not have been a greater contrast than between Frankle, aged sixty-five, in his twenty-fifth year in the Senate and the eager young newcomer, Wilkins. Yet there was every reason to believe the former would be sympathetic.

Frankle had come to Washington when environmental issues were just beginning to be taken seriously. Furthermore he came from a state that took them more seriously than most.

A big man with white curly hair and grizzled features, he had won his spurs when the committee under Ed Muskie's leadership initiated the Clean Air Act and a variety of other worthwhile measures.

Yet he had won the trust of his party and the grudging respect of his Republican opponents for his determination to pursue the truth rather than jump on bandwagons. Over the years, as he had risen in seniority, becoming the chairman of one full Senate committee and two sub-committees, he had come to be suspicious of zealots because he had seen too many companies fail, too many good men and women thrown out of work, too many communities impoverished by ill-considered action. More than many of his colleagues he felt a responsibility to get it right – and damn the consequences. Of course he was helped by being enormously popular in his state and relatively safe from electoral defeat.

Wilkins, on the other hand, had been carried to success on an environmental tide.

And the post-election polls showed it was the younger voters who had swept him to office.

This he knew was a fickle constituency. Demanding. Impatient.

He had to get results to hold them.

Also, he had not connected well with business people in his constituency. Most of them had financed and voted for his Republican opponent.

So, at least for the moment, the political benefit for Wilkins lay with the environmental cause.

In any case, he genuinely believed in it.

Wilkins took MacAnally and Jay Sandbach to the meeting in Frankle's big office in the Russell Building. The veteran senator came round his desk and, shaking their hands, led them to a rectangular seating area – two armchairs and a sofa. Taking a well-worn chair himself, he began slowly stuffing a pipe with tobacco. His first concern, he said, was his own programme.

'I simply don't have space for a lengthy hearing, Chris,' he told the younger Senator. 'This pressure you people are applying is making life damn difficult.'

He looked at MacAnally. 'We've had dealings before, Sam. Every time I see you I find myself confronted with what you believe is the most urgent issue facing the nation. Just how serious is this plantacon business?'

'It's the most serious issue your committee is likely to face, Senator. We're talking about the intelligence of millions of children. People all over the country are concerned. They want the facts opened up and you're best placed to do it.'

Frankle sighed. 'I don't like being pressured by public hysteria, Sam,' he said. 'On the other hand, if you can stand your case up, it would be irresponsible for me to block a hearing. Give me all the information you have. I'll think about it.'

As they stood to leave, Frankle put a friendly but firm hand on Wilkins' shoulder. 'If I take this up, you'd better be right, Chris. I wouldn't easily forgive anyone who made me and my committee look fools.'

Wilkins nodded. 'I understand. I'm not actually wanting to look a fool myself, Hal.'

Frankle gave him a searching look, then dropped his hand and smiled. 'That's good enough for me.'

But when they were outside Wilkins turned to MacAnally. The environmentalist glimpsed, just for a second or two, a look of panic in the young senator's eyes. 'Christ, Sam, I hope we *are* right about all this.'

MacAnally laughed. 'You wanted the issue, Chris. Well, now you've got it. But no one said that winning was going to be easy.'

'Goddamn it, Sam, I'm not talking about *winning*. I'm talking about *being right*.'

'You didn't really ask about this when I first raised it with you . . . ' MacAnally teased him. 'Is Tom Gamell getting to you?'

But Wilkins, remembering the look in Frankle's eyes, wasn't in the mood for humour.

'Damn you, Sam, be serious. Tom is only taking care of my interests. As I would expect my senior aide to do.' He stopped walking and turned to the environmentalist.

'But you heard Frankle. We *are* right, aren't we?'

MacAnally, steering him with a reassuring arm towards a taxi, said, 'Yes, Chris. We're right.'

Then when they were in the taxi and on their way towards Dupont Circle, he said to Wilkins, 'Look, the key, as far as you're concerned, is to raise genuine fears based on genuine research and then make relatively moderate demands. A hearing. A bill – but phasing out plantacon, rather than introducing an immediate ban.

'And you should all the time be stressing that in the unlikely event that further research proves plantacon is safe, little will have been lost. They can just start using it again.

'It's OK for you to sound moderate. We don't mind how moderate you sound. The more moderate the better. *We'll* do the tough talking.

'You press on the Hill for hearings, for the truth to come out. Leave us to prosecute the case in the public arena.

'It's the old nice guy, bad guy technique. You be the nice guy, concerned and reasonable. We'll be the bad guys, inconveniently impatient.'

After they had dropped Wilkins off at the restaurant where he was due for lunch, Jay Sandbach said, 'He looks to me like he's running scared.'

MacAnally wasn't worried. 'Frankle put the fear of God into him. Don't forget, this is Wilkins' first shot at the big time. And Tom Gamell isn't helping. If your own chief aide is unenthusiastic it's bound to make life difficult.

'But Wilkins will be OK. Once things start to move and we have him on television every day he'll decide the fame and the public support are worth risking even Frankle's wrath.

'Still, why not commission an opinion poll in

Connecticut asking whether people approve of Wilkins'
campaign on plantacon.

'My guess is it'll give him at least eighty per cent
support.

'That'll stiffen his backbone.'

Frankle leaned back in his old leather chair, took off his
glasses, rubbed his eyes, and sighed. 'I'm getting too old
for all this,' he groaned at the staff director of his committee, Ed Kellerman.

'What do you think?' asked Kellerman, nodding at the
plantacon file Frankle had dropped on his desk.

'I think we've got to have a hearing. And soon. There's
a case for the industry to answer and the health of a lot of
kids at stake. Anyway, MacAnally and company have
stirred up so much fuss that half the Congress is asking to
be let off the hook. What can we drop from the hearing
schedule to make room for it?'

Kellerman produced the list of hearings planned for the
winter. 'There's the one on factory emissions.'

Frankle groaned. 'That'll bring at least three colleagues
down on my head. Still, I guess it's not that urgent. I'll
promise them first shot next session.'

'You haven't forgotten Eberhard and friends are
coming this afternoon to persuade you not to have a
hearing?'

Frankle sighed even more wearily than before.

'I'll hear what they have to say,' he said.

Frankle restrained a smile.

You had to hand it to Ed Eberhard.

Not only had the veteran Senator from Texas come in
company with Nicola Kowalska, a lobbyist who he knew
to have a rising reputation on the Hill, but also with
Alexander J. Emerson (known to everyone as A.J.), once

a Congressman and now chairman of Frankle's own state party.

Emerson's legal firm, it now emerged, represented an air freight company. A fourth member of the group was his client, Art Geiberger, the air freight company chairman.

Frankle greeted Emerson even more warmly than if they were alone. This he knew would in itself discharge ninety per cent of his obligation to the lobbyist, namely to impress Emerson's client with Emerson's friendship with the senator.

It was Eberhard who kicked off. 'Hal, I know you've been under a lot of pressure from Chris Wilkins and the environmental lobby over this plantacon affair and I thought it could help you if we filled in a few gaps.

'I take it you know that as many scientific studies clear plantacon as purport to incriminate it?'

Frankle nodded.

'And I guess you know the cost and energy loss that would be involved if plantacon were to be banned?'

Frankle nodded a second time.

'What you may not know is what we're proposing. We're not suggesting the concerns should be ignored. We're suggesting they should be explored, but given the considerable doubts about whether they're justified, we don't believe they should be explored at the expense of the airlines or the customer or the nation losing the advantages of plantacon.

'We propose further intensive research. The industry will finance it but it can be commissioned and supervised by the Environmental Protection Agency or any other agency you wish to nominate. It can be carried out to a timetable, say over three years to get it right.'

Kellerman, lounging in a corner of the room, interjected, to Eberhard's barely disguised annoyance. 'That's three years of using children for research purposes, isn't it, Senator? Wouldn't that be rather hard to justify?'

Eberhard ground his teeth. 'It would be if there was any reasonable evidence that they were being harmed, young man.

'Fortunately there's no evidence of that.

'Even so, the industry is prepared to spend a lot of money for public reassurance purposes. I don't see how you can ask more than that.'

He turned back to Frankle. 'Hal, you know as well as I do that if you held hearings on every scare story the Senate would grind to a halt. I know you've got a heavy schedule of hearings ahead. Surely this is the best way forward.'

Before Frankle could answer, Geiberger, a tall, lean man in his late fifties, spoke.

'If I may, Senator, I think you should understand that in our state,' (he stressed the 'our'), 'there are three small airlines, two in freight and one small passenger airline, that have thrived since the introduction of plantacon, increasing employment and state government revenues. At least two of us would go to the wall if it were not for plantacon. With respect to these environmentalists, they don't seem to care about these things.'

Emerson leaned forward. 'I don't think arguments like those of Art Geiberger have had a fair hearing to this point, Hal.' He paused, then added, 'I think you know that Art's company has been a good supporter of ours.'

Frankle gave a friendly nod in the direction of Geiberger. He would bet his bottom dollar the businessman had pragmatically donated to both parties in the state.

'I hear what you say, Ed and gentlemen,' he said. 'You can be clear that I don't want to harm the airline industry in any way.'

He nodded to Emerson, flatteringly. 'What concerns A.J. concerns me. And of course I'm sympathetic to your

problems, Art. But do remember that, while there may be
a bill before it, the Committee's decision to have hearings, if it takes such a decision, will be purely to reach the
truth on this matter.

'I, for one, would enter such hearings with an open
mind. You have my word on that.'

'Would not the research programme I've proposed
have the same effect?' asked Eberhard.

'Possibly, Ed. And I will consider that. But the real
problem, as you know, is that a considerable number of
members of Congress in both houses are under pressure
from their constituents to address this problem and they
may only be satisfied with a hearing.'

He stood up. 'This has been most useful. Good of you
to come all this way, A.J. and I'm particularly pleased to
see you, Art. You just feed in via A.J. any information
you want me to consider.' He ushered them to the door,
but, indicating to Kellerman he should leave too, he
asked Eberhard to stay behind.

'A drink?'

'Don't mind if I do. A bourbon?'

'No problem.'

He poured them both a glass and sat down in front of his
desk beside the other.

'Ed, you must *know* I'm going to have a hearing. The
letters are pouring in from all over the country. But I
meant what I said. I'll not be adopting a position. I'm
interested in the truth.

'But, tell me, are you really sure this stuff is safe? How
come the scientific studies show such contrasting results?'

Eberhard looked into his glass. 'Hal, if I thought plantacon was harming children I would not be sitting here.'

'But there's something wrong about all this.

'I can't put my finger on it but I know it.

'I'm convinced by the industry, and I intend to make

MacAnally and his crowd eat their words or come up with more than a few unconvincing studies and a lot of deliberately engendered hysteria.'

He put down his glass and rose to leave. 'If you go ahead with the hearing I would hope I could have the best possible opportunity to press my concerns and those of the industry?'

Frankle grasped his hand. 'You'll be doing everyone a favour if you do, Ed.'

Eberhard held his hand for a moment and added: 'And I hope you won't rush ahead. We need to get the emotion out of this thing and have it coolly considered.'

To this Frankle didn't reply.

Kellerman returned as Eberhard left. 'Boy, I could've laughed when I saw A.J. and that air freight man with Eberhard. Talk about applying all the pressures . . .'

Frankle smiled. 'All right, but just the same, take care with this one. Don't lock us into either side of the argument.

'We're responding to public concern to get at the truth, we're not taking sides.'

Eberhard met Wilkins in his Capitol hideaway. This was a bit of one-upmanship. Only the most senior senators have an extra office for themselves in the Capitol building itself.

Greeting the young senator with a drink, he sat him down on one end of a deep leather sofa, sitting himself at the other end.

'Well, Chris, you're making quite a mark for yourself in this place. Well, good luck to you, good luck to you.'

Wilkins smiled. 'That's kind of you, Senator, but I suspect you're not wishing me good luck with my plantacon bill.'

'No, young man, I'm not.' He paused to light a cigar,

offering Wilkins one, but the younger man declined. 'May I offer you some advice as an old hand here?'

'I would welcome it.'

'I've seen many men come to this place anxious to make their mark, establish themselves.

'There are a number of ways of doing that. One is to demonstrate political maturity by working with and cooperating with others. That in my experience is the best way to achieve real influence.

'Another, of course, is to grab one headline-catching issue after another and run with it, hoping to become a national figure as a result.

'What I want to say to you is that the second route may seem the easier but it's the high risk one, for two reasons: first, if the issue goes wrong, you're exposed and no one listens again. Second, even if you succeed, it's often at the expense of many colleagues here, who can block you in other ways for the rest of your career. My advice is take it easy.'

'You mean abandon the plantacon issue?'

'I mean take it easy. There's a lot at stake. Enormous sums of money. Jobs. Energy savings. If you're wrong on this, as I believe you are, you'll do immense damage to a lot of people for no reason. Be reasonable. I'm not asking you to withdraw your proposal at this stage, I'm not asking you not to press your case at the hearings. But let the matter be dealt with responsibly, on the scientific evidence, on the merits of the case. Call off the dogs . . . MacAnally and the other people who are stirring up public anxiety and making it impossible for reason to prevail.' He paused, then added, 'And don't be quite so nakedly ambitious.'

Wilkins looked back at him. Although he had said he would welcome advice, he didn't like the patronising tone. 'You mean leave it all to people like you . . .?'

'What do you mean by that?'

'You would call them "People we can trust". People who deal in smoke-filled rooms and make deals to satisfy their paymasters or their own interests and to hell with the innocent out there whom they're supposed to represent. No thanks.'

'That's not what I'm saying.'

'That's what it sounds like.'

'That's because you hear what you want to hear. Believe what you want to believe. That's the kind of man MacAnally is. That's what will ultimately bring you both down.'

Wilkins struggled to control his annoyance. 'With respect, Senator, if you think this is just about playing politics you under-estimate me. No, sir, I will go further. You insult me. There's also the effect on our children to consider. I haven't come to this place just to get on with colleagues, much as I would like to do so. It may seem naïve to a politician of your kind, but I actually want to do some good for my fellow human beings. Plantacon pollution could be an appalling environmental scandal. I believe I'm doing what a senator should do in raising it.'

'No, Senator,' Eberhard said, looking at the younger man coldly. 'It's the responsibility of a senator gravely to weigh all the interests of the country in the balance, not conduct crusades. That's the role of your friend MacAnally.'

'The interests of the country or the interests of the airline industry, Senator? What is it that you're specifically asking me to do, Senator? What does "take it easy" mean? Withdraw my bill? Abandon the children of this country in the interests of big business? You may have been bought but I haven't.'

As soon as he said the word Wilkins regretted it.

Eberhard rose, his face hard.

'*Bought?* You have a lot to learn, young man.'

'Do you deny your re-election campaign was backed by the airlines?'

'No, why should I? My campaign may well have received contributions from the industry. And, yes, I support the industry generally; it happens to be a huge provider of employment and tax revenue in my state. It deserves support. Are you suggesting you've received no funds from local business? You know it's a nonsense and so do I.'

'I don't know. I may have. But they don't buy my uncritical support.'

'And who says the airlines have mine? You are, it appears, one of the more arrogant of the self-seeking zealots who have come into this place recently. Well, I'm here to tell you that you're wrong about plantacon. You will lose this battle and you will lose your reputation and I for one will not be sorry.'

Wilkins rose. 'Your day and the days of wheeler-dealers like you have gone, Senator. It is you who will lose.'

Eberhard walked up to him until their faces were close. 'You have a lot to learn and I'm going to teach you most of it.

'I understand you have another bill coming up. One to extend the period of unemployment benefit to Connecticut workers who lose their job as a result of natural disasters.

'Must be popular with the unions.

'A nice little vote winner.

'Well, *that bill is dead.* I will put a hold on it, filibuster it, block it at every turn. I will call in every favour to see that bill dies.

'And that's only a start. You've only just won that seat and if I was you I should start fundraising now, because every cent raised from industry in your state is going to your Republican opponent next time. And money will flow in from outside.

'Frankly, I think yours is going to be one of the shorter political careers.'

Wilkins rose. 'Goodbye, Senator.'

Eberhard looked at the door as it closed in his face.

'By the time I'm finished with you, young man,' he swore, 'there'll not be a door open to you . . . here or anywhere.'

Nicola Kowalska had suggested lunch well away from Capitol Hill so they met at La Tomate, an Italian restaurant not far from the offices of the *Progressive Review*, near Dupont Circle. She was sipping a mineral water and studying the menu when she felt the appraising gaze of MacAnally, as he stood for a moment just inside the door. He strolled over, waving to one or two others in the restaurant, and she found herself looking into frank eyes and a good-natured grin.

'Ms Kowalska,' he said, 'now tell me, what's the aim of this lunch? To persuade me I'm wrong or to offer me a thick wad of used one hundred dollar bills?'

She laughed. 'Just for that, you can pay for the lunch, Mr MacAnally.'

'Call me Sam.'

'OK, I'm Nicola.'

They ordered and over lunch found themselves engaged in an inquest into the motorcycle emissions affair, the lobbying campaign that had made Nicola's name.

'Doesn't it worry you that a lot of people may suffer because the industry won that one?' MacAnally asked.

'No, because I don't believe they will suffer. Not enough to justify damaging the industry and eroding the freedom of the people to have bikes and ride them.'

'You only take on business if you believe in your client's case?'

'As a rule I take the view that everyone's entitled to representation, and not just in the courts of law. These days the state enters into every aspect of the life of the citizen, and the company; they need help to promote or defend their interests. The citizen has people like you; the company has people like me.

'Sometimes I think the arguments are well balanced, sometimes my client's case is weak, sometimes your case is weak, but I would only have qualms about acting for a client if I really believed someone would be seriously harmed if I and the client won.'

She paused to pick at her food, then added, 'And in the case of plantacon I don't think anyone would be.'

'Ah, I wondered when you would mention plantacon.' MacAnally looked at her carefully. 'Let's be frank with each other. What did you hope this lunch would achieve?'

'Well, first of all, Mr MacAnally—'

'Sam.'

'Sam . . . you may see this as a war but I don't. I don't think in those black and white terms. I want to know whom I'm dealing with. And I want to open up channels of communication. If you're genuinely interested in truth you'll want that too.'

She waited for a reply but he didn't comment so she continued.

'So I want to be able to talk from time to time and I hope this meeting will make that possible.

'Also, I want you to know what our side really feels. I've talked to airline people, to the oil industry, to your "friend" Dieter Partrell, and to others. And they're not covering up. They're genuinely convinced you've got it wrong. That's important. That's what I particularly want you to know.

'It may be in your interests to pretend otherwise but these are not bad people, Sam. They do not believe plantacon is doing damage. They do not believe they're a threat to the country. Rightly or wrongly, they think *you* are.

'And I want to talk about the timing of the hearings. I know you want them soon to keep up the momentum of your campaign, but surely truth matters to you too. We need time, time to conduct more research. To have a proper scientific debate in scientific circumstances.'

While she talked MacAnally listened intently, but also studied her. Despite his instinct for black and white battles, with no holds barred, he liked this young woman who was so earnestly representing the other side. He was disconcerted by her good looks, impressed by her intelligence, but above all beguiled by her serious approach. MacAnally was used to bargaining or game-playing or just plain fighting with lobbyists who didn't really care, played the game for its own sake, who were in it just for the money, not lobbyists who felt just as seriously about their case as he did about his.

'OK,' he said. 'Yes to opening channels. You ring me if you want to talk and I'll talk.

'No to postponing the hearings. You're only trying to take the heat out of the issue, buy time to influence congressmen behind the scenes and take the pressure off them from their constituents. And you hope delay will bore the media so that the story fades.'

He held up a hand as she began to protest. 'Don't worry – I don't blame you – I would do the same in your shoes.

'As for your other point, if the industry cared about people as much as it likes to claim, why can't it stop using plantacon for two or three years while there's an exhaustive scientific study of the matter? OK, it'll lose some money, but if it's right and we're wrong, it'll ultimately get all the benefits back. I'll tell you why. It's because they all want the profits and they want them now and they don't care about the price anyone else pays.'

'You disappoint me, Sam. You're treating everyone in business as stereotypes, as if they're not parents or citizens or neighbours themselves, as if they're all one uncaring breed. Is this how you keep going? By persuading yourself that there is a deadly enemy out there that has to be destroyed at all costs? Are you one of those self-indulgent sanctimonious zealots who can only operate in a goodies and baddies world in which he's always cast as the goodie and anyone who makes money or employs anyone or is related in anyway to business and industry is evil?'

'Oh, my God.' He pretended to hide under the table. 'This *is* strong language. Now who's dealing in stereotypes.

'If I was like that we wouldn't be having lunch now, Nicola. We've cooperated and worked with industry before. But you're concentrating on attitudes to each other instead of the merits of the case.

'You say everyone in industry genuinely believes plantacon is OK. I don't. I genuinely think it's a dangerous pollutant.

'Now, what do we do about that? We each put our case before the authorities and the people and let them decide.

'That's what *we're* doing. We're building up a head of steam behind hearings and we'll present our case to those hearings. Publicly. And open to challenge. What's so bad about that?'

'Nothing, if that's all you're doing. But your so-called head of steam is built up by unnecessarily frightening people. Already it's having all sorts of repercussions. Property values are falling around airports – not that they were ever high – and people are trying to get out in a panic, losing money and sometimes even giving up jobs in the process. You don't seem to realise the extent to which you're frightening people.

'As for the hearings, you're not intent on establishing truth. You're pushing for hearings that will decide what *you* want them to decide. You won't just present information. You'll build up a whole political storm around the hearings. You're not being fair in all of this.'

'What's fair? For companies quietly to pollute communities and poison the brains of children because they were so anxious to get to the profits that they couldn't wait to test the process and demonstrate to themselves that it was safe? Then for them to refuse to act when the problem is identified, using loaded scientific studies and all their money and influence to stifle people's concerns? Is that fair?'

Nicola was about to answer when they were interrupted by a journalist dining at another table. While he and MacAnally exchanged a few words she decided the lunch had achieved as much as it could.

'OK, Sam,' she said as she waved for coffee, 'at least we've established where we both stand. At least we're talking.'

His face softened. 'Talking to you will be fun.'

'I'd prefer not to be patronised.'

'I'm sorry. That was not intended. I mean I've enjoyed our lunch, enjoyed meeting you. That's all.'

'OK.' She stirred her coffee. 'You can't compromise at all on the date of the hearings?'

'Sorry.'

'What are you afraid of . . . the evidence disproving your case?'

'No, Nicola, children being poisoned. Every day is one too many.'

She sighed. 'What if the industry was to finance a major

international scientific symposium within six months, organised independently, and if it was to finance all the necessary background research?'

'No one stopping it. But that won't stop the hearing.'

'Maybe the Committee will think it worth postponing the hearing?'

'You wouldn't say that if you had seen their postbags.' She picked up the tab. 'OK. Let's leave it that.'

'Next time I'll pay,' MacAnally said.

'Next time?' She met his eyes unflinchingly.

He looked at her, surprised. 'I thought you wanted to keep channels open . . .'

'And I thought . . . ' she reddened. 'Sorry, I misunderstood . . . Right. To the next time then.'

He watched her walk off down the street. And wished she wasn't working for the airlines.

She felt his eyes on her. And wished they had met under other circumstances.

The following day Wilkins spoke to the Senate, and introduced his 'Air Pollution Child Safety Bill' to require a phase-out of plantacon over twelve months.

Ed Eberhard spoke after him. He began by condemning unbalanced and emotive campaigns calculated to arouse fear without foundation.

Then, looking at Wilkins, he said, 'I hope my colleague from Connecticut will allow a veteran of this Senate to advise him to be judicious in his choice of causes to pursue. I recommend to him the words of the Texas preacher: "Ambition is the disease of the young. And the cure is experience." '

'Will the Senator yield?' It was Wilkins, livid.

'Of course I'll yield to the Senator from Connecticut.'

'Would my distinguished colleague, drawing on his years of experience, not also feel that one should be judicious in one's acceptance of campaign contributions?'

At this thinly disguised suggestion that Eberhard was influenced by financial considerations there was consternation throughout the chamber. The majority leader looked round at Wilkins and frowned.

The Vice President, who was in the chair, suggested that the Senator 'may wish to re-phrase his remark so that it would not be thought he was making an unacceptable suggestion about a colleague'.

Wilkins realised from the look on Eberhard's face that he had allowed the crusty old Texan to provoke him into a foolish remark. He would have no choice but to retreat.

He muttered an apology and left the chamber furious with himself. And even more furious with Ed Eberhard.

Senator Hal Frankle also left the chamber, concerned. He didn't like the heat that was being engendered by this plantacon business.

Within twenty-four hours Frankle announced that public concern justified an early hearing to establish the facts. The bill would be considered as part of this process.

ECO welcomed the hearings and pressed for them to be held urgently.

For the industry, Nicola Kowalska issued a press release also welcoming the hearings as 'a clearing up of the emotional and unjustified attacks on plantacon' but said she hoped that the Committee would not act with unseemly haste. It should allow both sides time to research the issues further.

But the next day Frankle named the date.

There would be no delay.

Hearings would begin in two weeks.

PORTLAND, MAINE

Kathy Smith was having a late-night drink with her husband in their home in Portland, Maine, when the call came.

It was from a reporter on a local TV news show, a woman she had seen on her screen many times.

'There's a meeting of workers in a hangar at the Jetport tomorrow,' she said. 'It's about plantacon. We're going to film it. Obviously we'd like to get your side of the story as well.'

At first Kathy was pleased. 'I'd be happy to help,' she said. 'What do you want me to do?'

'Well, the thing is, we need to show the strength of parental concern. We wondered whether you could get some mothers and children to come with you, perhaps with one or two placards – you know, *Ban plantacon*, that kind of thing – and we'll film you outside the hangar. Then we'll do an interview.'

Kathy began to feel less enthusiastic. 'Do we have to have the children – and the placards? It sounds as bit like rent-a-crowd. I'm trying to conduct our campaign in Maine at a more thoughtful level.'

'I understand that, but television is about pictures, Ms Smith. Without them it'll be difficult to justify the story. You do *want* the publicity, don't you?'

Kathy took the hint. No children, no placards – no publicity for the campaign.

'Yes . . . yes, of course.' She thought for a moment. They did need the publicity. 'OK, we'll be there. What time?'

'Three.'

She spent the next hour ringing around.

By midnight she had persuaded a dozen women to attend. With their children.

WASHINGTON, D.C.

That same night, the one before the plantacon hearings began, Sam MacAnally went to a reception given by Senator Leighton Taverner. He couldn't really afford the time but the senator was being helpful to Wilkins, and he also expected one or two other members of the committee there . . . a friendly contact could only help.

What he didn't expect was to find Nicola Kowalska there also, mixing assuredly with both senators and staffers and looking sensational in a simple black dress. She nodded to him and they circled each other for half an hour before he finally captured her alone.

'Hi. How's it going?' he asked.

'No problem,' she replied with a confident smile. 'So you got your hearing.'

'I'm sorry,' he grinned.

'You will be.'

He laughed. 'You know,' he said, 'this is the first time this has happened to me.'

'What?'

'Being able to talk to the enemy organiser. I rather like it.'

'Do you really see me in those terms? As the enemy?'

'No. Not you personally. But Partrell and company . . . yes I do. And I've no doubt they think the same.'

'It's a pity it has to be like that.'

'Maybe. Anyway,' he said, 'I want to thank you for suggesting lunch. It was a good idea.'

For a moment they ran out of things to say, yet both lingered. Eventually . . . 'You look terrific in that dress,' he said.

'Thank you.' She smiled at him.

'I guess you're not free for dinner. You know, last meal before facing the firing squad . . .?'

'I'm sorry,' she said. 'I have to have dinner with Senator Myers. Sorry.'

And with an even brighter smile she left him.

MacAnally looked after her, disappointed.

Because Senator Myers was on the committee. He didn't want him charmed by his opponent.

And because . . . well, it would have been . . . useful . . . that was all he would concede to himself . . . it would have been useful to have another chat with Nicola Kowalska.

He left to go back to his flat to study for one last time the evidence he would give tomorrow.

He took some lettuce and some tomatoes and onions from the fridge and made a sandwich, opened a can of beer, and relaxed on the couch, his feet resting on the coffee table.

As he reached for the file his eyes fell upon a picture of Marie.

She was smiling at him.

For the first time he was able to look at her without descending into deep depression.

He felt her smile encouraging him tonight.

Giving him heart for the battle tomorrow?

Giving him heart to get on with his life, to go on out there and live?

He looked down at the file.

And thought about the woman he had to beat in the plantacon campaign.

Nicola Kowalska.

It had been a pity she wasn't free for dinner.

The ECO 'hearings group' consisted of MacAnally and three of his top team, Jay Sandbach, Liz Fletcher, and Adrian Carlisle. They combined with the Democratic senator, Chris Wilkins, his chief administrative assistant Tom Gamell and legislative assistant, Carl Hanson, and the Republican senator, Leighton Taverner.

The group's task was to influence the structure of the hearings, assemble an impressive team of witnesses, help its friendly senators to undermine the credibility of the other side, and feed the media its own slant on the hearings day by day.

It established its headquarters in what it called the Bunker, a small room in the basement of the Russell building, usually the office of Taverner's press aide.

Such was the interest in the controversy that, instead of the committee's usual room in the Taft building, the opening sessions were scheduled for room 318 of the Old Senate Office Building – the room that became famous to television viewers during the Watergate hearings.

The day began well. Sam MacAnally, who was to be the opening witness and who would outline the anti-plantacon case, made appearances on both *Today* and *Good Morning America* and arrived in the caucus room confident.

His testimony and responses to friendly questions from Wilkins took all morning and went well.

The view of the 'hearings group' over a sandwich and beer in the Bunker was that MacAnally had 'hit all the bases'.

No one anticipated the grilling MacAnally was to get in the afternoon.

Eberhard had arranged to question MacAnally immediately after lunch.

'Tell me, Mr MacAnally,' he began, 'what is an environmentalist?'

MacAnally hesitated. 'Well, it can be one of a number . . .'

But the senator, noting the hesitation, moved quickly to exploit it: 'Mr MacAnally, I was hoping for a clear answer, not a list of options. Let me approach the question differently. Are *you* an environmentalist?'

MacAnally hesitated a second time.

'Come now, Mr MacAnally, is this so difficult? You received, I believe, the award for Environmentalist of the Decade. I have in my hand a sheaf of press clippings describing you as "America's leading environmentalist". Are you an environmentalist or are you not?'

'Yes,' said MacAnally, annoyed at his own hesitation.

'Good. Now let's establish what that means. Do you have academic qualifications? A degree in environmental science, shall we say?'

'No, but . . .'

'Well, what are your academic qualifications?'

'I have a degree in politics and economics.'

'Politics? *Politics*, you say.' Eberhard looked round the room with a grin. 'Well, gentlemen, it appears we have a rival.

'So you're a *politician*, Mr MacAnally?'

'I didn't say that, I said I studied politics at college.'

'Ah, of course. You're not a politician. You're an environmentalist. The trouble is I'm having difficulty in establishing what that means, Mr MacAnally. You have no academic qualifications to be an environmentalist. Do you serve as an apprentice, are you employed and trained to be an environmentalist? Are you elected?'

MacAnally struggled to control his anger. This was unexpected.

'I tried to explain to you earlier, Senator, there are

people who have academic qualifications in one of a number of forms of environmental science . . .

' . . . There are people who spend their lives working to protect plants and wildlife and places of beauty . . .

' . . . There are people who devote their leisure time to working in local groups campaigning to protect their communities from pollution . . .

' . . . These could all fairly describe themselves as environmentalists. There is no single answer.'

'And what are you, Mr MacAnally? Not a scientist?'

'No.'

'Not actively protecting plant and wildlife?'

'Well . . . no.'

'Not joining with friends to protect a local community?'

'No.'

'Well, then, where do you fit in?'

MacAnally, increasingly irritated by the line of questioning, still endeavoured to keep cool.

'The environmental movement consists of a variety of organisations and individuals, often working separately, occasionally cooperating.

'The organisations need organising.

'I have over the past few years played an organisational role.'

Eberhard looked up from the papers in front of him, as if surprised.

'Oh, I see . . . you're an *organiser*, Mr MacAnally. An environmental *organiser*? But an organiser of what?'

'What do you mean *what*?' MacAnally snapped back.

'Well, *what* do you organise?'

MacAnally tried to sound as if he were educating an idiot. 'People, Senator, people.'

'Oh, you organise *people*, do you, Mr MacAnally? What people?'

'All organisations consist of people, Senator. Even political parties.'

There was laughter. MacAnally privately rejoiced in his first strike.

'You should know,' he continued, 'having been elected to a position of leadership yourself, that organisations need leaders. Rightly or wrongly, my colleagues accept me in that role.'

Eberhard, however, was unrelenting.

'*Accept*? Mr MacAnally. Not appoint?'

'Well, no . . .'

'Not elect?'

'This would have been difficult as I founded ECO myself.'

'I see.' Eberhard shuffled his papers. 'Forgive me, Mr MacAnally, I'm not feeling too intelligent this afternoon. I'd like just to summarise what I believe you've described:

'You have *no* academic qualifications to be an environmentalist.

'You have *not* worked in national parks or places of that sort.

'You are *not* one of a number of local people dealing with a specific identifiable problem.

'You have *not* been officially appointed.

'*You* have set up an organisation and you are the non-appointed, non-elected leader of it.

'*And that makes you an environmentalist*?'

MacAnally was furious now, yet knew he dare not show it. He endeavoured to strike a tone of exaggerated patience. 'I'm an environmentalist in so much as I care passionately about the environment and devote all of my time to working to protect it, Congressman. That also defines an environmentalist.'

Eberhard, becoming more genial the more MacAnally

became tense, smiled. 'A good definition, Mr MacAnally. My problem is that *anyone* could be that. Anyone at all.

'Anyone could care passionately, anyone could devote all their time to this work, but my concern is why should the majority of the people of this country, and we in particular, their elected representatives, be expected to take any notice of them?

'If everybody who cared passionately about something and devoted a lot of time to it were given a hearing by Congress the government of this country would grind to a halt.

'I've been trying to establish your *qualifications*, Mr MacAnally, your *qualifications* for taking the time of this august body, your qualifications for being listened to by anybody . . . other, that is, than the publicity you get for your views . . . other, that is, than your ability to whip up hysteria.

'Because aren't these your *real* qualifications, Mr MacAnally . . . the ability to get attention, to create fear and bully people into doing what you believe is right? Aren't these, in fact, your *only* qualifications?'

MacAnally had had enough. 'What you've described are the qualifications for being a politician,' he half shouted at Eberhard.

'And isn't that what you were educated in? *Politics*?' It was Eberhard who half shouted now. 'You're not an environmentalist, Mr MacAnally. In so much as there is such a thing, you're not it. You're a politician without a constituency, a self-publicist in need of a cause.'

Wilkins, who had sat slumped in his chair, stunned by the way things were going, disconcerted to see MacAnally clearly embarrassed by the unexpected attack, now called to the Chairman in protest. 'This is not a suitable line of questioning. The senator from

Texas has had his fun. Can we now get back to plantacon.'

But Eberhard would have none of it. 'Fun? *Fun?* On the contrary, Mr Chairman, this is the *only* relevant line of questioning.

'This man and his colleagues, aided by my young colleague, the senator from Connecticut, are attempting to discredit and undermine a great industry, attempting to persuade us to ban a product that saves fuel and saves money. The effect of such a ban will be billions of dollars lost and billions of gallons of crude oil lost. We are entitled to know who they are and what their qualifications and motives are.'

He turned once more to MacAnally. 'Isn't the truth that you will always disbelieve business and industry, that you see them as anti-social, whereas people like you, who have contributed not one iota to the standard of living of the American people, are always to be believed?'

MacAnally countered strongly. 'There may be some extremists in our movement who think like that. Every movement has its extremists. But I do not. I respect the contribution of business and industry. I ask only that, if they put a product on the market, it's safe . . . that they don't frivolously use up finite resources . . . that they don't cause health-endangering pollution. Is that so extreme a position?'

'I see. Is this the same man who has described the airline industry as "only concerned about the bottom line", the manufacturers of plantacon as "child poisoners", who has been quoted in *Time* magazine as saying "the biggest threat to the world apart from nuclear war is the unaccountable, undemocratic power of multi-national companies"?'

'I don't withdraw those comments. Nor do I see them as contradicting what I have just said.'

'I see. Now, let's talk about this organisation of yours, the Environmental Campaigns Organisation . . . this ECO. You said it has one hundred and three local groups in the US, groups that have been campaigning for a ban on plantacon in their areas?'

'That's right.'

'Who are these people?'

'They vary. They can be local teachers, librarians or accountants, timber workers or car mechanics. The common denominator is that they're concerned about environmental issues and have come together to help ECO.'

Eberhard looked around the room with raised eyebrows. Then, with contrived surprise in his voice, he asked, '*Teachers*, Mr MacAnally? *Timber workers*? *Car mechanics*? What qualifications are these for persuading their fellow citizens they should worry about plantacon?'

'Naturally they're a local expression of our national campaign, they're briefed . . .'

'Yes, *briefed by you*, Mr MacAnally. You have *no qualifications* – you admit that – and yet you're briefing others without qualifications and on the basis of this you want us to undermine a great industry.

'I have a letter from one of my constituents, Mr MacAnally. I won't read it all, but the gist of it is in the final sentence.

' "*Please vote for a ban on plantacon and protect my children from this evil.*"

'I went to see this woman, Mr MacAnally. She is a housewife who had not even heard about plantacon – didn't even know it existed – until she received a leaflet from your local organiser.

'So I went to see your local organiser. She is an office worker who also hadn't heard of it either – until she received information from you.

'I put it to you, *no one in this movement really knows what they're talking about*.

'You send a message to the office worker and she sends a message to the housewife and they then start to pressurise me.

'But the pressure really comes from *you*, not them.

'They're just innocent dupes.

'It comes from *you* and you've told us you have no qualifications.

'So,' he looked triumphantly round the crowded and silent room, 'why should we give this matter any more time at all?'

MacAnally was aware that the credibility of the whole environmental movement was being threatened by this merciless cross-examination. He looked to Frankle, hoping to indicate that the question couldn't be answered briefly.

'Senator, for the last half hour you have been questioning my qualifications and those of my fellow environmentalists. And, yes, I *do* use that word environmentalist and am proud of it.

'What you don't seem to understand is that your qualifications for your position and my qualifications for mine are similar.

'We are both ordinary men without special credentials. Yet you feel able to participate in the taking of a wide variety of decisions requiring highly specialist input. Including this one, about plantacon.

'How can that be?

'The answer is that you're a representative of the people, chosen – at least in theory – for your intelligence and judgement. It's not expected of you that you be an expert, but that you be able to weigh the often conflicting evidence of experts and the pressures from vested interests and then do what you believe, on balance, is right.

'You are there because you're believed to care about the community and to be able to take decisions in its best interests.

'Well, like you I'm not a specialist.

'And I'm not a scientist.

'But I would argue that specialists and scientists and so-called experts should never be allowed to take the decisions, only to advise and assist the decision-making process . . . assist us to decide. We, all of us, have ultimately to apply our judgement.'

Eberhard's face hardened. '*Us?* But there's a difference between us, isn't there, Mr MacAnally? I'm *elected* and you're not.'

'Quite so, but that's why you have the decision and I do not. I am, if you like, the prosecutor of this case. The industries are the defendants. But *you* are the judge.'

'But what gives *you* the right to prosecute?'

'It's my right. It's the constitutional right of every individual, of every citizen, to petition his government for the redress of grievances.

'The trouble with politicians like you, Senator, is that you believe that political parties should be the only vehicle for people to participate in the life of their community and country. That is not, fortunately, the case, nor is it healthy. It ignores the fact that some of the most fundamental reforms have been initially promoted from outside conventional politics, and that some of the worst injustices have been corrected from outside conventional politics.

'The civil rights movement was one of the great non-party-political forces for good in this country.

'And who is to say that the motor car would ever have become safer if it had not been for Ralph Nader?

'In fact, almost every environmental outrage has been identified and exposed by non-party-political groups.

'It's worth saying, too, that we have no formal power. Only the power to care, the power to become informed, the power to argue our case, and the power to win support and capture your attention.

'Yes, Senator, I have the temerity to be here, arguing that plantacon should be banned. But you and your colleagues have all the power . . . the power to ban it or reprieve it.

'Why should you be so afraid of us? Why should you not welcome the fact that we have at the very least identified a possible problem?

'And why should the industry be concerned about our existence, provided it's able to answer our concerns? After all, *that is all we want – that our concerns be answered.*

'So, Senator, why don't we address the real question – *is plantacon safe?*

'Or are you saying that it's a question that should not be asked? Should not be addressed?

'You challenge my right to raise the question, Senator; well, I challenge your right to deny me the answer.'

There was a burst of applause from the gallery. The Chairman banged down his gavel. But Eberhard just looked back at him impassively, then nodded to the Chairman to indicate that he would leave it there.

PORTLAND, MAINE

Kathy Smith felt uneasy the moment she got to the Jetport.

She had no difficulty in finding the hangar. There was already a TV crew outside, together with a bunch of mothers and children.

From inside the hangar she could hear someone using a loud speaker. She couldn't hear the words. But whoever it was, they were being rewarded with frequent gusts of applause.

But what worried her was another group. There were about thirty of them. Young, dressed like hippies, wielding banners. Some had their faces painted. As she got closer her fears were confirmed: they were members of the ECO Warriors.

She knew all about the ECO Warriors. They were a militant outfit, operating well outside the parameters of the conventional environmental movement. Wild. They staged headline-catching stunts, sometimes verging on violence.

The ECO Warriors didn't really care about environmental protection; their aim was revolution.

In terms of their own objectives they were, of course, ineffectual. They had about as much chance of getting results as they had of swimming the Atlantic.

What they did do was embarrass genuine environmentalists.

But you couldn't tell them that; in their view *they* were the genuine environmentalists.

Now they were latching onto the plantacon campaign.

The last thing Kathy wanted was to get ECO's campaign mixed up with the ECO Warriors. So she walked over to talk to the TV reporter.

The woman looked harder than she expected. The smile 'as seen on TV' lacked warmth in real life. Her make-up made her face look as if it were encased in cement.

'What are these people doing here?' Kathy asked.

The reporter pretended to be surprised herself. 'I had no idea they were coming,' she said. 'I only mentioned it to one of them who I happen to know.'

Like hell, Kathy thought. The ECO Warriors didn't go to the kind of cocktail parties this woman attended.

'Look,' she said. 'We can't get the public confused about who ECO is. These people are not involved in this campaign. They're not even genuine environmentalists. I'll simply have to take my people home.'

'That would be a pity,' said the reporter. 'Because if you're not around I'll have to use them to represent the environmental case. I can't have no one.'

Kathy felt trapped. That would be a disaster.

'Well, I don't want them in the picture,' she said.

The reporter was all reassurance. 'No problem.'

Then she told Kathy the plan. When the workers came out of the meeting Kathy and the mothers and children would be lined up. The reporter would ask the workers' leader to say what they had decided in the hangar, then Kathy Smith would reply.

Kathy was liking it less and less. 'I thought I was having a separate interview,' she said.

'It will be. It's just that it'll be in the same place as the other one. It saves moving the cameras.'

Kathy wished Molly Macintosh or someone was there to advise.

Her instincts told her to get out.

But how could she? If she did, the ECO Warriors would step in. And God only knew what damage they would do to the cause.

So, feeling more and more apprehensive, she gave in.

From the hangar there came a roar of applause and then the doors were flung open and men poured out, blinking in the sunlight.

The reporter stepped forward, Kathy on one side, the cameras and microphones on the other.

'Mr McCarthy,' the reporter called out to a big burly man wearing a suit and carrying a clip-board. 'Can you tell us what you and your colleagues have decided?'

The big man came over, surrounded by workers.

He looked annoyed at the presence of Kathy's group, hesitated, then decided to ignore them.

'We feel the public should be told the other side of the story,' he said. There was a touch of Irish in his accent. 'We think people should know what plantacon's done for this area. The jobs it's created. Our industry is being maligned and we've had enough.'

A cheer went up from the surrounding workers. 'Good on you, Mick,' someone called out.

'What do you say to this, Ms Smith?' the reporter asked.

'We're not trying to malign the workers,' she said. 'No one suggests they knew that plantacon was a threat to our children. Nor do we deny the benefits of plantacon . . .'

She stopped. Her voice was being drowned by a chanting sound behind her. She swung round.

So did the cameras.

To her horror Kathy saw that the ECO Warriors had come forward. They were waving their placards menacingly. Their leader was calling out '*Plantacon*' and the others were replying, '*Out, out, out*'.

Kathy tried to speak but was drowned out.

'*Plantacon!*'

'*Out!*'

'*Plantacon!*'

'*Out!*'

'*Plantacon!*'

'*Out, out, out!*'

The workers now began to shout back.

The exchanges became increasingly abusive.

Kathy tried to indicate to the reporter that they should move away but the reporter brushed her aside.

Kathy had become a bit player in the drama . . . one whose scene could easily be cut.

'Get some pictures of the workers shouting back,' the reporter urged the cameraman.

Then a placard flew threw the air and landed in the middle of the group around McCarthy, the workers' spokesman.

One broke away from the others, clutching his head. It was bleeding.

At this a roar went up and the workers moved forward towards the ECO Warriors.

More placards were thrown.

Some of the Warriors were tearing the posters off so that they had pointed stakes they could throw like spears.

The workers moved to a pile of discarded pieces of machinery near by and began to hurl them back.

Kathy called to the mothers and children. 'For God's sake, run. Back to your cars.'

But one of the children, a little girl . . . one of Kathy's pupils, Betty Hunter . . . had already panicked and broken away. Instead of running away from the ECO Warriors she was trying to find a way between them.

As she did so a piece of iron came flying from the workers' group.

'Betty,' screamed a woman's voice.

The metal hit the little girl on the back of the head.

She pitched forward on her face.

And lay still.

Both groups stopped.

For a moment all was quiet.

Except for the whirring of the camera.

This was going to make a great story.

WASHINGTON, D.C.

As the environmentalists had anticipated, Senator Charles Myers of North Carolina was the next questioner.

Myers had scored a zero on the League of Conservation Voters' scorecard of votes on environmental issues. He took up the attack where Eberhard had left off.

'You listed the scientific studies. You have no scientific education, Mr MacAnally, have you?'

'No.'

'You couldn't have carried out such research yourself?'

'No.'

'Yet you not only consider yourself suitable to review the research but also to attack scientific research funded by the industry.

'You have asked the public to trust the scientific evidence that supports you, but not the scientific evidence that doesn't.

'Who do you think you are, Mr MacAnally? On what grounds should anyone consider your views on scientific matters of any value whatsoever?'

'I only outlined the studies and the results.'

'No, you've done more than that, Mr MacAnally, you have *accepted* their work. You have built a campaign on their work. You are asking us to take momentous decisions on the basis of their work. At the same time you have asked us to reject the work of other scientists.

'I have a clipping from the *New York Times* in front of me. You are quoted as saying "The so-called scientific studies in defence of plantacon come from scientists who work consistently with industry and are paid for with industry money. Why should we believe them?" You did say that, didn't you?'

'Yes.'

'You're choosing the scientists you think we should believe and those we should not. Isn't it the case that you don't have a lot of respect for science or scientists unless they support your non-scientifically established views . . . your prejudices?'

'I take the pressures on them into account.'

'Ah yes, the conspiracy theory.' Myers looked down the row of senators. 'But shouldn't we, as politicians, take our decisions on the basis of scientific consensus? And if there are gaps or discrepancies in the scientific information, shouldn't we respond to those gaps by commissioning more research, rather than by premature, expensive and often unnecessary legislation?'

MacAnally looked at the chairman. 'This is not an easy question to answer. Perhaps I could have some time to do it?'

Frankle looked pointedly at Myers and said, 'I don't think that's a problem, Mr MacAnally.'

'Of course the scientific evidence is of paramount importance, and where a scientific consensus exists it's likely to be decisive.

'But the scientists who've looked at the environmental and health effects of plantacon are divided. There is no consensus to help you to a decision. So you're forced to choose who to believe.

'We must beware the danger that, when science can't produce a definitive answer, the scientists, for all sorts of reasons, some good, some bad, become launched on a never-ending search for one. In one way we should admire their determination to solve the problem. But the effect can be to sacrifice people, even generations of people, to research.

'Those with a vested interest in delay rely on these uncertainties. Each study that purports to defend the product or process is enthusiastically welcomed; each study that reinforces the need for regulatory controls is hypersensitively challenged. And always they demand more and more research.

'Thus does the inability of scientists to reach accord play into the hands of the polluters.'

Hal Frankle intervened. 'You argue that science is not the infallible aid to decision-making we would like it to be?'

'I'm really saying, sir, that science can be no more infallible than the scientists, and that scientists are no more infallible than anyone else.'

Myers exploded. 'This is outrageous. This man, without any scientific qualifications at all, is ready to question the integrity of anybody who gets in the way of what he wants to achieve.'

MacAnally was now the calmer. 'Sir, all I'm saying is that scientists are no more or less fallible than any other human being. No one is, I hope, suggesting they're superhuman. There are able and clever scientists and there are incompetent scientists; there are hardworking scientists and lazy scientists; there are idealistic scientists and self-centred scientists; there are honest scientists and corrupt scientists.'

'So all you have to do is question a scientist's integrity and his work should be written off?' Myers growled.

'No, sir. But if there's a question-mark over his neutrality on a particular issue, his views on that issue have to be treated with reservations. What are the differences between industry's scientists and the ones who incriminate plantacon? Their qualifications and fields of expertise are similar. The only obvious difference is the source of funds for their work.

'It's surely fair to say that, given the needs of the industry to defend plantacon, it was more likely to purchase scientific expertise from those known to have its interests at heart.

'I'm not saying the scientists deliberately sold out.

'I'm saying they were chosen with their prejudices in mind.

'A scientist cannot be assumed to be objective if there is every reason to believe that he's so attached to an established position that it would require a disproportionate weight of evidence on the other side to change his view.'

There was a lengthy pause, then the Chairman turned to Myers: 'Senator?'

Myers theatrically took off his glasses, gave them a brief polish, then suddenly leaned forward.

'Is it not equally possible to argue, Mr MacAnally, that, science being a complicated business, it's too easily open to misrepresentation by people like you?

'That in the public arena the scientist doesn't stand a chance when challenged by the campaigner?

'That you use scientists just like you claim industry does, choosing those with prejudices or known social or political positions . . . choosing those predisposed to interpret data the way you want them to?

'You point out that the scientists opposing you are all employed by the industries. Your conclusion is that they have in some way been corrupted by them. I could argue that your scientific supporters are all known to be non-industry scientists, people who live on public funds and who have a vested interest in being seen to be acting in the so-called public interest. Have they not been corrupted too? If not by money, then by publicity, or the flattery of public support?'

'No more, I hope, than you or your colleagues, Senator.'

There was laughter, but before a red-faced Myers could answer the Chairman intervened. 'Senator, I think the issues you have raised have been well aired. Can we move on?'

Myers looked as if he were about to insist on his right to keep questioning, but then changed his mind and retired from the fray.

The next questioner was a Democrat, Earl Coulter, the senator from Georgia, the home base of Delta. 'Is energy conservation a concern of you environmentalists?'

'It's a concern of the environmental movement, yes.'

'Do you accept that the use of plantacon in airline fuel has created a significant energy saving?'

'Yes.'

'Is the saving of money . . . the consumer's money . . . an environmental concern?'

'It's not an environmental concern, but as citizens we welcome it.'

'Do you accept that plantacon has benefited the public?'

'Financially, yes.'

'Do you accept that a ban on plantacon will cost billions of dollars to the airline industry and related industries, and also many jobs?'

'There is nearly always a price to be paid . . .'

'Yes or no. Will it cost billions of dollars?'

'Yes, but . . .'

'Yes. That's the answer, Mr MacAnally. *Yes*.'

Wilkins appealed to the Chairman. 'There's no need for senators to play at Perry Mason. If we're to reach the truth we must hear all that the witness wants to say. I believe Mr MacAnally wanted to add to his answer.'

The Chairman looked at MacAnally.

'I wanted to add, Mr Chairman, that of course there is nearly always a price to be paid for environmental protection.'

Coulter pressed. 'Quite so. And the price of the removal of plantacon is enormous. Don't you think that calls for *conclusive* evidence of harm?'

'What is *conclusive*, Senator?

'This involves complex issues encompassing scientific data from many fields. As I've said, the research so far has demonstrated that what is conclusive to one scientist is inconclusive to another. It could take years to reconcile the differences and all that time our children would be the guinea pigs.'

The Chairman intervened. 'I take it you think we should act on the basis of risk, Mr MacAnally. But how do we decide that?'

'Sir, any responsible doctor, when taking decisions about an individual patient, errs on the side of prudence.

'What does he say when proposing rest or remedial action? "*Better to be safe.*"

'If that is the policy for the individual patient, surely it should be the policy when it comes to public health, to questions affecting millions of men, women and children.'

The Chairman sat back and Eberhard, asking if Coulter would yield the floor, asked sarcastically. 'And how do you suggest we evaluate risk, Mr MacAnally? On the basis that whatever concerns you should concern us?'

'No, Senator. There are three factors:

'First, there is *the nature of the risk*. In this case it's damage to the intelligence and learning ability of children.

'Second, there is *the number of individuals at risk*. Here we are not talking about a handful of children but millions all over the world.

'Third, there is *the practicality of individuals themselves being able to avoid the risk.* Children have not voluntarily chosen to be poisoned by plantacon, nor can they act themselves to prevent it. They have to rely on you . . . yes, even you, Senator.'

Coulter was replaced by Cal Calhorn, the senator from Tennessee. 'Mr MacAnally, this campaign of yours must have cost a lot of money. Where did it come from?'

Wilkins rose. 'Really, this is irrelevant.'

But Eberhard, furious at the younger committee member, was anxious to hammer home the advantage. 'If the Senator from Tennessee will yield the floor? Mr MacAnally has argued that the industry has a vested interest in covering up pollution. We want to know where the vested interests are on the other side.'

'Surely it's the *public* interest Mr MacAnally raises,' said Wilkins.

'Then the answer is *public* money. Is that right, Mr MacAnally. Did all the money come from the public?'

MacAnally hesitated. What was Justin Lord if he was not a member of the public? He had no vested interest. His contribution may have been huge but not in proportion to his overall wealth. A few million from Lord was the same as a few thousand from a less wealthy donor.

'The money came from the public,' he said.

Eberhard looked at him hard but then nodded to the Chairman and sat back.

'I think that will do for today,' said Frankle looking tired.

MacAnally sat back in his chair, suddenly aware that he was wet with sweat.

So exhausted was he that he was hardly aware of the questions from reporters as Jay Sandbach quickly guided him out of the room and down to the Bunker where they closed the door and breathed a collective sigh of relief.

'Shit,' said Jay Sandbach speaking for them all, 'that wasn't a lot of fun.'

The door opened and Wilkins came in. 'Sorry, Sam,' he said. 'There wasn't a lot I could do to stop the son-of-a-bitch. Don't worry. You did well and we'll have our turn when the other side show up.'

MacAnally wasn't so sure. After a press conference designed to put a favourable spin on the day's proceedings, he got away and took a taxi back to his flat, pouring himself a stiff drink when he got inside.

He collapsed into a chair. He looked at Marie's photograph and he wished she was there. He wanted her opinion. He wanted her encouragement. He wanted her love.

And he wanted her to help him believe in himself.

For at one point during the questioning he had felt stripped bare . . . and he knew that what was revealed had not looked at all good.

He remembered what Marie had said, that she was worried they were entering a more dangerous game. '*I just have a feeling it could all go wrong,*' she had said.

It had felt like that today.

It was not a good thought to go to bed on and he didn't sleep well.

Nicola Kowalska lay in bed and listened to a late-night radio programme reporting on the day's events.

As she heard a recording of Sam MacAnally's voice, tinged with anger as he tackled Eberhard's relentless questioning, she found herself thinking about the campaigner.

She had been impressed by him when they had lunch.

Not his logic. She genuinely believed that he had an unbalanced view of the world and that to American business he was potentially dangerous.

No, it wasn't his logic that impressed her.

So what was it?

His humanity? She liked that.

His good humour? He wasn't at all the aggressive, one-dimensional character she had expected.

No, she concluded, it was something else.

She couldn't think what it was.

Or . . . truth be told . . . she wasn't going to admit what it was.

Even to herself.

So, convinced that her side had experienced their best day since the campaign began, she turned off the radio and endeavoured to lose herself in a good book.

Less than half a mile away Eugene Remington sat in his hotel room gloomily looking at a printout of his finances.

He was not a reckless man but he had let himself get carried away. He now needed more than a million dollars a year to sustain his lifestyle.

It would be all right if plantacon was cleared. The airline could expand, and he and his co-founders could increase their annual salary and bonus.

He could even consider selling off some of his interest in the company to pay off the hefty mortgages on the latest properties – and to cope with his latest extravagance – the quarter of a million dollars he had contributed to underwriting his wife's new Broadway play.

It was not her fault she was costing him money. He knew that. The fact was that for all his outward assurance and his success, he had lacked confidence in his ability to win her on personality alone, for there were plenty of equally famous and wealthy rivals competing for her attention. So he had from the start thrown money at her. And he had never stopped. She hadn't asked him for the additional houses. She *had* suggested he finance the play, but that was because he had always acted as if funds were unlimited and, when the production had run into financial trouble, he had been the obvious saviour.

No, it wasn't her fault.

But nor did he want to have to tell her he had overstretched.

For God's sake, he thought, even now it was only basically a cash flow problem.

Provided plantacon was saved.

And – he began to cheer up – it looked as if it would be.

The first day had been theirs.

And if Eberhard and the others could do that much damage to a professional operator like MacAnally, what could they do to the environmentalists' other witnesses?

In the same hotel, but a floor above, Dieter Partrell was talking to Charlie Orbell on the phone.

'You've done well, Charlie,' he said grudgingly. 'We're using some of your information tomorrow. And more the day after.'

He paused, wondering whether the phone was safe. Then decided it must be.

'Charlie, those friends of yours . . . the ones we used a couple of years back . . . I want you to get in touch . . .'

He talked on for nearly five minutes.

In the background he could hear music.

The tune that was nearly always playing in the seedy little Lower East Side bar.

'Mac the Knife.'

In Baltimore, Todd Birk also listened to the radio summary of the hearing.

He didn't really understand what was happening but it appeared as if the Commie environmentalist MacAnally had been given a roughing up.

Maybe Remington, Kowalska and company knew what they were doing after all.

He wondered whether Theodore Jordan was listening. And what he was doing.

The second day of the hearings began badly with the morning newspapers.

Environmentalist rattled by senator's questions, reported the *New York Times*.

The *Wall Street Journal* headlined the story: *MacAnally's halo slips as environmental credentials questioned*.

The *Washington Post* was the best of them from MacAnally's point of view. Under the headline: *Plantacon revolution could be disaster* it began with the allegations MacAnally had made. But it too reported:

Bombarded with questions about his credentials by Senator Ed Eberhard (Rep., Texas) and others, MacAnally looked less at ease.

He acknowledged that he and others in the environmental movement lacked academic or scientific qualifications.

Senator Eberhard commented after the day's hearing, 'MacAnally has been shown to be little more than a self-publicist and anti-industry propagandist. His attacks on industry scientists are based on prejudice. If this is the best the environmentalists can do I cannot see how we could possibly consider banning plantacon.'

The paper's editorial was even more damaging:

There are two issues involved in a hearing such as the one into plantacon.

One is the specific issue of whether this fuel additive is a public health hazard.

The second is the reliability of both the industries involved and the environmental movement.

Mr Sam MacAnally and his supporters may not have liked the questions he faced at yesterday's hearing but they were nonetheless fair. We have a lot to thank environmentalists for but, given their growing influence, it is right that we should know exactly what their credentials are. This is especially so considering they feel able to robustly criticise the motives and actions of those they decide are their opponents.

Yesterday's hearing left the questions about plantacon unanswered and the hearings must address them today.

But it raised new questions about the environmental movement that Mr MacAnally and others will have to answer in more depth over the coming weeks and months.

This was bad enough but for MacAnally there was much worse.

He sat looking in horror at the new, fast-rising tabloid, the *New York Express*.

This paper's front page headline was:

ANTI-AIRLINE 'GREEN' LOST PARENTS IN AIR CRASH.

The story began:

Sam MacAnally, the so-called environmentalist or 'green' who spearheads a campaign that could lose the airline business billions of dollars, cause higher air fares, and waste valuable reserves of energy, has particular reason to dislike aeroplanes and their owners.

It emerged yesterday that MacAnally, currently testifying before a Senate committee in Washington, lost his parents in an air accident caused, it was later ruled, by negligence by maintenance engineers.

A close friend of MacAnally says, 'Sam never got over it and never forgave the aviation industry.'

The story fell short of saying that MacAnally was motivated by revenge but the inference was clear.

MacAnally threw down the newspaper in anguish. Memories of his parents came flooding back. How could

the sons of bitches do this? How could Nicola Kowalska
have stooped to this?

And if they had gone to the trouble to dig out this story,
what else had they discovered? About the other witnesses? How would their backgrounds stand up to a
campaign of denigration? And how long could Lord hope
to remain anonymous?

And, on top of all this, there was something else.

Most of the papers had a side story.

About a demonstration in Portland, Maine, that had
gone badly wrong.

A little girl had been hit by a flying missile.

Even now she was lying in hospital in a coma.

The papers described a battle between workers and
ECO members. MacAnally knew this couldn't be possible. ECO was dedicated to non-violent campaigning.

But it was the worst kind of publicity.

He hoped that the child was all right. He would ask
Molly Macintosh to ring the family.

As he dressed, throwing his clothes on and moving
around his apartment like an angry bull, he remembered
once more Marie's worried face and her fears.

'They won't get to me, Marie,' he muttered.

But would they get to others?

Was the little girl in Portland, Maine . . . Betty Hunter
. . . was she the first victim of something uglier than he
had ever encountered before?

The hearings group met briefly. The only question was
whether MacAnally should return for a further bout of
questioning by Wilkins. Eventually they decided to try to
repair the damage of the first day with a brief thirty
minutes or so.

Gaining the floor, Wilkins began. 'Mr MacAnally,
yesterday questions were raised about your credentials

even to testify before this hearing. I would like you to explain once more your role in the environmental movement.'

MacAnally nodded. 'My organisation is a legitimate part of the democratic process, an organisation of citizens with a particular concern for environmental protection.

'Such an organisation needs a variety of contributors, just as a political party or a business corporation does. There is a technical and scientific input and we have qualified people to advise and contribute in these areas. There are fundraisers and membership organisers, there are administrators, there are lawyers.

'And there are campaigners, people with experience of coordinating these skills, organising a campaign on a particular issue and representing it to the public. They may not be specialists on the particular issue but they are specialists at organising a campaign on the issue.

'I am an environmental campaigner . . . or, if you like, a campaigner on environmental issues.

'I like to describe myself as an advocate in the court of public opinion. I represent my case, rather as a lawyer represents his client.

'A lawyer does not devote his career to any particular client. He brings advocacy experience and knowledge of the process to the cause of many clients. I try to do the same to any cause my organisation decides is urgent and should be responsibly raised.

'The other side also has *its* advocates, often millions of dollars' worth of advertising agencies, public relations consultants, lobbyists, lawyers, etcetera. They have their chance to put their case too.

'You, in your role within the governmental process, are the judges.'

Wilkins smiled. 'Thank you, Mr MacAnally. One last

point: what would be your preferred outcome of this hearing?'

MacAnally looked along the line of senators before him.

'I would prefer plantacon to be cleared.

'Of course I would prefer that the public and the industry do not have to live with the consequences of a ban.'

He paused. The room went quiet. 'That is what I would prefer. But I fear it won't happen. So far, all the sceptics on your committee have done is to attack me and the environmental movement. We are, of course, accustomed to that, accustomed to being attacked personally, accustomed to being abused and sneered at by those who cannot answer our arguments and our evidence. Unfortunately for Senator Eberhard and others, it's becoming less and less an effective form of defence the more we are proved to be right on one issue after another. The American people will not feel better about plantacon because I've been attacked by Senator Eberhard or anyone else; they will only feel safer when our case has been undermined. I repeat, I hope they can do that. I hope that I and my colleagues can leave these hearings free of our concerns about plantacon. The opening day suggests it will be otherwise.'

Eberhard flushed with anger but didn't attempt to respond and MacAnally rose. As he walked to the back of the room he noticed Nicola Kowalska sitting, watching intensely.

'Congratulations on the *Express* story,' he said. 'You've got your side into the gutter in record time.'

She flushed angrily and began to reply but he brushed past her and retook a seat well away from her.

David Abernathy was the next to testify and from the moment he arrived it was clear that after his early hesitancy he was enjoying his moment in the spotlight. He had put on a slightly flamboyant off-white suit with a silver shirt and darker silver tie and wore a flower in his button hole. He smiled at the cameras and looked, thought MacAnally, over-eager. He hoped the enthusiastic scientist was not going to go over the top.

He was soon reassured. Abernathy presented his findings carefully and clearly and even his conclusion was not overstated. 'Mr Chairman, my study leaves little doubt that children in the vicinity of this airport are absorbing plantacon at levels that are adversely affecting their intellect and behaviour.'

Wilkins had indicated he had no immediate questions so it was Eberhard who Hal Frankle called to begin the questioning.

'Dr Abernathy, let me for a moment make a comparison between plantacon poisoning, if there is such a thing, and lead poisoning. Lead is an environmentally produced substance, isn't it? Whereas plantacon is manufactured, it's a synthetic substance?'

'Yes, sir.'

'And lead is non-degradable?'

'Yes.'

'But is there any evidence that plantacon is also non-degradable?'

'I didn't do work on this,' Abernathy replied. 'But many of its properties are the same as lead and it could well follow, therefore, that it too is non-degradable.'

'But it could be degradable, just as it could be non-degradable?'

'I would have to do the work . . .'

'And if it's degradable it will not accumulate in children's bodies. And if it doesn't, it's unlikely to do permanent damage? I mean, assuming it does any damage to children at all, that damage must be only temporary?'

Abernathy protested. 'No, sir, I don't think so.'

Eberhard interrupted. '*Think*? Dr Abernathy. Not a very scientific word. Do you *know* . . . one way or the other?'

Abernathy looked along the row of senators and addressed them all . . . indicating by a conspiratorial smile that he expected them to understand his argument even if the obstinate Senator from Texas couldn't.

'Gentlemen, you need further testimony on whether plantacon is degradable or non-degradable. I can only say that I have no reason to believe that it's degradable. But even if it is, it doesn't follow that the damage it does is just temporary. Plantacon is a neurotoxin, a brain poison. Excessive exposure to such a neurotoxin, say at a level of around eighty micrograms per decilitre of blood, could cause severe behavioural disturbances, abdominal pain, anaemia, nerve palsy, epilepsy, convulsions, paralysis, coma and even death. At lower levels of exposure, and we don't know if there is any safety limit, neurotoxic poisoning can lead to reduced IQ, behavioural problems, and learning difficulties. The damage could be permanent.'

'*Could*, Dr Abernathy?' It was Eberhard, his voice raised now. '*Could*. That's the point. You *don't know*, you can't know, because you haven't had time. You're not presenting us with definitive evidence, but a possibility. And you expect us to demolish the economics of the aircraft industry on that?'

Abernathy smiled at him, maddeningly. 'I'm not asking you to do anything, sir. I'm just presenting the results of my study.'

Eberhard looked at him coldly.

'You're not suggesting that the level of alleged poisoning of children by plantacon fits within the definition of clinical poisoning?'

'No, sir, we're discussing low level exposure.'

'If at all.'

Abernathy didn't reply.

'Now you suggest that children living near the airport, those you claim have the greater plantacon content in their blood, had IQs averaging a few points lower than the children living in areas further away. You also claimed they were suffering other behavioural problems. Is that right?'

'That is a brief summary.'

'Good. Now, I am right in thinking that differences of three points in IQ are not regarded as statistically significant by scientists . . . that three points could be an acceptable margin of error in the study?'

'That is a generally held view. However it doesn't automatically follow that they're not significant. It's just that on their own they hardly represent definite proof of an effect.'

'Not definite proof?'

'Not on their own. But if you have more than one study, as we do, and they show the same trend, then it's more likely the result is significant.'

'Well, we're just considering *your* study, Dr Abernathy. And your study shows, on average, a six and a half point IQ difference between the two sets of children. But you have acknowledged that a three point difference is not statistically significant, that it could involve error of some kind. So we're really looking at a three to three and half point difference between the IQs of the groups of children.'

'I think that's a gross distortion. We're looking at individual IQ deficits ranging between five points and eight and a half points. That is what my research revealed. And, as you know, my result has been replicated by similar work in other countries.'

'It's also been contradicted, hasn't it, Dr Abernathy. I believe we will be hearing from scientists to that effect.'

'Yes.'

'Why do you think that is?'

'I don't know. I would need to know more about those studies. There is a need for scientific discussion about the studies, perhaps further work.'

'Ah, now we're getting to the crux, Dr Abernathy. *Further work? More discussion?* What you're saying quite clearly is that *some doubt remains*.'

Abernathy looked round the room, then at MacAnally, helplessly.

'I suppose so,' he said. 'But then there's always room for further research on any problem. With respect, sir, it's your duty as politicians to decide when there's a case for precautionary action.'

Eberhard looked at Abernathy contemptuously. 'Ah yes, we've heard all this from Mr MacAnally. Precautionary action? Err on the side of caution? Do you know what that sounds like to me, Dr Abernathy: it sounds like you're saying if you can't prove your case we must just act anyway, out of hysteria or because of the fear that you've generated.'

Abernathy began to protest but Eberhard waved a hand to silence him.

'Now let's look at the other possible causes of the differences between the two children. There could be other factors could there not? Lead pollution for instance.'

'I checked for lead.'

Eberhard looked surprised.

'You *checked for lead*?'

'Yes, sir. As the symptoms were the same as for low level lead exposure I thought it right to check for lead. They all had some lead in their blood.'

Eberhard looked triumphant. 'So the problem could be caused by lead pollution.'

'No, sir.'

'Why not?' The senator, frustrated by Abernathy's replies, was almost shouting.

'Because there was little difference between the lead in children further away from the airport and those nearest to the airport, so it could not account for the IQ and behavioural differences.'

Eberhard looked furious but pressed on. 'But it could account for *some* of the IQ and behavioural problems, could it not?'

'They did not have an abnormally high lead content in their blood.'

'But *some* lead in their blood?'

'Yes, possibly . . . some.'

'Well, I'm not suggesting the lead accounts for *all* of the IQ difference, but it could account for some. Maybe twenty or twenty- five per cent?'

'I can't say that.'

Eberhard looked at him hard for a moment, then ignored the answer. 'So if you take the area of statistical irrelevance, say three IQ points, and add a possible lead effect which could possibly account for twenty or twenty-five per cent of the IQ deficit, that would damn-near add up to an explanation for the brain damage? Without plantacon being involved?'

Abernathy looked around the room with a grin.

'Frankly, sir, there are a lot of "possibles" in that . . . this is absurd stretching of your argument. It is convoluted. Your figures don't even add up. It's nonsense.'

'Nonsense?' Eberhard's voice was cold and sharp as a knife. '*Nonsense?* You have said the children's blood contains lead. Lead is a neurotoxin known to have the effects you have identified. You *admit* it could be a contributing factor. You also *admit* that three of the percentage points would have been statistically insignificant. So why is it so convoluted to suggest that, taking your two admissions together, there is at least a small possibility that you have identified low level lead poisoning?'

Abernathy spoke firmly, looking straight into Eberhard's eyes: 'Because, as I've explained, there was *no difference* in the levels of lead in blood between the three groups but there *was* a noticeable difference in IQ deficiency and behavioural difficulty. Therefore it has to be assumed that the brain-damaged children have been affected by *something else*.'

For a fraction of a second Eberhard looked flummoxed. Then he shook his head. 'You do seem anxious to be proved right at all costs, Dr Abernathy. OK, let's move on. There are other factors that could explain these problems, aren't there?'

'Of course and within the limits of time and money available I tested for them.'

'Explain what the other factors could be.'

'Social factors. Family problems. Poor housing. Poor diet. That kind of thing.'

'And you took them into account.'

'I did.'

Seeing the Chairman becoming restless, Eberhard turned to his colleague and said, 'Just a few more minutes, Mr Chairman, please.'

He shuffled some papers.

'Dr Abernathy, you know we will hear testimony from reputable scientists, some with many more years experience than you, that they carried out similar studies and were unable to replicate your results. You've already said you can't explain that and you think further work is required. Is it just possible that you got it all wrong? I'm not trying to be offensive, Doctor, but isn't that at least a possibility?'

'It's always a possibility. It would be an arrogant man who claims *never* to make a mistake. But I cannot see how it could be so in this case.'

'But you *could* have got it wrong?'

'I don't believe I did.'

'But you *could* have?'

Abernathy shrugged. 'I suppose so.'

'Isn't the answer "yes"?'

'Very well. Yes.'

'Thank you.'

Eberhard leaned back in his chair as if finished and then as the Chairman began to call another representative he suddenly leaned forward. 'Sorry, Mr Chairman, just one more point. When did Mr MacAnally commission this research?'

'He didn't.' As soon as he said it Abernathy knew he had stepped into a minefield. He lost some colour and nervously wiped his brow with a handkerchief.

Eberhard moved in like a snake with his victim trapped against a wall. 'He *didn't*? Well, who did? We were told this was paid for with public money.'

'It *was* – it was commissioned by a member of the public. But it was an anonymous contribution.'

Eberhard looked amazed. The whole room was silent now and Frankle himself was unable to resist stepping in.

'Wait a minute, Senator,' he said to Eberhard, then turning to Abernathy he said, 'are you telling us that a member of the public came along and gave you a sum of money to carry out this research and that you cannot or will not name him to this hearing?'

Abernathy wriggled in his seat. 'Yes, sir.'

'This is highly unusual, isn't it? Has this ever happened to you before?'

'Research is commissioned by all sorts of organisations and individuals. Sometimes for their own reasons it's kept private.'

'Have you ever had a member of the public commission a study of this kind before and then insist on anonymity?'

'Well, no . . . but it didn't seem so strange. He was concerned to establish whether plantacon was a hazard.'

'But what made him concerned?'

'You would have to ask him.' Once more Abernathy could have bitten his tongue.

Eberhard leapt in. '*Of course* we would like to ask him, Dr Abernathy. *But that requires you to name him.*'

'I'm afraid the terms of my contract don't allow that, sir.'

Eberhard almost roared at him. 'So while the environmentalists cast doubt upon the integrity of scientists who don't support their claims, who they say are working for vested interests, their *own* research is financed by someone who remains anonymous and could have a vested interest himself?'

He turned to his colleagues. 'I believe this hearing is increasingly a waste of time.'

Wilkins, looking serious, stepped in. 'With respect, Mr Chairman, there is no evidence of vested interest. In any case the issue is not who financed the research but whether these deeply serious findings withstand examination. If they do, then millions of children in the vicinity of airports are being damaged. The Senator from Texas can make debating points all he likes, can try to discredit those who testify, environmentalists and scientists alike, but it's plantacon that is under examination here and there is too serious a question over it for these hearings not to pursue the matter further.'

The Chairman looked at the clock. 'I will adjourn this

hearing for three days. We need time for tempers to cool.'

The hearing broke up in tumult.

PORTLAND, MAINE

Betty Hunter came out of her coma at nine that evening.

The local TV news show interviewed the relieved mother as she left the hospital.

The story had been its lead item for forty-eight hours.

Kathy, desperate for news, had watched every programme.

They had shown the violence.

They had shown the ECO Warriors placards – often with only the word ECO appearing.

They had shown the child lying on the ground.

They had referred to a battle between workers and environmentalists . . . but . . .

. . . They hadn't mentioned plantacon. Not once.

The impression created by the TV coverage was that ECO was a violent group who attacked workers and didn't care whether children were caught in the crossfire.

Kathy sat forward in front of the TV set, her head in her hands.

Campaigning, she decided, tears in her eyes, was harder than it looked.

TOKYO

Before he could tackle the crisis developing in the Washington hearings MacAnally found himself facing yet another problem.

Jake Katzir had found discrepancies between the work of Raynald Warner and that of the Japanese scientist Seiichi Tezuka and was worried that the other side would use them to raise doubts about the quality of the whole ECO scientific package.

Also Machiko Yanagi, running her first major campaign, reported that she was struggling.

The media were abandoning the story and her frontrunner in the Diet was being blocked at every turn.

Japan was becoming a weak link in the ECO international operation.

MacAnally called in Katzir and Adrian Carlisle. 'We've got a three-day break in the hearings, then one day of hearing, then a weekend. If you two were to miss that one day, you would have six days available. That's plenty of time to fly to Tokyo and back.

'You, Jake, must iron out the scientific problems with Tezuka. It's vital that, if there are any inconsistencies between our studies, we can explain it convincingly.

'And you, Adrian, can sit down with Machiko and see what her problem is. I need to know whether we should send an experienced campaigner in to back her up.'

The two flew to Japan that night.

Katzir locked himself away in a hotel room with Tezuka for forty-eight hours, then telephoned Carlisle who had spent the same time holed up in Machiko Yanagi's flat.

'How's it going?' he asked.

'OK. Despite her reservations, *I* don't think it's Machiko's inexperience that's the problem, and I'm saying that with her sitting beside me. I think she's done all that she could. It's just extremely difficult to campaign here.'

'So there's not a lot you can do to help?'

'No, I wouldn't say that. We've come up with a

number of ideas. One is that we should stage an Asian-Pacific conference in Japan. We can give your man Tezuka another chance to publicise his work and bring Cossens from Australia and David Abernathy too. And leading environmentalists and politicians from other countries. Make a big thing of it. It'll get the issue back in the media. Also, the Japanese are impressed by visiting politicians and experts. We should get a few people listening who aren't doing so now.'

'Sounds good.'

'How are things with Tezuka?'

'OK. I don't think the discrepancies are real at all. It's just that there are differences in the way some of the data has been presented.'

'Well, why don't we all meet up for dinner. About nine. We can put the idea of the symposium to Tezuka. Then we can take the package back to Washington tomorrow.'

Katzir checked with the scientist and came back to the phone. 'You're on. Professor Tezuka is taking me to have a drink with a couple of colleagues and we'll meet you at nine.'

'Good. Machiko suggests somewhere in the Akasaka district. Hang on, I'll put her on the line and she can tell you how to get there.'

The arrangements made, Carlisle went back to his hotel, packed, and telephoned MacAnally to update him.

It was ten past nine when he met Machiko Yanagi at the exit to Akasaka subway station and the two began to walk to the restaurant.

It was a warm night and the streets were crowded with mainly young people. The restaurants and bars were packed.

Machiko felt uplifted. Carlisle had boosted her

confidence and morale. She now knew what she could do to revive the campaign.

And they had a convivial evening to look forward to.

She was just pointing out their destination – the restaurant was about fifty yards away – when there was a huge explosion.

In an instant the gaiety and vitality of the evening were gone – replaced by fear and panic. There were screams, the sound of people running. Cars braking.

Of all this they were only half aware. Because, as the bomb exploded, Carlisle picked up Machiko and literally threw her into a doorway, falling on top of her, protecting her from the bits of glass and debris as they flew by.

As he did so he felt a sharp pain in his thigh. He gasped and fell away from her.

'Don't move, Adrian,' she said. 'You've got a big piece of glass embedded in it.' She looked more closely. It was about a foot long and shaped like a knife, hanging out of his leg. 'Oh God,' she said, 'it's really big. Grit your teeth, I'm going to have to pull it out.'

He groaned and bit his lip as she did. He felt the blood gush down his leg.

She sat him up, and undid his belt and pulled down his trousers to uncover the wound. Taking some clean tissues from her shoulder bag, she told him to press them over the cut while she got help.

It was only then that she became aware of the mayhem. People had emerged from bars and cafés and all begun running in the direction of the noise. She could hear sirens. She saw the traffic had been stopped; many drivers were tooting their horns, not knowing the reason for the jam.

But that was not all she saw.

Her heart nearly stopped beating.

'Adrian,' she cried. 'The explosion. *It came from the restaurant we were going to.*'

'Christ.' He groaned, then, moved so that he was sitting with his back to the shop door, his injured leg stretched out in front. He said, 'I'll be OK for a few minutes. Go and see if the other two are all right.'

She began to run, pushing her way past the crowd.

She could see now that the whole front of the restaurant had been blasted away.

There was glass and debris everywhere. She felt herself running over broken plates and cutlery and bits of wood.

The police were quickly cordoning off the restaurant. She tried to break past but was firmly held back. Ambulances and fire engines only were allowed close-up. Already the latter appeared to be getting the blaze under control.

The crowd was quiet, standing watching, whispering.

Then she saw stretchers being carried out. Some were covered.

On one of them was Jake Katzir.

She shouted to a policeman that this was her friend, and at last managed to slip by and reach his side.

Thank God, she thought. He's alive.

And although injured and covered in blood and dust, he didn't appear too badly hurt.

He grabbed Machiko's arm and held it tight. 'Christ, I was lucky. I went out the back, to the washroom. I was just about to come back when it happened.'

'Tezuka?'

He shook his head. 'He never stood a chance. The bomb must have been planted in our corner of the restaurant.'

Then he began to shake.

He held her arm so tight it hurt.

'Machiko, tell Sam to remember what I said. There's something very wrong. This is one too many.'

As soon as he was in the ambulance, she ran over to another and told the attendant about Adrian. He collected a colleague and they took a stretcher back to the doorway.

For an awful moment she was afraid Adrian had died too. He had fallen into the corner of the doorway, his head lolling to one side. The tissues had slipped from his fingers. His leg and the ground around it were soaked in blood.

'It's all right,' one of them told her. 'He's breathing. He must have fainted.' They picked him up and carried him to the ambulance. Machiko clambered in too and sat holding Carlisle's hand as they raced through the city streets to the hospital.

There she waited for nearly an hour until she was told Carlisle was comfortable and that she could see him.

He was sitting up in bed, his whole leg in a thick bandage. He looked pale but managed a smile.

'They told me you were waiting,' he said. 'Thanks. The doctor said you'd pulled the glass out so cleanly that there wasn't a single splinter left. But I haven't been told what happened.'

She wondered whether he was in a fit condition, but he seemed alert enough, so she told him about the bomb in the restaurant . . . that Jake was only slightly injured, but that Tezuka was dead.

'It was a terrorist group, Adrian. It's their third bombing in the past month. They call themselves the Avengers. I never did get to understand what they were all about.'

'Christ, another couple of minutes and we would have got it too.' He lay back.

She noticed he was shaking.

'Look, I think I'd better let you get some sleep.'

He tried to sit up, then fell back on the pillow. 'Look, I must ring Sam first. Can you get them to bring me a phone?'

'Why don't I ring him?'

'No, I must talk to him myself.'

They located MacAnally in his flat, just about to leave for New York.

Carlisle told him what had happened.

MacAnally collapsed into his couch. 'Christ, that's *three* of our scientists. *I don't believe this*.'

'That's what I wanted to say, Sam. Three deaths . . . I know they can all be explained but . . . we've got to at least consider the possibility that the other side are getting to them.'

He told MacAnally about Jake Katzir's warning to Machiko.

MacAnally listened silently, then, telling Carlisle that the two of them mustn't hurry back until they were properly fit, he ended the call, grabbed his coat and briefcase and headed out the door to find a taxi to National airport.

Surely, he told himself, it *had* to be an awful coincidence.

He couldn't believe anyone had set out to kill the scientists.

He knew it was always possible for a campaign to turn nasty. He had been faced with some minor violence before. But murder?

Who by? The airlines? Out of the question. Partrell? That awful man Birk?

No, he didn't believe they were up to it.

No, it just wasn't on.

Still, even if it was a coincidence, they'd better draw

the attention of someone to it. But who? The deaths had been in three different countries. The FBI? Interpol?

He didn't know where to begin.

He would have to seek advice.

NEW YORK

On the plane he read the newspapers. It was another bad day for the campaign. Every newspaper headlined the row over the anonymous funding of the research.

The *New York Times* headline was typical: *Secret funder of plantacon research*, it said.

Others ran separate stories on the scientific debate, also with unhelpful headlines: *Other possible causes of damage to children, hearing told*.

It was left to the *New York Express* to once more deal the low blow.

MacAnally groaned as he looked at its front page.

ANTI-PLANTACON SCIENTIST CHEATED AT COLLEGE.

The story hardly measured up to the headline but it was damaging enough.

New York University researcher Dr David Abernathy, at the centre of a controversy over his claims that plantacon is brain damaging children, was sentenced to be suspended for a term from Ohio University for alleged cheating during examinations, it was revealed today.

The story told of an incident when Abernathy was eighteen. Only in the last paragraph was there to be found his side of the story.

Dr Abernathy said last night that he had denied the charge at the time and still did. An appeal later had been upheld.

When they met in his cupboard-sized office at the

university he was virtually sobbing with rage. 'Sam, I appealed the charge and the Board found the evidence wanting. I was cleared. I was never suspended. It's a lie.'

'They've been clever,' MacAnally replied. 'They only said you were *sentenced* to be suspended. Christ, it's the dirty tricks brigade again. Forget it David,' he urged him. 'No one you care about reads that paper. And anyone who does will see by the last paragraph that you were cleared. You did brilliantly at the hearing.'

Abernathy shook his head. 'If all this shit doesn't stop, Sam, you can count me out. I don't know who's feeding them these stories but they've got to be investigating our backgrounds. Where will it end? I tell you, I can't take much more of this.'

MacAnally wondered what was really worrying Abernathy. He was positive now that the young scientist was gay. Was he afraid the tabloid papers would make a big thing of this? Humiliate him publicly?

He told him how painful he had found the *Express* story about himself – about the death of his parents. 'I know it's hard, David, but this is a *hard* business. I don't blame you for hating the people who are doing this, but the way to deal with them is to beat them.'

The researcher looked half-convinced. 'Yes, I guess you're right.' He put on a brave face. 'Don't worry, Sam. I'll stick with it.'

'Good man.'

But MacAnally was not as sanguine about the newspaper campaign as he pretended. With every story in the *Express* the depth of the other side's research was becoming clear.

And he feared that this was only the beginning . . . that these were gentle openers compared with what was to come.

The sub-committee's interest in their funding was also a problem.

Clearly Justin Lord was worried too. When he called on him at the WTC, MacAnally saw no sign of the good humour evident on his earlier visit.

Lord still flatly refused to have his name made public, but did make some useful suggestions about how Wilkins should handle it in the committee.

They discussed the bombing in Tokyo . . . and that three of the five scientists were now dead.

Lord shook his head in dismay, then said, 'You're the man with the experience, Mr MacAnally. *Do people get killed?*'

'There've been suspicious deaths among campaigners. There was the Silkwood case. But I find it hard to believe it's happening in this instance. It's not as if any of the three deaths are inexplicable. In every case the police are satisfied by the obvious explanation.'

'Well, I can't advise you, Mr MacAnally. My only thought is that your Senator Wilkins could raise the matter with the head of the FBI so that some liaison could go on between the three police forces, maybe to double-check the circumstances.

'I tend to share your view that it would be paranoic to imagine someone's killing our scientists but it would be irresponsible not to at least draw attention to the links.'

'Actually, that's a good thought,' MacAnally said. 'I'll ring Wilkins tonight.'

WASHINGTON, D.C.

The following morning Chris Wilkins – having had an embarrassing phone conversation about the deaths of the scientists with the head of the FBI, who had politely suggested that the senator had been reading too many thrillers – told the reconvened hearing what Lord had suggested to MacAnally they could say about the funding.

'Mr Chairman,' he said, addressing Frankle, 'this question of funding is irrelevant. It's been blown up out of all proportion. In any case, I've checked the facts. The money to pay for Abernathy's research was only part of a larger sum donated to ECO to fund this campaign and it just so happened that the benefactor acted directly in the case of the research. Had he made his donation direct to ECO and let *it* pay for the research this wouldn't have even been an issue. We have assurances that there is no vested interest.'

Eberhard began to argue but Frankle quickly intervened. 'Cancelling the hearings won't help anyone,' he ruled. 'Nor is such a step justified simply because the funding of the research is anonymous. I would prefer to have all the facts but that's up to Senator Wilkins and his colleagues. If they wish to leave this in the air that's up to them, and it's up to the committee to decide later what weight to put upon that secrecy. I suggest we proceed.'

So they moved to the witnesses for industry. Remington was called first. He could not have been more plausible.

The industry was taking the matter seriously. It had already conducted preliminary research and the scientists would all testify there was no problem . . . just the same, it was setting up its own scientific inquiry and would report within a year.

He spelled out the advantages of plantacon and concluded: 'Mr Chairman, my industry is deeply safety conscious, deeply environmentally conscious. Despite his unwarranted attacks on plantacon we admire

Mr MacAnally and his organisation. We share their overall concern for the health and well-being of our fellow citizens. We are family men and women ourselves. Why should we want to put our own children at risk? So it's only after careful consideration of all the evidence that I say to you that it's our view that there are no grounds for throwing out the enormous benefits of plantacon on the basis of unsupported and discredited research anonymously funded . . . and because of an emotive campaign that has played on the fears of concerned parents. We must ask for your support for our maligned industry.'

Wilkins was first to question him:

'Do you live near an airport, Mr Remington?'

'No, sir.'

'To your knowledge do any of the members of the Board of Executive Airways?'

'I'm not sure . . .'

'Then let me tell you. I have here the home addresses of all your Board members. None do. So this claim to be equally concerned as parents is nonsense, is it not?'

'Sir, you have no grounds for questioning our sense of public duty.'

'I am merely questioning your right to say you are just as affected as the communities who have testified at this hearing. Clearly you are not. Now let's move on. Did your company, when it asked the oil companies to add plantacon to Jet-A, carry out environmental checks or ask for assurances that there was no environmental hazard?'

Remington licked his lips nervously. 'We asked if there was any safety downside.'

'By safety you had in mind the effect on those handling it?'

'Yes, of course.'

'But not environmental safety?'

'We had no reason . . .'

'Exactly, you couldn't imagine a reason so you didn't ask for it.'

'Well, no . . .'

'You claim to be environmentally conscious but you didn't check whether there was an environmental downside to plantacon, did you?'

'With respect, there was no reason—'

'Did you or did you not?'

'No, sir.'

'Thank you.'

Wilkins left it at that.

Remington was followed by industry's scientists, all five of them, each of whom confirmed they had found no evidence of fallout near the airports and no evidence of harm to children.

Wilkins asked questions stressing their links with industry. His aim, he told them, was to establish why, out of all the scientists in the world, they had been chosen.

He began with Kendrick. The scientist was looking as calm and suave as ever.

'Your research was funded by the aviation industry?'

'It was commissioned by Fuel Efficient Industries.'

'FEI. The manufacturers of plantacon?'

'Yes.'

'But with funding from the whole aviation industry?'

'I believe so.'

'Now I'm not necessarily going to draw any particular conclusions from your answer, but I must ask you to confirm this, yes or no: each of the funders of your research had a financial interest in exactly the result you produced, is that not so?'

'I suppose so.'

'I did ask for a yes or no, Dr Kendrick. Surely my question *can* be answered straightforwardly.'

'Yes, then.'

'Quite.' Wilkins paused. 'You are, are you not, an industrial research scientist . . . a consultant to industry?'

'Yes.'

'All your work comes from industry?'

'For the past few years.'

'Most of it from the aviation industry?'

'About sixty per cent.'

'About sixty per cent of your income comes from this industry. You could almost say you work in this industry, couldn't you?'

'No, sir, I'm independent. I will work for anyone.'

'Yes, but sixty per cent of your income comes from this industry. It would not be too inaccurate to describe you as a scientific researcher who works mainly in the aviation industry?'

'At present, possibly.'

'I see. All right, let me put it like this. You're a scientific researcher who *at present* works mainly in the aviation industry.'

'I would prefer to say *for* the aviation industry.'

Wilkins looked round the room with a raising of the eyebrows. 'Let me try again. You're a scientific researcher who *at present* works mainly *for* the aviation industry?'

Kendrick nodded, now looking harassed, aware that by prevaricating he had made things worse.

Wilkins pressed on. 'Now if you work for an industry it would follow that you would at least hope that the results of your research would be helpful to that industry. That is fair, isn't it?'

'I don't think like that. I just do the research, objectively.'

'But you would feel *happier* if the result was supportive of the industry. You certainly wouldn't be hoping your research would undermine the industry you work for?'

'I don't think like that . . .'

'Let me put it this way: would you be *pleased* if the research undermined the industry?'

'Of course not, but it would not concern me too much either. I would have done my job.'

'Come now, Dr Kendrick, you presumably earn a good living working for this industry. Irrespective of how objectively you conducted the research, you would surely *prefer* to present a result to them that they were likely to welcome, wouldn't you. Isn't that only human?'

'I suppose so.'

'So isn't it possible that if a detail arose that required a judgement, and if you were committed to that industry, and worked for that industry . . . isn't it just possible that unconsciously you would lean, instinctively rather than deliberately, in favour of a judgement favourable to it?'

Kendrick was now red in the face. 'Sir, in your own way you are suggesting I load the results for those who are funding me. I resent that.'

Wilkins kept calm. 'No, sir. I'm not suggesting you do it deliberately. But we have a coincidence here. The five scientists in different parts of the world who have found a result unfavourable to the industry are all earning their income in the public sector, are genuinely independent of the industry. The five who have found a result favourable to the industry all earn at least part, and in your case sixty per cent of your income, from that industry. That's my problem. I repeat, I'm not suggesting you deliberately fixed the research. I want to make that clear. I'm not suggesting that. I'm suggesting that understandable loyalty and faith in the industry that employs you could unconsciously affect your work.'

'No, sir. That's not so. Anyway, this work required little judgement.'

'Oh? But you have had to consider other factors, social factors, etcetera. Couldn't you have unconsciously been looking *too hard* for another explanation of Dr Abernathy's result? Could you have unconsciously given greater weight to these factors than these more independently-minded scientists did? Not deliberately, but unconsciously? As a fallible human being wanting in good faith to find a satisfactory explanation?'

'No, sir. I deny that. In any case I was doing my own work, not reviewing Abernathy's.'

Wilkins looked round the room. 'Then the puzzle remains. Two sets of results from two groups of scientists, one working for the industry and one not. Do you have an explanation for it?'

'No, sir. I only know I stand by my work. And I would be happy to work with other scientists to follow it up.'

'Dr Kendrick, have you seen the results of an opinion poll carried out a short while back for the League of Conservation Voters – on the credibility of environmental scientists?'

'I believe so. I can't remember the details.'

'Let me remind you. More than sixty-six per cent said they would rely on the opinion of an environmental group scientist, while only fifteen per cent said they would trust a government scientist and only six per cent – *six per cent*, Dr Kendrick – said they would trust the findings of a corporate scientist. What does this suggest to you, sir?'

'It suggests that the public are ignorant on these matters. On what basis can they form such an opinion? It is ludicrous.'

'I grant you that it's unfair, Dr Kendrick – unfair to a lot of good scientists. But let me suggest to you why they have formed that opinion. Could it be that they take note of the behaviour of industry generally. For instance, the tobacco industry. A Senate committee once had to endure a procession of thirty-eight consecutive witnesses with scientific credentials who denied the causal relationship between smoking and disease, despite the overwhelming evidence of that relationship.

'Could it be that such scientists are the cause of the credibility gap?

'Could it be because the public have heard too many scientists, representing polluters, denying that the pollution exists, denying that harm is being done, only to find that subsequent, independent research has proved them wrong?

'Could it be that on issue after issue the environmentalists have been personally attacked, called emotive, hysterical, or worse, accused of having all sorts of motives, when in fact they have been subsequently proved right?

'Could it be that people have found the environmentalists more reliable? Is that why two thirds of the public trust them rather than other scientists? And that only six per cent of them trust people like you?'

Kendrick was silent.

Eberhard asked only two questions. 'Dr Kendrick, has your integrity ever been publicly or privately questioned?'

'No, sir. I have a record stretching over twenty-five years and I believe it's a respected one.'

'And the source of your funding is, of course, public knowledge, unlike that of Dr Abernathy?'

'Yes, sir.'

'Quite.' Eberhard looked at his colleagues meaningfully, and at Wilkins maliciously, and sat back satisfied.

The questions to the other four industry scientists and their answers were on similar lines.

The day ended and the hearings group met that night over dinner to discuss the position.

Wilkins looked despondent. 'It's not been going well, Sam. We've had three bad days.'

'You did the best you could today, Chris.'

'I'm not sure it's good enough. Their scientists looked and sounded convincing. We should have brought the Australian scientist over. We missed a trick there.'

'Don't worry. You did brilliantly with the differences between the studies. You really dented their credibility.'

But, truth be told, MacAnally was worried. As he made his way home he thought that, contrary to what he had told Wilkins, the industry was getting the better of the hearings.

Somehow they had to turn it round before it was too late.

If the hearings ended badly it could take years to get the campaign back on track.

They desperately needed a break.

The next day they got one. In the form of Dieter Partrell.

Partrell's testimony was nearly all to do with the benefits of plantacon. He produced impressive projections of energy savings over the next ten, twenty-five, and sixty years. He suggested that as it became even cheaper to produce it, and as the product was further developed, the savings could be even greater.

Eberhard who had opened the questioning eventually came round to the environmental effects.

'Plantacon is a neurotoxin, isn't it, Mr Partrell?'

'Yes. That's why we've introduced unparalleled safety

measures in our factory and in our distribution system. I'm happy to say that since it's been on the commercial market there has not been one reported accident involving plantacon, not one leakage that would affect the public.'

'And of course at the airports it's added to the fuel in tiny quantities.

'It represents only two per cent of the total volume.'

'Did you consider the possibility that it would be – to use Mr MacAnally's words – blasted out of aeroplane exhausts so that it became an environmental hazard?'

'We believe the bulk of it, probably as much as ninety per cent, is burned with the fuel. The remaining ten per cent is insignificant. We judge, I believe correctly, that it would just be "blasted" into infinity.'

'Do you believe it's safe?'

'One hundred per cent, sir.'

Wilkins began amiably. 'Of course, if there is no environmental hazard, your company has performed a major service, Mr Partrell, and I would be the first to welcome it.'

Partrell nodded appreciatively.

'Now, you acknowledged that it's a neurotoxin, a brain poison in simpler language?'

'I did.'

'You said that because of this you took what you described as unparalleled safety measures? What are these?'

Partrell described the protective clothing including hoods and gloves used by the men handling the chemical, the specially designed unbreakable canisters for its transportation, the detailed safety regulations that could only be ignored on threat of instant dismissal.

'And you said there had been no *reported* accident

after the product came on the commercial market. I think those were your words.'

Partrell hesitated. 'Yes,' he eventually said.

'*After* it came on the market. What about before?'

'There is always a danger during the developmental process that—'

'Just answer the question: was there an accident *before* it came on the market?'

Partrell began to redden and sweat. 'Yes, there was.'

'Four men were killed.'

'Yes.'

'What happened?'

'One was poisoned by an undetected leak. In the case of the other three, there was a spill. They were handling the chemical at the time. They were badly contaminated.'

'Badly contaminated? Isn't it true that they suffered physically and mentally, that they died in agony and insane?'

Partrell raised his voice. 'They died tragically and we were as you would expect appalled. But there is always a risk in a developmental process. We learned the lessons. Tragic as it was, it was not a case for not proceeding.'

'I'm not suggesting it was. I'm saying that four men died a terrible death and that shows what the product is capable of if someone is exposed to it in large doses. Is that not so?'

'Yes, but they won't be because . . . .'

' . . . Because the accidents are never likely to be repeated, Mr Partrell? That is a confident claim.'

'We have done all that's humanly possible.'

'Did you test to see what plantacon exposure could cause to human beings, especially children, at lower levels of exposure?'

'No. There was no need.'

'No need? No need? It's being suggested that children are being seriously damaged at low levels of exposure. What do you mean, *no need*?'

'I deny that.' Partrell's temper was getting out of control. 'All we have is these damn environmentalists, determined as always to damage industry, interested only in publicity, making accusations they can't substantiate.'

'You think environmentalists are only trying to damage industry, Mr Partrell?'

Partrell's company lawyer laid a restraining hand on his arm but the big man would have none of it. 'Yes,' he roared. 'What have they done for this country? What have they made? What have they sold? Where is their contribution to its wealth – the money that pays for their university education and enables them to work in government-funded jobs while the rest of us earn our living? This man MacAnally has attacked one industry after another, as if we're enemies of our country instead of being the source of its wealth. It's they who are the enemies, the parasites.'

Wilkins held up a list. 'I have here a list of one hundred major organisations covering the fields of child welfare, education, and many other related areas, all of whom believe plantacon should be phased out . . . are *all these* parasites?'

'They are just taking what MacAnally says at face value. Why should they? What right has he to make the claims he does?'

'You don't like Mr MacAnally, do you, Mr Partrell?'

'The man is a threat to the American way of life.'

'Do you know a Mr Charlie Orbell, Mr Partrell?'

The industrialist looked stunned. Mopping the sweat that was running down his face, he turned and whispered to the company lawyer.

The lawyer appealed to the Chairman: 'We don't see the relevance of this question.'

Wilkins, scenting blood, moved in quickly. 'The relevance is that Mr Orbell is a private detective who has been for the past six weeks in Mr Partrell's employ and has been investigating the personal life of Mr MacAnally. And Dr Abernathy. He is the man who produced the rubbish that has been paraded across the front pages of the *New York Express* the last few days. Isn't that true, Mr Partrell?'

The businessman said nothing.

'Are these the ethics of your business, Mr Partrell? Isn't it the case that you'll do *anything* to protect your product, that you'll do *whatever is necessary* to discredit public servants and scientists, that you *couldn't care less* about the public health and environmental questions before this committee, that *it is you*, not Mr MacAnally, who is the parasite?'

Partrell exploded. '*Bullshit,*' he roared.

Wilkins shouted back: 'You don't *care* about the children you're harming, do you? Just like you don't care about the four men who died?'

'So a few men died, *so what*?' Partrell roared, then stopped as his lawyer nearly broke his arm.

The room exploded in a buzz of comment. Eugene Remington and Nicola Kowalska, sitting near the back of the room, looked at each other in consternation. The ECO group were openly jubilant.

The Chairman banged his gavel. 'I don't think this testimony is getting us very far, gentlemen,' he said. 'We shall adjourn.'

The hearings group gathered in the Bunker and collapsed in laughter.

'Partrell's undone just about all they've achieved on

the opening days,' Jay Sandbach said.

'How the hell did you get the stuff about the detective?' MacAnally asked Wilkins, still amazed at the turn of events.

Wilkins, who had been looking pleased with himself, grinned. 'Let's just say I have a friend on the *New York Express*.'

Jay Sandbach calmed them. 'Look, I don't think we should go over the top. OK, Partrell made an ass of himself, but my guess is he hasn't changed the weight of the evidence. It's going to be a close-run thing.'

That sobered them up. But it had been their best day and that night MacAnally slept well for the first time in weeks.

The meeting of the Environmental Pollution Sub-committee the day after the plantacon hearings was one of the stormiest any of its members could recall. Not only was it clear that two of their number, Eberhard and Wilkins, hated each other's guts, but they were also totally committed to their own side of the case. The result was stubborn intransigence combined with personal pointscoring that drove Hal Frankle to the edge of his patience.

Finally, he exploded. 'I won't have any more of this,' he said. 'As Chris and Ed have no wish to compromise, let alone behave in a manner that befits the Senate of the United States, I propose to take a decision.

'I'm not convinced there's a case for a ban on plantacon.

'But I'm convinced that when there is widespread public concern, and there undoubtedly is, and when the information available is so contradictory, we need to take steps to sort it out.

'Therefore I propose to set a date for a mark-up on

Chris's bill but I for one would like Chris to know that, *on existing evidence*, I would not favour a bill that bans plantacon outright. There will need to be a compromise proposal.'

'How can there be?' asked the bewildered Wilkins.

'That's up to you, Chris. But that's my view on the basis of what I have to say were a particularly unpleasant set of hearings.'

He paused and looked round the room. 'So we move to a mark-up.'

The decision was announced in time for the early evening news programmes.

Round One had resulted in a narrow victory for the environmentalists.

But, as Senator Eberhard confided to the industry's war council later that night, Frankle's qualifying remarks had made it a hollow one.

There was a long, long way to go, and in the war council's view the environmentalists had shot their bolt.

The issue would now get bogged down in detail.

And when it came to *detail* the industry's lawyers and lobbyists were the best money could buy, the governmental institutions would all be on their side, and public opinion would have little effect.

Yes, concluded the war council, MacAnally and their friends, reputed to be having celebratory drinks in The Monocle, may have won this battle. But the probability was they were losing the war.

The President gripped Sam MacAnally's arm with one hand and shook hands with the other.

'Sam, good to see you. Come and sit down. Coffee?'

'Please, Mr President.'

'Good.' The older man leaned forward slightly. 'Sam,

I was told of the loss of your colleague and friend, Ms Doutriaux, I'm really sorry.'

MacAnally was both taken aback and moved. This caused his hand to shake. He quickly put the coffee down. 'Thank you, Mr President. It was a blow.'

'I can imagine.' The President paused for a moment. 'But now you're back in the fray you've been far from idle. Tell me about this plantacon business.'

MacAnally sketched out the details of the scientific studies. 'I believe it would be criminally irresponsible not to act, Mr President.'

The President looked thoughtful. 'But there have been contradictory studies, have there not?'

'That's so, sir, but all funded by the industry.'

'That does not necessarily invalidate them.'

'No, Mr President, but on their own they're hardly a full answer to the charge. Of course we have a scientific dispute, but our point is that where we're faced with the risk . . . let me put it no higher than that . . . of widespread damage to health we should at least protect people until the dispute is resolved. That's why we propose a plantacon phase-out, not an overnight ban. That allows time for further scientific study.'

'And what if that's inconclusive?'

'Then possibly the industry may have to do without plantacon for a while. After all, if it's subsequently cleared, it can be re-introduced. It all comes down to one question: given the scientific controversy, who pays the price for the ongoing research, the industry or the children?'

The President sighed. 'You make it sound so simple, Sam. But I have to take other factors into account. For instance, one of the biggest challenges we face is to conserve our resources of energy until we develop alternative sources. Plantacon is making a significant difference. It also has real social effects, making it possible for more people to fly more cheaply, opening up air travel to people who could never afford it before. And it's doing wonders for our balance of payments, and that helps everybody. These are considerable benefits.'

'And I welcome them, too, Mr President, especially the energy saving. But at what cost? If the earlier studies are right, and I believe they are, the price we're paying is far too high.'

'Hmm. Well, we'll have to see what Congress says.'

MacAnally pressed. 'Sir, would I be right in thinking that if Congress decides the risk justifies a ban, or at least a temporary one, that you would not veto the bill?'

The President smiled. 'Now, Sam, you know better than to expect me to answer that. Let me just say that I care about the children of this country as much as you do.'

He poured them each another coffee.

'Do you think there's a case for a Presidential study commission?' he asked. 'To look into the whole question? It could be expanded to include aircraft emissions generally.'

'With respect, sir, we both know study commissions are a delaying tactic. If this wasn't urgent maybe that wouldn't matter, but a lot of children could be harmed while we wait for the result.'

'*Could* be harmed, Sam. That's the point. We don't really know.'

The President leaned back in his armchair. 'Tell me, what else should I be worrying about besides plantacon?'

For twenty minutes MacAnally reviewed some of the major environmental issues.

He got the impression from the President's questions that he was better informed than he pretended. 'You make it all sound so bad, Sam,' he eventually said.

'I'm sorry, Mr President, I don't want to appear so negative. I'm afraid it's your misfortune to have inherited the record of neglect by your predecessors.'

'That's fair – but you can't expect me to do all that's necessary within the term of a Presidency.'

'No, sir, but every President who leaves these problems untackled is leaving his successor with a worse problem. I'm hoping you'll make a real start.'

The President smiled. 'Well, we'll see what we can do, Sam.'

There was a knock on the door and a young, brown-haired man in his mid-thirties entered. The President waved him over.

'Jack, come and meet Sam MacAnally. Sam, this is Jack Donaghue, my domestic affairs advisor. I've asked him to keep in touch with you. I'd like you to raise with Jack any matter you think I should know about. Let's keep communication going.'

Sam rose. 'I would welcome that, Mr President. Thank you.'

The President put his arm round him and walked him to the door of the Oval Office. 'As for this plantacon business, we'll do what's best for the country, I assure you of that.'

It was only when MacAnally was out in the cold and the rain that it struck him that 'what's best for the country' could have meant anything . . . anything at all.

Part Six

NO HOLDS BARRED

LONDON

In response to an ECO-commissioned opinion poll, a staggering ninety-five per cent of people replied 'yes' to the question: '*If it is proved that plantacon emissions from aircraft could harm children's health, would you be willing to pay higher air fares in order that the additive can be phased out?*'

Olly Witcomb gave the poll result exclusively to *The Sunday Times* and thus ensured it made the front page.

In the meantime, Nick Bell got an adjournment debate. Usually this would be replied to by a junior minister but the Secretary of State, Tom Muldoon, decided to speak himself.

Olly, worried about the aggressive tone his friend had been adopting, met Bell for breakfast on the day of the debate. 'Be factual, concerned, but *sane*, Nick. You're getting all the publicity you want now. There's no need to go over the top.'

The MP took Olly's advice, concluding his moderate speech with what most MPs felt was a reasonable appeal.

'Mr Speaker, to concerned parents, public relations

double talk, political manoeuvering, scientific point-scoring won't do.

'Is this harming our children or is it not?

'Mr Speaker, I'm not saying plantacon is guilty. I'm not saying the industry is guilty. I'm saying *there is a case to answer*.

'Will the Minister admit that?'

He sat down to 'hear hears' from an impressed Labour front bench. From the gallery Olly Witcomb caught his eye and nodded enouragingly.

Muldoon had expected a hysterical, blatantly publicity-seeking performance from Bell and had prepared a speech mocking the young back-bencher. Inwardly cursing, he now jettisoned part of it.

But worse was to come.

As he ploughed pedantically through his civil servants' brief, Bell rose.

'Will the Right Honourable Gentleman give way? We know there's scientific dispute . . . the Minister doesn't need to spell it out. I didn't ask him whether plantacon is a dangerous pollutant, whether children are being harmed, or even whether he will ban plantacon. I asked whether he thought there was a case to answer?'

Muldoon rose. 'I've made my position clear. There is as yet no evidence to justify a ban on a product that's so helpful . . .'

Labour's shadow environment minister rose. 'Mr Speaker, can the House have a yes or no? *Is there or is there not a case to answer?*'

'There's a case for keeping the matter under review and that is what we will be doing.'

The shadow minister leaned languidly over the dispatch box. 'With respect, Mr Speaker, the Right Honourable Gentleman knows very well that these things are not the same. "Kept under review" does not call for definitive action. Acknowledging that there is a case to answer does. Which is it to be?'

Muldoon's patience had been strained enough. 'At present we have two sets of contradictory studies. No signs of damage. Not one child produced who can be said to have definitely suffered from plantacon pollution. In all the circumstances it will be kept under review but I see no case at this point for specific action.'

There were shouts of shame.

And what worried the watching Prime Minister was that they came from both sides of the house.

Muldoon groaned. *The Times* headline had been bad enough . . . *Uproar in house as Minister refuses plantacon inquiry* . . . but now both the *British Medical Journal* and *The Lancet* had published leading articles criticising him for not instigating an inquiry.

After that day's Cabinet meeting the Prime Minister called him aside for a quick word. 'I'm a bit worried by this plantacon business. We've got an election coming up and some of our marginals are in the vicinity of airports. Play it carefully, will you.'

But the pressures continued to mount.

Local authorities all over the country began demanding more information.

The only good news for Muldoon was that the unions, concerned about jobs, were for once supporting the employers.

Then came a fresh blow. The political headlines were stolen by a spectacular by-election win by the Liberal Democrats in a normally safe Conservative constituency near enough to Birmingham's airport for plantacon to have become an issue.

The Liberal Democrat candidate had organised a petition calling for an inquiry. Conservative ministers, visiting the constituency to support their candidate, found themselves faced with a barrage of aggressive questions.

It was of course possible the Government would have lost the by-election anyway, but the decisive nature of the Liberal Democrat win and the exit poll evidence that the plantacon issue had weighed heavily with voters living near to the airport could not be ignored.

The Prime Minister took the unusual step of calling a special meeting of ministers responsible for transport, energy, environment and health. But what especially unsettled Tom Muldoon was the presence of the Party Chairman and it was he who spoke first.

'You, as departmental ministers, obviously have to consider a number of factors, but my responsibility is to look at this politically.

'*Politically* the position is this:

'There are no votes in protecting airlines or even airline fares.

'There are no votes in energy conservation, worthy as it is.

'There are few votes in doing the right thing on preventative health grounds.

'But there *are* lost votes if we're found to be negligent.

'All the key words and phrases on this issue – Environment. Children. Big business v the citizen . . . they're all electorally touchy ones.

'Of our thirty seriously marginal seats, sixteen are in the vicinity of airports. Our private opinion polls show seventy per cent of people are concerned about plantacon pollution. It only takes a few votes to swing those seats.'

The PM looked enquiringly at Muldoon. 'Secretary of State, you're the lead minister on this?'

'Well, Prime Minister, of course I understand the

Party Chairman's concern about the *political* position.
But I have also to consider what's *the right thing to do*.
Unfortunately the case for action on plantacon is still less
than convincing. We have totally contadictory evidence,
very little of it from this country.

'It is, of course, dangerous to reject out of hand the
possibility of pollution; plantacon particles are
undoubtedly emitted from aeroplanes. Some of the stuff
must be falling to the ground. And, of course, it is a
neurotoxin. But, on the other hand, the price for
controlling the use of plantacon will be extremely high.
It's not a black and white question.'

The Party Chairman interrupted impatiently. 'Really,
Secretary of State, it's the political question—'

But the PM stopped him. 'We know that, Party
Chairman, but the Secretary of State is right – there are
wider questions.'

Muldoon now suggested the compromise he had
devised during a sleepless night. 'We could announce a
major independent scientific inquiry—'

'Won't the environmentalists say we're just putting off
a decision?' the PM interrupted.

'That's what I was going to say: we can balance the
research with a request to the airlines to reduce
plantacon use to, say, fifty per cent of the present level
just until the inquiry reports.'

Ted Ingham, the Secretary of State for Transport, was
having none of it. 'Prime Minister, I must object.
Frankly I find these political points introduced by the
Party Chairman somewhat distasteful. We're supposed
to be governing responsibly.

'And does the Environment Secretary appreciate the
likely cost of his compromise? It would cost the industry
millions and millions of pounds. And raise air fares. To
do this on the evidence available for reasons of political

expedience would be monstrous.'

The Energy Secretary chipped in. 'And there's the lost energy.'

The Prime Minister, disconcerted by the divisions, began to sum up. 'As I see it there *is* a case to answer. That's the right position for any Government to take.

'And there *are* votes at stake. That's the political position we can't ignore if we're to survive.

'On the other hand I don't want to undermine the airlines, in particular British Airways, And Humphrey Brooks's lot – UK Ambassador. I like what the Environment Secretary proposes. It gives something to both sides.'

Ingham, unusually, interrupted the summing up. 'Prime Minister, I must protest. We're giving in to environmental lunatics. Their evidence looks increasingly scrappy. This is the worst kind of political expediency. I'm sorry, but if you ask for a fifty per cent cutback I may have to consider my position.'

There was a stunned silence.

The PM fiddled with his pen.

A ministerial resignation at this point and on an issue like this would be a disaster. Inevitably Ingham would emerge heroically as the man who sacrificed high office for principle; in his resignation speech he would be bound to accuse the PM of opportunistic and weak leadership, of bowing to every pressure group that threatened votes. The PM's and the party's position was too weak to risk it.

On the other hand, if the PM backed down under Ingham's threat his own position would be weakened anyway.

If he wasn't careful this plantacon business could put him in a no-win situation, literally end his occupation of No. 10 Downing Street.

Then Muldoon came up with a face-saving way of postponing the decision.

'Why don't we wait until we find out what the US Senate sub-committee plans to do. We'll know in a few days. We could then reconvene and take a final decision.'

The Prime Minister gratefully accepted the proposal.

Unfortunately the plan misfired.

It misfired because the *perception* of what was happening in the US differed from the *reality*.

While in theory the industry's war council had been right about what was really happening in the US Senate Environmental Pollution Sub-committee – that there was no real support for an outright ban – it had overlooked one factor: *the effect that the decision to mark-up a bill would have on the public and, even more significantly, around the rest of the world*.

In the US itself it was assumed that if the sub-committee had decided to even consider a bill, the pollution must be real.

In every other country including the UK the decision to move to a mark-up was reported as a victory for the environmentalists.

This, of course, was what MacAnally wanted: the more it was *believed* throughout the world that plantacon was likely to be banned in the US, the more likely other countries would be to take tough decisions themselves.

Nicola Kowalska, on the other hand, did her best to correct the 'misunderstanding'.

She encouraged her representatives in other countries to undertake detailed briefing of the media, politicians, bureaucrats and others, to communicate what was *really happening* in the US.

But the message was difficult to get across and,

because it was based on reports of a confidential meeting of the sub-committee, it lacked conviction.

Furthermore the industry couldn't get to the public as effectively as the local ECO campaigners, and the public were getting the message from ECO that the industry was losing.

It was bad luck for the UK government that the American news broke on the day questions were due to the Transport Secretary, Ted Ingham.

Ingham had been primed with a 'safe' answer to any question arising from the US sub-committee's decision. He was to say:

'We note with interest the action of the American Senate sub-committee in exploring a bill. We have, of course, no knowledge of what kind of bill will emerge and whether it stands any real chance of being passed. We will continue to keep the matter under close review.'

But Nick Bell wasn't going to let him get away with that, and, as the acknowledged frontrunner on the issue, once more had no difficulty in capturing the Speaker's eye.

'Is the Government really intending to continue risking our children's health despite the fact that the US, who stand to lose at least ten times the energy and the money we would lose, are considering a phase-out of plantacon?'

The Prime Minister wished that the more flexible Muldoon had been at the dispatch box instead of the fiery Ingham; this was a moment for showing some sympathy for Bell's position, some concern for the nation's children. But Ingham had no intention of letting down the airlines.

'The US is not considering phasing out plantacon. One small sub-committee of the Senate is to look at a proposed bill. Really, the honourable member is becoming a bore on this issue,' he abrasively replied.

Bell shouted across the chamber. 'Is there no end to the Government's obstinacy? Or is it that the Conservative Party is so in debt to industry that it has to do what it's told?'

Ingham looked at him coolly.

'I'm not aware of my party having received any contributions from the aviation industry,' he replied. 'No doubt the honourable member will on reflection wish to withdraw that disgraceful remark.'

The House was silent. Bell got a nod from the Speaker and rose. 'No doubt,' he said, 'the Right Honourable Gentleman will wish to apologise to me, Mr Speaker, when I tell him that I have information with me to the effect that two petroleum companies and one airline made contributions to his party's funds at the last election worth £15,000, £20,000 and £30,000 respectively. The airline was UK Ambassador.'

The Labour back-benchers loved that. There were cries of 'Answer that . . .' and 'Corruption . . .'

Ingham, furious, hit back: 'Naturally if I'm misinformed I will accept what the Honourable Gentleman says.

'But it's not illegal for any party to receive donations from industry just as it's not illegal for the Labour Party to receive donations from the trade unions.

'I do, however, take great exception to the suggestion that these donations have affected our judgement on this matter. The fact that I clearly did not know of these donations will have been noted by the whole House.'

The shadow minister rose. 'May I ask the Minister why these companies would give the money if it was not to affect his party's judgement?'

'Why do trade unions give the Labour Party money?' snarled Ingham. 'Because they choose to support a party which they believe, misguidedly in this case, will create the best circumstances for their members. They are not buying specific policies. Or maybe they are? Maybe the Labour Party is judging our behaviour on the basis of its own dishonourable conduct.'

That did it.

Labour back-benchers were on their feet howling for Ingham's blood.

It took the Speaker ten minutes to re-establish order.

Olly Witcomb left the gallery in high spirits. Ingham's aggression had helped Bell to make plantacon a party political issue. This could only work to the campaign's advantage.

The Times' leader the next day addressed the issue:

The aviation fuel additive plantacon may save conventional energy but it is certainly causing a great number of people to expend a great deal of theirs. Why is this so? It is because the allegations about it are serious but the scientific evidence is conflicting. What should we expect a responsible Government to do in these circumstances? The solution is so obvious that it is extraordinary it has not been adopted. It should set up an inquiry.

Olly Witcomb now organised a lobby of MPs by constituents and kept the issue high on the agenda by using his local coordinators to ring in to radio phone-in programmes, write letters to newspapers, and organise petitions.

The Party Chairman called on 10 Downing Street with the results of some alarming private opinion polls. One showed that less than ten per cent believed the Government was acting decisively to protect children from possible pollution by plantacon.

What would really have pleased Olly, if he could have

seen it, was a party poll showing that a month earlier only five per cent of those questioned had ever heard of plantacon; now ninety-seven per cent were aware of it. This was a triumph for the campaign.

Later that night he got a phone call from Hal Robbins. 'I should advise you to be in the House tomorrow, Olly,' he said. 'I think you'll be pleased with the way things are going.'

The House had been packed for Prime Minister's question time and, once it was over, members, instead of leaving in droves as they usually did, waited expectantly in their places. The word was out that ministers had grasped the plantacon nettle and everyone wanted to see how it was being handled.

The Secretary of State for the Environment rose. 'With permission, Mr Speaker, I would like to make a statement.'

It was brief. The Government was setting up an urgent inquiry into the plantacon affair. In the meantime it was asking the European Community to seek to persuade all European airlines to make a voluntary fifty per cent cutback in the plantacon added to fuel.

'We hope,' Muldoon told the House, 'that plantacon will be found to be safe and that the reductions will be necessary only for a short while. But we feel it best to err on the side of prudence.'

Ted Ingham, the Transport Secretary, sat silently beside him. He had seen the PM the previous night and offered his resignation, but the latter's plea that his experience was essential to the nation – plus a hint of promotion in an early reshuffle – had persuaded him to stay.

Muldoon's front bench opposite welcomed the inquiry with only a passing rebuke for the delay in announcing it.

Nick Bell was less grateful. 'What will the Secretary of State have to say to the fifty per cent who are harmed while this is going on? And what will he do if the European Community refuses to cooperate? Or the airlines refuse to respond?'

Muldoon shook his head. 'Mr Speaker, it is clear we can never satisfy the Honourable Gentleman. I can only say we will do our best to persuade the Community, and the Secretary of State for Transport will be going to Brussels within a few days.'

The headlines next day were unequivocal.

Environmentalists win on plantacon, said the *Guardian.*

Airline pollutant grounded, said the *Mirror.*

Humiliating Government back-down on plantacon, said the *Independent.*

Vicar caught in bath with topless model, said the *Sun.*

Even ECO couldn't win them all.

British Airways said it would comply with the request for a voluntary cutback, but added that it would wish to reconsider the position after interim research results were published. It believed this should happen within six months.

UK Ambassador was less enthusiastic.

Its public affairs head Trevor Richardson called in Peter Kingman, who had by now been winning a reputation as a whizz kid – or as Richardson's hit-man, depending whose side you were on in the boardroom battle between Richardson and the company chairman.

'I have a plan, Peter,' he said. 'In at least one respect we can actually make this plantacon business work *for* us.

'We've been trying to find a way to force the trade

unions to help us reduce overmanning. Now we can . . . on the back of plantacon.

'We're going to tame the unions – and we're going to blame it all on these irresponsible campaigners.

'By the time we're finished the unions will hate environmentalists.'

Richardson knew the increased unemployment wouldn't be welcomed by the Tories either, not with an election approaching.

That didn't worry him a bit.

It would be Pinky Brooks's turn to 'take the flak'.

So the company announced that while it was willing to consider the fifty per cent voluntary cutback if all its competitors did the same, it would be forced to make economies including *the suspension of 5,000 workers*.

Within half an hour Sir Humphrey Brooks was telephoned and asked if he would like to join the Prime Minister for a drink at No. 10 Downing Street.

Brooks went bright pink. This was just the kind of thing he liked to drop into the late-night gossip at his club. *Had a word with the PM last night, you know . . . asked me for a drink . . . I told him . . . etc., etc.'*

But, unfortunately for Brooks, the PM was in no mood for a friendly chat.

'Humphrey,' he said as soon as the door was closed behind them, 'forgive me for being frank. We did not give you a knighthood and look favourably on your applications for a share of our air space in order that you could go firing thousands of workers on the brink of an election. What the hell do you think you're doing?'

Brooks went a light pink. 'We hope it'll only be temporary, Prime Minister,' he said.

'Oh, no, you don't. You're using this issue to offload workers. Permanently.'

Brooks went medium pink. 'Well, we do have a

serious problem of overmanning . . .'

'Well, whose fault is that? It's your damn misma-nagement.'

Brooks went dark pink. 'Well, really, Prime Minister . . .'

'Look, Humphrey, let me make this plain to you. Either you stop antagonising the trade unions and throwing workers onto the dole queue until after the election, or you could find us unsympathetic – extremely unsympathetic – to any further requests you make.

'If you're not careful you can forget your expansion plans right now.

'Now I'm busy, Humphrey. Forgive me if I ask you to finish your drink on your own.'

And with that he left.

For the second time in his life Sir Humphrey 'Pinky' Brooks went through the colour barrier.

When he left Downing Street he was bright red.

Olly Witcomb was in high spirits – ecstatic at the progress of the campaign, and looking forward to dinner with Sally in her flat.

This, he was positive, would be the night.

He showered, put on clean underwear and shirt and, taking a bottle of wine, climbed to the top floor.

There was a note attached to it:

'Olly: was told today that I'm one of those to be made redundant as a result of your plantacon campaign. Thanks. Sally.'

He rang her bell but there was no reply. He thumped it hard, then looked under it, but there was no light on.

He left the bottle of wine by the door and went downstairs.

He looked again at the headline in his evening newspaper.

'*ANOTHER VICTORY FOR ECO.*'

He had been over the moon when he first read it.

Now he couldn't care less.

Peter Kingman, sitting in the corner in his capacity as public affairs spokesman, felt sorry for Sir Humphrey.

The little man had arrived already a medium pink. And was rapidly on his way up the register.

He was under fire from two directions.

For one thing, he hadn't told the board about the £30,000 donation to the Tory Party and, about this, his fellow directors were extremely unhappy. They had been embarrassed by the publicity. And felt they should have been consulted.

More seriously, however, two or three directors had been telephoned by the supporters of the PM during the night. And told that the company could find itself in real trouble with the Government if it caused electoral problems by firing workers at a politically sensitive time.

Brooks would probably have survived the meeting intact if he hadn't made the mistake of trying to turn the fire on to Trevor Richardson.

'Perhaps Trevor could comment,' he murmured. 'After all, he is responsible for our political policy. Also for dealing with this plantacon business.'

Richardson smiled, but his eyes were cold. 'With respect, Sir Humphrey, I wasn't consulted on the donation to the Tory Party. I was told in a memo from you.' He produced a slip of paper. 'I have a copy with me. It is dated May of last year . . . just a few weeks before you received your knighthood in the Birthday Honours, I believe.'

Brooks went bright pink. And began to sweat profusely.

'As for plantacon, Sir Humphrey, it's fair to say that

I've been responsible for bearing the burden of the current crisis. But, with respect, I must point out that it was your decision to press ahead with the purchase of additional aircraft that put the company into this vulnerable position. That decision did not fall within my area of responsibility. But I did express the view at the time that we should proceed more cautiously. I have a copy of that memo with me too.'

Another director spoke. 'Let's be frank, Mr Chairman,' he said to Brooks. 'We voted you into your position because of the political goodwill you could bring with you. As I see it we're getting damn-all goodwill, and your business decisions are proving disastrous.

'We're in danger of upsetting the Government, upsetting the unions, and upsetting our shareholders by reducing our profits to nil to pay for new aircraft we probably won't need – at least not while there's a threat to plantacon.'

Brooks, embarrassingly pink now, made his second mistake.

Failing to appreciate how few friends he had, convinced of his indispensability, and – above all – unaware of a number of damaging calls Richardson had made to Board members over the past few hours, he decided to call for a vote of confidence.

One of his friends, desperate to save him, suggested that it wasn't necessary.

But Brooks insisted.

The Board voted by six to four that it no longer had confidence in its Chairman.

NEW YORK

Eugene Remington sat in the back of his chauffeur-driven car in a state of shock, the *Wall Street Journal* clutched tightly in his hands.

The news from the UK was bad enough.

But the story published alongside it was even worse.

For once his urbanity failed him. 'Bastards,' he hissed to himself.

The target of this remark was not, as was to be expected, the environmentalists, but instead the petroleum industry, and the cause of his anger was a story headed: '*Petroleum companies consider plantacon ban.*'

It read:

At least a temporary ban on the aviation fuel additive plantacon became more likely today after representatives of the oil industry made clear they would not oppose it.

David Johnston, chairman of the public affairs committee of OILO (Oil Industries Liaison Organisation), said after a meeting yesterday: 'While my colleagues in the industry are confident plantacon will be cleared of being a hazard to health, we take the view that a temporary voluntary ban on it by the aviation industry could be in the best interests of both the industry and the public.'

Mr Johnston argued that a voluntary decision not to use plantacon would 'place useful pressure on everyone in the industry to tackle the real issues rather than just produce a PR solution'.

'Hypocrite,' thought Remington. *Just produce a PR solution* indeed! If ever there was a consummate PR man it was Johnston. He didn't breathe unless there was a PR reason for doing it.

And why was he doing this now?

Obviously the fuel suppliers, with nothing to lose, in fact with greater Jet-A sales to gain, had decided to remove themselves from the firing line and leave their airline customers to face the heat alone.

And they were acting together hoping that this would protect them individually.

Well, Remington would see about that.

Relations between the two industries had always been uneasy. The airlines believed the fuel suppliers had loaded their costs on to them rather than motorists. During the 1990–91 gulf crisis, for example, the price of Jet-A had risen far more dramatically than ordinary gasoline for cars.

It was time they were taught a lesson.

Remington reached for his car phone and rang Johnston.

'David, what the hell is going on?'

'I'm sorry, Eugene, but we think this is in the best interests of everybody.'

'Balls. *Your* best interests. Don't pretend it's in ours. And why didn't you warn us?'

'Frankly I didn't expect the decision, and I didn't expect it to leak to the press. It is, after all, only a recommendation of the public affairs committee. The full board are yet to confirm it.'

'Balls again. You know that now your decision's been leaked it becomes damn-near inevitable that the board will confirm it. If it doesn't, it looks as if it's acting irresponsibly, contrary to advice.'

'Look, Eugene, we exist to serve our industry. You can't blame our member companies for doing what they believe is best for them. And for the public.'

'*The public.*' Remington finally lost his temper. 'Bullshit, David. Christ, you're a two-faced bastard at the best of times – and, believe me, this is *not* the best of times.

'That you're covering your own backs, I can just about understand. But the *public interest*? You wouldn't know or care what the words mean.'

Johnston remained cool. 'OK, we're doing what's best for us. But you could at least consider that this happens to *coincide* with the public interest.'

Remington held the phone so tightly in his hand that his knuckles went white. 'What about the aviation industry? We're a major customer of your industry. Don't we deserve some consideration?'

'Of course, Eugene. You have our sympathy. All we've done is support the idea of a temporary ban so that plantacon can be cleared. Then everyone'll be happy.'

'*Sympathy!* Bullshit, David, *bullshit*. What you're doing is having your cake and eating it. When plantacon is cleared you'll benefit from the growth in our sector. But if the environmentalists are allowed to win, no matter how undeservedly, you'll benefit by selling more fuel. In the meantime you want to look good to the public so you're abandoning us to the wolves. What I'm trying to tell you is that you and your God-damned committee are cynical bastards and you can tell them that from me, each and every one of them.'

'Eugene, this isn't getting us anywhere. I repeat it's only a recommendation from our committee. If you feel strongly, put your point of view to the Board.'

'Oh, I will. Don't doubt that.' And he hung up.

His car was trapped in heavy traffic so he continued to use his car phone, dialling next the chief executive of Jet-A Supplies, the company that supplied his own airline. He and Cliff Anderson had been college friends and still played golf together. While this friendship had not been the decisive factor . . . Remington was too tough an operator for that . . . it had undoubtedly helped Anderson's company get the Executive Airways account.

'Cliff,' Remington began, abandoning the usual pleasantries. 'Have you seen what your industry's public affairs people are up to?'

'You mean on plantacon?'

'Of course I mean on plantacon. I'm not having this, Cliff.'

'Well, I'm sorry, Eugene. As you will know, I've not been involved . . .'

'But you will be, Cliff. When it comes to the Board. And I want that recommendation rejected. This could not have come at a worse time.'

'Well, of course I'll listen to what the others have to say, Eugene, but . . .'

'Don't bother listening to *them*.' Remington's voice was cold and harsh. 'Listen to *me*. I want your assurance that your voice and your vote will oppose that recommendation or you lose our account from midnight tonight.'

'But all the others . . .'

Remington interrupted once more. 'No, Cliff, "all the others" won't take the same view. Let me tell you why.

'We'll mobilise a majority of companies to oppose it and we'll all switch our orders to them.

'The minority who support this recommendation can forget the aviation industry. We'll never buy their fuel again. We're not going to be abandoned in our hour of need, Cliff. So, I'm starting with you. You better decide whether you're on the side of your customers and you had better decide *now*. I'm giving you thirty minutes. Ring me back.' And he hung up.

The phone rang almost immediately. 'You shouldn't hang up on an old friend, Eugene. Of course you have my support. That wasn't in question.'

Remington smiled. 'You're right, Cliff. I should have known.'

There was a pause. Then Anderson spoke once more. 'Look, Eugene, just for reassurance, for my own Board, this plantacon *is* safe, isn't it? These environmentalists have got it wrong?'

Remington spoke slowly and firmly. 'It's safe, Cliff. Completely safe.'

The other sounded relieved. 'Ok, Eugene, that's good enough for me.'

'And another thing, Cliff. We're going to win. Goddamm it, we *are* winning.'

By now Remington's car had made its way across Manhattan to Park Avenue. From his office he set up a conference call with colleagues in other airlines and after that he (and they) spent most of the day on the phone.

By lunchtime the following day an emergency meeting of the Board of OILO had overruled its public affairs committee.

> 'While we understand why this particular committee should be concerned about the public relations aspects of this controversy, we are satisfied that plantacon is completely safe and that the aviation industry has acted with typical responsibility throughout,' the Board press release stated. 'Even a temporary ban would be unfair to the industry, to the flying public, and to the nation as a whole.'

Unfortunately the damage had been done.

The press commented more about the oil industry's turn-about than about its continued support for plantacon.

Jackie Brown, writing her weekly environmental column for the *Washington Post*, was scathing.

What are we to make of the behaviour of the oil industry?

On one hand its public affairs committee, presumably showing a commendable concern for the public interest, called for a temporary ban on plantacon.

On the other hand the Board of OILO, dominated by men with an eye on the bottom line and determined to preserve its cosy friendship with its customers in the aviation industry, says plantacon is safe and a ban is not justified.

This industry is facing both ways.

Lionel North was equally scathing about the industry, but from a different point of view.

Who were these lily-livered men within the petroleum industry who support a temporary ban on plantacon?

Public relations men!

Need I say more?

Their only concern is the public image of their companies. They are ready to abandon one of the great developments of the last few decades, and in the process abandon one of their major customers, to maintain temporary public goodwill, irrespective of whether their action is justified or not.

Thank God for their seniors, the Board of OILO, who rightly told these unprincipled operators to get back to their three-martini lunches and leave the big decisions to big men.

As for plantacon, the position remains the same. While its benefits are demonstrably great, the case for a ban is totally unconvincing. The environmentalists are losing. As well they should.

On balance, however, the response to this latest turn of events favoured the Jackie Brown view rather than that of Lionel North.

Sam MacAnally was quick to build on the advantage he had been given.

'The industry's public relations pro-plantacon façade is beginning to crack,' he told a hastily summoned press conference. 'The public affairs experts in the petroleum industry know plantacon is going to be proved poisonous. They are trying to remove their industry as a target for public criticism before it's too late. Whatever you may think of their motives, their behaviour is eloquent testimony to the strength of our case.'

The ECO campaign was given further stimulus by news of the UK decision to ask European airlines to make a voluntary reduction in plantacon of fifty per cent until more facts were available. Many newpapers published leading articles suggesting the US should follow the British lead.

The industry war council had an emergency meeting and Nicola Kowalska for the first time found herself under real pressure. Its members were beginning to panic.

'What horrifies me,' said the representative of a plane manufacturer, 'is that we're dealing in perceptions instead of realities. The sub-committee is only committed to *consider* the detail of the bill. The chairman who decided on the mark-up said himself that he wouldn't consider a ban. Yet people *think* the Senate has virtually decided to ban plantacon.

'Likewise, the British, for political reasons only, are merely asking for a voluntary cutback while they carry out research. Yet people *think* they've accepted that plantacon is a threat and abandoned it.

'Now one unimportant sub-committee of the petroleum industry loses its nerve, and its decision is promptly overturned by its Council. Yet people *think* the oil industry are anti-plantacon too.

'We can't win.'

Nicola Kowalska tried to calm them. She pointed out that they always knew they would have a credibility problem. And they knew how fickle both the media and politicians were.

'These are only the opening rounds. We must be patient. When it gets to the detail, when they really have to weigh the consequences of a ban in the balance, things will change.'

But that night as she bathed and, in her dressing-gown, dried her hair in front of the fire in her Philadelphia apartment, she felt less confident.

While she wasn't too worried about the Senate sub-committee, it would have been more helpful if they had decided not to proceed to a mark-up.

Although she had no doubt the British government was playing for time, and the European Community would never get the fifty per cent voluntary cut, it was causing governments in other countries to consider action too.

She couldn't believe how easily MacAnally had orchestrated such a world-wide scare.

She had been confident that his case was too flimsy to win any concessions at all.

But he *was* getting concessions. The facts, the need to be fair to the industry . . . all this seemed to be irrelevant.

She thought about MacAnally.

He was looking so confident on television these days.

And when they had passed each other in the Capitol building he had given her a smile that had not only been friendly but, she had thought, sympathetic.

Damn it, she didn't want his pity.

She wanted to win. She needed to win.

She could imagine where the blame would be pinned if plantacon was banned. Even if Remington was understanding, Partrell, Birk, and a lot of the others would say they should never have entrusted their cause with her. She was too young. She was a woman. She wasn't up to it.

She envied MacAnally his assurance. And his freedom from clients and their demands.

Yet, while she feared that he could be the cause of her downfall, she couldn't dislike the man.

On the contrary, she admitted to herself that while she didn't like what he was doing, she liked Sam MacAnally.

He was the most interesting man she had met for years.

And attractive.

But – goddamn it – he was on the other side.

That made her feel sad.

And lonely.

WASHINGTON

A hundred miles south of Philadelphia, Sam MacAnally fell into bed in his Washington flat, exhausted but content.

The campaign was going as well as expected.

In the US they were regrouping on two fronts. In Washington Jay Sandbach was coordinating the campaign to influence the sub-committee mark-up and to guarantee the votes at the full committee stage. Round the country Molly Macintosh was orchestrating a big drive to ensure that the senators who were not on the committee came under heavy pressure when the decision finally came to them.

He had spoken to Monique de Vos that day about the campaign she would now run to get European backing for the British request for a voluntary cutback.

Liz Scullen and Mike McKenzie were confident the UK decision would help in Australia.

Machiko Yanagi remained doubtful whether the Japanese would respond as positively as the British but was hopeful their plans for later that month would help.

And all other member countries had been told to use the British decision to good effect.

As he considered these initiatives he became drowsy. And began to think of Nicola Kowalska.

He wished she wasn't running the industry campaign. He liked her.

He fell asleep. And suffered the recurring nightmare. Marie was in a car with Warner. The car was out of control. There was a lorry. And a crash. And then he was standing beside a grave. Looking down. At Marie's coffin. Then he was looking across the grave to a shadowy figure in black on the other side. Slowly she lifted her veil . . .

He woke up, already sitting up, sweat pouring off him, his heart beating fast . . .

The face under the veil . . . the face looking at him full of sympathy . . .

It had been Nicola Kowalska's face.

He fell back on the pillow, breathing heavily.

And felt sad.

And lonely.

BRUSSELS

The day the British decided to make their approach to the European Community there were meetings all over Brussels.

Monique de Vos was at a number of them. And Pierre Courtois was at even more.

Monique's first meeting was with Claude Chevallier at Environment, DG XI.

Chevallier had been worried because the British approach to the Community would have to be made by their aviation minister (i.e. the Secretary of State for Transport) and this meant the first major discussions at a European level would be between transport ministers and officials.

This would make it much harder for the matter to be kept within the remit of the Environment directorate.

He had taken the matter to the top of DG XI and the Environment Commissioner had agreed to take the matter to the President himself.

But Chevallier knew that the head of the air transport division of DG VII (Transport) was getting similar support from his commissioner.

The question would, therefore, have to be settled at a meeting of commissioners chaired by the President of the Commission.

And Chevallier was pessimistic.

He told Monique he would telephone her as soon as he had news.

Pierre Courtois had been with Alain Jurgensen, head of the air transport division. Jurgensen had been optimistic. He couldn't see how Transport could fail to be given charge of the issue.

Jurgensen, too, said he would telephone with news of the outcome.

The President of the European Commission listened to the argument rage around him for an hour.

Logic was, of course, on Transport's side. It was an aviation industry matter and the cooperation of the industry would be vital.

But the President didn't like the Commissioner for Transport and had heard a lot about his colleague, Alain Jurgensen, and his links with the aviation industry. Jurgensen, he had been told, was due to leave shortly and would then become a highly-paid PR man for one of the airlines.

He thought about compromising and giving the matter to Energy, but they would be even less open to both sides of the question.

At the end of the meeting he frustrated them all, the commissioners for Transport, Energy and Environment, by reserving his position.

He wanted a few days to think about it.

The news that the President had not automatically ruled in favour of Transport caused consternation or euphoria according to which camp you were in.

Between the monthly plenary sessions of the European Parliament, two weeks are reserved for parliamentary committee meetings, with the third week kept free for meetings of the party groupings. These take place in Brussels, not Strasbourg.

Daniela Bonetti set about organising a hearing and committee debate. Dr David Abernathy was flown over from the United States to testify. He received a lot of publicity. Monique de Vos then sent him on a tour of European capitals to do more interviews.

Olly Witcomb and Nick Bell also came to Brussels to testify.

The airlines sent over the sympathetic American scientist Dr Bryce Kendrick, and the lobbyist Erhard Piermont took him on a tour of Commission officials and other opinion-formers in Brussels and also Paris and Bonn.

Pierre Courtois was here, there, and everywhere, as he and Hans Fischer tried to strengthen DG VII's case.

Courtois was, however, feeling increasingly uncomfortable. It was not proving easy going. And he was finding it more difficult to get to see people than he was used to.

Then a strange thing happened. He received an invitation to an ECO reception for Belgian MEPs and MPs and other leading political figures.

Given his strained relations with Monique de Vos this was the last thing he expected.

His vanity, however, led him to the conclusion that she was missing him. This was her signal that she wanted to see him again.

He remembered the way she had humiliated him on the airport bus at Strasbourg.

OK, he would go.

And afterwards he would fuck her.

Then he would never speak to her again.

When he arrived the reception was well under way. He was greeted at the door by Monique herself, albeit with a frosty smile rather than the warm welcome he had expected.

'Come and meet the new President of ECO Europe,' she said, moving her head slightly to avoid his attempted kiss on the cheek.

She took him across to Philippe Van der Haegan.

Courtois almost stumbled in shock.

Van der Haegan the President of ECO Europe?

It couldn't be possible.

Van der Haegan was one of the most influential figures in Belgian politics. A man of enormous stature who could make or break politicians' careers.

He was also Pierre Courtois's father-in-law.

The two shook hands. Courtois was unable to hide his surprise. 'I had no idea you were a supporter of the environmental movement,' he said.

'Maybe you should keep in closer touch with the family,' Van der Haegan said coldly.

Courtois flushed. 'Yes.' Then he laughed uneasily, pretending he thought it a joke. 'I had better.' Then he added, 'This damn Euro parliament takes me away too much. The sooner I can get a transfer to the Belgian Parliament the better.'

He looked at his father-in-law hopefully. 'How are your enquiries about that vacancy on the list coming along?'

Van der Haegan looked puzzled. 'Vacancy?' Then, apparently remembering, he said stiffly 'Oh, we've chosen someone for that.'

And walked away.

Courtois, shaken, began to circulate.

And as he did so became increasingly concerned. Something was wrong. People who would have previously gravitated to one of the rising stars of Belgian politics were now avoiding his eye. When he joined a group he was coolly greeted and then the conversation carried on as if he were not there. He glanced wildly around and caught Monique looking at him. He thought he saw a triumphant glint in her eye.

The reception was beginning to break up when Van der Haegan called to him. 'Oh, Pierre, I would like to see you for a few minutes tomorrow. Would ten in my office be convenient?'

Courtois shook his head. 'I have a committee meeting in the morning.'

But the older man acted as if he hadn't heard.

'Good. Ten, then.'

Courtois went to his car, his mind full of what had happened.

Clearly he had neglected his contacts in Brussels. He would need to put a lot of work in, and do it quickly.

Maybe this plantacon business would have to be left to others.

In any case the last thing he wanted was to find himself in a head-on battle with his influential father-in-law.

He drove quickly up the Avenue Louise and through the Bois de la Cambre, the trees outlined in his headlights, until he came to the exclusive suburb of Waterloo. The house he shared with his wife had been a gift from his father-in-law.

As he parked he noticed the house was dark. That was strange. His wife always left the downstairs lights on, even when she went to bed. She spent a lot of time there on her own and believed the lights would deter anyone from attempting to break in.

He opened the door and went in. It was not only dark, but cold. He switched on the lights and called her name. There was no answer. He quickly ran up the stairs and opened the bedroom door. The room was empty, the bed untouched. He went to the children's rooms. They were also empty.

He ran back downstairs and then noticed the envelope on the dresser by the front door.

He opened it. The note was brief.

'Dear Pierre. My father has sold the house, but you have it for a month. That is now all you have. Goodbye.'

He sat on the stairs and looked at the piece of paper in dismay.

And for the first time in weeks he forgot plantacon.

He thought only of Monique de Vos. What was it she had said? *'You'll never win again, Pierre, from now on you're a loser.'*

Philippe Van der Haegan's office was in the spacious family flat in the Avenue Louise.

Courtois, who stepped from the old lift onto the

landing at the top floor, was accustomed to being greeted warmly and taken directly in to see his father-in-law but this time he was kept waiting for nearly thirty minutes.

He sat, nervously, crossing and uncrossing his legs, his copy of *Le Soir* unread, his eyes looking sightlessly out of the window at the monumental Palais de Justice.

In his mind he ran over the things he was planning to say.

But he never got the chance.

Van der Haegan was sitting behind his large desk. Lying on it was a file. He silently passed it to Courtois.

It was a series of reports by a firm of private detectives. Page after page of them.

Reports about the extra-marital activities of Pierre Courtois. Courtois with a statuesque blonde in Rome, a dark-haired *señorita* in Madrid, a brunette in London. And with countless other women. There were reports of meetings with women in restaurants, at airports, in cars, in parks. There were copies of hotel registers and credit card slips.

There was also a list of tape-recordings and transcripts of their contents. A particularly striking one contained three voices . . . one was that of Courtois; according to the report the others belonged to the fifteen-year-old twin daughters of the President of his party.

Courtois put the file down and looked in despair at his father-in-law.

'I suppose it's no good saying I'm sorry. That I had already decided to stop this . . . this behaviour.'

Van der Haegan said nothing.

Courtois stumbled on. 'I would like to talk to Suzanne.'

The older man shook his head.

'You've disappointed me, Pierre. That I can live with. But you've broken Suzanne's heart and that I cannot and will not forgive. You're no longer a member of my family. And I think I can promise you that your political career is over.'

He stood up and looked at Courtois contemptuously. 'You will leave Brussels. You will stay in Strasbourg until the next European elections, when you will not be a candidate. You will, to all intents and purposes, disappear.'

Courtois rose too. 'This is too much. You can't make me do that.'

'Oh yes, I can.' He opened a drawer and took out an envelope. 'I have some papers here that show that you have been systematically stealing Suzanne's money for years. Using it no doubt to chase other women.

'I also have papers that confirm you took a bribe to support the pharmaceutical industry when the Community was considering a regulatory directive. You know that the Chief of the Fraud Squad is a close friend. I have had an informal chat with him. He seems to think you would be looking at a minimum of seven years in prison.

'Even if there were not that, there are, of course, these files. A private viewing for any potential constituency chairman would, I think, put a swift end to any further political ambitions you may have.' He sat at his desk.

Courtois felt as if he was falling down a deep pit. His stomach turned. He could hardly breathe. He looked at Van der Haegan desperately.

'Philippe, can't you . . .?'

'Don't even ask.'

Slowly he turned and walked to the door.

Then, rage briefly replacing panic, he turned. 'Tell the President,' he shouted, 'that his twins have fucked half the party executive . . . the half, unlike you, who can still get it up.'

Van der Haegan looked at him with contempt. 'Up? What do you know about *up*, Pierre?

'There's only one way you're going.

'And that's down.'

He rose and, walking across to the door, carefully and emphatically slammed it in the younger man's face.

Courtois stumbled out into the big reception area, and from there into the street.

The Avenue Louise is wide, divided by tramlines, and near the der Haegans' building it is lined with banks, travel agencies, shops and cafés. As Courtois passed them in a daze, stumbling occasionally, bumping into other pedestrians, going he knew not where, he almost knocked down Erhard Piermont coming out of the expensive Copthorne Stephanie Hotel.

'Pierre. Just the man. Come and have a cognac. I want to talk to you about plantacon.'

Courtois looked at him wild-eyed, at first uncomprehendingly. Then he answered briefly and savagely.

'Fuck plantacon,' he said.

'From now on you're a loser,' Monique had said.

'There's only one way you're going and that's down,' Van der Haegen had said.

He walked on.

Until he disappeared into the crowds on the Boulevard Waterloo.

And into oblivion.

The President of the European Commission advised colleagues in writing of his decision.

Transport would deal with the specific UK proposal of a temporary cutback in plantacon use.

But *Environment* would be responsible for coordinating the scientific inquiry into plantacon and making recommendations for longer-term action.

Monique de Vos was ecstatic. 'We've won the opening skirmish,' she told MacAnally over the phone.

'Does that mean we're definitely going to win over there?'

'No. But we're ahead. You could say we've loaded the dice. The whole issue will be raised as an *environmental* one. That means that environmental considerations can't be ignored. In effect, it's now just as much the responsibility of the airlines to prove plantacon is safe as it's ours to prove it's not.

'And you can bet the other side's feeling sick.'

She hung up, sat back on her couch, and, clenching her fists, held them up in front of her in triumph.

Then she thought of Pierre Courtois.

And repeated the gesture.

She had, she told herself, dealt with two pollutants in one day . . . a chemical one and a human one.

For a third time she gestured with her fists in triumph.

WASHINGTON D.C.

Senator Taverner wrote to Senators Frankle and Wilkins to say that he intended to ask the American aviation industry to adopt a similar voluntary measure – a fifty per cent cut – as that proposed by the British.

'Such a step combined with the commissioning of further scientific research could make a bill and a full ban unnecessary at this time.'

This led to a series of meetings in both Washington and New York.

At the ECO offices MacAnally called a team meeting. 'We're winning' he began enthusiastically. 'There's no doubt about it.'

Then, tempering his own enthusiasm, he warned, 'But this is just the time to be careful. We're about to enter the compromise zone and that's when the other side is at its most dangerous.'

'So what are we ready to settle for?' asked Sandbach.

'Why should we settle at all?' Adrian Carlisle indignantly replied. 'Why not keep right out of what Sam calls the compromise zone? Why don't we stick to our stated objective, a ban within eighteen months?'

It was the quiet-spoken Jake Katzir who replied. 'Because at the moment we're a player. If we keep out of the compromise zone we could find the whole thing is settled game, set and match, without our participation or influence. The industry and everybody else, even the White House, will say that they're responding responsibly while we're simply impossible to satisfy. And you'll be surprised how many of the newspapers will accept that. The public too.'

MacAnally looked sympathetically at Carlisle who appeared to be considerably agitated by what he was hearing. 'Don't panic, Adrian,' he said. 'Just because we're ready to entertain an element of compromise to stay in the game doesn't mean we don't still want to win. We don't have to compromise that much . . . just enough to guarantee we're centrally placed in the debate.'

'I have an idea,' said Sandbach. 'Why don't we welcome Senator Taverner's initiative and also the UK and Australian decisions and say that we, too, would welcome an immediate fifty per cent reduction in the use of plantacon and further scientific studies.

'However, we would not withdraw the bill but, as a compromise, we would stretch our time scale for a full ban to two and a half years, even three, thus allowing time for the research to either justify the ban or not.'

Before the group could debate this suggestion the meeting was interrupted by a phone call to MacAnally from Justin Lord.

MacAnally was surprised. It was the first time Lord had called MacAnally himself. He slipped out of the meeting and took the call in his own office.

He updated Lord on the state of the campaign and on the Sandbach proposal.

'I have a proposal of my own,' said Lord. 'Will you at least consider it?'

'Of course.'

'I've been thinking. Why not offer a different approach . . . stress that it's not *plantacon* you're concerned about, but plantacon *emissions* and plantacon *pollution*.

'What I'm suggesting is that you don't promote a bill to ban plantacon. Instead you promote a bill that sets a standard for plantacon *emissions*. And the standard would be so close to nil that it doesn't matter.'

MacAnally was taken aback. 'What's the difference?'

'It's a subtle one but it could have considerable public effect. The difference is that you will not be so vulnerable to the charge of being *anti-plantacon* or *anti-progress*. You would be showing that you're just *anti-pollution*.

'It will focus the debate even more. And it will be holding out to the industry the real hope that if they can stop or control the emissions they can continue to have the benefits of plantacon.'

MacAnally wasn't convinced it was a credible strategy but, when he reported back to the group, they were enthusiastic.

Molly Macintosh argued that while there wasn't in substance a lot of difference between what Lord was proposing and what they had been aiming for anyway, it could be presented to the public as a generous attempt to find a compromise.

Jay Sandbach felt that many members of Congress would prefer to vote for a measure controlling pollution than for a measure banning plantacon.

'I can see them going back to their home states and telling irate aviation industry unions, *"Look, I would never have voted for a ban. But we have got to control these emissions of a dangerous neurotoxin. Join with us in insisting your employers tackle that problem."*

'The point is that it confuses the issue but only to the industry's disadvantage. They'll be going round saying, *"For Christ's sake, this makes no difference. As we can't control the emissions it's still a ban by another name."* And we'll be able to reply, *"You just can't satisfy these people. We tried to compromise but they wouldn't listen."* '

Carlisle joined in: 'And we'll be able to say that they're conceding that there are significant emissions and that they can't control them. It's brilliant.'

Dominic Young had been listening carefully. 'Actually,' he said, 'this is probably the industry's ultimate fallback position anyway. What they won't like is to have it coming from us and to have it coming this soon. And, of course, the standard they would suggest would hardly reduce emissions at all.'

And he warned them, 'Don't forget, the industry can easily use that formula to delay action.'

'Then we must stay right in there to see that they don't,' said MacAnally.

He and Sandbach went directly from the meeting to see Wilkins.

'Let me get this clear, Sam,' Wilkins said. 'You want me to come up with an amended bill that sets a standard – a maximum level – for plantacon emissions? That maximum level would be so low that it would stop them using plantacon altogether. So the effect would be the same as a ban.'

'Yes, but the process is different. Your bill will come as a complete surprise. Everyone expects it to ban plantacon. Instead it will only regulate its use; it will seek to make plantacon safe. Who can argue with that?'

'But can that be done?'

'That's not your problem. That's the industry's problem. The point is that you'll be able to acknowledge the financial and energy benefits of plantacon, but then simply and straightforwardly insist that industry takes steps to ensure the economic upside is not matched by a pollution and public health downside.'

Tom Gammell, who had remained concerned about Wilkins getting himself out on a political limb on the issue, looked impressed. 'I like it, Senator. It's in line with what Hal Frankle wants. It's going to seem more moderate and reasonable than proposing a ban and it wrong-foots the industry. What are they going to say? "Sorry, folks, we can't control emissions"? That's not going to sound good.'

MacAnally nodded. 'The game will be the same but you'll have moved the goalposts. And, believe me, the goal you'll be aiming for will be an easier target.'

NEW YORK

The aviation industry was also beginning to face up to the need for compromise.

Eugene Remington, fresh from an embarrassing encounter with his accountants, had also had a disappointing meeting with his fellow Board members.

He had tried to force a decision to buy more planes and expand Executive Airways, but they were unwilling to do that until the plantacon issue was settled.

He had no choice now but to act decisively to deal with his own finances.

He had taken advice about whether he could sell part of his share of the company but was told that no one wanted to know about buying into airlines while the controversy raged around it.

He was going to have to tell his wife that either the Sante Fe ranch or the new Aspen ski lodge would have to go. And that there would have to be considerable economies all round.

He was, therefore, grim-faced as he told an emergency industry meeting in the Waldorf Astoria: 'We've got to change our approach. We've got to make a gesture that gives away the minimum but makes us look less insensitive to public concern. And we have to give our political friends some help if they're to protect us.'

Everyone was there. From the airlines that is. Remington had not invited representatives of the oil industry or Dieter Partrell of FEI. He no longer trusted OILO. And Partrell would not want to know about a compromise. He would have to be confronted with a *fait accompli*.

That had left Todd Birk. After some heart-searching Remington had included him. Birk would find out about the meeting eventually and Remington didn't want to feed his paranoia any more than necessary. In any case he hoped even Birk would see the way things were going and be willing to compromise a bit.

Remington had spent a week talking to colleagues in other companies and spent the morning closeted with Nicola Kowalska. Now he put his plan to the meeting.

'There is a growing momentum behind Wilkins and

the environmentalists. The UK initiative for a voluntary fifty per cent cutback has not helped and other countries may follow suit. The advice we have from our Washington advisors is that we have to be seen to compromise.

'I propose that we do two things: first, we make the best of Senator Taverner's initiative. We build him up, cater to his ego, and get him on our side.

'Thus we show Congress we're open to reason, and we improve our public relations. And we buy time.'

'You mean concede a fifty per cent reduction in plantacon?' Birk was aghast.

'No, Todd, I don't. But Senator Taverner's proposal has two parts, first, a fifty per cent temporary ban that we, by compliance, can make a voluntary ban, and, second, more research.

'I propose that we offer full cooperation with the research. We'll even offer to pay for it ourselves. We do this to show our complete confidence in plantacon. But – and this is the key – we build into the plan an *interim report* on the earlier stages of the research. And *only* if that interim report supports the environmentalists' five studies rather than our own, do we make a voluntary cut of fifty per cent.

'Now, as we know that the interim report *won't* support the ECO studies, we'll never have to make the cutback.'

'How do we know that the scientists doing the new studies won't be as biased as the first lot?' asked Birk.

'Those scientists may not have been biased. They may just have been wrong,' Remington said, then before Birk could protest: 'But we'll insist that the scientists forming the official inquiry are agreed between the EPA, the American Academy of Science and ourselves. All three parties will have a veto. It won't guarantee a scientific bias towards us but it should protect us from one against us.

'Anyway,' he added, 'I repeat, as we know plantacon *will* be cleared, we have no problem.'

The meeting looked impressed. Even the truculent Birk looked less angry than usual. 'Let me be clear,' he said. 'We voluntarily cut back on plantacon by fifty per cent *only* if the interim results support the environmentalists' case?'

'That's right.'

'How long will that take?'

Remington smiled reassuringly. 'By the time we all agree on the scientists and their brief, and by the time the work is done, I reckon we're looking at well over a year.'

Birk sat back.

A year.

A lot could happen in a year.

He said no more and the meeting ended in agreement.

HOBOKEN, NEW JERSEY

Dieter Partrell went so red his secretary was convinced he was about to have a heart attack. Crashing down the receiver after taking the call from Todd Birk, he looked out of the window and across the Hudson and roared a series of oaths in the direction of Manhattan. His secretary, accustomed to his language, nevertheless blanched at the obscenities.

Those chicken-shit airline people were selling him out.

Meeting without him present.

Coming up with a chicken-shit idea that put the whole enterprise at risk.

When there was no need to do it. No need at all. They had hardly started their defence of plantacon yet. They hadn't taken the gloves off yet.

'Get me Charlie Orbell,' he shouted at her. 'No, talk to him yourself and tell him to fucking get over here now. And by now I mean he's already late.'

WASHINGTON D.C.

Senator Hal Frankle looked at the two men glaring at each other across his desk and wished that things on the Hill were as gentlemanly as they used to be in the old days. Then senators could be involved in a major dispute and still have a quiet drink together in the cloakroom behind the Senate floor or in one of their respective offices, always searching for accord and compromise in the interests of both the Senate and the country.

He had never seen Ed Eberhard so hostile and young Wilkins was white-faced in his anger.

'Senator,' Wilkins said to Frankle, 'I'm trying to be reasonable. I'm introducing a revised version of my Bill that gives hope to the industry. It does not ban plantacon. It merely sets an emission standard.'

'A *nil* emission standard. You know damn well it's the same thing,' Eberhard protested.

Wilkins ignored him. 'Furthermore, provided the industry accepts Senator Taverner's proposal of a voluntary cut of fifty per cent while research continues, I'm further adapting my bill to allow two and a half years before compliance – that's an extension of a year. I think that's a most generous gesture. If Senator Eberhard is confident of his case he should have no problem with it.'

He looked earnestly at Frankle. 'The senator from

Texas and others may call me hot-headed but I've tried to find a way of representing the concern of my constituents about plantacon without excessively undermining the industry. I believe this compromise bill does that. I would like you to schedule a mark-up in the sub-committee as soon as possible.'

'Your constituents weren't concerned until you whipped up all this hysteria,' Eberhard said, finally given his turn.

He looked at Frankle. 'Hal, you and I know that if we can persuade industry to act voluntarily, this is by far the best thing. The industry has shown a great sense of public duty by agreeing to an expensive compromise. It has offered to pay for all the research itself despite the fact that it will be independently done. And it has agreed that if early interim findings support a cutback it will go along with a fifty per cent reduction until the work is completed.

'There is no need for this bill. God knows, we have enough work piling up in the Senate without debates and votes on bills that are unnecessary.'

Frankle looked at Wilkins. The young man almost pleaded for support. 'Senator, it all comes down to whether or not you believe that plantacon is already harming children. If you do, as I do, then there is little room for compromise. Yet, despite that, I have compromised. But the airlines' proposed compromise would have the effect of postponing any controls on plantacon for years. All that time they continue to pocket the profits while children are being poisoned.'

Frankle sighed and said, 'You both make convincing cases, gentlemen. Let me consult colleagues on the sub-committee over the next two or three days and I'll come back to you.'

Wilkins hesitated, then nodded his thanks, and left.

Eberhard remained sitting deep in his armchair. Finally, slowly, he stood. 'Hal,' he said. 'We've both been here a long time. Sometimes we've been strongly opposed, sometimes we've voted together. I don't know or care whether you like me but I think you know I'm an honourable man. So believe me when I say to you that I do not intend a great industry to suffer at the hands of hotheads who take over this great place and use the privilege of being here for self-promotion irrespective of who is harmed in the process. No, sir, I will not let that happen.'

And he left.

Frankle looked dispiritedly at Ed Kellerman who had been observing the meeting from the corner. 'Damn it, Ed, I like them both. And I think they're both genuine on this. They both think they're doing the right thing. But out of it all . . .' he paused, and rocked back in his chair, 'out of it all, if we're not careful, wrong could come.'

MacAnally had proposed to Nicola Kowalska that they meet at Chadwicks, an American restaurant on Wisconsin Avenue just inside the North West city line. She was late and, from a table in the corner by the window, he watched her pay her cab driver and walk in, hand over her coat and come towards him. Reluctantly he admitted to himself that he liked her. He was physically attracted to her. But he also liked her style – and admired her courage.

'A spritzer,' she said in answer to his opening question, then before he could speak further she leaned forward.

'Look, Sam, before you say a word I want to make one thing clear. I had nothing – repeat *nothing* – to do with the *Express* stories. They are not my style. I was shocked by them.'

She leaned forward even further so that he could smell her perfume. He looked unsteadily into her eyes as she added, 'It is very, very important to me that you believe me. Will you take my word on this?'

He responded instantly. 'Yes. I believe you.'

She relaxed and he grinned and said, 'Christ, I dare not. You're so intense about it. Why is it so *very, very* important?'

'Because just as you take pride in what you do, so do I. We've had that conversation before. I could not take pride in it, or my success, if I stooped to that. It hurts me that it was done by someone on our side.'

'Partrell?'

'In a way I feel sorry for him. He's got most to lose and he does feel really bitter that his miracle product is under threat. But he frightens me. I get the feeling he'll do whatever it takes . . .'

'And you won't?'

'No, will you?'

MacAnally paused. 'Almost. Almost . . . but not quite.'

'You're that ruthless?'

'I care that much. You see, if I'm right – just consider that for the sake of argument – then millions of kids are being poisoned and most of your friends simply don't want to know. So, yes, I would do whatever is necessary.'

'Then how can you complain if—'

'If they do the same? That's easy. Because I'm protecting lives and they're only protecting money. We're playing for different stakes.'

She looked at him silently for a moment. 'I could argue this with you. That they're also protecting their freedom against unwarranted attack, that they're also fighting for truth and justice, albeit justice for themselves . . . but what's the point. You're the white knight on the charger and all they ever pretend to be is businessmen.

So let's get down to business. I want to explore the possible compromises.'

'Ok, but why don't we get some food on the table too?' He once more looked amused at her intensity. After they had ordered – he a hamburger, she grilled sea food and salad – he said, 'Do you speak for anyone on this?'

'My side doesn't know I'm here. But if we can identify common ground it's got to help.'

'Quite,' MacAnally said. 'Well, let's consider the questions:

'One, is plantacon a menace? We say Yes; your side says No.

'Two, does it need to be removed from the environment? We say Yes; your side says No.

'Doesn't seem much room for compromise there.'

'Come on, Sam. We can compromise by agreeing that there is sufficient scientific controversy to justify a greater effort by everybody to establish the truth. That's not much of a compromise to ask of you. After all, you're convinced truth is on your side.'

'Agreed. But, assuming we're right, that raises another question: first, do we allow you . . . sorry, your side . . . to continue poisoning children while we wait for truth to be established. We say definitely not.

'But having said that, we *have* compromised. We've stepped back from demanding a total ban within eighteen months; we're ready to accept a fifty per cent voluntary cut now while a bill is introduced establishing a plantacon emission standard for two and a half years hence. Frankly, this is a huge compromise on our side and one we'll have some difficulty in defending to our own supporters.'

'But that's why this discussion is so helpful. We're nearly there,' she replied. 'We've agreed to the research.

We've agreed it should be independently done but funded by the industry. All we've asked is that the fifty per cent cut awaits the interim results. If you're proved wrong, the industry will save a great deal of money. If you're proved right, that cut will then take place.'

'But, if we're right – and we are – we'll have lost a few months of action to protect children. And the bill.'

'But, Sam, you won't need the bill. If the interim report shows you're right, you'll be getting the fifty per cent cut. But it won't stop there. If the completed research shows you're right there is no way the industry could keep using plantacon. You'll have won without a bill.'

'Why are your side so afraid of a bill?'

'I guess for the same reason you're so keen to have one. Why is that?'

'Because it will mean Congress, acting on the *risk* of damage to health, will have taken a position.'

'In other words, it's not to do with the substance of the issue. It's a matter of principle.'

'If you like.'

'Christ. It's just game playing. Game playing by people who can afford to play with principles.'

'Whereas your friends can't afford to have them. Is that what you're saying?'

'No, I'm not.' She sighed.

He grinned sympathetically. 'Anyway, I was simplifying. There are two differences of substance between our positions: first our proposal will lead to an immediate cut in plantacon pollution of fifty per cent. Not a cut that won't come for at least a year.'

'Why a year?'

'Because by the time this deal is negotiated by lawyers, then the scientists are chosen and gathered together to decide on the nature of the work, then they undertake the work, then they reach accord on the wording of their findings, and then time is found to debate it and argue over it, at least a year will have passed. So that's the first objection.

'The second difference in our positions is that we want progress on a bill. So that when the research confirms the hazard we can get some action.'

'But what if the research doesn't support your position?'

'It will.' He sighed, wearily. 'Look, there's hardly been one environmental debate that has not followed the same course. First our science is ridiculed. Then the industry produces its own. Then a lengthy debate takes place. Finally we're proved right – but we've lost years. We've been *through* all this. You haven't.'

The food arrived and for a moment they ate silently. Suddenly they both began to speak at once.

'Sorry, you go first,' he said.

'No, no. What were you going to say?'

'Only that maybe we could take a few minutes break from plantacon. Tell me about yourself?'

'What do you want to know?'

'Where you come from? How you got into this?'

So she briefly described her background. And then demanded the right to hear about him. She looked sad as he told of his parents' death, then excited as he described his career.

'God, I wish I was on your side instead of ours,' she admitted. 'It's so much easier.'

He looked surprised. 'Why do you say that?'

'You have all the advantage of believing you're on the side of the public good. Virtue. Self-righteousness. You don't have to defend your motives. It makes things a lot

easier. It also means the media listen to you more
sympathetically. And the public. We start with a huge
disadvantage. Yet I can't understand why. Industry is
the way whereby people are able to earn the money to
eat and drink and keep warm and pay for their leisure.
We create the work and we create the products and the
services. Yet we're distrusted and treated as enemies,
our motives always questioned.'

'Don't you think that's because of industry's record?'

'Partly. We get tarnished by the bad apples more than
you do. But you forget that much of the pollution and
environmental damage caused by industry was not –
maybe *could not* – have been anticipated. Much of the
criticism of industry, many of the findings, are
retrospective. Take the lead in gasoline case that you
like to quote. At the time lead was first added to gasoline
no one knew the level to which emissions would build, or
that at that level of exposure children could be harmed.
The first real scientific questions were only raised in the
mid-Sixties, thirty years after lead was first added. So
while the car and petroleum industries may have caused
damage to health by that process, they were doing so
unwittingly until quite recently.'

'Sure, but look how they resisted taking the necessary
action when we *did* know.'

'They could have found it simply impossible to believe
it was necessary. After all it was new thinking, and there
was scientific controversy, just as there is now over
plantacon.'

Then, pushing her plate away, she said, 'Can we come
back to plantacon? Is there no way your side will accept
our proposals?'

'None at all.'

'What about a clause in the bill?'

'What kind of clause?'

'Some kind of qualifying clause. Like basing the emission standards on the level of risk of health damage established by current scientific knowledge.'

He laughed. 'Oh boy, Nicola, full marks for trying.'

'You won't compromise on a thing will you?'

'It's not for me to do so. You're asking me to compromise on children's health. I don't believe I have that right.'

He said it self-righteously and suddenly she was mad at him – at the implication that he cared about children and she didn't. Damn him.

'Bullshit.' For the first time she raised her voice. 'You've already modified your position and called it a compromise. Now you say you can't compromise with children's health. You know what you do – you play with words. You don't play fair. You people are self-righteous phonies.'

He looked at her coolly. 'I think we've taken this as far as it can go.'

'You bet we have.' She waved for the check.

He looked at her, a little sadly. 'Look, do you have to go? We've dealt with the business. Why not stay and have a coffee and another drink?'

She rose. 'No thank you, Mr MacAnally.'

'Sam.'

'Goodnight, Mr MacAnally.'

He watched her walk to the exit and snatch her coat from the stand. A moment later he saw her waving at a taxi in the street.

She never looked back.

It reminded him of the occasional rows he had experienced with Marie.

But there was a difference. After those he would go home and find her waiting. They wouldn't say a word. Just fall into bed.

Tonight there would be nobody waiting.

No Marie.

And no Nicola Kowalska.

He ordered another drink and sat there, too depressed to move.

When Nicola got back to the self-catering hotel where she stayed in Washington she took off her coat and let it fall to the ground, tossed her handbag into one corner of the couch, and half fell into the other. And cried.

For the first time in years.

She told herself it was because she was exhausted.

The Environmental Pollution Sub-committee met in executive session.

Frankle waited till they were settled and then, speaking with quiet authority, opened the meeting.

'Gentlemen, I don't like this plantacon business. I don't like the way public opinion is being stirred up, emotions are running high, and Congress is being put under political pressure to approach a technical matter too quickly and not too dispassionately. I don't like the way personal animosities are getting into this thing.'

He looked at both Eberhard and Wilkins.

'And I don't like the confusion that surrounds the whole affair. Is plantacon safe or isn't it? I honestly don't know and the hearings didn't help. What I do know is that we must take a position. The public want an answer and they're looking to us for it.'

'Unfortunately, Hal, they've already decided what answer they want. On the basis of media manipulation and stirred-up hysteria.' It was Eberhard.

Before Wilkins could protest, Frankle frowned and said, 'Let me finish, Ed, if you don't mind.

'I've already said I don't like the pressure we're under.

But I guess that's what we're elected for. Now I've called this special meeting because the industry have come up with an offer. They'll back the research wholeheartedly. And if *interim results* suggest there is a pollution problem they will make a voluntary reduction of fifty per cent until we get the final results.

'However, Chris argues we should get legislation ready so that if the science then justifies a ban or a phase-out there will be minimal delay.

'The common ground between the two of you is that more research is necessary. My proposal is that we accept the industry offer, but proceed with mark-up sessions on Chris's revised bill and then if the sub-committee votes in favour, and the full committee votes in favour – and I am not prejudging those votes – we will take it on through the Senate at reasonable but not hysterical speed, making clear in our speeches in the Senate that our final individual positions will be determined by the interim research findings.

'That way we make the best of the two things on hand: the industry's offer and the Wilkins' initiative.'

He turned to Wilkins: 'Chris?'

'I happily accept your proposal, Senator.'

'Ed?'

'I object most strongly, Hal, for two reasons. First, this campaign is not justified. We're reducing the standing of the Senate by allowing ourselves to get drawn into it. Second, it's a waste of time when we have so much else to do. The industry's proposal meets any sane man's concerns.'

'Are you suggesting I'm not sane, Ed?' Frankle asked with a twinkle in his eye.

'Of course not, Hal, but I think your bending too far to meet extremist positions.'

'Maybe. But I was impressed by Sam MacAnally's

point that we should err on the side of caution. It's a valid position.'

'This is all a bit unusual, Hal,' said Leighton Taverner, frowning. 'How can we go back on our Senate votes?'

'It's not too difficult, Leighton. We simply arrange for the House to amend the bill so that we can't support it. Then it can die in conference between the two bodies.'

Eberhard snorted. 'Really, Hal. This is too much. Is this the way honourable men should behave?'

Frankle looked at him wearily. 'Ed, if you're right about plantacon, this precedure will protect it. If you're wrong, it will protect our children's health. It's a genuine attempt to establish the truth and do what is best. I don't see how a man of honour could oppose it.'

WASHINGTON POST

PLANTACON BILL NOW FIRMLY ON CONGRESSIONAL AGENDA

by Jacqueline Brown.

The bill promoted by Connecticut Senator Christopher Wilkins to control aircraft emissions of plantacon is now firmly on the Congressional agenda.

The Environmental Pollution Sub-committee chaired by Senator Hal Frankle is to begin mark-up sessions next week.

The bill, if it becomes law, will set a zero standard for plantacon emissions within two and a half years, with intermediate reductions.

It has the support of the ECO campaign led by environmental campaigner Sam MacAnally who said yesterday that it represented a generous compromise on calls for an immediate ban.

'We are doing all we can to protect public health while enabling the airlines to extricate themselves from

dependence on plantacon or, alternatively, to find a way of controlling emissions.'

Nicola Kowalska, of the industry's plantacon liaison committee, said the bill represented a sellout to hysterical campaigning. The industry had offered a compromise that more than met public concern. It would strongly oppose the measure.

IS THERE NO SENSE IN THE SENATE?

by Lionel North

The plantacon affair has gone from farce to tragedy.

How can an experienced sub-committee chairman like Sen Hal Frankle have allowed himself to be talked into even considering a bill so scientifically unsupported?

And what chance does industry have if, when it offers a compromise at considerable expense to itself, it's treated like a criminal asking for time off for good behaviour?

It's time the President set up one of his study commissions.

But not on plantacon.

It should investigate the roll of single issue pressure groups and the way they work. They are becoming a cancer on our democratic process.

NEW YORK

David Johnston couldn't believe this place.

When he'd accepted Dieter Partrell's invitation for an after-hours drink he'd assumed the bar Partrell suggested would be at least reasonably comfortable and sophisticated.

Instead it was about as sordid a place as he had ever seen.

He looked with distaste at the whore at the end of the counter, wiped the bar-stool with his handkerchief and sat gingerly down.

He had never liked Partrell. He suspected few did. He was a brutish man. But he would never have guessed that Partrell frequented dumps like this.

Unless . . . Johnston began to feel uneasy . . . could it be that the business Partrell had in mind *called* for a place like this?

He could still remember the contempt on the plantacon manufacturer's face when he had been less than helpful at the Waldorf-Astoria meeting.

'You drinking, or thinking of buying the place?' The barman lodged a toothpick between a couple of teeth and looked at Johnston with the scorn he reserved for losers. That, of course, was what he assumed Johnston was – despite the expensive suit and shiny shoes. You didn't come into this bar unless you were at the end of the line. This was a loser's bar.

Johnston ordered a martini. The barman went to get it, shaking his head as if to say, 'Jeez, does this guy think he's somethin', or what?'

'To hell with this,' Johnston thought. 'I'm getting out of here.'

Then he saw the burly figure of Partrell in the doorway. The big man came over, hauled himself on to a stool, called for a bourbon, and looked at Johnston coolly.

'Christ, Dieter, what on earth are we doing in this place?' Johnston protested. 'I know you're worried about plantacon but FEI can't be in this much trouble.'

Partrell downed his drink. 'It's the haunt of a friend of mine,' he said.

He ordered another drink.

Johnston began to feel increasingly uncomfortable. There was something not right about this. He half rose to go. 'Look, Dieter, I don't know what game you're playing but if this is the best you can do . . .'

'Sit down.'

'I beg your pardon? I don't like your tone—'

'*Sit down.*'

Johnston sank back on to the stool. 'What is it you want, Dieter? Say it and let me get out of this dump before I catch something nasty.'

'A bit late to worry about that, isn't it?'

'What do you mean?'

'I mean the people you've been mixing with could have given you a much nastier disease than you'll get in this place.'

'Look . . .'

'No,' said Partrell, his voice brooking no argument. '*You* look . . .'

And he placed in front of Johnston a photograph.

The oil man froze.

He remembered part of the evening well. It was while his family were in Montego Bay. He had come back for another one of their damned plantacon meetings. Partrell had taken him out for dinner afterwards. And a drink. Several drinks. OK, a barrelful of drink. And at the end of it all Johnston had found himself back in his hotel room with these two girls.

One black, the other white.

Coffee and Cream they had called themselves.

He had drunk too much to remember what happened . . . what they did.

All he knew was that he had woken up alone. There was no sign they had been there. He had almost persuaded himself it never happened.

But of course it had. And Partrell had the photograph to prove it.

And if the photograph was anything to go by, it had

been a hell of a night.

He sighed and then, surprising himself with how calm he felt, he said, 'OK, Dieter I presume this is blackmail. What do you want?'

The big man leaned across until his red face was almost in Johnston's. The smell of alcohol was overpowering.

'Cooperation, David,' he said. '*Cooperation* with your good customers, the airlines. It's what they were entitled to anyway. So, no more trying to play it both ways. From now on the oil industry backs plantacon all the way.

'Otherwise Mrs Johnston gets this photograph. And so will a few people in the oil business. And your airline customers.

'Need I say more?'

Johnston sighed again. 'No, Dieter,' he said, 'you needn't say more.'

He got up.

'I just wish you'd chosen to blackmail me in a decent bar.'

He looked around him, then added, 'Still, this place suits you.'

And on what he hoped was rather a good note he left with what dignity he could muster.

Partrell glared at the whore at the end of the counter, ordered himself another drink, and waited for Charlie Orbell.

He didn't really see why he should wait for the little creep. But the photograph had done the trick. Orbell had earned his money. You had to give him that – he always earned his money.

He felt an itch under his arm and began to scratch himself.

Johnston had been right about one thing.

This was a lousy bar.

BALTIMORE

Todd Birk was frantic.

The goddam environmentalists were winning.

He was likely to be asked to voluntarily cut plantacon use by fifty per cent.

Well, he had said little at the New York meeting but the motherfuckers could forget that. He couldn't afford to cut it by one per cent, let alone fifty. And he was damned if he would.

If that bunch of ex-college boys in New York were ready to cut their plantacon use, that was their problem.

He wondered if Federal Express would make the voluntary cut. That would give him an extra edge over them.

As for the additional research, Birk didn't trust that either. Because Dieter Partrell wasn't in charge of it.

Partrell was the one man in this whole affair Birk trusted. The one man he knew thought the same way he did. The fifty per cent must be catastrophic news for Partrell. What would he do?

Then there was Jordan and company. Their shares had fallen further as a result of the latest newspaper stories. He couldn't believe Jordan would let the environmentalists win. Even if blood had to be spilt to avoid it.

Birk had a feeling that the rules of the game were about to change.

WASHINGTON, D.C.

That night the ECO headquarters near Dupont Circle
were burned to the ground.

Sam MacAnally was woken at three o'clock by the
police. When he got down to 19th Street he had to fight
his way past a crowd of onlookers. There were four fire
engines at the scene but they were concentrating on
controlling the spread of the blaze. It was clear to
MacAnally at a glance that they had rightly concluded
that his own offices couldn't be saved.

Flames were pouring from the windows. Sparks were
being carried by the wind as far as Dupont Circle. Tears
pouring down his face, caused by the smoke, he stood
and watched all that he had built up, years of
accumulated records, from campaign files to membership lists, and all their equipment . . . the 'machine' that
was ECO . . . being destroyed before his eyes.

Including the whole file on the plantacon campaign.

NEW YORK

Eugene Remington sat at his breakfast table, engrossed
in the television coverage of the fire. The blaze made for
some spectacular pictures. And the interview with a
white-faced MacAnally was dramatic.

The environmentalist was asked whether he believed
the fire had been deliberately lit.

'I've never been a believer in conspiracy,' he said. 'But
it's a coincidence that it should happen at this time.'

'Have you received any threats?'

MacAnally paused. 'No more than usual,' he said laconically, and ended the interview.

Remington now got into the back of his car and, as it slid away from the kerb, began wondering: surely no one in the industry group had done this?

Then he thought about Partrell and his nasty little detective, the one uncovered by the hearings.

And of the newspaper stories Partrell had planted about MacAnally and Abernathy.

And about Todd Birk and his heart-felt desire to 'nuke the bastards'.

They were capable of it. No doubt about that.

Then he began thinking about his own financial problems. About his desperate need for plantacon to be cleared so that the company could expand.

It was all so unfair.

Damned unfair.

He had earned his success. Worked for it. Taken risks for it.

Now these damned environmentalists were threatening it all.

Remington didn't believe that burning down ECO's headquarters would deter MacAnally.

But he had to admit to some satisfaction at the inconvenience it must have caused.

If Birk and Partrell had arranged the fire, he wasn't going to complain.

Provided they stopped there.

There were limits and they had reached them.

BALTIMORE

Todd Birk dropped the newspaper on his desk and reached out for a can of beer, flipping the tab off, and swilling it with deep satisfaction.

Jordan had obviously struck the first blow.

That should scare MacAnally and his friends off.

WASHINGTON, D.C.

Nicola Kowalska watched her TV set with horror tinged with relief that MacAnally hadn't been in the building.

She listened closely to the questions about possible arson.

And she thought about Partrell and Birk.

Could it be. . .?

No, she couldn't believe it.

Dare not believe it.

Senator Hal Frankle read the *Washington Post*'s account of the fire with deep concern.

He rang Ed Eberhard. 'You've seen this about the fire, Ed?'

'I have, Hal.'

'I don't like it.'

'Nor do I.'

'We'd better get some kind of accord on this thing and get the heat out of the issue. Before someone gets hurt.'

'Hal, I've already spoken to Eugene Remington. He's convinced no one on our side would allow this. But the

word will be put out to every corner of the industry, just
in case there's a lunatic somewhere. Everyone will be
told that any violence would be totally counter-
productive.'

'Well, I hope it works, Ed.'

'So do I.'

MacAnally decided to have an international 'summit
meeting' to discuss how to rebuild ECO and its
plantacon campaign after the fire.

They met in Jay Sandbach's condo up Connecticut
Avenue just before the bridge over Rock Creek Park.
Jay was the only one of them with a big enough room for
the meeting. They sat around, some on chairs, some on
his comfortable couch, some on cushions on the floor.

From the US there were Jay, Molly Macintosh,
Dominic Young, and Adrian Carlisle and Jake Katzir,
both now fully recovered from their experience in
Tokyo.

Olly Witcomb had come from the UK, Monique de
Vos from Belgium.

Liz Scullen came on behalf of both Australia and
Japan.

About the burnt out headquarters there was one piece
of good news. Dominic Young had kept a duplicate set
of computer discs at home covering all of the financial
records including the fundraising and membership lists.
MacAnally could have wept with gratitude for his
colleague's caution. They all congratulated the beaming
Young.

'We'll issue an immediate financial appeal, for funds
to replace equipment,' MacAnally said.

'Weren't you insured?' asked Liz Scullen.

'Yes.'

'Well, then, why the appeal?'

The Americans laughed. 'In this business,' said Young, 'you launch appeals on the back of anything. Anything at all. We'll make a profit on the fire.'

The bad news was that they were now without their detailed planning records for the plantacon campaign, including Molly Macintosh's priceless card index system.

There was a grassroots organisation out there, somewhere, but Molly no longer knew where it was.

She was going to have to spend weeks looking in telephone directories from all over the US tracing the addresses and phone numbers of the names she could remember.

Jake Katzir was more worried than any of them. 'We were the sole custodians of all the scientific records. All of the original notes from Barnes and Warner have been destroyed completely. We only had copies of the records of the other three so they're okay.'

Jake now opened up the wider discussion about the status of the campaign. 'Look, while I'm bemoaning the loss of these records I have to say we're becoming more and more vulnerable on the scientific front. We can't explain the differences between our studies and theirs except by attacking their integrity and there's a limit to the extent we can get away with that. Three of our scientists are dead and, as I've said, the original records of two of them no longer exist.'

'But it looks as if we're going to get a deal whereby more research is carried out, paid for by the industry, but done by scientists we help to choose,' Liz said. 'Why do we need to do more ourselves?'

'I would just feel better if we do. This is all going to come down to the science. We need to be as well informed and well equipped with research as we can. I have no doubt that, in addition to the official scientific inquiry, the industry will commission its own backup studies. Then, if the official inquiry doesn't come down on its side, it will use them to confuse the position further.'

'You're right, Jake,' said MacAnally. 'I've been meaning to act on this for some time but I've kept getting sidetracked. I'll talk to our sponsor and see if we can't get another set of studies moving.'

They now began a review of the state of the campaign.

Everyone backed the idea of a fifty per cent voluntary ban coupled with more research, provided that while the research was being conducted a Bill was being prepared to phase out plantacon once its dangers were confirmed.

The Americans were confident this could be achieved in the US, and Witcomb felt things were going his way in the UK.

Monique de Vos was less sanguine about some of the European countries. 'It's going to be a long hard battle,' she said. 'Some of the countries are taking a hard line in defence of their airlines. But the environmental movement is growing in strength, so we're not without a chance.'

Liz Scullen reported that, provided the Americans took the lead, there was a good chance Australia would follow.

It was Jake Katzir who raised the issue of the dead scientists. And the fire. 'I can't understand why you're so sanguine, Sam. I feel like we're under attack.'

MacAnally told them that Senator Wilkins had called just the previous day with a report of his contacts with the FBI.

'There have been exchanges of information. All three local police forces are sticking by their explanations.

'According to the Japanese police the bombing had been expected. They just hadn't known where it would be.

'The New York State and British police see no reason to revise their verdicts that the Warner and Barnes deaths were caused by an accident and by suicide.'

He paused. There was a sympathetic silence. They all knew he had carefully avoided mentioning Marie.

Then he continued, 'Believe me, I've thought about it a lot, but I can't bring myself to believe anyone's launched a world-wide campaign of murder.' He laughed. 'Honestly! It's not on.'

'What about the fire?' Adrian Carlisle asked.

'The police haven't found any evidence of arson. But I must admit I keep thinking of that man Birk's threats. You saw his face. That man hates us.'

'I *did* see his face,' Carlisle said ruefully, 'and I don't want to see it again.'

'OK, well, we'll just have to be careful. We'll have a security guard on our new office.'

That night they went out for dinner together before the others returned to their own countries. Liz found herself sitting next to Sam.

'So you think you've got Australia under control?' he asked.

'I wouldn't go that far. I think it'll be OK. But we could do with a bit of help, Sam. Any chance you could come over and do a few media appearances?'

'I doubt it. But we could send a team. Adrian and Jake. They're going to Japan anyway.'

'Christ, going back to Japan?'

'Sure.' He put on a macho look, throwing back his shoulders and thumping his chest like Tarzan. 'Nobody scares ECO.'

She laughed. 'What are they going to do there?'

'Well, the idea is to have a big symposium. Send your man Cossens from Australia. Also a few outside politicians, maybe this guy Bell from England, and

Mullalay from Australia. Possibly even Chris Wilkins. I'm told this kind of thing will get massive Japanese media coverage and galvanise their politicians into taking some action.

'And you think some of your team could then come on to Australia?'

'Why not? They'll be almost there already.'

'Great. I'll get organising it.'

She looked closely at him. 'You're looking a bit low, Sam. Is it the fire?'

'No.' He laughed. 'Not at all. That building was getting too overcrowded. A lot of that stuff should have been burned years ago.' Then more seriously he said, 'Dominic had copies of the stuff that would have been irreplaceable. The lists. Obviously it's a damned nuisance but we can rebuild our library and the rest in a relatively short time.'

'So what's the matter?' She paused. 'Is it Marie?'

He sighed. 'Of course I miss her. But you know, Liz, it's extraordinary, good in a way, and terrifying in another, how life goes on. For a while I thought the hole inside me was there forever, but then one day it seemed smaller and every day after that smaller still. We survive, don't we? We go on.'

Then he put his arm around her and gave her a hug. 'Stop worrying about me. I'm just tired, I guess.'

But when he got home he suddenly felt deeply depressed. And lonely. Liz's questions had unsettled him. He poured himself a Scotch and lounged on the couch. Then the phone rang. For a moment he thought about letting it ring, but he picked it up.

It was Nicola Kowalska. 'Hi,' she said, 'am I disturbing you?'

'Yes,' he said, 'but I was feeling sorry for myself. So I'm happy to be disturbed.'

'I heard about the fire. I'm really sorry.'

'Thanks.'

'That's what I rang to say. I know we're on opposite sides but . . .'

'Sure. It's good of you.'

'Sam. . .?'

'Yes?'

'You don't think . . . you don't think anyone could have . . . done it deliberately?'

He sat, without replying, trying to get hold of the question. It had all happened so fast, the fire, finding alternative premises, sorting out insurance, dealing with the immediate problems, setting up the review meeting. Apart from the brief discussion at the ECO meeting he hadn't really had time to consider how it was started.

'I don't know,' he said eventually. 'Why, you think it's someone on your side?'

'Well, not exactly . . .'

'What do you mean, not exactly?'

'Well, Eugene Remington and the big boys wouldn't want to know.

'But Todd Birk . . . well, actually I like to pretend that Todd Birk is not on our side. Just a menace to us both. And if Partrell was my only client I would pack him in.'

'You think one of them was behind it?'

'No. No . . . At least . . . well, I don't know what to think . . . no, I'm not saying that. I just wondered what you were thinking.'

'Well, now I'm thinking about it.'

'Oh, God,' she said, 'I've fed your paranoia.'

'Don't forget who had the idea first.'

She laughed. 'That's true.'

He put his feet up. He was enjoying talking to her.

'Nicola,' he said.

'Yes?'

'I'm sorry we're on opposite sides on this.'

'So am I.'

'Are you?'

'Yes.'

Her voice sounded smaller.

For a moment he was silent.

'Are you still there?' she asked.

'Sorry, I was just thinking. Look, let's have dinner. Tomorrow night. How about tomorrow night?'

'I'd like that.'

'Good. I'll ring you in the morning to fix where and when.'

'OK.'

He put down the phone. The depression had lifted. He began looking forward to tomorrow.

As he climbed into a bath he thought to himself that he hadn't looked forward to tomorrow for a long time.

He slept late and was woken by a call from Jay Sandbach on Capitol Hill. 'You'd better get down here, Sam. We're in trouble.'

'What the hell's happening?'

'You've forgotten it's the first day of the mark-up. Eberhard is trying to undermine the compromise. He's mobilised a number of the committee behind some clauses in the Bill that would be catastrophic. We're trying to get to the individual members to get a majority to oppose them but it won't be easy.'

MacAnally was in a cab within five minutes, studying his rough notes on what Sandbach had told him.

Eberhard, supported by Charles Myers of North Carolina, had introduced an amendment stating that enforcement of the emission standards should be suspended until 'equivalent energy savings could be achieved by other technical means'.

A second amendment suspended enforcement until 'scientific consensus on the dangers, if any, caused by plantacon can be established'.

Both were unacceptable to ECO. The argument for the second would sound reasonable to people who believed that scientific consensus was possible to achieve. But it wasn't. At least not on an issue like this.

As for the first amendment, there was no guarantee that an alternative energy-saver *could* be found.

Yet MacAnally could imagine people saying to each other, 'Well, it makes sense to me. Plantacon goes if the scientists agree it's a problem . . . and if we can save energy in other ways.'

It had been shrewd.

When he got there he found Sandbach walking down the corridor towards him. 'They've broken for the day.'

'Did they vote on the amendments?'

'No, thank God. Wilkins managed to stall it until tomorrow.'

'How's it looking?'

'I think it's going to come down to Frankle's vote. Eberhard has the same support he had before but Cal Calhorn was going his way. I must say Chris Wilkins was very good. He argued that the industry were playing it both ways, secretly trying to undermine their own offer. I think his arguments swung Calhorn back onto neutral territory and Chris is having lunch with him now.'

'What did Frankle say?'

'He didn't. He didn't comment. But he's no fool. He knows what's going on.'

'I wish Frankle was more committed to this cause.'

'Sam, you get at Ed Kellerman. He's right behind us and he thinks the sun shines out of your eyes. He's worked for Frankle for a long time and the old man respects him. If he is prepared to go out on a limb I think he'll talk Frankle into blocking the amendments.'

They split up.

MacAnnally got Kellerman on the phone and arranged to have dinner.

It was only much later that he remembered that he was supposed to be having dinner with Nicola Kowalska.

He rang her office but she had gone for the day.

And they wouldn't tell him where she was staying in Washington.

Cursing his luck, he went to meet Kellerman. At least that meeting produced good news. The staff director to the committee told him that Frankle was wise to what Eberhard was trying to do.

'Hal knows you'll never get a scientific consensus, at least not in the short term. It's a ludicrous proposition. He also knows that there's no guarantee that plantacon can be replaced by another energy-saving device of equal value. In fact its extremely unlikely.

'But, just the same, he reckons if you could find a way of balancing the phase-out of plantacon with some progress in energy saving it's got a better chance of going through Congress.'

'How difficult do you think it will be to get a bill past the Senate?'

'Well, as you know, the Senate doesn't usually overrule the work of its committees. But this is different. We're not going to get a unanimous committee recommendation. And there are a lot of vested interests on this. Members with airline or other industry connections. Members on other committees, concerned with energy, or exports, or trade, or defence, who will be under a lot of pressure from those sources.

'I tell you this, you would never have got an outright ban. I think you've done damn well to get the compromises you have. Especially as the scientific case is less than convincing. Still, you're winning on public pressure so far. Are you going to be able to keep that up?'

'The fire didn't help. It destroyed all our records. But, yes. We'll re-launch the grassroots campaign around the time of the Senate vote. And I hope to commission more scientific research too.'

As he walked back to his apartment MacAnally thought about the scientific research. He had for the first time been unable to get Lord on the phone. So he had sent him a fax:

> 'Need for more scientific studies to support our case is becoming crucial and urgent. The three million dollars is nearly all spent, one and a half million on the TV commercials and air time, one million on the initial grassroots campaign, and half a million on the headquarters campaign. Could you bring yourself to finance some more research?'

So far there had been no answer.

He let himself into the apartment.

It felt particularly empty tonight.

Then he remembered his failure to cancel the dinner with Nicola Kowalska.

What must she think of him?

He didn't know the answer, but he did know that he cared about the answer.

Much more than he would have expected.

He grabbed a classified phone book and ticked the hotels he thought she would be most likely to choose.

What did he know about her. She worked out of an office in K Street, and therefore would choose somewhere reasonably close.

She was well funded, so it would not necessarily be a cheap place.

She was in Washington a lot, so it was possible the arrangement was temporarily permanent. It would most likely be a self-catering place.

He ticked three likely ones and telephoned them all. The third had a Ms Kowalska staying there. Would he like to speak to her? He said yes, then no, then hung up and paced up and down the room. Then he picked up the phone, began to dial, then put it down.

Then, on an impulse, he grabbed his keys, walked out and down the stairs and signalled a cab. Five minutes later he was at her place. The doorman recognised him and provided the suite number. He listened for a moment at the door and thought he could hear music. He rang the bell.

She was wearing a soft mohair sweater and jeans. Her hair was rumpled and looked softer than he recalled it. For a moment she stood, astonished, as he began to mumble apologies. Then she took his hand and led him in and suddenly they were in each other's arms.

For several minutes they stood there, kissing, exploring each other with their hands, gently, each not daring to speak. Then she drew apart from him and led him to a sofa in front of the fire.

She had already opened a bottle of Chablis and poured him a glass.

He realised she still hadn't spoken.

So he just sat and looked at her.

Then he said, 'I really am sorry about dinner. The whole day went wrong.'

'I know,' she said. 'I was at the mark-up session this morning. I can guess what you've been up to ever since.'

'Well . . .'

But she put a finger to her lips. 'Let's not talk about it.'

He relaxed. 'No.'

He pulled her to him and she rested her head on his chest, putting her feet up on the other end of the couch.

'I like you, MacAnally,' she said.

'I know.'

'You do?' She lifted her head and half turned to look at him. 'You're an arrogant son-of-a-bitch.'

'Sorry. I didn't mean it like it sounded. I really meant I knew we were attracted to each other.'

He let his hand slip down over her sweater, until it cradled a small but firm mohair-covered breast.

But she took his hand and gently removed it. Then she sat up and looked at him, her eyes serious.

'Sam, listen to me. I'm not going to pretend I haven't thought about this . . . about being with you . . . but we've got to get this plantacon affair out of the way first. Otherwise we won't stand a chance.'

He sighed. 'I know you're right. It's just . . .'

'Don't say it. I feel the same. But I don't want a casual affair with you. And I don't want problems and that's what it'll be like while we're involved in the plantacon business. There'll be one problem after another until it poisons whatever we could have had. I want either a real, lasting friendship or I want to forget it before I get hurt. Believe me, I've thought a lot about this, Sam. Because I do like you.'

And she leaned forward and kissed him again.

'OK.' He rose. 'I know you're right.' He took her in his arms. 'Take care,' he said.

He held her tight, walked to the door, and then, standing just outside, he said with a grin, 'And I'm going to beat the shit out of you over plantacon.'

She laughed and threw a cushion at him.

'Don't you believe it, Mr Environmentalist. You've met your match this time.'

He caught the cushion. He could smell her perfume on it.

'Just for that,' he said, 'I'm going to keep your cushion. I'll bring it back the day the Senate votes for our bill.'

And, absurdly happy, he carried it off into the night.

For the second day running MacAnally overslept. He arrived at the mark-up session a quarter of an hour late but in time to hear Kellerman's predictions being confirmed. Frankle opened the meeting by rejecting the first Eberhard amendment and saying that he would consider adaptations of the second. In the meantime he would oppose them both.

They voted and Frankle's casting vote settled it. Eberhard, however, warned he would re-introduce his amendments in the Senate itself.

As they left MacAnally saw Nicola Kowalska in the lobby. He walked up to her and smiled into her eyes. 'Hi.'

She smiled back.

There was no one near. 'Tell me,' he said with a grin, 'What would you do for me if I called off our campaign?'

She laughed. 'Cook you the best home-made Polish meal you've ever had.'

He put on a disappointed look. 'Is that all?'

'What do you mean, "is that all?" You haven't tasted my cooking.' And with that she walked off to talk to her colleagues.

'What was MacAnally saying?' Alexander Green, the industry lobbyist, asked curiously.

She looked at him impassively. 'Maybe he's wondering if we're going to give up,' she said.

'I hope you made it clear he could forget about that.'

'Oh yes,' she said. 'I made my feelings clear.'

SYDNEY

The ECO team and accompanying stars – Dr Bruce Cossens and Senator Keith Mullalay from Australia, the Labour MP Nick Bell and the Tory MP Hal Robbins from England – gathered at Doyles for a fish and chip celebration of the success of the Japanese initiative.

As expected, the symposium and the visiting contributors had received saturation coverage from newspapers, radio and television.

Machiko Yanagi could not have been happier and was now more confident that the Japanese would respond positively to the American lead.

(She had also spent two memorable nights with Mike McKenzie. They had decided that Machiko would go to Australia as soon as the plantacon campaign was over. They would get married and explore the Great Barrier Reef for their honeymoon. Mike was planning to stop working fulltime for ECO and take up a post as lecturer at the University of West Australia. Machiko, they hoped, would then become Liz Scullen's co-campaigner.)

Now the team was in Sydney to repeat its performance for the benefit of the Australian media. As the lager flowed and the overseas visitors including Jake Katzir and Adrian Carlisle sat and wondered at the beauty of the harbour, Liz noticed Cossens leaning quietly on the wall, his feet resting on the sand. She strolled over with a couple of lagers.

'I hear you were a big hit in Tokyo,' she said.

He grinned.

To her surprise, it didn't seem so maddening this time.

Had she changed, she wondered, or had he?

'Maybe my TV days are just round the corner,' he said. 'I've had an approach from Channel Nine.'

'Really? What for?'

'A weekly "What's happening in science?" feature. Late at night. When everyone's in bed. Still, it's a start.'

'What about plantacon?'

'No problem. I'm yours to the end.'

'Good.'

'Talking about being yours . . . how about coming up to my place when the party's over?'

She hesitated. Then caught sight of his face in the light from the restaurant. There it was, that vulnerable look again – that little boy look – the one she found so appealing.

'OK,' she said.

When she woke the sun was shining onto the bed. It had been a warm night and one of them had thrown the covers off. He was lying on his front, naked, his face buried in the pillow.

She looked at his strong sun-bronzed back, the muscular white buttocks she had gripped so tightly as he had thrust into her last night, and the long legs.

She remembered how gently he had touched her.

To her surprise he had been nervous. She got the impression that for all the outward show of confidence he hadn't had a lot of experience.

All of that she had liked.

She lay looking at him for a few minutes, then quietly got out of bed and went to the window to look over the bay. She must have been standing like that for several minutes when she felt his arms encircle her, then his hands come up to cup her breasts.

She snuggled back into his arms and for a while they didn't move, didn't speak.

Then she turned, kissed him, slipped her hand down and squeezed him affectionately, and said, 'Does this place of yours serve coffee?'

He grinned – she didn't mind it at all now – and let her go with a friendly slap on the backside.

'Sure,' he said. 'And steak and eggs if you like.'

'I like,' she said, and fell back onto the bed. She heard him run the shower, then heard him moving in the kitchen and soon she caught the smell of cooking.

She got up, showered herself and, slipping on the tee-shirt and jeans she had been wearing for the party, joined him in the kitchen.

'I've got an idea,' he said. 'I bet the Yanks and the Poms have never seen good surfing. Why don't we ring up their hotel and suggest we party on the beach today? It's Sunday. There's not a lot else to do.'

So she rang the hotel and got hold of Adrian Carlisle. 'Great idea,' he said. She heard him talking to someone else. Then he said, 'Jake thinks so too. Apparently he fancies himself as a surfer. Shall I ring the English MPs? I don't see Hal Robbins on a surfboard but the Labour guy Bell will probably want to come.'

They picked them up in Cossens's car about three hours later – Carlisle, Katzir, Bell and Mike McKenzie – and, cramming them all in, made for Bondi beach. Cossens recommended another one, better for surfing, less crowded, but Carlisle and Bell both said they couldn't go home and say they'd been surfing if they couldn't say it was Bondi.

Liz should have known that Cossens wouldn't be able to resist showing off.

Still, even she was impressed.

He rode the giant waves effortlessly, a flying bronzed

figure on a red surfboard, drawing admiring looks from everyone at their end of the beach.

Jake Katzir soon retired. He paddled out of the water, his body incongruously white compared with the Australian surfers and, dropping his board, said, 'That man Cossens is damn good.'

'And doesn't he know it,' laughed Liz as Cossens came flying in, carried by a wave almost onto the sand at their feet.

He flopped down beside her, the water gleaming on his chest. She looked at the small bathing costume, and at the substantial bulge, and for a moment wished they were back at his place in Watson's Bay, and she could free the hard and soft parts of that bulge and repeat what they had done last night.

Then he was on his feet once more. 'One more ride,' he said. 'I'm going to go a bit further out this time.'

She lay back on her towel, while Mike McKenzie opened the ice box and got out some tubes of lager. He tossed one to Bell, Katzir and Carlisle as they watched Cossens working his way beyond the waves.

'Bet he comes down this time,' said Bell. Liz sensed he was envious of Cossens's physique and skill.

'You're on,' said McKenzie. 'A dollar.'

'I'll have a piece of that action,' said Katzir.

'So will I,' said Liz, sitting up to watch.

They saw Cossens lazing in the water, then positioning himself to catch the first wave.

It was Bell who saw it first. 'That speed boat's getting awful close, isn't it?' he said.

Liz looked up, then froze in fright. A black powerboat, low in the water, was heading towards Cossens at tremendous speed.

She leapt to her feet, shouting a warning, waving madly.

He couldn't hear her but saw her wave and, with his free arm, waved nonchalantly back.

Then it was upon him. It must have hit him square-on. They saw him fly into the air, the surfboard going in the opposite direction.

The boat itself swivelled around in the water, almost capsized with the impact, then, putting on speed, it raced away towards the far end of the bay.

Half crying, half shouting his name, Liz ran into the sea, followed by the others. She was a strong swimmer but became aware of two men passing her, life-savers, who had seen the incident from their tower.

She swam on but by the time she got to Cossens the two life-savers were already turning, preparing to take him back to the beach.

Liz looked at the white face, at the battered and broken body.

She didn't need them to tell her he was dead.

WASHINGTON, D.C.

The news of Cossens's death did not reach MacAnally until he was about to leave for the crucial Senate debate. He steadied himself against the wall, badly shaken.

'Was it deliberate?' he asked Adrian Carlisle, who had been allotted the task of breaking the news.

'We don't know. The power boat raced off but the police think it could have been some crazy kid who panicked and fled. Maybe one who had taken his parents' boat without permission. They're searching for it now.'

'Well, what do you think?'

Carlisle hesitated for a few seconds, then said, 'I feel

the same as when we were hit in Tokyo, Sam. I thought
it was a helluva coincidence then. I think it more so
now.'

'OK, you tell the police the whole story so they look
into it properly and don't automatically treat it as a
one-off.'

He knew now he had no choice but to think the
unthinkable.

That the other side were killing their scientists.

One could be explained.

Two could be explained.

Three was becoming too much of a coincidence.

But four? Surely four meant only one thing . . .

He had better warn Abernathy to take care.

He telephoned the researcher's number but there was
no answer.

He rang the office and asked his secretary to chase
Abernathy at the university or wherever he was.

He should be told that MacAnally was concerned
about his safety.

That he should keep out of sight until they could talk
that night.

Then, late now, he headed for Capitol Hill and the big
debate.

The plantacon affair had been bogged down in
sub-committee meetings, negotiations between sub-
committee members and the industry, and sub-
committee members and the environmentalists, then full
committee meetings, but at last the full committee had
voted by a narrow majority to send the bill on to the
Senate with a favourable recommendation.

It was now up to the full Senate to decide whether to
vote in favour, and thus send it on to the House of
Representatives.

There had been over the last few days one of the most intensive arm-twisting exercises since the Senate had been called upon to support the Bush Administration's decision to fight the Gulf War.

ECO had broken down the list of one hundred senators into a number of groups.

There were about twenty who were firm supporters, either because they always supported the environmental lobby or had no choice but to respond to public opinion in their constituencies.

There were about thirty who, as Jay Sandbach put it, were so locked into defence or business interests that they would support plantacon even if it were slowly poisoning the entire nation.

So, of the remaining fifty senators, the Wilkins' Bill would need the support of thirty-one for a majority.

It wasn't going to be easy.

MacAnally, as well as coordinating the whole campaign, had been responsible for holding their existing twenty together, and Sandbach had led the lobbying team to corral the other thirty-one votes. Their press team had built up the media heat and Molly Macintosh had concentrated her efforts entirely on mobilising voters in the states of the fifty senators who were still up for grabs. Senators had not been able to go back home without meeting concerned members of the public, at the airport, at their offices, at every event they went to. On the other hand they were also heavily lobbied by business interests.

In Washington itself Eberhard had been as good as his word. Malevolently, he had expended considerable energy in destroying Wilkins' other bill, the one that would have helped the unemployed in his state. He had also arranged for presentations to undecided senators. They were shown how house prices around airports were falling. How airport hotels were two-thirds empty as travellers decided to stay in the centre of cities. All the time they were being told how flimsy the evidence was, how enormously beneficial plantacon was. The message was clear: as responsible senators they must not give in to the hysteria.

The Wilkins' line had been more straightforward. No state would forgive a senator who supported plantacon if hundreds of thousands of children in the state were later found to have been brain-damaged as a result.

On the eve of the debate – at about the same time as Cossens had been demonstrating his surfing skills on Bondi beach – both organising groups had met in Washington.

The industry's war council was told it was desperately close.

Wilkins had come up with a clever tactic. He had talked to undecided senators and told them that they could play it both ways. They could vote for the bill and thus demonstrate to their constituents that they cared about their children. But, in their speech, they could say that they were doing so without prejudice to their vote on the amendments when it came back from the House of Representatives. In other words, they would be giving it fair passage for the next stage without finally committing themselves. There was always the option of opposing the House amendments and then allowing the bill to get bogged down in conference committee.

This ploy of Wilkins had, lobbyist Alexander Green warned the war council, been well received.

On the other hand, Ed Eberhard's brutal campaign of promises and threats had been effective too.

Nicola Kowalska had been more upbeat. 'Obviously I would like the Senate to kill it tomorrow,' she had told them. 'But look what we've achieved. No one any longer is talking about a ban on plantacon. Despite huge publicity and mass hysteria the environmentalists still can't count on a majority of the Senate. And the publicity and hysteria cannot be kept at this level.

'In the meantime the opportunities for delay are endless. And delay is crucial because all the time this is being discussed and debated the research continues, research that will clear plantacon and end the whole affair.'

They had left the meeting feeling fairly optimistic.

But, then, so had the ECO group. Wilkins had come to the meeting himself and reported that his tactic was working. 'I think if there were a straight vote, ban plantacon or don't, we would lose. But colleagues are telling me that they're impressed with how reasonable we're being.'

Thus the scene had been set for the Senate debate.

Up in the gallery MacAnally saw Nicola sitting with Remington and winked at her. She nodded back.

Frankle opened, commending the compromise approach, then yielding the floor to Wilkins. Taking care not to use emotive language, the young senator described to an attentive chamber the benefits of plantacon. 'Be in no doubt, Mr President, plantacon was potentially a great development.' He paused to let his fairness register in the minds of his colleagues, most of whom were quietly acknowledging to themselves that it was an impressive start by their youngest member.

'I say "was" because unfortunately there is sound scientific evidence to suggest it is also potentially a disastrous development.' Then, taking even greater care to appear uninvolved emotionally, he described each of the five studies. He also referred to the follow-up studies. 'I do not deny there is scientific confusion here.' But he pointed out how the second studies had all been funded by the industry and undertaken by scientists who were well known for their connections with industry. And he argued strongly that when there was doubt, public authorities had to act with caution. He described the huge public support for a ban on plantacon. And at the end of a solid, factual but unemotional speech he said this:

'Mr President, my bill is not the decisive response to the plantacon peril I would have liked to introduce. It is a compromise. Provided the industry accepts the wise proposal of my good friend, the Senator for Montana, Senator Taverner, of a fifty per cent voluntary cut while further research proceeds, I have built in a time-scale of no less than two and a half years before my bill takes effect. Furthermore I have not sought a ban on plantacon. Only sensible emission standards. Thus the industry has two and a half years to devise a way of controlling emissions and if it does so all of the advantages of plantacon can be retained without the disadvantages. But if it cannot do that, and if the research does not clear plantacon, it must concede that, for all the advantages, this is an uncontrollable and unacceptable pollutant.'

He sat down to an approving tapping of desks. Hal Frankle turned and smiled. The majority leader also indicated that he had been impressed.

In the gallery Sam MacAnally decided that Wilkins had been the right man for the plantacon campaign. He had grown in stature, learned quickly.

Leighton Taverner spoke next, commending his compromise proposal.

Then it was the turn of Ed Eberhard. 'Mr President, let's be clear what we're debating.

'It's not, as has been suggested, a compromise. Zero emission standards are the same thing as a ban. No one has evolved a way of completely controlling aircraft emissions because no one has been able to produce a catalytic coverter that will work in jet aircraft.

'So whatever else the Senate does it should be clear that it is deciding the fate of plantacon, not just introducing some minor control as the Senator for Connecticut would suggest.

'But before I come to the issue I want to talk about how this issue comes before this distinguished Senate. Does it come as a result of carefully considered recommendations from the EPA or any other well-established body? No, it comes as a result of what the increasing number of pressure groups in our society call a "campaign".

'Now, what is a campaign? It is a small number of people who are drawn together from motives that can vary. They can be political, or just plain self-publicising. But these self-appointed guardians of the public good then seek by using a gullible media and appealing to people's fears and emotions to apply unreasonable pressure on what is, thank God, a reasonable system of government.

'Facts, logic, reason, responsibility, compromise between conflicting pressures, all count for nothing with these people. But they must count with us. We are here to take responsible decisions. To *be* that *reasonable system of government* I have described.

'Now, what are the facts? The facts are that we have conflicting studies. Forget all the outrageous high moral ground positions of the Senator for Connecticut, or the slanders on the industry's scientists. The fact is that we have conflicting studies. Now what does a responsible body do when faced with conflicting studies? Answer: it calls for more information. More research. It demands an investigation to establish the truth. Is that satisfactory to the Senator for Connecticut? No, on the basis of a complete contradiction he wants us to take up a clear position. He wants us to act as if one side is right and the other wrong. Why? Because he says we can't take the risk. If we take that to its logical conclusion every senator can come up with any proposition, no matter how unproven, but say we must act because we can't take the risk of him being wrong.

'I am proposing two amendments. One ensures that if we proceed with this measure it will be because it is justified by research. How can he reject that? How can he claim to be confident of his case if he rejects that?'

Wilkins rose. 'Will the Senator for Texas yield the floor?'

Eberhard sat down.

'The Senator from Texas knows there can never be one hundred per cent scientific accord. What he demands is impossible. By proceeding with the bill while we await the results of further research, we are making the children the beneficiaries of the research instead of its guinea pigs. All we have asked is that the industry suspends its activities until we can establish the truth.'

Eberhard rose again. 'We heard all this at the hearings. But it's a dangerous logic. As I've said, it means that any scaremonger or self-publicist with a bee in his bonnet can cause great losses while his ludicrous claims are investigated.'

He then developed the case for plantacon, stressing energy conservation. Finally he concluded:

'It is not plantacon on trial in this debate. It's this Senate. The way whereby it takes decisions. The equal justice it gives to our great industries as well as to so-called citizen groups.

'We have heard a lot about compromise. I will compromise. Pass my amendments and I will vote for the bill. Reject them and I will reject the bill.'

Towards the end of the evening Hal Frankle rose.

'It is not unfair of my good friend, the distinguished Senator for Texas, to say that this debate is about more than plantacon,' he began. 'He is right to say it is about how decisions are taken and about what factors should infuence them.

'Let me begin by reminding my colleagues how often in the past we have been called upon to balance conflicting considerations. And what have we done? We've worked day and night to identify honourable compromises. By honourable I mean compromises that genuinely achieve the best balance between the rival pressures. Compromises are often called shabby. Compromises of the kind I describe are not shabby. They often represent the right conclusion for the common good.

'But sometimes we cannot compromise. Sometimes we have to take a decision that hurts. The environmental cause often faces us with tough decisions. What the environmentalists have argued for years is that we cannot claim to care about our children, about our responsibilities to the generations to come, if we're polluting their habitat, their planet, the air they breathe, the soil in which they grow their food, the water they drink. And if we're destroying places of beauty. Already in this century we *have* done immeasurable environmental damage. We *have* done it recklessly, wantonly, selfishly, irresponsibly, but – and this is our excuse to history – we also did it in ignorance. We didn't hear or didn't believe the few voices who cried out in warning. But now, because the damage is all around us, we know they were right. Not about every detail. But the broad thrust of their message was right.

'Is there room for compromise? Yes, usually there is. When we became aware of the pollution caused by motor cars we didn't ban them. We insisted that over a reasonable time-scale they be made clean. Let me assume, for the moment, that plantacon is proved to be endangering children's health. Is this one of those issues where there is room for compromise? My answer is yes. We should not ban the product. But we should seek to control the emissions. And if, ultimately, we must phase plantacon out altogether we should do it in a way that gives the industry every opportunity to find another energy-saving solution.

'However, where we cannot compromise is in protecting children's health and intelligence. If, and I say if, plantacon is a threat to these, we *must* act.

'But is it?

'We don't know.

'I deplore the way both sides in this debate have attacked the integrity of the other. This Senate must not and will not be influenced by such charges. The answer is clear. As my good friend, the senator for Texas says, we must have research.

'So why a bill? Because my friend, the Senator for Connecticut, says we should be prudent and establish acceptable emission standards now so that if the science supports them, they can be quickly implemented.

'It's an unusual situation. I cannot recall it before. But to me it makes sense. I say to my distinguished colleagues, none of you would be compromising your intelligence, your genuine concerns either for the environment or industry, in voting for this bill. You are sending it on to the House without finally committing yourselves. For there are mechanisms that can be used to ensure its failure if the research justifies that failure. That is my position. It may be difficult for those outside the Senate to understand but it is the right response. I ask your support for my committee's recommendation.'

He sat down. The Vice President had to bang his gavel to halt applause in the gallery. Colleagues came over to slap him on the back.

It had been a decisive speech.

The Senate voted by 57 votes to 43 to approve the Bill.

And to reject the Eberhard amendments.

NEW YORK

Todd Birk was called in to see Theodore Jordan who – he was told – wanted a full update on what was happening.

He had a dreadful journey from Baltimore, torn between a desire to drink the bar dry to steady his nerves and the need to stay sober in order to be able to handle the meeting well.

When he'd last spoken to Jordan he'd felt a chill emanating from the other end of the phone so physical that he had wondered whether Jordan had his office in a refrigerator. In fact Jordan's office looked more like a lawyer's, full of books, dark oak panels, expensive red leather armchairs, tasteful desk-top lamps leaving the room semi-dark. Jordan himself was about sixty, bald, tall, and walked with a limp. But it was his eyes that struck Birk most forcibly; they were like lasers, staring into his soul.

There was no small talk, just the cool courtesy. 'Mr Birk. Do sit . . . and tell me what's been happening.'

He told the silent Jordan what the war council was thinking, what the effect of the Senate vote would be. He also told him that he, Birk, was not going to make a voluntary cutback in plantacon. No sir. Jordan could count on his money from Birk.

But, to Birk's surprise, Jordan appeared disinterested

in Birk's business. It was clear that he had bigger fish to fry. He asked a series of probing questions about the effect of a fifty per cent plantacon reduction on the profitability of the industry generally.

Eventually he said: 'Thank you, Mr Birk. That is helpful. You can assume we are considering what steps to take.'

Birk wished this cold man would tell him what he was thinking. And what he was doing.

It was clear that Jordan had invested a lot of his clients' money in the aviation industry.

And Jordan's clients were probably the kind of people who even frightened Jordan.

Birk shivered at the thought. What kind of people must *they* be?

As he stumbled gratefully out into the night he wondered about the significance of the meeting.

He was convinced Jordan was about to make a move. The questioning had been chillingly methodical; it was almost as if Jordan wanted to be in full possession of every conceivably relevant fact before proceeding with whatever he planned to do.

What would that be? How far would he go? Birk had been warned before he ever went to Jordan that there were no limits. Having met him, he believed it. Jordan ruled by creating fear – even in the hearts of men like Todd Birk.

He wondered whether he should have mentioned the fire.

But then decided it had been wiser not to.

You didn't have casual chats with Jordan. Least of all about arson. Not unless you wanted to find your own hangars in ashes.

He saw a call box on a corner and on an impulse rang Dieter Partrell.

It was time he told him about Jordan.

Time they got their heads together.

Because, Birk admitted to himself, he was beginning to feel a little bit isolated. Lonely. Out on a limb.

And if things were going to turn really nasty he wanted company.

HOBOKEN, NEW JERSEY

Dieter Partrell looked deep into his drink, as if for hope or inspiration.

There wasn't any there. So he downed it and ordered another.

He had heard the result of the Senate vote a couple of hours ago. It was a disaster. How could those fools fall for the environmental campaign? Didn't they understand MacAnally's science was completely discredited? That there was no need to do a thing about plantacon?

He thought about the call later, from Todd Birk.

Good man, Birk.

Kind that made America great.

Now the air freight man wanted to see him. He had implied things were happening that would cheer Partrell up. Well, he could do with cheering up.

There was a nasty coughing at his elbow. He looked at the newcomer with distaste. Charlie Orbell looked greasier than ever. But he restrained himself from saying so.

'Charlie,' he said, looking carefully around. 'The fire. Did you read in the *Post* today that the police now suspect arson?'

Orbell grinned toothlessly, and, leaning forward, breathed all over Partrell who recoiled at the stench.

'Don't worry, Mr Partrell, it'll never be traceable. It was all handled by a friend of mine who used someone far removed from me or from you. He knows what he's doing. He's pulled off more insurance fires than you've had Eighth Avenue hookers.'

'Well, that's not saying much. I haven't had any Eighth Avenue hookers.'

Orbell looked sceptical. 'If you say so,' he said. 'Anyway, you're safe.'

'Hmm. What else is happening?'

'Well,' the grin looked slightly crazy. 'You're not going to like this. I've been following MacAnally and guess whose place he went to late at night?'

'Don't play games, Charlie. Just tell me.'

'The little blonde bit.'

'What little blonde bit?'

'The woman who appears on television talking about plantacon. Nicola someone . . .'

'Kowalska! Nicola Kowalska?'

'That's the one.'

Partrell leaned forward and grabbed Orbell by the lapels.

'*Are you sure?*'

'Let go, Mr Partrell.' He shrank back, shaken. 'Of course I'm sure.'

'Jesus Christ. If that bastard's fucking our campaign coordinator no wonder we're doing so badly.'

'You're doing badly, then?'

'Oh, shut up.' Partrell glared at him.

'I shouldn't shut me up, Mr Partrell. There's something else.'

'What?'

'I think I know where their money's coming from.'

And for the next few minutes he had Partrell's undivided attention.

When he finally finished talking, Partrell leaned back and looked at him with grudging admiration.

'You may smell, Charlie,' he said, 'but you're fucking good at what you do.'

If Orbell was flattered by this, he didn't show it.

Partrell thought for a moment. Then, screwing up his nose and leaning forward so no one could hear, he said, 'This is what I want you to do. . . .'

After the detective had gone, he drank on.

Kowalska would have to be dealt with. That would be easy. He could just imagine the reaction of the war council to the news that their wonder girl was screwing MacAnally – but not quite in the way they had intended.

Then he would decide how to handle the Justin Lord involvement. That was a turn-up for the books.

And then . . . he had to do what he could about the science. This couldn't be left to chance. There had to be ways of getting the right people on the commission of inquiry – and influencing the others.

There was still the science.

WASHINGTON, D.C.

Eugene Remington, who was having dinner with Nicola Kowalska, was depressed.

While in theory ECO was still a long way from even a fifty per cent ban on plantacon, they were suffering too many setbacks.

He couldn't believe how his life had fallen apart.

A matter of weeks ago he was on top of the world.

Expanding airline.

Great wealth.

Superb homes.

Beautiful wife.

Now what did he have?

They couldn't buy more planes.

The airline offices were being picketed by environmentalists.

He had a major cash flow crisis.

He was selling the Aspen place with considerable loss of face.

And he had just experienced the first real row with his wife. His bank manager's refusal to go along with the underwriting of her production meant she was off Broadway. And she didn't think that was funny – not funny at all.

He looked at the fresh-faced woman sitting opposite him.

She was damned attractive.

And tonight he felt lonely.

Maybe . . .

But she was talking business. And somehow he didn't have the energy to change the subject. To her. To him. To them.

No, it wasn't on.

Not tonight.

Wearily he focused on what she was saying.

'Eugene, I know it seems as if we're losing but these are still the preliminaries. The whole thing is still wide open. Don't forget it's in the government's interest to keep plantacon. Our strategy *will* work. I'm absolutely convinced of it.

'If the science is on our side, we'll win. There's no doubt about that. And we know it will be. So don't worry.

'In the end it *will* all come down to the science.'

Sam MacAnally, Senator Chris Wilkins, and the whole

gang celebrated the Senate vote late into the night.

Everyone believed outright victory was now on the cards. The bill was expected to do even better in the House of Representatives. As Jay Sandbach pointed out, the congressmen who would consider it there came from smaller constituencies. They were more vulnerable to public opinion. And the new environmental campaign at the grassroots was just beginning to build up.

MacAnally had kept the details of Cossens's death from the others during the day, not wanting to affect their concentration as they feverishly lobbied senators to keep their vote together. Now he still kept it to himself, not wishing to spoil their moment of triumph.

He did his best to look cheerful but was sobered by the news from Australia and distracted by his inability to get hold of Abernathy. Where the hell was he?

As he walked home to try the scientist's number for the umpteenth time, he turned his mind to the controversy over the conflicting studies.

They needed more work of their own.

Why hadn't Lord responded to his request for additional resources?

Presumably the financier believed the battle was won.

He must persuade Lord that it wasn't all over yet.

There *was* still the science. . . .

Later still his bell rang. He answered it and there stood Nicola Kowalska. White-faced and trembling.

He drew her in and hugged her.

'What's the matter?'

She withdrew from his arms and, throwing her coat and bag into a chair, collapsed onto the couch. 'It's that bastard Dieter Partrell,' she said. 'I just had a call from him. Sam, he was horrible. He said . . . well, never mind what he said. The thing is, his nasty little detective saw you come to my apartment.'

'Christ,' he said, pouring them both a drink. 'What did he say?'

'He was horrible. Just horrible.'

'Oh, Christ. I'm sorry. Are you going to be in trouble?'

'No. *You* don't have to be sorry,' she said in a suddenly determined voice. He saw the steel in her. 'I let him finish and then told him that *of course* I'd been talking to you. It was my job. To keep in touch. I said I was trying to negotiate a deal. And if he screwed it up he would be responsible to everyone for his stupidity. That shut him up.'

But she hadn't finished. In fact, now that she was with him, her mood was changing rapidly, from anger to satisfaction at the way she had dealt with it. 'I then rang Eugene Remington and told him of our meetings. He didn't like it at first.' She giggled. 'Actually, for a minute I thought he was jealous. Anyway, I made it clear we met on business only. And he approves. In fact he made some suggestions as to how I should handle you.'

'Handle me? Did he just!'

She giggled. 'No, Sam – he didn't suggest *that* . . . but . . .'

She hesitated tantalisingly.

'Yes. . .?'

'Well, in a way you are the beneficiary of all this.'

'Why?'

'Well,' and she drew him across the couch towards her, 'I thought, to hell with you, Partrell, it it upsets you so much to think – to use his words – that I'm "fucking Sam MacAnally", then I'm damn well going to.'

He laughed, kissed her on the forehead, then held her at arm's length. 'It's not a good reason.'

'It's not the only one.' Then she stood up and held out her hand. 'Oh, come on, Sam. I don't know how all this is going to end, but I don't want to miss whatever we can have. I've spent too much time alone and too much time thinking about it. I'd rather spend the rest of my life regretting what we did than wondering what it would be like.'

He took her hand and led her into the bedroom.

He liked it best the second time.

When she was on top of him and he could look up into her shining face and fondle her small but firm breasts as she rocked back and forth.

And he liked it even better the third time, when they woke in the morning, and made love while they were half asleep. As if they had been doing it for years.

And he liked lying there, watching her walk from the room, naked, and then return, her hair wet, and stand in front of the mirror and dry it, still naked . . . smiling at him in the mirror.

He liked it all so much that he didn't move.

Until suddenly he was aware she was about to leave. He climbed out of bed, he now being the naked one, and took her in his arms.

'You remember what you said last night about not knowing where this was going. The plantacon business. Well, I don't know either. But it won't come between us. I promise you. I promise you.'

She kissed him, wrapped her arms round him and squeezed him, and then, before he could say all the other things welling up inside him, she was gone.

As she left, Orbell, hunched up in his car, blue with cold, tossed his cigarette out of the window, started the engine and drove slowly off.

Let her talk her way out of this one.

'Negotiating', she had apparently told them.

She would find it difficult to convince Partrell she had been 'negotiating' all night.

BALTIMORE

Todd Birk could hardly wait to get to his office and phone Jordan.

The information he had was red-hot.

So red-hot he wondered whether Jordan would even consider a reward – like cutting back the interest Birk had to pay on the loan. Or giving him more time to pay.

He had to wait a frustrating ten minutes before the cold voice came on the line.

At the sound of it Birk abandoned any thought of a reward. He must have been mad to even consider it. The man with the cold voice gave away nothing.

Speaking quickly, he told Jordan about his meeting with Partrell. Who had told him about the source of the environmentalists' money . . .

. . . And who had told him about Justin Lord.

LONDON

With the General Election approaching and his party beginning to trail in the opinion polls, the Prime Minister decided to reshuffle his top team.

He also took the opportunity for a face-saving rethink on the plantacon affair by moving Muldoon to Trade and Industry. And he kept his word to Ingham by promoting him to Home Secretary. His shock selection as Secretary of State for the Environment was Hal Robbins.

Within twenty-four hours of the reshuffle Robbins called in the new chairman of UK Ambassador, Trevor Richardson, and also the chairmen of British Airways and Virgin, and told them of the political imperative to further toughen up the Government's stance.

'We simply can't risk being caught out on this,' he told them. 'We have to be seen to play safe with public health.'

Within thirty-six hours of the reshuffle Hal Robbins telephoned Olly Witcomb and Nick Bell privately to tell them to expect good news.

Within forty-eight hours of the reshuffle he announced to the House that in the interests of international cooperation and because health doubts had not been resolved, the Government would give the European aviation industry only three months to agree to a voluntary cut in plantacon use.

Otherwise it would insist on a temporary ban.

This would affect every airline in and out of Britain.

But, of course, the policy would be kept under review.

The ultimate fate of plantacon would depend on the science.

The combined effect of the US Senate decision and the new hardline UK response sparked off fresh initiatives around the world.

In Australia, under pressure from the media and its political opponents led by Keith Mullalay, the Government set up a high level cross-party commission to ensure that scientific work proceeded apace. The New Zealanders, saving money, linked up with this instead of funding their own inquiry. Liz Scullen was appointed to it to represent the environmental movement ex-officio.

It was said that the death of Bruce Cossens had been a factor in the Australian decision. By investigating plantacon further, they were paying tribute to his work.

Both countries said they, too, would insist on a fifty per cent cutback in plantacon use, although they didn't name a date. This would be 'negotiated' with the airlines.

The Japanese authorities, under heavy pressure from airline interests, announced they would await the results of the US scientific studies before taking further action. Machiko Yanagi interpreted this as positive; at least they were now acknowledging there was a case to answer.

While the continental countries considered their individual responses, the European Commission was under fire from both the industry and the environmentalists. Claude Chevallier rang Monique de Vos to say that the matter had been debated 'at the highest level' within the Commission. A further programme of research was the likely outcome.

'Don't underestimate the power of the industry's lobbying, Monique. I've never seen anything like it. We're not going to get hasty decisions.

'It will all depend on the science.'

WASHINGTON, D.C.

'It will all depend on science.'

MacAnally was hearing it from all sides.

They were winning the campaign, but it was now vital that the official scientific inquiry confirmed their case.

He had a long conversation with Jake Katzir. Jake, who had come back from Australia extremely shaken, had been appointed to a committee set up to decide how the scientific inquiry should proceed. Also on it were representatives of the American Academy for the Advancement of Science and the Environmental Protection Agency. Ed Kellerman was representing the

Senate committee and there were also industry nominees.

As Katzir talked it became clear to MacAnally that he had done brilliantly at the first meeting.

He had pressed for the work to be done quickly. The committee had set a target date of a year; he told MacAnally this was the best they could have hoped for.

Katzir had also demanded that the scientists undertaking the research must be acceptable to the whole committee. Any member could veto any scientist or scientific institution. This had been accepted.

His most controversial request had been that the inquiry should not only determine whether harm was being done *now*, but whether plantacon had the potential to cause harm *in the future*. This had been hotly contested by industry representatives but had eventually been agreed.

To MacAnally's surprise Jake Katzir had also persuaded the committee not to review the studies done so far. They would, in effect, be treated as irrelevant.

'Why?' asked MacAnally.

'For Christ's sake, Sam, four of our five men are dead. They won't even be there to explain their findings. And some of the key records were destroyed in the fire. Our case has virtually been blown out of the water. I keep telling you, I don't like it. You know I'm not a conspiracy theorist, but if the other side had wanted to write off our studies they couldn't have done it better.' And he added darkly, 'Frankly, if I was David Abernathy I would be as worried as hell.'

MacAnally frowned. 'I can't get hold of him. Adrian finally found out from the university that he'd taken three days off. Apparently he was exhausted. But no one knows where he went.'

'Well, anyway, going back to the studies, I thought it

best to get everyone to accept a fresh start. That's why I suggested the existing ones be ignored. I thought it was rather clever, because in writing off ours I was also writing off theirs . . . don't forget, *their* scientists are still around to speak for their work. However, I would still like us to commission some work ourselves, so that we can be cross-checking what's going on. Do you think our sponsor will come up with the cash?'

'I don't know. I'm having trouble getting hold of him too. I'll have another go. Anyway, Jake, you've done superbly.'

'Thanks.'

MacAnally left his colleague, and once more told himself that he had an exceptional team. Katzir had been nearly killed once, and seen two colleagues die violent deaths, but he was still operating professionally. Dom Young was being wonderfully supportive; so was young Adrian Carlisle. In fact the whole team was in top form. MacAnally was proud of it. It was, he was convinced, the best in the world.

Later he began to feel increasingly uneasy about what Jake Katzir had said. About the science. And about the deaths.

His pride in his team was replaced by a sense of foreboding.

Despite their efforts, despite the fact that they *were* winning, he felt the whole thing was beginning to unravel.

He decided to go to New York. He would see Lord about the money and he could also look up David Abernathy who should be back by now.

He still didn't really believe it was necessary.

He still couldn't believe that the scientists were being murdered.

And he didn't want to frighten the young scientist.

But it was only right to warn him to take care.

NEW YORK

Theodore Jordan had built his empire on a theory.

That everybody had *something special* they were afraid of.

And everybody had *someone* they were afraid of.

It was a proven theory. Reliable.

It even applied to him.

He had been entrusted with a lot of money. Many millions. By people who treated him like a bank. When they wanted it back they expected to get it. With interest. And he had never failed them.

Over the past year, ever since Todd Birk had come to him, he had moved a lot of the money into airlines.

Thanks to the plantacon revolution it had increased enormously in value.

Then, with the pollution scare, the shares had dropped dramatically.

He had found himself with only three options:

He could sell at a loss and make up the difference himself. That would mean losing much of his personal fortune. That was unthinkable.

Or he could tell his clients that they were going to lose some of their money. That was even more unthinkable.

Or he could stop the rot.

The last was the only real option.

All this he had been thinking as he stared out the window. Now he looked at the two men standing in front of him.

They were his best. Especially the senior of the two, Canning.

And what they had done so far was first class.

'You've seen the note of my telephone call from Birk
. . . about Justin Lord?'

The senior of them, the thin, blond-haired one,
Canning, nodded.

'And you've seen the file we've compiled – the one
about Lord's involvement in this business?'

'Yes.'

'And you're clear what needs to be done?'

'Yes.'

Jordan turned his laser eyes on them. 'Don't fail,' he
said.

The senior of them, the thin, blond-haired one,
Canning, said they wouldn't.

LONDON

Olly Witcomb climbed the stairs wearily. He had spent
the evening with Nick Bell, who was ecstatic. His success
on the plantacon business had meant he was now on
Labour's front bench. Profiles of him as 'the Green MP'
and 'the public watchdog' had appeared in the Sunday
newspapers. His enthusiasm tonight had exhausted Olly.

Thank God he had done most of what he could on the
plantacon campaign. It would soon be over.

He had surprised Bell by not being in a celebratory
mood. 'Frankly, Nick, I haven't enjoyed it. I still feel
guilty about Barnes; I feel as if I drove him to suicide. I
don't even feel as if I have a victory. The whole thing's
going to hang about for at least a year while we wait on
the results of the research. And I've lost a girl because of
it, one I liked.'

Bell had laughed at him. 'Oh, come on, Olly, there are
plenty more girls, but there's only one plantacon

campaign. It's been brilliant.'

But Olly didn't feel brilliant. He felt thoroughly frustrated.

Until he got to his door. There was a note on it.

'Why not come up for a drink?' it said.

But it was the second sentence that caused him to bound up the stairs, two at a time.

'Bring a toothbrush,' it said.

SYDNEY

'I'm sorry, Liz, I didn't know you two had got together. I thought you didn't like him,' said Mike McKenzie as he and Liz Scullen walked slowly away from the graveside.

'I didn't at first. But *that* Bruce Cossens was a performance. The real one was . . .' she bit her lip.

It was the second funeral she had been to recently.

Her mother had died.

Not before giving her a last lecture from her death bed.

Now she looked at Machiko walking off with Mike, arm in arm, so obviously in love, and she felt alone and envious.

It had been a strange funeral. As far as she could see Cossens had no close relatives. And not a lot of friends. There had been colleagues from the university, and a few other people, maybe fifteen in all. As they stood round the grave it began to drizzle and this added to the forlorn atmosphere.

She felt sorry for Cossens. To be young and rich and yet die so little mourned.

He had been a strange man.

Strange . . . yet . . . he'd been all right.

As she looked for a taxi a tall man, balding, in his sixties, came over to her. 'Miss Scullen?'

'Yes.'

'Can I give you a lift into the city? I'd like a word.'

'Sure, thanks.'

It was an expensive car. As it headed towards the centre of Sydney he said, 'My name is Bernard Carr. I was Dr Cossens's solicitor.'

She feigned interest. 'Oh, yes.'

'As you know Dr Cossens came into some money recently. And bought a house at Watson's Bay.'

'Recently?' She tried to remember what he had said. 'Yes, he told me . . . family money.'

The solicitor laughed. 'Oh, good heavens no, Miss Scullen. Bruce Collens came from a long line of swagmen and scavengers. As far as I'm aware he's the first in his family to escape the life, the first to ever live in a city or become a professional.'

'Well, where *did* the money come from?'

'I have no idea, Miss Scullen. One day he had none. The next day he was rich. I didn't dare ask.'

'I see . . .'

'The thing is, Miss Scullen, and this is what I wanted to talk to you about . . .'

'. . . he left the whole lot to you.'

She looked at him, incredulous. 'What did you say? How could he? We only . . . came together . . . a day before he died.'

'Oh, the will was made well before that, Miss Scullen. Weeks back, in fact.'

She was stunned. He must have done it immediately after they met. Did he know even then, even when she was so hostile to him, that they would end up lovers?

How could he? And even if he had, it was still an

extravagant, premature, illogical, mad . . . stark-staring mad . . . thing to do.

Why had he done it?

And where had the money come from?

She became aware that the elderly solicitor was still talking.

'. . . and as I say, he left the whole lot to you. The house. And the money.

'I'll have to do the sums, Miss Scullen, but I'm prepared to say that you're now worth well over five million dollars. American.'

NEW YORK

Sam MacAnally climbed out of the taxi at the busy junction of 7th Avenue South and Bleeker Street. From there it was only a few steps to where Abernathy lived. Quiet, tree-lined, trafficless, it was hard to believe that Commerce Street was right in the heart of Greenwich Village. He walked past the Sojin vegetable restaurant and a number of brownstones until he came to a big, grey building in the middle of the street, its paint peeling off, its neglected appearance and the rows of door bells indicating this was an apartment house with an absentee landlord. As he climbed the stairs the front door opened and a girl emerged, tall, thin, dressed all in black, but with bright red hair all but covering a pale face. She was carrying a shopping bag.

MacAnally reached out and grabbed the door before it closed and, reminding himself of the number of Abernathy's apartment, climbed to the third floor. On the way he passed two other tenants; an old man, bent, making his slow way down the stairs; a young couple, who looked like students, emerging from a bedsitter with the shining faces of people who had just made love.

He could hear music, but Abernathy wasn't answering his door. He knocked louder, then tried the handle. The door opened.

Suddenly he experienced a sense of foreboding. He began to go hot and cold all over.

It didn't feel right.

He called out, 'David?' but there was no reply.

He called several times. Still no reply. Yet he sensed a presence in the apartment. He was convinced the scientist was there.

He walked slowly, hesitantly down the hall towards the study where he and Abernathy had met last.

He stopped outside.

The door was open an inch or two.

He called once more. 'David?' Then he reached out and gave it a push.

It swung open.

Abernathy was there all right, sitting in a chair, slumped forward across his desk, his head on the keys of a typewriter.

His head and the typewriter and the desk were covered in blood.

A gun lay on the floor beside him.

MacAnally choked, then putting a handkerchief over his mouth, walked slowly to the body. He reached out and touched Abernathy's shoulder, he didn't know why . . . it wasn't to find out whether the young man was dead . . . that was obvious. It was . . . well, useless really. But he wanted to do it.

He leaned over and looked at the sheet of paper in the typewriter.

To his horror he saw it was a letter to him.

'Dear Sam,' it began. 'I can't go on with this . . .'

That was all.

Either it was all Abernathy had wanted to say, or he'd been interrupted.

MacAnally struggled to get his brain working. What was he supposed to do? Ring the emergency number?

He reached over Abernathy for the phone . . . then he heard it.

A faint, scraping noise.

It was coming from the next room.

He stood still, his throat dry, breathing heavily.

Still he could hear the scraping.

He dropped the receiver back onto the phone and slipped into the hall.

He considered making a run for the street, but instead heard his voice call, 'Is anyone there?'

The scraping became louder, more urgent, as if in response to his call.

He edged towards the sound.

What was it thriller writers said about times like this? . . . 'hair stood on end, spine tingled, blood ran cold. . .'

Don't ever tell him these were clichés . . . Christ, *it was true*. It was all happening. And more . . . he didn't remember them saying that your legs wouldn't work properly.

He shivered as if chilled to the bone.

By now he had somehow reached the door of what he guessed was Abernathy's bedroom. For what seemed a lifetime he paused outside, then the scraping began once more.

He heard a moan.

That convinced him. Whatever . . . *whoever* . . . was in there, it or he sounded in a lot more trouble than MacAnally.

He flung the door open.

Lying on the floor, in a pool of his own blood, was a

small, thin, seedy-looking man. One leg was folded under him, the other was stretched out. He had been making the scraping noise with his shoe. He looked up at MacAnally in desperate appeal.

MacAnally bent down. 'Who are you? What happened?' he asked.

The man whispered a few words. MacAnally leaned over further and was rewarded with a whiff of the worst breath he had ever encountered.

'Orbell . . .' said the man. 'Charlie Orbell.'

'What happened?'

'They did it . . . killed them all . . . came to warn him . . . too late . . .'

He began coughing up blood. As MacAnally tried to lift him into a sitting position his skinny body shuddered. He went as if to speak but only made an awful rattling sound. Finally his head fell back onto MacAnally's chest.

MacAnally let it drop to the floor. The man was dead.

For a moment he stayed kneeling there, disbelieving. Then he felt the vomit rising in his throat.

He half ran to the bathroom and threw up. Then washed his face with cold water.

He couldn't believe what was happening . . .

. . . And in the confused hours that followed he remained barely conscious of what was going on. He telephoned the police in a daze . . . later went with them to the precinct in a daze . . . told them what he knew in a daze . . . more than one . . . endless detectives, none of whom he could now remember . . . and somehow, drained, exhausted, later that day found himself back on the Metroliner to Washington, still in a daze.

Blood. Guns. Dead bodies. Police. Conspiracies . . . to kill . . . danger . . . it was all insane.

It was what you read in books, saw in films . . . *it didn't happen*. Not in real life. Not to people like MacAnally.

He needed a drink. Desperately.

He went to the bar and ordered a whisky, gulped it down, had another, and ordered a third.

They warmed him. For the first time since he threw up in Abernathy's bathroom he began to feel human. The alcohol worked its rejuvenating way up and down his system, warming his inside, resurrecting lifeless limbs, setting his brain to work.

Inevitably there came the questions.

Orbell?

Orbell?

Orbell was the man who worked for Partrell.

What did he mean, *'they killed them all'*? All the scientists? All five? And who were 'they'?

What was it Nicola had told him? Partrell and Birk had become 'as thick as thieves'.

Had they become as thick as murderers too?

Why not? They were both brutal men . . . utterly ruthless . . . the kind of animals only found in the darkest corners of the business jungle.

Birk and Partrell would do whatever they believed necessary to protect plantacon.

Birk in particular. The man *was* an animal . . . a brute.

His heart beat faster and faster as awareness and anger grew.

Birk. If Birk had killed Warner *he had also killed Marie*. He felt a pain in his chest, tears stinging his eyes . . . at her memory . . . her climbing on top of him, engulfing him . . . brown mischievous eyes flashing at him from above . . . laughter as the bed bounced and squeakingly complained as they made love.

Marie. So soft. So special.

And Birk . . . that . . . that *bastard* had caused her to be killed.

Birk.

He remembered that fleshy face, contorted by fury, breathing alcohol fumes and roaring abuse at him on the night of the Baltimore meeting.

It was Birk who had killed them.

Birk the animal. Birk the brute.

The train was slowing. He looked out of the window. Already they were at Baltimore. Driven now by an uncontainable rage, he grabbed his bag, leapt from the train, and shouted to a taxi to take him to the airport. To the headquarters of Airlift International.

Part Seven

Real War . . . Real Blood

BALTIMORE

Birk rose to his feet, his fleshy face contorted with rage.

'Listen, MacAnally, don't get me wrong . . . I would've been more than happy to kill the motherfuckers with my bare hands . . . and you also . . . and your trouble-making friends . . . the whole fucking lot of you.

'You lot will probably bankrupt this country . . . destroy what I've spent a lifetime working for.

'Before you're finished you'll do more damage to America than the goddamn Commies ever looked like doing; you'll wipe out whole industries, lose good, honest working people their livings, devastate the whole fucking economy.

'And what will you fucking care?

'Most of you don't know what real work is. You spend years getting educated at your parents' or the taxpayer's expense, then what do you do? Do you get proper, productive work to repay them? Like hell you do! You set yourselves up as judge and jury on those of us . . . most of us . . . who have to spend years of our lives fighting our way up from the gutter to what is laughably called a goddamn living. What do you care about the damage you do with your big mouths and your manipulation of the media? Anyway, what's the media if it isn't another bunch of assholes like you? And politicians too. You're all the fucking same. You all think you know what's best for those whose work you couldn't do . . . or whose work you think you're too damn clever to do . . . whose work produces the money you live on. What fucking chance do we have? I tell you: no fucking chance.

'Then what do you do? Then you have the fucking cheek to come into my office and accuse me of murder. Jesus wept!'

MacAnally, who had been standing eyeball to eyeball with Birk, stepped back, shaken by the other's aggression, and then collapsed into the badly scratched metal chair between the desk and the open door.

He had swept into the air freight man's office on a wave of uncontrollable, unthinking fury and now, as he looked into that livid, indignant face, he knew instinctively that he was hearing the truth.

He felt deflated, ashamed, but also bewildered. 'But if it wasn't you, or someone working for you, who was it?'

'How the hell do I know? Maybe there's a God after all and he's wiping the whole lot of you out. And good fucking luck to him.'

MacAnally didn't react to the abuse. He was too confused, too tired, and, anyway, what could you expect if you burst into a man's office and branded him a killer? 'I simply can't believe the airline companies or the oil companies would countenance it . . .'

Birk exploded. 'That's *fucking typical*. You've spent a fortune persuading everybody that the airlines and oil companies are amoral, anti-social, capable of any criminal act you like to charge them with . . . but now you're saying they've too much integrity to sanction murder. Why don't you make up your fucking mind whether they're goodies or baddies, Mr God Almighty MacAnally?

'And while you're about it get off my land before I throw you off it.'

MacAnally put a hand on each of the arms of the chair and slowly raised himself . . . as if he were suddenly aged. He walked to the door and then, remembering, he stopped. 'Mr Birk, the accusations I made . . . I was distraught, but I know that's no excuse . . . I had no right to make them.

'I know you don't care one way or the other, but I'm sorry . . .

' . . . And I'm also sorry if our campaign harms your company. That's not what we want . . .'

Birk interrupted contemptuously. 'Oh, *fuck off.*'

MacAnally did.

Back to the taxi, its driver leaning on its engine, smoking a cheap cigar, and looking curiously at the smouldering figure of Birk standing at the open door . . .

. . . And back to the Amtrack station, just in time to catch the next train to Washington.

It was early evening now, and the train was full. He stood in the bar, avoiding the speculative eyes of those who recognised him, and considering the enormity of his behaviour.

How could he have made such an accusation without proof?

Was Birk right? Was he beginning to think he was God?

And what about Birk's attack on environmentalists? It was a crazed, distorted view, of course. And yet . . . was there some justification for the air freight man's hatred?

Were they becoming too obsessive, too uncompromising, too tunnel-visioned?

Were they being unfair to a lot of people in industry?

And, if the answer was yes, was his leadership partly responsible for that?

He rememebered what he had told Nicola: that citizen groups were advocates in the court of public opinion. They had no power other than the power to persuade. And they had no obligation to present a balanced case. *'We present our case to the best of our ability. They present theirs. And it's the politicians who must be the judges.'*

But was it as easy as that? Was the analogy a fair one?

Had they gone too far in allowing the ends to justify the means?

He no longer knew.

He only knew that, to his surprise, he felt sorry for Birk. He didn't like the man. But he could see pain behind the bluster, and he, MacAnally, understood better than most how pain could fuel anger.

In Washington he went directly to Nicola's apartment and told her what had happened . . . about Abernathy's death. And Orbell's. And about his confrontation with Birk.

She listened with mounting horror, then, when he described his behaviour in Baltimore, disbelief.

'Sam, how could you. . .?'

'I know, I know . . . but, imagine how I felt, suddenly knowing . . . not just thinking it, but *knowing* that the scientists had been murdered, all five of them . . . and Marie too.

'I just went wild. Birk seemed the obvious one. You would have thought so too if you'd heard the threats he's been making.

'Afterwards, on the train, I could see that it didn't

make sense. It would have called for a more sophisticated operation than he could set up.'

Nicola shook her head, bewildered. 'I still can't believe it was murder, Sam. I've been working with these people. They may not all be angels . . . but murderers? It's not possible. Unless . . .' She paused, thinking.

'Unless what?'

'Unless there's someone else . . . someone affected by plantacon . . . maybe with a lot of money invested . . . someone who hasn't surfaced during the campaign. Someone that no one on either side is aware of.'

While she conjured up a meal from the bits and pieces in her fridge, MacAnally paced up and down the room, thinking about what she had said – 'maybe there was *someone else.*'

It *was* possible.

While she began to open a bottle of wine, he reviewed aloud what they knew of the scientists' deaths.

Warner. At the inquest it had emerged that Warner's brakes had failed. It was automatically assumed by everyone that the crash was caused by the falling apart of an inadequately maintained old car.

No one had looked carefully to see whether the brakes had been tampered with because it was unimaginable that anyone would want to kill a harmless old scientist – or the young woman whose presence in the car could not, anyway, have been predicted.

But the brakes *could* have been tampered with. It *could* have been murder.

As he spoke of Marie he flinched with pain. And momentarily became quiet.

Her death had been unplanned. She had just happened to be in the car at the wrong time. If any of the deaths was an accident, it was hers.

Nicola handed him a glass of wine, taking care not to look at him, leaving him to deal with what she guessed were painful memories.

Then he continued, pacing, speculating.

Barnes. The British scientist suffered from uncurable cancer. All that lay before him was humiliating deterioration and pain. He had no enemies. Suicide was the obvious conclusion for the coroner to reach.

But the note had been typewritten. He *could* have been murdered – and the note written for him.

Tezuka. The police were convinced he was the victim of the latest in a series of terrorist bombings. And it couldn't be denied there were similarities.

But it was an extraordinary coincidence that it should happen in that particular restaurant on that one night – and that the bomb should have been planted so close to this one man.

The bomb *could* have been intended for Tezuka. It *could* have been murder.

Cossens. His death remained a mystery. If it had been caused deliberately then little attempt had been made to make it look like an accident.

The police were keeping open the possibility that it had been some wild kid, maybe full of beer, who had not been paying attention to who and what was in the water and who, after hitting Cossens, had fled the scene and was now lying low, hoping to get off scot free.

But half of those who witnessed it were convinced the powerboat had been aimed directly at the scientist.

It not only *could* have been murder but to many people it *looked* like murder.

Abernathy. He had been upset by the article alleging cheating at college. He had been worried by the growing scepticism about his research. And he had been cagey about his private life.

But he hadn't been *that* distraught. And he had thrived on the notoriety he was getting.

To believe Abernathy's death was suicide you had to accept the coincidence of two suicides out of five dead scientists . . . you had to accept that the young New Yorker was desperately unhappy when there was no real evidence of it . . . and you had to explain the presence of Orbell.

That was asking too much.

Of all the deaths this was the one that not only *could* have been murder but obviously *was* murder.

'The fact is,' MacAnally concluded, sinking into a chair, 'every one of them could have been murdered and two of them definitely were, Tezuka and Abernathy.'

Nicola, who had been listening carefully, said, 'Yes, but there's an explanation for who murdered Tezuka . . . the terrorists. And Orbell could have been the killer of Abernathy.'

'How do you mean?'

'Maybe he killed Abernathy, but somehow, maybe in a struggle, also accidentally shot himself. Or maybe Abernathy shot him . . . anyway, imagine that he didn't know he was dying . . . that he was hurting a lot but thought he would live. While he was lying on the floor he could have worked out a way to explain his presence there . . . by pretending someone else was the killer and that he came to warn Abernathy. And you fell for it.'

MacAnally stared at her. 'You're not *still* arguing the five deaths were unrelated to plantacon?'

She shook her head, confused. 'I don't know . . .'

'Anyway . . .' he took up her argument, 'if Orbell was trying to cover-up his involvement in Abernathy's death he would have said 'they killed *him*''. What did he mean when he said "they killed *them all*"?'

'He could have been delirious . . . he could have been

trying to invent a way out for himself but just not been able to make sense . . .'

'Hang on a minute,' MacAnally said, leaping up and beginning to pace about again. 'We're getting hopelessly confused.

'You're actually arguing my case – that Abernathy was killed because of plantacon.

'If Orbell *was* the killer, then he was *sent* to do it. Because of the research.'

He paused. 'And who was Orbell? *He was Partrell's man.*'

Nicola looked at him, shocked. 'Partrell. *Dieter Partrell!* He *couldn't* have been involved.'

'Why not? He had more to lose than anyone. He hates me . . . he hates all environmentalists. And we know he hired Orbell. We know that because it came out at the hearings. Look . . .' He took her by the shoulders and looked into her face while he talked. 'Five scientists killed, one after another, the last of them killed by someone *we know* was hired by Partrell.

'Who had the biggest vested interest in the demise of them all? Partrell.

'He's as big a brute as Birk. But, unlike Birk, he *was* capable of arranging such an operation. I tell you, they were killed to stop them talking. To stop them confirming their findings, answering questions, validating the campaign.'

'But *Partrell*? I attended meetings with him . . . I know he was a crude bully but I can't believe . . .'

'Who *else* could it be?'

He sat down beside her on the couch. 'I don't buy your idea that it could be someone affected by plantacon that no one knows. It had to be somebody directly involved in the plantacon controversy. Now let's just think . . .

'*The airline companies?* I can't see it. They aren't that

amoral, and also it doesn't make sense. It was too big a risk. The damage it would have done to the industry if it were proved would have been colossal.

'*The oil companies?* No, for the same reasons, and because they didn't stand to lose that much.'

Birk? He had looked into the whites of the man's eyes and had seen the incredulity, the outrage in them when he had been accused. Birk had been telling the truth.

But still Nicola couldn't, didn't want to accept that it was Partrell. 'There were others who had a vested interest in protecting plantacon.'

'No, Nicola, none of them had that big a vested interest. Whoever commissioned the killings had to be desperate. Maybe so desperate that he was driven mad. Who could *be* that desperate? Only Partrell.

'And Orbell was Partrell's man. *That's* the clincher. For Christ's sake, Nicola, it *had* to be Partrell.'

'But why kill them after their studies were complete and in your hands?'

'He stopped Warner and Barnes from personally testifying to their research. He couldn't get to the other three in time – but he knew that the fate of plantacon rested on the scientific work that's now being commissioned. He wouldn't want any of it to go to the three scientists most likely to produce further work to endorse our case. Nor would he want them around . . . he just wouldn't want them around. Period.'

'But that's crazy. He would have to be mad.'

'Men have been driven mad by a lot less. I think he probably is crazy. He always struck me as a bit unhinged.

'If plantacon is banned he and FEI stand to lose a fortune. And, at least in the case of Partrell, he stands to lose all that he's struggled for – to be a top business tycoon.

'To him it must have seemed as if his life's work, his

whole life was at stake. If you're already on the edge, that's the kind of thing that would push you over.'

Nicola's heart sank.

He was right.

It was the only logical answer.

If you believed the five scientists had been murdered – and that was the only credible supposition – then Dieter Partrell was the only credible suspect.

BALTIMORE

If you believed the five scientists had been murdered – and that was the only credible supposition – then Theodore Jordan was the only credible suspect.

The more he thought about it the more Birk knew it was so.

Recently he had been unable to get to speak to Jordan on the telephone. So when he rang he laid it on the line. It was, he said, urgent that they spoke . . . essential . . . not to him – *to Jordan*. It was of crucial importance *to Jordan* that they spoke.

The tactic succeeded.

'Well, Mr Birk.' The air freight man, tough as he was, felt the usual tingling in his spine at the chill in Jordan's voice.

So he got right to the point. 'MacAnally has been snooping around my depot asking about the murders of the scientists.'

'*Murders*, Mr Birk? I understand three of them were accidents and two of them were suicides.'

'Mr Jordan, he *knows* they were murders. I just hope your men have been careful. Because they'll soon prove the connection between you and me . . .'

He heard a click and there was a long pause.

For a moment he thought Jordan had hung up.

Then came a reply, in a voice so inhumanly cold that Birk shuddered.

'Mr Birk, I hope you're not saying . . . and on an open telephone line . . . that *we* were responsible for the deaths of these men?'

'Well, I . . . that is . . . I thought. . . .'

'You disappoint me, Mr Birk.'

'You mean . . .'

'Mr Birk, I'm going to be extremely generous. I'm going to forget this ludicrous conversation.'

'But . . .'

'I don't think I'm making myself clear. You will *not* suggest this to me or anyone again. You will *not* even think it. *And if anyone else gets hurt, you won't think it then either. Is that clear?*'

'Of course.' Birk was relieved. 'But who. . .?'

'Goodbye, Mr Birk.'

Birk found himself holding a dead receiver in his hand.

Slowly he put it down. He looked out at his planes, perched quietly on the edge of the runway like giant birds in the dark of the night, and groaned at his stupidity in ringing Jordan.

It had only been after MacAnally had left that he thought of Jordan.

And when he did, it all seemed obvious.

Jordan *must* have had the scientists killed.

He had the motive.

And he was the only one involved in the plantacon affair who Birk knew would actually *do* such a thing.

And then he had begun to worry. Really worry. If it came out . . . if Jordan was investigated . . . the trail would lead to him.

Why? Because, while Jordan was responsible for the murders, it was he, Birk, who had provoked them.

He had telephoned Jordan, wound up Jordan, hoping that he would act.

And when Jordan acted, people got hurt.

But what was Jordan telling him now? That he *hadn't* arranged the murders?

Or that he, Birk, must not *think* about Jordan arranging the murders?

Goddamn it, he didn't know the answer.

Because Jordan had been ambiguous.

But – and Birk cursed himself for his impulsive and clumsy call – that was hardly surprising, because there was no way Jordan was going to confirm the killings over the phone.

Birk didn't know what to think any more.

Except that killing the scientists didn't make that much sense to him.

If they were going to get someone, it should have been MacAnally.

He frowned, concentrating. What was it Jordan had said? '. . . *If anyone else gets hurt, you won't think it then either . . .*'

Anyone else?

Christ, *they were going for MacAnally*.

He poured himself a hefty drink.

And looked at his planes.

And thought of all the work he had done, all he had endured to get them – the work, the humiliations.

Saving those planes mattered more than any goddamn thing in the world.

Yet somewhere, deep down in his soul, there was a niggle of doubt.

Conscience began to gnaw at his confidence . . . in his own way Birk had been a honest man . . . what had happened to him that he could now stand by while another man, even a dangerous hot-head like MacAnally, was murdered? . . . yet what choice did he have?

No, goddamn it, he had no choice. . . .

Still his conscience gnawed away . . . so he took another stiff drink to still it, then another . . . until finally he fell asleep, his head on the desk.

NEW YORK

Todd Birk was on Dieter Partrell's mind as he sat in the back of his car while his driver negotiated their way to the World Trade Center.

He had been amazed by what Birk had told him . . . of the sums of money he had borrowed from this man Jordan . . . of Jordan's financial interest in plantacon . . . of Birk's belief that Jordan had arranged the murders of the five scientists.

Partrell smiled to himself. At least it hadn't crossed Birk's mind to accuse *him*.

Birk had turned out to be a useful ally.

Maybe he could get him on to the FEI board.

Partrell could do with a friend there.

He reviewed the position:

Everyone was getting into a mess in Washington. Kowalska and Green and the others had been right about their capacity to delay . . . at the rate the politicians were going plantacon was safe for at least three years. That alone would guarantee Partrell was a wealthy man for life.

But that, of course, wasn't good enough.

He wanted FEI to become a mighty empire.

With him at its head.

As its wealth grew it would establish its own oil company, begin to buy up others . . . until it totally controlled the delivery of plantacon-added fuel to the aviation industry. What was stunning about the plan was that it was all so easy: it couldn't be stopped. Because FEI would have the money to buy the oil companies . . . and it alone would control the availability of plantacon.

That's how he had always seen it and, before MacAnally came on the scene, that's the way it had been heading.

That's why these environmentalists had to be beaten. Destroyed.

Well, they had made a good start with that.

As for the oil industry, David Johnston was now making all the right noises to the media and the politicians. Thanks to Johnston's liking for 'coffee and cream' – Partrell chuckled at the memory of the two girls in the photograph – there would be no more trouble from OILO.

The international campaign was still being fought and, while he was reluctant to give credit to MacAnally, the motherfucker was damned effective. But the news from Japan was good. And he was assured that a number of countries with state-owned airlines were swinging the industry's way; indeed, the poorer countries, who should have had the sense not to have an airline in the first place, couldn't afford to do much else.

Now all he had to do was sort out this man Justin Lord.

Surely that wouldn't be difficult.

Lord was a businessman.

Clearly MacAnally had got to him in some way, but Partrell was in no doubt that Lord would understand the industry's point of view.

And if Lord could be persuaded to stop bankrolling MacAnally, maybe even to announce that he no longer supported the campaign, it would do a lot to undermine the environmentalist's organisation and his credibility.

Partrell felt buoyant. For the first time since that damned war council had been set up he felt that he had got control of the situation.

Christ, if he had left it to that Ivy League chicken shit Remington, and his girl campaigner, he would have ended up with damn-all.

Well, hang on a minute. He had to be fair. They had done their bit.

They had helped buy time.

He wondered what MacAnally must be feeling like. All his scientists dead. His offices burned down. He and his friends the subject of a series of nasty stories in the *New York Express*.

And then there was his affair with the girl campaigner. Kowalska. Wait till Partrell unleashed that one on an unsuspecting world.

All he had to do now was cut off MacAnally's source of money and the campaigner would be in deep shit.

He arrived at Lord's office full of confidence.

That confidence lasted as long as it took him to pour out his company's troubles. 'You're not one of these unproductive so-called campaigners, Mr Lord,' he concluded. 'You understand business. You must appreciate our concerns.'

Lord rose and, as courteous as ever, replied, 'I do, sir. I would like to see you succeed. You deserve it. It really is a tragedy that you haven't yet found a way of controlling the plantacon emissions.

'But I'm afraid,' he added mildly, 'you do me an injustice when you suggest I've been in some way deceived into supporting this campaign. Do you really think I'm so gullible that any campaigner can walk into this office and persuade me to give him a million dollars? I initiated the campaign, Mr Partrell. Because unfortunately your product is a threat to health.

'My advice to you is to stop ducking your responsibilities, stop trying to find an easy way out. Try to find a way to control the emissions. That's what will keep you in business.'

He looked at Partrell's reddening face. 'That's your only hope, sir. What will not work are bully-boy tactics, no matter how extreme they become.'

Partrell rose to face this infuriating man. 'Are you suggesting. . .?'

Lord interrupted him. 'I think we've conducted our business, sir.'

Partrell held his ground for a moment. 'I don't know why you've wanted to keep your name secret, Mr Lord, but if I was you I would read tomorrow's *Express*. Because that's where I'm headed, right now.'

Lord smiled. 'Given the public support for controls on plantacon, Mr Partrell, you will probably make me a hero.

'That's not what I sought.

'But I can live with it.'

TORONTO, CANADA

The pilot's voice came over the intercom, warning of their impending landing at Toronto. MacAnally, looking out of the window at the expanse of Lake Ontario and the beautiful, bustling city on its shore, realised he had spent the whole flight worrying about the plantacon affair, time he had planned to use to prepare tonight's speech.

It was a fundraiser for ECO, the kind of event he hated . . . a home so lavishly furnished and full of servants that its annual upkeep would exceed ECO's budget; elegant women and overweight husbands, listening politely to his little speech, patronising him over the buffet afterwards, their reward the pictures in the society pages that weekend, his time justified by their competing with each other to donate the largest cheque.

He had wanted to cancel it but Nicola, concerned he was becoming obsessive, had argued he should get back on his campaigning schedule and bundled him into a taxi to the airport.

Christ, he thought, I don't believe all this.

A few months back I was in Washington receiving that award, not a trouble in the world.

That seems a hundred years away.

Now, I've lost Marie.

We've endured the most bruising campaign the movement has ever known.

Five good men have been murdered.

And I've spent the last twenty-four hours talking almost non-stop to detectives.

What a mess. What a bloody mess.

He wondered whether they'd arrested Partrell yet.

The detectives had given him the impression they were not going to waste any time . . . not after he had repeated to them the case he had made to Nicola. 'It's circumstantial,' the senior one had said, 'but good enough to get him in for questioning. And to get a few search warrants.'

Just the same, they had made it clear that Partrell's guilt would not be easy to prove. 'If he's got any sense at all,' the detective had said to MacAnally, 'he's had all this commissioned at least one removed. We may never be able to trace the killings to him.'

SYDNEY, AUSTRALIA

The kindly old solicitor looked across his desk at Liz Scullen.

'That's it, Ms Scullen,' he said, closing the portfolio. 'The whole estate is worth just over five million American dollars.'

Liz felt as if she was listening to him from a distance. It was all so unreal.

'But where did it come from?'

'Well, I'm afraid it's not for you to ask or for me to answer. I'm afraid the details are protected by the terms of the will. But his bank manager is an old friend. I can tell you this much: it came from America.

'In one transfer. About a year ago.'

She sat thinking. Then she said, 'You realise I can't accept it.'

He smiled. 'I think you have to, Ms Scullen. Because it's yours. There's no family. No one else.

'Of course, what you do with it is up to you . . .'

TORONTO

He was jolted out of his reverie by the plane landing. He only had a carry-on bag and so, after quickly dealing with the immigration formalities, he walked directly from the plane to collect the keys for the rental car he had reserved.

The car park was just across the road running alongside the arrivals building. He quickly identified the vehicle. He tossed the bag on to the back seat and went to open the driver's door.

As he did so, he saw a car pass his own – on its way to the exit. From a few feet away and even in profile the driver was unmistakable.

It was Adrian Carlisle.

He called out a greeting but the car was moving too fast for Carlisle to hear.

As he climbed into his own car, pulled out of the parking space and began to drive back past the terminal and follow the signs to Highway One, he wondered: what the hell was Adrian doing in Canada? MacAnally recalled him saying that he was going to be in New York all week.

There was a queue of cars to get onto 401 West. He could see Carlisle's car about fifty yards ahead. He slipped into the same lane.

Christ, he thought, what am I doing? *I'm following him.* What has this plantacon business done to me? I'm now trailing a colleague's car like a seedy private eye.

Yet, somewhere, deep in his subconscious, he felt an answer to that question beginning to form.

It was an answer he didn't want to know.

He felt as if he was waking from a deep sleep – only he was not escaping a nightmare, he was entering it.

He made a desperate attempt to evade it, to shake it off.

He didn't want this.

He didn't *want* to know. *No, no, no – he didn't want to know.*

Yet, he had to know.

And, as he drove, he began to let his mind edge towards the truth.

It had been exceptionally good timing that someone like Carlisle should have popped up offering his undeniably

*useful services just when the plantacon campaign was
about to be launched.*

Carlisle's car moved into the fast lane. MacAnally
followed.

And at last, almost choking with pent-up anger, bitter
tears welling in his eyes, he permitted himself to think
the unthinkable.

*Carlisle was the one man who had been on or near the
scene of all the deaths.*

The pace of the traffic increased. They were on the 427
following the signs to downtown Toronto and he could
see the high CN Tower and the half-egg shape of the
Skydome ahead.

*Carlisle had travelled with Marie to Ithaca but – luckily
(as they had all thought) – had not been in the car when
the brakes failed. He had the opportunity to tamper with
those brakes. While Warner was with Marie.*

They were getting nearer the city. The traffic coming
the other way – after-work traffic – was heavy, but on
their side of the highway it was moving fast. On either
side of the road were small factories and plants for light
industry. Between the buildings to his right he could
glimpse the lake and the occasional small yacht.

*Carlisle had been in New York when Abernathy was
killed. MacAnally knew that because they had travelled
there together. They had parted on arrival, MacAnally to
make an abortive attempt to see Lord, and Carlisle . . . he
had said he was meeting a friend. He could easily have
killed Abernathy. And, when Orbell showed up, he could
have killed the detective too.*

The traffic was heavier now, as workers from factories
outside Toronto came onto the highway, city-bound.
They slowed. He had to take care to keep his car out of
the sightline of Carlisle's rearview mirror.

Carlisle had been in the UK when Barnes had died.

And he had not been with Olly Witcomb that night, because Witcomb had arranged to see the Minister. So where had Carlisle gone?

The other car moved into the inside lane. MacAnally followed. They left the highway following a sign to Trippling Avenue, then dipped into the thin factory belt between the highway and the lake. MacAnally observed a machinery company, a marine equipment company, a tyre and auto centre.

Carlisle had been in Japan when Tezuka died. Had he been on time he would have been blown up too. But he wasn't *on time. He was late. Once more saved by amazing good luck. True, he was hurt in Tokyo, but Carlisle had probably considered that a small price to pay for removing himself from suspicion.*

And, of course, Carlisle had been in Australia when Cossens died. Had three hours' notice of the surfing. Could easily have arranged the 'accident'.

Carlisle must have been Partrell's man, infiltrated into the ECO to look after Partrell's interests. A hired killer.

It was unbelievable.

No, actually, it wasn't . . . *it was entirely believable.*

It explained a lot.

It explained it all.

The car in front turned into the car park of a big square building. It was windowless except for some small slots in the doors at the top of the fire escapes, one on each of its four walls. There was no sign, no identification of any sort.

MacAnally pulled up outside and watched Carlisle, briefcase in hand, disappear through a small side door.

He looked at his watch. It was 5.30 p.m. and the dinner was 8.30 for 9 p.m. He still had a couple of hours before he checked into the hotel and changed. Should he ring the police?

God, what would he sound like to the Canadian police? An environmentalist from the US – 'a goddamn liberal' – turning up at a Toronto police station raving about five murders and blaming someone without a shred of real evidence.

Why not wait until he got back to New York? In any case, the New York police probably already knew about Carlisle . . . they were probably getting the truth out of Partrell at that very moment.

He doubted that Carlisle was going anywhere.

He didn't look like a man on the run.

He looked like a man going confidently about his business.

No, he wouldn't go to the police in Toronto. He would fly back to New York instead of Washington and report to the detectives he already knew.

But he did have enough time to try and see what Carlisle was up to. He got out of the car and, keeping close to the wall, he walked round the building. Once at the back, checking that no one was watching, he quickly climbed one of the fire escapes, two steps at a time. The door at the top had a window just a few inches deep.

He looked down into a huge, cavern-like space, a gigantic factory floor. Men in white overalls appeared to be involved in some kind of engineering work. He could see parts moving along an assembly line. But he couldn't work out what was happening – what it all meant.

He climbed back down and walked back to the car.

What could this place have to do with Adrian Carlisle?

Now men were starting to leave for the evening. MacAnally watched a man in his early twenties begin to stroll down the street.

MacAnally looked at his watch. He had about an hour before he must check into the hotel, change, and make the speech.

Amazed that he was doing this, appalled at what it had all come to, he followed the factory worker for a number of blocks until they came out on to the lake side.

The man headed for a big, cheerful-looking place, advertising country and western music from the cocktail hour until 1 a.m. He entered and, after waiting a couple of minutes, MacAnally followed.

The interior was decorated like a huge barn, but with tables and comfortable leather chairs in front of the brightly lit stage. Buying himself a Bud Lite at the bar he wandered around for a few minutes and eventually threw himself casually into a chair at the table where the young man was drinking and tapping his fingers in time with the band.

Apart from a friendly nod and a 'Hi' he took little notice of him for almost ten minutes until the band took a break. He grinned at the other. 'The band's not bad.'

'Damn good. They're always damn good,' said the man in a lazy drawl. He had blond hair, a bland, round, unintelligent face.

'You obviously come to this place a lot,' MacAnally said.

'I like to come in after work for a few beers with my pals.' He looked around the bar. 'None of them made it yet.'

'What do you do?'

The factory worker looked at him sharply, but MacAnally pretended not to be really interested in an answer. Instead he was calling for another beer. 'And one for my friend here.'

'Thanks.' The young man waited but MacAnally didn't press the question. As if reassured, the young man said, 'I just got a new job – working in a factory. Just down the road. Making some machinery.'

'Yes?' MacAnally contrived to sound bored.

But the more the campaigner appeared to lose interest, the more the young man felt compelled to keep his attention. 'For aeroplanes,' he said.

MacAnally looked impressed. 'Really. What, for jets?'

The young man looked cagey. 'Actually, it's all a bit hush-hush.'

MacAnally tried to look even more impressed. 'Oh,' he said, 'military stuff.' And he pretended that he expected no more.

But, no matter what he had been told about keeping his mouth shut, the factory worker wanted to talk now. Wanted to impress. 'Actually no. Commercial.' He looked around, then leaning towards MacAnally said, 'We've been told it's secret, but I can't see why. Except that I guess no one else has come up with it so they're trying to get control of the market.'

'I don't understand,' said MacAnally, once more feigning indifference, but aware that the band was beginning to return to the stand and that he didn't have a lot of time.

'Well, you know all this fuss about pollution from jets. Plantacon and that stuff?'

MacAnally felt his throat go dry. He gulped down some beer while he struggled to contain himself. 'Yes, I think I read about it but I don't remember exactly what.'

'Well, they're going to ban it but our people have a piece of machinery, the equivalent of the catalytic converter we have on our cars, that could solve the problem. No one's ever been able to make one work in a jet engine before. So it's a helluva technical breakthrough.'

The band was tuning up. MacAnally, his heart beating fast, took the risk of pressing for home. 'You mean your people have *invented a solution to the plantacon pollution problem*?'

'Sure. But you could say it was the other way round.'

The band was playing now and MacAnally had to draw his chair up and shout at the young man who unfortunately was now himself losing interest, concentrating on the band.

'What do you mean, *the other way round*?'

His companion looked back in surprise, as if he had forgotten the conversation. 'Oh, well, they invented the converter before anyone got concerned about the plantacon. So you could say it's the plantacon that solved their problem.'

'Which was how to persuade the airlines to pay to put the catalytic converter in their planes?'

'Yep.'

'Amazing.'

The band was playing 'Country Roads'. MacAnally tapped his fingers in time . . .

> *'Country Roads. Take me home.*
> *To the place I belong.*
> *West Virginia, mountain momma,*
> *Take me home, country roads . . .'*

Usually, when he heard the song, his mind would drift back to a battered old Chev, a small boy sitting in the back seat, looking out of the window for hour after hour. But now he was trying to grasp what he had learned. Because it didn't make sense. Surely Partrell wasn't trying to have it both ways? Finally, in the brief gap between numbers, he rose. 'Good luck with the new job . . . who did you say it was with?'

'CAT.'

'Cat?'

'Clean Air Technologies.'

'Yeah, well, good luck with it.'

'Thanks. See you around.'

He walked quickly to the rented car and, his mind reeling, he drove to the Inter-Continental on Bloor Street, booked in, telephoned his host and said he had been delayed but would be there in fifteen minutes, and put a call through to Dominic Young in Washington.

'Dom . . . Clean Air Technologies, it's a manufacturing company based in Toronto. Do whatever you have to do to find out who owns it and telephone me at this number.'

'It probably won't be possible tonight.'

'Try. If not, first thing in the morning . . . but I'll check with you after my speech, at about eleven.'

'Sure. Why's it so important?'

'It's complicated . . .'

'Great,' Young said dryly.

'I'll tell you when I see you. Just believe me, it's important.'

BIRMINGHAM, ENGLAND

Elizabeth Barnes was a spinster, aged fifty-seven. She worked in the local library.

She had never been in a solicitor's office in her life.

And she couldn't understand what the man was saying.

A will?

Her brother's will?

Money left to her.

That was good of him.

A few hundred pounds would be useful.

How much?

Five. He was saying five.

Five hundred pounds.

She took a handkerchief from her purse and wiped away a tear.

Dear Trevor.

No, he was saying . . . dollars . . . why dollars? . . . not five hundred . . .

What was that?

Millions . . .

Five *million*. . .!

Five million American dollars!

Elizabeth Barnes fainted.

Right there.

In her chair.

In the solicitor's office.

The first solicitor's office she had ever been in.

NEW YORK

Young had no news for MacAnally that night but the campaigner finally got an answer while waiting for his plane at the airport.

'Sam, it's not been easy. Had it been in the US I could have given it to you last night.'

'Ok. What have you got?'

'That the company is a subsidiary of another Canadian company called Technology Developments.'

'Who owns that?'

'Well, the directors are three men I've never heard of, Al Schwartz, Matthew Pool Jnr, and Ken Washington.'

'Well, if you've never heard of them there's no way I have . . .'

'Quite . . . but hang on a minute. Technology Developments is itself a subsidiary of The Technology Consortium, but before I give you another list of people you've never heard of let me tell you that the Technology Consortium is a subsidiary of a company called Technology Finance.'

'Well, who the hell owns that?'

'Well . . . wait for it . . . it's a subsidiary too, only not of a Canadian company . . . of an *American* company.

'A holding company called T.I.I. – Technology Investments International.'

Young waited for a reaction.

MacAnally couldn't think what he was supposed to say.

'So?'

'So, Sam, T.I.I. is owned by someone we *do* know.'

'Don't tell me . . . Dieter Partrell?'

'No, Sam, not Partrell.

'This company, T.I.I., is owned by Justin Lord.'

TOKYO

'No, sir.'

She wept.

She was distraught.

Why was this man . . . this solicitor . . . saying this . . . confusing her?

Didn't he know she was in mourning?

And how could he have bungled like this?

'No, sir,' she said, 'there has to be some mistake. I can assure you my husband could not have that money. All he had was a professor's salary. That's all he ever had.

'That's all we ever wanted. This five million dollars . . . *American* dollars . . . it has to be a mistake.'

He began to argue . . . to explain . . . to show her . . . but she didn't want to hear any more.

She rose to her feet. Upset.

'The only way he could have got that sort of money was by doing something . . .'

She stopped. Snatched up her purse.

'No,' she said.

Defiantly.

Definitely.

'No. It's a mistake. I don't want that money. I don't want to hear from you . . . leave me alone.'

And she left.

He looked after her in dismay.

He had never experienced anything like this before.

Yet . . .

. . . she had a point.

The only way Tezuka could have got five million American dollars – in one lump sum – was, as she had put it, 'by doing something' . . .

. . . wrong.

NEW YORK

MacAnally had spent the flight to Washington and the subsequent shuttle to New York in a state of shock.

His mind seemed to be working on two levels. At one he was struggling to make sense of what he now knew. At the other it was coming to terms with the numbing probability that he and ECO were facing catastrophe.

There were only three possibilities, one of them a probability.

One – please God make it *the* one – was that Lord had found out about the pollution and then, *and only then*, realising how desperate the airlines were to keep using plantacon, had got his engineers to work and they had invented what many believed was the uninventable – a catalytic converter that could be fitted to jet aircraft to control exhaust emissions.

This was at least an acceptable explanation. While Lord should have told MacAnally he had a vested interest in the success of the campaign, it was at last a legitimate activity. Lord was, after all, in business.

It was, however, inconsistent with what the factory worker had told MacAnally. That the catalytic converter had been invented *before* the pollution was known about.

The second possibility was that Lord's engineers had invented the converter and that, fortunately for Lord, the pollution problem had coincidentally arisen to justify the airlines spending a lot of money adding it to their aircraft. All Lord had done was use MacAnally to guarantee that everybody knew about the problem.

This was consistent with the factory worker's story. But damn lucky for Lord? Far too damn lucky to be believable.

The third possibility was the terrifying one. And, alas, the most probable. It was that Lord or someone working for him had devised a catalytic converter that would operate in jet aircraft. But it was expensive. He knew that the airlines wouldn't contemplate it. So he invented a reason why it would have to be used. He invented what appeared to be an appalling new form of aircraft pollution – plantacon pollution.

Justin Lord had fooled MacAnally and he in turn had led ECO and, in fact, the whole environmental movement into involvement in a gigantic fraud, one that could cost industry and the country billions of dollars.

Presumably any day Lord's Canadian company would announce the technological breakthrough and be greeted as the saviour of the industry – of FEI, and of the airlines.

And presumably, with a compromise solution at their

disposal, the authorities would quickly dictate that Lord's catalytic converter must be fixed to every jet operating from every country.

With the technology patented, Lord would be able to name his own price to a huge captive market.

Lord would no longer be just a rich man. He would be one of the richest in the world.

But how had he done it? After all, the studies had been carried out by five scientists in four countries, all of them respected . . . and all of whose studies reinforced each other.

Five scientists.

MacAnally's heart almost stopped beating.

Five scientists, now all dead.

Up to now he had made the logical assumption, the assumption anyone would have made, *that the murders were commissioned by the other side.*

But what if they had been arranged *by his own side*? By Justin Lord? Using Adrian Carlisle? Arranging the deaths of his and MacAnally's own witnesses?

Not wanting to believe it, MacAnally went back to the beginning, hoping to identify reasons for rejecting his theory.

Unfortunately it all worked the other way.

Lord had been the first to raise a question over plantacon.

Lord had commissioned all five scientists.

What if they had been blackmailed or bribed into producing the result he wanted?

Poor old Dr Warner with a desperately sick wife. Had he needed the money to care for her? And after she died had he – no longer needing the money – trying to do what was right, because he was a good scientist . . . had he decided to unveil the fraud? Is that why he had been killed?

And David Abernathy? He adored MacAnally and was proud of his links with ECO. Had he, too, become riddled with guilt? Or frightened that the new research would expose his dishonesty? Or was he being blackmailed; he had been strangely edgy whenever questioned about his private life. He had mentioned to MacAnally that he was going to see Lord, ostensibly to ask for more money for research. Had it been to plead with him to drop the project? Was that why he was killed?

As for the British man, Barnes, presumably once he knew he was dying he no longer saw the point in getting the money he was going to be paid. Perhaps he, too, told Lord he wanted out.

As for the others, maybe by then Lord had simply decided that if Cossens and Tezuka were eliminated too, his secret would be completely safe.

For the one thing – *the only thing* – that Lord could never, *ever*, under any circumstances, want revealed was that the science was a fraud.

Mistake, yes. Scientists could be wrong. But fraud – that had to be secret forever.

It was all so terrifyingly obvious now. Lord had a much better reason for wanting the scientists out of the way than the others, even Partrell.

And Carlisle was not Partrell's man. He worked for Lord.

MacAnally thought of Partrell, probably at that moment being interrogated by the police. Christ, Partrell was yet another person he had falsely accused.

And Orbell. While doing whatever he was doing for Partrell, he had stumbled upon the truth. About Lord and the catalytic converter. And the murders. So he had been killed too, perhaps doing the one worthwhile thing he had ever done . . . going to warn Abernathy.

As the plane dipped over New York, MacAnally looked out on the World Trade Center, the harbour, the Statue of Liberty, Ellis Island . . . he thought of his first meeting with Lord. And his trip to Ellis Island.

He had fallen for the man's extraordinary charm, hook, line, and sinker.

And Dominic Young's investigation into Lord's background had failed because he had unknowingly used Lord's man, Adrian Carlisle, to do the research.

They had been conned.

He had been conned.

And now there would be hell to pay.

ITHACA

Ellie Hendon, unlike her older brother Raynald Warner – her *late* older brother – had a keen sense of fun.

Now she looked at the lawyer and giggled . . .

Five million dollars?

Wow, this was some mistake.

Raynald could never have earned that sort of money . . . he was too impractical . . . too unworldly . . . it was absurd.

Ridiculous.

A joke.

She began to laugh.

Her husband, who had experienced a few seconds of flickering hope . . . smiled wanly . . .

. . . Then, because her sense of humour was infectious, he too began to laugh.

Even the lawyer allowed himself a smile.

He marked the file, '*Check with bank – error likely*'.

'Oh well,' he said. 'It was good while it lasted.'

That really set them going.

They all laughed now. Fit to bust.

They had heard of computer errors before . . . but this one had to be the screw-up of the century.

He should, of course, have gone straight to the police.

But he wanted to see Lord. He wanted to hear Lord admit it. He wanted to confront the man who had killed Marie . . . who had made him such a fool.

Tight-lipped and white, MacAnally stalked through the terminal at La Guardia and commanded a taxi to the World Trade Center. All the way there, oblivious to the taxi bumping up and down on the uneven road and the aggressive driver tooting and swearing at other cars, he became angrier and angrier.

He remembered Lord standing in the window, reciting the words on the Statue of Liberty . . .

'Sea of shining hope . . .'

How impressed MacAnally had been.

And all the time it was more like a sea of shining bullshit.

How could he have been so easily fooled? He had destroyed himself, destroyed ECO. They would never survive this. No one would ever listen to them again.

On arrival he went straight to the 98th floor and without waiting to be announced walked past the receptionist and into Lord's office.

Albert Abernathy was a sorry-looking sixty year old. Skinny. Failure all over his face.

His had been a disappointing life.

His wife had left him soon after David went to college.

His hardware business had failed.

His son David had been bright . . . had done well . . . kept in touch . . . but he was gay. And Albert had never been able to come to terms with that.

He looked at the lawyer who had insisted on this meeting.

What problems had David left behind?

Actually, quite a problem, said the lawyer.

In fact, a puzzle.

One helluva puzzle.

Five million dollars' worth of puzzle.

They didn't know what to make of it.

'Well,' said the lawyer, 'the way I look at it . . . you've got two choices. You can tell the bank it's a mistake. Or you can take the money and run. What's it to be?'

Albert Abernathy bit his lip.

His *had* been a disappointing life.

He thought of Florida.

The sea. The sun.

A little fishing boat.

'I'll take the money and run,' he said.

Justin Lord was sitting behind his desk, signing letters. If he was surprised or annoyed at Sam's unscheduled and abrupt invasion of his office he didn't show it.

'Mr MacAnally, what a pleasant surprise.'

MacAnally walked up to the desk, put his hands on the front and leaned over it.

'Did you really think it would work, Lord? That you could get away with it?'

The dealer sat back, pushed away the pen, and sighed. 'Ah. At last.' He rose. 'I'm a little disappointed in you, Mr MacAnally.'

MacAnally was infuriated. 'Disappointed? *You're disappointed?*' He shouted. 'You have. . . .'

Lord interrupted him with a gesture towards the centre of the room. He himself walked round the desk and threw himself into one of the leather chairs.

'Sit down, Mr MacAnally . . .'

'I'd rather stand.'

'Please yourself . . . yes, I'm disappointed it's taken you so long. I thought you were a clever man. I've been expecting you to come for weeks.'

MacAnally couldn't believe his ears. 'You thought I would find out and go along with this. . .?'

Lord leaned forward. 'Mr MacAnally, you *have* gone along with it. You've been the key player. Without you, without your ego, without your ambition, this would have been impossible.

'It wasn't your strength that enabled us to win, it was your weakness. You were so keen to have an issue you could make your own, world-wide, and a stage to exercise your abilities on, and you were so self-indulgent and self-righteous in your automatic rejection of what the other side was saying, even its scientists, that you were the ideal man for what we needed to do.

'If you had been fully in the know and personally paid by me you couldn't have done it better.'

MacAnally finally sank into the chair nearest him, stunned.

'So it's true.'

'Yes, Mr MacAnally. You remember the cousin I talked about? Well, you were so anxious to get on with organising your victory over the airlines that you forgot all about him. He was – is – in fact a much more brilliant man than I described. For years people have assumed that it would be impossible to make a catalytic converter work in a jet engine. He's proved them wrong. When he told me about it I realised the potential was tremendous.

'But there was a problem. The converter was expensive. Too expensive to be justified by the prevailing level of concern about environmental pollution from aircraft.

'What I needed was a huge furore about a particular pollutant . . . then, by emerging in the nick of time as the solution to the problem, we could get our converter literally forced upon the whole industry. We would not only make a huge fortune but appear as public benefactors.

'That's when I heard your speech, Mr MacAnally. And when I met you, when I saw the look in your eyes when we talked, I knew you were my man.'

'Look?'

Lord stood and walked over until he stood above the environmentalist. 'Yes, Mr MacAnally. The look. It told me one thing I needed to know. It told me you *wanted to believe* what I said. You wanted to believe it so badly that you read the research the way you wanted to read it. You interpreted every detail in a way that supported your case.

'*You needed a campaign as much as I needed a campaigner*.

'We were made for each other, Mr MacAnally. Such partnerships are rare. We should both be proud of it.'

'Proud!' Yet his indignation was weakened by a terrible realisation that what the other said was true. He remembered what he had said to Marie. '*We need an issue. Black and white . . .*'

Throughout his career he had urged his colleagues, 'use research to establish the truth, not just to prove yourself right'. But he had *wanted* the charges against plantacon to be true. Because he had *wanted the campaign*.

He had gone to see Warner and Abernathy, wanting to be reassured.

He had not commissioned any original research of his own – despite Jake Katzir's pleas.

He had not even considered the possibility that the

industry's research was legitimate. He had automatically assumed its scientists had been bought.

He realised Lord was sitting looking at him. 'So the question is, Mr MacAnally, what do we do now? There are, it seems, two options. The best one is that you get your rightful reward. A share in the profits.'

He walked to a desk drawer and drew out a slip of paper and tossed it onto the coffee table between them. 'As I said, I've been waiting for you.'

MacAnally gasped.

It was a cheque for ten million dollars.

'Take it. Either use it to fund some other campaign or retire somewhere and live well.'

He saw MacAnally beginning to rise in protest but, by force of personality, he waved him back into his chair. 'It's the only way you can win. What else can you do? Go out and say you were wrong? You'll be finished. Your movement will be discredited. As it is, what harm is done? Plantacon will be saved. But at the same time aircraft will become more environmentally friendly. It's an achievement . . . one you can be proud of.'

In MacAnally's eyes the round little man had swollen, become bigger. His face looked like that of a giant toad.

He rose. 'You were right, Lord. You read me right the first time. I was blinded by the size of the challenge . . . the opportunity you presented me with.

'But you're wrong now. You must be mad . . .' he corrected himself . . . 'you *are*, of course, mad . . . to think you can get away with it, to think that I or the environmental movement will shut up about this.

'Yes, I may be finished. But so what? The alternative is to share complicity in murder, including the murder of my girlfriend, to share complicity in a gigantic fraud. I wouldn't even contemplate it. No money would make me do it.'

'You can't bring them back.'

'Christ, you just don't care, do you? You're mad. And the maddest thing about you is to think I would take your money and become part of it.'

Lord rose and walked to the desk and pushed the buzzer. He sighed. 'A pity. But I expected you to say it. And that's too bad. Because, as I said, there were two options. You must know what the second one is.'

The door opened and Adrian Carlisle walked in accompanied by another man, tall, thin, dark complexion, with unfeeling eyes.

Carlisle grinned at MacAnally. 'Well, hi, Sam, good to see you.'

MacAnally saw red.

Even more than Jordan, Carlisle represented betrayal. He had been trusted.

He had been drawn into the family.

And from that position of trust he had killed. Even killed Marie.

Enraged, he lunged at him, but the other man, Carlisle's companion, grabbed his swinging arm and effortlessly forced him to the ground. He tried to struggle to his feet but saw an arm raised above him, then felt a blinding pain, and then . . . nothing.

Nicola Kowalska had been trying to concentrate on the business being discussed at a client meeting but finally gave up on it. Complaining of a bad migraine she left and began walking, unseeingly, down Madison Avenue, several times bumping into irritated passers-by.

She was terrified that MacAnally was about to make a fool of himself.

He had only had a couple of minutes to talk to her from Toronto airport and hadn't made any sense.

What had he said? It was not Partrell, it was Justin

Lord. But how could it be? Lord was on MacAnally's side. Had funded all the research.

How could Sam have got so confused ... got it wrong?

She recalled how tired and wan he had looked when he left for Toronto and how distraught he had sounded on the phone. She wished now that she had not insisted he go. The strain had been too much. He had cracked up.

It was, she knew, hardly surprising when you considered the pressures he had been under, what with the plantacon campaign, and the loss of Marie, and then the murders arranged by Partrell.

Now he was on his way to see Justin Lord. To make what kind of accusations?

She must stop him before he went too far.

She looked at her watch. There was a chance she could get to the World Trade Center first and head him off.

She waved wildly at a yellow cab and sat, frantic, in the back, urging the driver on while they drove down Madison Avenue and then across town in the heavy early evening traffic. It was slow going but she consoled herself that it would be slow for Sam too.

Round the back of the World Trade Center, near the entrance to the Vista International hotel, they got stuck in an unmoving line of cars. She thrust a ten-dollar bill at the driver and leapt out, planning to go round to the front entrance. She could ring up to Lord's office and find out whether Sam had arrived. If he hadn't she could hopefully prevent him doing so.

She stopped to avoid being run down by a big black car – a stretch Cadillac – emerging from the underground car park. As it passed she caught a glimpse of the faces of the men in the back. One was Sam. Looking strange ... strained. The other was his aide, Adrian Carlisle.

So it was too late.

He had already been up to see Lord. Oh God. What had he said to the man?

Poor Sam. He had really blown it this time.

Why hadn't Adrian Carlisle stopped him. Sam was exhausted; out of control. But what was Carlisle's excuse?

Then she recalled what Sam had said. *'It was not Partrell, it was Lord.'* But there was something else. Something jumbled up . . . something about Adrian Carlisle. *'Carlisle did it.'*

Did what?

She had assumed that it was some remark by Carlisle that persuaded Sam that Lord was to blame.

But what if . . . suddenly she remembered his face in the car. His head had been slumped forward. It had sort of rolled as the car passed and his eyes had looked at her but there had been no sign of recognition.

'Carlise did it.'

That's what he had said.

'Carlisle did it'

Did it! Did what? For Christ's sake, *did what?*

Surely not. . .?

Then she knew it. It explained so much.

Carlisle was Partrell's man.

A plant in MacAnally's campaign.

And now he had Sam.

They were going to kill Sam too.

She ran towards the row of cabs outside the hotel and, pushing aside an indignant-looking businessman she leapt in and, as she had seen people do in movies, ordered the driver. 'Follow that car.'

Sam MacAnally was suffering from a blinding headache. All he could think about was the pain.

He was aware of being in the car, of Carlisle sitting

beside him, but only had the vaguest memory of what had happened. He opened his mouth to speak but no words came. He wasn't functioning properly. He decided to concentrate on watching where they were going. Twice he lost concentration completely. At one point he was aware of being in a tunnel. Then he saw a sign to the New Jersey Turnpike. The next thing he knew they were pulling up outside what looked to be a factory.

Then he blacked out.

When he came to he was lying on a piece of sacking in the corner of what appeared to be a huge empty warehouse. The man who had hit him was standing by the door, smoking a cigarette.

Then he became aware of Carlisle standing over him.

He tried to speak but still couldn't form any words.

The pain in his head was blinding.

The blackout came as a blessed relief.

Joe Paretsky had a cheerfully fatalistic attitude to life.

'I'm going to die young,' he would assure his passengers as he wrestled with the increasingly insane mechanical tide sweeping down the man-made canyons of Manhattan. 'Look at me. Overweight. Driving in this madhouse of a city. A heart attack. . .? I tell ya, it's goddamn' guaranteed.'

If his passengers bothered to lean forward and look at Paretsky's unhealthy 280 pounds of flab they could conclude it wasn't worth the argument.

'Then there's these things . . . Killers,' Joe would continue cheerfully, waving a grotesquely big but cheap cigar in the air, as if to clear the smoke.

'Then there's the fucking muggers. I tell ya I don't stand a chance. I'm dying, I tell ya. Keep looking. I'm dying before your eyes.'

And all he wanted to do before it happened was have

just one of the experiences taxi drivers in movies had. 'Fifteen years I've been driving a cab in in New York. Know what I mean? Fifteen fucking years. Not picked up one movie star. I tell ya, not one celebrity. No disrespect but all I get is people like you.'

Now, today, Joe Paretsky was having the time of his life.

'Fifteen years,' he said. 'Fifteen years waiting for someone to say "follow that car". Ya can count on it, lady. That motherfucker . . . excuse me . . . doesn't stand a chance.'

It had been easy to follow it because the traffic, heading home to New Jersey, had been heavy and progress slow.

And, of course, their eyes were always on the car in front. The Cadillac. The one containing MacAnally. And Carlisle.

It never crossed their minds to look behind them.

Had they done so they would have seen another limousine move out from the line of cars at the World Trade Center.

Also a black car. Also a stretch limo. Only this time a Lincoln. With the kind of tinted windows that hid from view whoever was inside.

But they hadn't done so . . . they hadn't looked back.

They only had eyes for the car in front.

Paretsky was beside himself. 'Ever watch Kojak, lady? I watch it all the time. Even the repeats. I tell ya, that guy's somethin' . . . and this is just like it.'

Once out of the tunnel they had turned left, past the Newport Center Mall, up to Columbus Avenue, a wide street, battered for too many years by commuter traffic so that it now looked down at heel and fading fast. From there the car ahead swung into Jersey Avenue, then at Rolley's Tavern, its ground-floor bar still open but all the windows upstairs boarded up, they turned right into Grand Street, passing under a rusty old overhead bridge. Then they entered Pacific Avenue. Nicola saw a wedding party leaving an old grey church, black matrons in big hats, men looking uncomfortable in tight-fitting suits.

Pacific Avenue appeared to disintegrate as they drove down it. Clearly once a busy centre of warehouses and local industry, it was now half-dead. A few cars were parked outside a warehouse selling arts and crafts from the People's Republic of China. A truck was loading up at a grocery wholesaler's. The rest was high wire fences, anonymous-looking buildings. Industrial territory. Factories. Dumps . . . dumps of old tyres, dumps of rusty machinery. Outside one was a pile of mangled machinery as if a huge iron monster had disgorged its insides.

The car ahead turned from Pacific Avenue into a side street, factories and warehouses on either side, and then swung in at the gates of one.

Paretsky drove slowly past, but already the Cadillac was virtually out of sight behind the grass that had grown high and wild in front of the building.

They reversed and looked at it. On one side of it was a car dump, vehicles, tyreless, stripped of all useful materials, piled three high. On the other was an old timber yard with some pieces of old wood and oil drums lying outside.

The building, set back from the road, was itself new-looking. Could have been a factory waiting to open. Could have been a warehouse. But there was no sign of life.

Nicola told Paretsky he could drop her but he wouldn't hear of it. 'No way, lady. You gotta be kidding. You think I'm going home to tell my wife about this and, when she says what happened next, I'm saying I left you in the middle of nowhere without knowing what's going to happen? You gotta be out of ya mind.'

He suggested they get out. He parked the cab thirty yards up the street, in front of the car dump, and they slipped past the factory gates and into the long grass. From there they watched MacAnally being dragged into the building.

'What do we do now?' he said.

'I don't know.'

How could she know? An hour ago she was in an ordinary client meeting . . . Nicola Kowalska, cool, professional, rising star of the public affairs world, discussing proposals, looking at research . . .

. . . Now she and this taxi driver were lying in rubble and grass on a factory site in New Jersey acting out an episode from Kojak . . .

. . . And *he* was asking *her* what they should do!

'I don't know,' she repeated. 'What would Kojak have done?'

'Kojak?' he said. 'Radioed for backup.'

She gasped. Of course. 'Well, for Christ's sake do it,' she said. 'Radio for help.'

With one eye she watched him run back towards the cab, bent almost double to keep the long grass between him and the building. With the other she looked at the door the three men had entered.

She didn't see the third car, the other black car, the Lincoln, the one with the tinted windows, cruise up the street and stop just a short distance from Paretsky's taxi.

MacAnally didn't know how long he had been unconscious but it couldn't have been that long because the second man was still in the same place, still smoking.

The pain was lessening and at last he found his voice.

'Carlisle,' he said weakly, his voice seeming to come

from a distance. 'Carlisle. You killed Marie. You killed them all.'

Carlisle stood above him. 'I'm sorry about Marie, Sam. I really am. I liked her. It was an accident. She wasn't supposed to get hurt.'

'We trusted you.'

Carlisle laughed. 'You've been too trusting, Sam. Christ, you're naîve. You're a fucking good campaigner but you really don't know what's happening out in the real world.'

'But how could you do it? Why?'

'Money, Sam. A lot of money. More money than you could dream of. Billions.'

The headache returned. He winced in pain.

'Enough to kill me too, I suppose.'

Carlisle sounded genuinely regretful. 'I'm sorry, Sam.'

'Well, why don't you get on with it?'

And he meant it.

He hurt.

He was exhausted.

He was demoralised.

Let Carlisle do his thing. It would be a blessed relief.

The younger man laughed again. 'Don't be impatient, Sam. Your time'll come soon enough.'

'You killed them all, didn't you? But why?'

'There was too much at stake, Sam. Too much at stake to take chances. You remember you told me that scientists live in a world of their own. Well, you were right. None of them could be trusted to take their money and shut up. Warner and Barnes were already threatening to pull out. And Abernathy was afraid that the new work would discredit him. As for the others, how did we know what they would do one day? These were the only five people who knew your campaign was a fraud, Sam. The only ones who knew what we were really doing. They had to go. It was the only way.'

'But if our studies were all false, the new research would have shown there was no pollution from plantacon. You'd be finished anyway.'

'We don't think so. That's the extent of your success, Sam. That's why you're such a genius.'

'Even if – as will undoubtedly be the case – the new research contradicts our studies, *the question will still remain*.

'You've created too much hysteria. And you've created too much distrust . . . of industry . . . of the authorities . . . even of science. No one knows what to believe any more . . . except, they believe it's better to be safe than sorry.

'That's your triumph. *You've sown such seeds of doubt that truth no longer prevails.* You've created an illusion, Sam, and it's not going to go away. An illusion so powerful that huge sums of money will be paid to cater to it.

'You've stirred up such a controversy, so much public concern, that we figure that if the catalyst technology is revealed soon, at least a year before the latest research into plantacon is complete, that everyone will say: *what the hell? Let's deal with this. Here's an answer, let's apply it.* Even the airlines will say it. Because the cost of the catalytic converter, prohibitively high before, becomes acceptable as an alternative to losing plantacon.

'It's also a ready-made answer to any other environmental criticism of the industry.

'That's the beauty of it, Sam. Thanks to you, they'll be glad to pay for the converter, irrespective of the scientific verdict on plantacon. It's their environmental insurance policy.'

MacAnally knew it was true.

The new studies wouldn't change things.

He had done too well.

If Lord got the catalytic converter on the market soon, *everyone* would settle for it as a solution.

Lord would make a colossal fortune; presumably Carlisle as well. As he had said – billions.

It would be an environmental victory.

It would be a way out that industry, boosted by the survival of plantacon, could afford.

And it would be the ideal face-saver for the politicians. They could pass laws controlling emissions and the emissions would be controlled. That way they would look like they cared. But the energy would still be saved; their tax income from the airlines would remain high; their industrial friends would remain friends.

Everyone a winner.

Everyone but MacAnally – and the dead scientists. And Marie. And Orbell.

The only thing that would have changed all that was a confession by any one of the five that they had been blackmailed or bribed. That the science was a fraud.

And that they couldn't now do.

His eyes misted, his head began to throb even more painfully than before. Why the hell didn't Carlisle get on with it? Take him out of this misery.

In one clearer moment he asked, 'And how will you explain my disappearance?'

'Tapes, Sam. Tapes of you and your friend Ms Kowalska. Rather intimate, I'm afraid. The letter you're leaving behind is rather sad, really. When you realised that the scandal was going to break . . . the newspaper story that you were screwing your supposed opponent, and that you had inadvertently sold out the anti-plantacon cause by letting her have access to all your planning documents . . . you decided to protect ECO and the environmental movement by resigning and getting away from it all. South America, I believe. Helping the Indians in the Amazonian jungle . . . that kind of thing. The whole gesture is characteristically idealistic, Sam. People will, of course, assume you'll turn up eventually but, by the time it's clear you're not going to, nobody's going to look hard. They'll just think you died in the jungle.'

'It's crazy. You can't get away with it.'

'Actually, it isn't. It will all sound perfectly reasonable to the people we need to convince. The police. The media. And the public. Your friends may be sceptical, but who will listen to them?'

'Come on, let's get on with it.' It was the other man, dropping his cigarette and coming across the empty space to join them.

'OK. Sam, I'm afraid we're going to have to tie you up.' MacAnally felt his arms being pulled behind his back and some thin cord being roughly wound around them. 'We're leaving a little box to keep you company, Sam. In about an hour it will make a small bang. Not much of one. Not enough to be heard away from this site. But it will start a fire. By the time anyone notices it, the place will, alas, be ablaze.'

The other man came back and stooped over him. He felt a gag being stuffed into his mouth.

Carlisle called back. 'Sorry about the gag, Sam. But . . . what was it you said . . . better to err on the side of prudence . . .'

He laughed as he went.

The headache returned.

And once more MacAnally blacked out.

The light was beginning to fade.

It had been ten minutes since Paretsky called for the police, yet there was still no sign of them.

Then the two men . . . Carlisle and the other one . . . came out from the building and stood by their car, talking quietly while the driver searched in his pockets for the keys.

Keys. What was it about keys that worried her? Then she remembered; they hadn't locked the door to the building. Her heart sank. If Sam was all right . . . alive . . . surely they would have locked the door.

'Stay down. Just let them go,' she said to Paretsky. 'We've got to get in there as fast as we can.'

But the cab driver was now starring in his own drama.

And ' there was no way it was going to end in anti-climax.

These men had to be held till the police came.

He'd ram the goddamn car. That's what he'd do.

Deciding to get the cab and hit them at the gate, he began to run back to the street for the second time, an overweight, panting, but determined figure, bent double in the long grass so that he couldn't be seen.

But just as he reached the gate he found himself running directly into the path of another limo. Not unlike the first. Except this was a Lincoln. It had those windows that blacked out your view of the driver and the passengers . . .

. . . It was moving fast . . .

. . . And without a sound.

Straight towards Joe Paretsky.

To avoid being hit, he dived, face down, onto a pile of rubble near the gate.

While he lay there, covered in dust and stunned, the Lincoln swept on, braked in front of the Cadillac . . .

. . . and from it a man sprung . . . a man holding what Nicola recognised as some kind of machine-gun . . .

What followed she was to re-live in nightmares for the rest of her life:

. . . gun fire . . .

. . . Carlisle falling across the bonnet of his car, face down . . . then slowly sliding to the ground . . .

. . . the other man, jerking under the impact of the bullets . . . like a marionette . . .

. . . blood spurting from huge tears in their clothing . . .

. . . and she . . . thinking that MacAnally had to be the ultimate target . . . that he had to be warned . . . she screaming 'Sam' and recklessly rising to her feet.

. . . the killer slowly turning and looking at her, the gun still in his hand . . .

. . . standing only about ten yards away . . .

. . . she stopping – becoming aware of the danger . . . the two of them looking into each other's eyes.

He was thin, blond-haired, no one she recognised.

Then . . .

. . . he smiled.

That's what she would always remember.

The moment when the nightmare ended . . .

The moment when HE SMILED.

And because this stranger, this smiling killer wasn't interested in harming her . . .

. . . or MacAnally either . . .

. . . he stepped back into the car, and it began to move swiftly but silently away . . .

. . . past a bewildered Nicola . . .

. . . straight at an astonished Joe Paretsky who, to avoid being hit, had to throw himself back onto the heap of rubble.

As the Lincoln disappeared into Pacific Avenue they both heard the sound of approaching police sirens.

Joe Paretsky, covered from head to toe in dust, was scratched all over. His hands were bleeding. And he was fed up. His knees began to buckle. He sat back down, and put his head between his hands . . . because he was tired of diving into heaps of rubble . . . and his over-taxed heart was beating far too fast.

He'd had enough of this.

'Kojak can keep it,' he muttered.

But Nicola didn't hear him. She was running to the building.

She pulled open the door. It was a huge empty warehouse. She peered into the gloom.

Then she saw him.

He was lying on a piece of sacking in the far corner. She ran to him and fell down on her knees, half laughing, half crying.

'Oh, Sam,' she said. 'Oh God . . . thank God . . .

' . . . Oh, Mac-O.'

He opened his eyes and blinked at her as she removed the gag.

'What did you call me?' he whispered.

'Mac-O,' she said, hugging him.

'Oh, no,' he said. 'Not you too.'

EPILOGUE ONE

'*Can I ask a question, Mr Jordan?*'

'Go ahead, Mr Canning.'

'*MacAnally caused all the trouble; why did we save him?*'

'Because we need him to put it right, Mr Canning.'

New York Times

PLANTACON CLEARED AFTER FRAUD REVELATIONS

COMMODITIES KING LORD ARRESTED FOR MURDER

*TOP ENVIRONMENTALIST MACANALLY APOLOGISES . . .
RESIGNS*

*After yesterday's sensational disclosure by top environ-
mentalist Sam MacAnally that the campaign to get the
airline fuel additive plantacon banned was based on
fraudulent scientific evidence, the campaign's main
financier, 'commodities king' Justin Lord was arrested
and charged with fraud and complicity in the murder of
two US scientists.*

*Congressional sources predicted that plantacon would
be fully cleared within a matter of weeks.*

*MacAnally, who disclosed details of the fraud at a
remarkable press conference in Washington, apologised
to the industry for the damage the campaign had done and
said he would be resigning as director of ECO and
withdrawing from public life.*

*At the press conference MacAnally said he had
discovered that the five scientists on whose work the
campaign was based had been bribed and blackmailed by
Justin Lord to falsify their findings and discredit
plantacon.*

*MacAnally said that the deaths of all five scientists,
thought to be an extraordinary coincidence, was no
accident. He charged Lord with complicity in their
murders.*

*Lord's Canadian company was on the point of a
technological breakthrough, the production of a catalytic
converter for aircraft engines. Plantacon pollution, if
proven to be a threat to health, would have created the
ideal market conditions to launch it.*

MacAnally admitted ECO had been irresponsible in not conducting more thorough scientific research before making its charges and said he took personal responsibility for what he described as 'a shameful fiasco'.

He urged people not to lose faith in the environmental cause. 'Nearly all of the claims of the environmental movement have been proved right. This one major failure, which was mine alone, should be treated by the movement as a salutary experience, one to learn from, but not be used by others as an excuse to avoid their responsibility for environmental protection.'

Speaking for the aviation industry, Eugene Remington Jnr, who chaired its plantacon defence coalition, said that everybody would be pleased that the benefits derived from plantacon would continue to be available to the industry and the public.

David Johnston of OILO said the oil industry was 'never in doubt that plantacon would be cleared'.

Dieter Partrell, of plantacon manufacturers FEI, expressed satisfaction, but said the company had instructed its legal advisors to sue ECO for defamation.

On Capitol Hill, Senator Christopher Wilkins, Dem., Conn., said he was considering how he should respond to the news. Senator Ed Eberhard, Rep., Texas, said he hoped the environmental movement had learned its lesson.

On other pages:

Editorial: time for environmentalists to take stock – page 7

Jacqueline Brown: Give credit to MacAnally; man of courage and integrity – page 8

Lionel North – Goodbye and good riddance to campaigner MacAnally – page 9

Wall Street Journal

DRAMATIC RISE IN AIRLINE SHARES . . . FORTUNES MADE

Airline shares rocketed yesterday in the aftermath of the plantacon scare.

As investors competed to benefit from the expected expansion of the industry, the shares broke all records, rising considerably higher than they were before the plantacon controversy broke.

Some investors are believed to have made overnight fortunes.

To my friends at ECO all over the world

From Sam MacAnally

By now you will know I have resigned. I hope that at your forthcoming conference you will vote to close ECO down. We must admit our error, and be seen to pay the price. We owe that to the environmental cause.

I hold myself wholly responsible for what has happened.

There were warnings and I didn't listen.

There were rules to follow – rules that I have always urged upon you – and we failed because I myself broke them.

Campaigns must emerge naturally from the cause itself. They should not be artificially created, whipped up, to accommodate wider organisational or personal needs. They must be genuinely, urgently *needed* . . . needed because a serious problem cannot be tackled any other way, or because an injustice cannot be righted any other way, or because people cannot be protected any other way.

We ... I ... took the decision that we should campaign before doing all we could and should have done to have a proper dialogue with the industry and with the regulatory authorities. We never really *justified* the campaign ... we never really proved to ourselves that there was no other way.

The second rule we ... I ... broke was the one that says *we must always research, research, and research some more* before we go public. I *wanted* to believe the studies I was presented with. I wanted to believe them because I wanted the campaign too much. I wanted to believe them so much that I only half-heartedly checked them out. I rejected requests for more studies ... studies we could have commissioned ourselves. I also rejected the other side's studies on the basis of the same prejudices, the same stereotype assumptions that they make about us.

I write, first, to say how sorry I am that I let you down.

But, above all, I want to urge you to stay with the environmental cause. I have harmed it. But not fatally. It remains the great cause of our time ... it calls for the most urgent attention by the whole human race. Immediately, it's about protecting health; in the longterm, it's about conserving resources, preserving beauty, and keeping our earthly habitat clean and safe so that the species can survive.

So the environmental movement must survive and grow stronger.

What happened to ECO should be seen as a lesson . . . that the movement must be built upon truth, upon integrity, upon greater understanding of the realities of people's lives and the pressures upon them, by greater partnership with those whom we too easily identify as enemies.

The planet will not be saved by a few. It must be saved by the many. That means we have to find new ways of addressing people, involving people. All people.

I know you. I know environmentalists all over the world. You are people full of love and vision and one day history will say that you saved the world.

Not just by campaigns.

But by who you are and by what you do with your own lives.

You have to persuade more people to be the same.

The fate of our children and their children depends upon it.

Sam MacAnally

EPILOGUE TWO

THREE YEARS LATER

New York Times

PRESIDENT OPENS THIRD PLANTACON FACTORY

The President of the United States was in Houston yesterday to fulfil one of his last public engagements before retiring. He opened another factory built to produce plantacon, the revolutionary aviation fuel additive.

It is the third factory built for Fuel Efficient Industries in the past year and reflects the spectacular growth of the company over the past three years.

The opening also marked the promotion to company President of its former Director of Public Affairs and Marketing, Mr Dieter Partrell.

Also present at the event were Eugene Remington Jnr, whose company Executive Airways has now risen to become one of the world's top ten, Mr Todd Birk, recent winner of a series of lucrative contracts expected to propel his Airlift International into the top rank of air freight companies, and Mr David Johnston, newly elected President of OILO.

Hartford Courant

DEFEATED SENATOR TO LEAVE STATE

Christopher Wilkins, the junior Senator for Connecticut who was sensationally defeated in the primaries and who admitted afterwards that it would be futile to seek a second term, is to leave the State altogether.

Wilkins said he planned to accept a business offer and move to California.

Wilkins lost the support of the Democratic party after championing the anti-plantacon cause and later being forced to withdraw his Bill and apologise to his colleagues on the Senate floor and to the manufacturers FEI.

Dallas Star

STATE MOURNS VETERAN SENATOR

The State of Texas today mourns its veteran senator, seventy-one-year-old Ed Eberhard who died yesterday.

In a cruel irony Senator Eberhard, a lifelong defender of the tobacco industry and foe of the environmental movement, died of lung cancer.

New York Times

DISGRACED FINANCIER DIES IN PRISON

Former billionaire financier Justin Lord, who became known as the 'commodities king', and who was sent to prison for life on six counts of murder and one of fraud, all arising from the plantacon affair, died yesterday.

He was found on the floor of his cell. He had apparently suffered a heart attack.

He was seventy-seven.

Melbourne Age

ANONYMOUS GIFT FUNDS ENVIRONMENTAL RESEARCH CENTRE

An anoymous gift of five million American dollars is to be used to fund a research centre to assist environmentalists to strengthen the scientific backup for their campaigns.

The gift was announced by the centre's co-directors, Mike McKenzie and his Japanese wife Machiko Yanagi.

Both were involved in the ill-fated ECO plantacon campaign. They said it was that experience that persuaded them the centre was necessary.

The Guardian

DISGRACED ENVIRONMENTALIST APOLOGISES TO COURT

Olly Witcomb, the young environmentalist who led the anti-plantacon campaign in Britain, apologised to the airline UK Ambassador in the High Court yesterday.

Mr Peter Kingman, who took over as public affairs chief for the airline when Mr Trevor Richardson, now Sir Trevor, replaced Sir Humphrey Brooks as chairman, said that given Witcomb's lack of financial resources the company was only seeking token damages of £1.

It was, however, determined that Witcomb should be held publicly accountable for his actions and be made to apologise for the adverse comments he had made about the airline and the aviation industry.

Witcomb was accompanied to the court by his fiancée Sally who, ironically, was recently promoted to purser by her airline employer – UK Ambassador.

Le Monde

CONTROVERSY OVER EURO JOB FOR ANTI-PLANTACON CAMPAIGNER

Euro MPs yesterday criticised the decision by the European Commission to appoint former ECO coordinator Monique de Vos to a position in DG XI, its environment directorate.

De Vos was involved in the campaign to ban plantacon.

The decision was defended by her division head Claude Chevallier who said that Ms de Vos, who had been a valued employee of the division in the past, was 'like anyone else, entitled to make a mistake'.

However, in view of the MPs' concern, her work would be subject to special supervsion.

Washington Post

DISCREDITED ENVIRONMENTALIST WEDS FORMER OPPONENT

Discredited environmentalist Sam MacAnally, whose organisation ECO was bankrupted after being sued by Fuel Efficient Industries for its role in the plantacon scandal, and who is now a community worker in the deprived northern hill towns of New Mexico, yesterday married Nicola Kowalska, who acted for the airlines during the dispute. Kowalska is giving up her own career as one of America's leading political lobbyists to live with MacAnally in Santa Fe.